Courage on Cemetery Ridge

A HISTORICAL NOVEL

THOMAS M. EISHEN

Courage on Cemetery Ridge follows *Courage on Little Round Top* as the second novel in the Courage at Gettysburg series.

Visit Thomas Eishen on Facebook for photo albums on the ground covered by the 1st Tennessee and the 13th Vermont

Also on Facebook, visit Battle of Gettysburg for the largest collection of photos of the Gettysburg National Military Park on the Internet

High Quality Gettysburg photographs are available for purchase at tommyeishen.com

Cover image by artist Edwin Forbes, courtsey of the Library of Congress

Book layout and cover design by Marie Stirk

Acknowledgments

Thank you to Michele Townsend for her help in fine tuning the manuscript. Your enthusiasm and professionalism were invaluable. To Brenda, thank you for your constant love and support for 38 years. Without you, this wouldn't be possible. Thank you to Marie Stirk for your work and guidance on the layout and cover design.

For Cheryl

A Note to the Reader

This is the story of two men and the events that brought them to the gentle slope of Cemetery Ridge during one of the most critical events of the entire Civil War, Pickett's Charge. I have strived to be faithful to the historical record including the personal histories of each man. The fiction is contained in the interpersonal relationships, gaps in the historical record, and the dialog.

Jacob Turney

The blood-red sun cutting through the cloud-filled morning sky was a bad omen, but no one said anything. The drums beat. Stacked together in their column of fours, rifled muskets at right shoulder arms, their footsteps kept time with the sound of the drums. From the front of the column, the foot beats of the artillery horses brought a muffled confusion to the rhythm. The rolling wheels of the artillery's caissons, limbers, and canons across the dry, hard packed road provided a dull background noise.

Each footstep and turn of a wheel brought them farther from the roads wet from the rains of the night before to ground, that hadn't seen rain for many days. As the sun rose, dust, heat, and humidity replaced the cool air of the early morning.

The sun worked its way higher in the sky, glaring down on them. Captain Jacob "Jake" Turney of Company K, the "Boon's Creek Minute Men" of Lincoln County, Tennessee, pulled down the brim of his battered, faded, gray slouch hat shielding his eyes from the harsh gaze of the sun.

As they marched over a small rise, Jake glanced up hoping to see signs of the town, but there was only another rise and—just beyond it— another steep ridge.

"Damn, another ridge," he whispered. His First Sergeant, Chuck Tuley, marching just to his right, chuckled.

"It ain't funny," Jake snapped back.

"Sorry, sir," Chuck said, but both of them knew Chuck wasn't sorry. He'd picked up his new pair of shoes off a dead Yankee at Chancellorsville.

The front of the column had "Little Game Cock" Brigadier General James Archer commanding the Third Brigade (commonly called Archer's Brigade), Heth's Division, Hill's Corps, Army of Northern Virginia, and his field staff were going over the top of the next rise. Next was Pegram's artillery battalion, five batteries totaling twenty guns. Next in line was Fifth Alabama Battalion followed by the Thirteenth Alabama Volunteer Regiment. Between Jake and the last rank of the Thirteenth Alabama rode his commanding officer, the regiment's twenty-four-year-old colonel.

Lieutenant Colonel Newton George wheeled his horse to the right, then touched the large brown mare with the soles of his worn-out riding boots. The horse darted ahead as the boy colonel expertly guided him between the column and the split rail fence that lined the road and his regiment.

Clean shaven, George looked even younger to Jake, but he rode tall in the saddle with the confidence of a man comfortable being in command. As the colonel passed the front rank, he made eye contact with Jake for an instant. The younger man's eyes seemed dull and distant. Jake wasn't surprised nor concerned about his cousin Pete's handpicked successor to lead the First Tennessee Regiment Provisional Army, Confederate States of America, better known as Turney's First Tennessee.

Jake heard the colonel's voice but couldn't make out what he said. He glanced over his right shoulder in time to see Private Willey Wood unfurl the color. The bright red background, blue crossed stripes, and the white stars of the new flag seemed to glow in the morning sun. Across the red background, the blue letters spelled out the names of the twelve major battles in which they'd participated. Only the name of Cold Harbor was a source of embarrassment for the regiment.

"I do believe we're gonna get some action today, boys," Private Albert Turney shouted loud enough, so most of the regiment had surely heard him.

"Quiet!" Chuck snapped at Jake's younger brother doing his part as first sergeant to keep order in the ranks.

Jake glanced over his shoulder and saw Albert looking at him with his familiar "what did I do?" expression.

"Eyes front!" Jake barked a sign of support for his first sergeant.

Jake wasn't surprised to see Albert's expression change to one of contempt just before he snapped his head and eyes to the front. Jake shook his head as his other brother, Jim, four rows back, flashed him a nervous smile.

Jake whispered to Chuck, "What am I gonna do with him?"

"Besides shooting him?" Chuck whispered back.

"Yeah, besides that."

"I don't know," Chuck replied.

Jake knew this was just the start. The closer they got to the enemy, the louder and more irritating Albert would become. It was the reason Jake gave for wanting to transfer him to another company. While it was never discussed, they were all changed by the fighting. For Jake, it was easy to see the change in his brothers since he knew them so well and he suspected they had seen the change in him too. For those he didn't know as well, he could only guess at how the war might have changed them based on how they behaved.

While Albert had stopped having the nightmares, he had always had the Turney temper; before the war, he had kept it mostly under control. To add to the fits of temper, whenever there was the threat of action, Albert would become nervous and jumpy, which led him to be obnoxious in the ranks and undermined the disciplined in the entire company.

Jake had tried talking to him, but it was a failure. How could he—as commanding officer—admit to a member of his company, even his own brother, that he understood his fears without admitting that he was just as scared? Jake couldn't bring himself to discuss his own fears, so he did as the rest of his men and ignored the issue, hoping no one noticed how it affected him.

After two years of fighting, most of the men who were left in the company had done a fair job of masking their fears. Jake looked back at James and he noticed how his shoulders were back to being slumped forward and how he kept looking at the feet of the man in front of him. Both were signs of how he was dealing with the growing fear in his soul.

Those who hadn't learned to deal with the fear were either dead or deserted. Some had taken their own lives or had purposely gotten themselves killed by the enemy. Some others had just lost their minds and jumped out of the ranks and into friendly fire.

At night in front of the campfires, they would all talk about how the man had been a coward, but no one ever talked about the fear they felt. Instead, they had all found a way to deal with the physical effects of the coming danger. Unfortunately for Jake, Albert's way was becoming an increasing problem for the company.

He went to the colonel and asked him for a transfer to another company, but the colonel replied, "If I got to put up with my brother, you got to put yours."

"But your brother doesn't cause any problems!" Jake had protested.

Newt had taken a step toward Jake then whispered, "And you think transferring him will solve his problem?" That ended the conversation because they both knew the answer.

Newt patted Jake on the shoulder. "Being our brother's keeper is a burden we will both have to endure."

"You are your brother's keeper." His father's proclamation was a heavy burden. One that Jake was tired of carrying, but one he had no choice but to endure.

Unable to transfer Albert, Jake had tried everything he could think of—short of talking to him about what was really bothering him—to fix his brother. Hounding him, yelling at him, putting him on extra duty, nothing worked. Oh sure, Albert would promise things would be different, but nothing ever changed.

A horse's gallop, cut short with a whinny just to Jake's left, meant the young colonel wanted to talk. Jake glanced to his left as Newt—the name his friends, family, and Jake, when they were alone, called him—jumped from the saddle. He held his horse's reins in his left hand and fell in next to his senior captain.

"Colonel."

"I see you're still having problems with Albert."

"I still think he'd do better in Company G."

"Davis doesn't want him in his company. He told me it was bad enough that he had to put up with the commanding officer's brother, he sure in the hell didn't want to put up with your brother as well."

Jake laughed. He was glad the colonel's younger brother Tom was a private in Captain Davis Clark's

Company G. It was one thing to have to look out for your own brothers, but quite another to be responsible for the commanding officer's family too.

"If Stuart was here we'd know for sure." Colonel George continued the conversation they'd started about an hour ago as they left from the little town of Cashtown, Pennsylvania.

"As we came though Pettigrew's lines, I asked a captain what he thought. He said it looked like militia to him," Jake said as the first bead of sweat formed on his forehead.

The colonel took off his forge cap and beat it against his right leg in a steady, familiar rhythm like he was keeping time to a song playing in his head.

"Pettigrew was sure it was Union Cavalry. I could see it in his eyes last evening, when he gave his report to General Heth. The man was absolutely convinced it wasn't state militia that followed him as he pulled back from the town. His aide ... I don't remember his name ... stayed behind and watched closely for several minutes. He agreed with Pettigrew. They were too organized and disciplined to be state militia."

"I still don't understand why he didn't deploy his brigade and mount an attack. Then we'd know for sure," Jake said.

"He was under orders not to bring on an engagement. Looking back on it, I think General Heth might have wished he'd given Pettigrew a bit more discretion or maybe sent a someone like Archer who had used a bit more initiative—"

"You mean disobey orders?" Jake cut Newt off.

"I think initiative is a better word than disobey," Newt chuckled with a nervous laugh that Jake knew all too well.

It was the same before every fight. The colonel would want to talk and talk, sometimes about the condition of

Company K or the regiment, but other times, like today, he'd talk about the decisions and actions of the generals or the army as a whole.

Beating his hat against his leg, the talking and the nervous laugh were all things Jake expected from his commanding officer just as he expected that once the shooting started, he would be a pillar of strength to the entire regiment. Like Jake's cousin Peter before him, Newton George was instinctively a leader of men, but the waiting, as he told Jake once in the strictest confidence, just about drove him crazy.

A distant yet distinct sound of a rifle shot suddenly cut through the heavy, humid air. A few seconds later came an answering of scattered fire, then a dark gray, angry cloud of smoke slowly rose from beyond the next rise.

Jake glanced at Newt as a sense of relief spread across his face. The waiting was finally over. Newt jumped back in the saddle and spun his horse so he faced the entire regiment, his eyes gleaming with excitement and confidence.

"State militia or Union cavalry," Colonel George purposely raised his voice so everyone nearby could hear. "It doesn't make any difference. After we get done with them, they're going to wish they'd never heard of the town of Gettysburg."

"We're gonna whup up on them, colonel!" Albert yelled as the men burst out in a cheer for their commanding officer. Newt nodded to Jake, and then he rode toward the front of the column.

Echoes from the Thirteen Alabama drifted over Jake. "Regiment; Company; ..."

Sergeant Major John Fitzhugh relayed the order to Turney's First Tennessee. "Regiment!"

Jake and the other company commanders barked, "Company!"

"Halt!" rang out from the Thirteenth Alabama a split second later. With the next step of his right foot, the sergeant major yelled, "Halt." Jake and the rest of the regiment planted their left feet, then brought their right feet next to the left executing the order like the veteran regiment that they were.

"Regiment!" the sergeant major barked again. He waited for the chorus of "Company," before he ordered, "Rest in place."

Jake wanted a better look at what was ahead, so he stepped over to the fence that lined the side of the road and climbed up on the second of four rails. The rise in their front was only ten to fifteen feet high, but just high enough to block the view of the front of the column. Beyond, about halfway up the next ridge, he saw a couple of horsemen come out from behind a white house on the left side of the road, and they galloped up the ridge.

A more organized volley from the front of the column chased after the riders, but with no effect as both men disappeared into the morning glare near the summit of the ridge. The smoke from the friendly fire rose up obscuring the white house. As First Sergeant Chuck Tuley joined him up on the fence, a lone rider—one of General Archer's aides—galloped past them toward the rear of the column.

"Sir, can you see what they're shootin' at?" the first sergeant asked Jake.

"A couple of cavalry troopers," Jake said as he noticed a large hill to the southeast. Through the glare and the smoke, it was hard to tell for sure, but from that hill, it looked like a series of ridges fanning out to the north and west with each one taller and steeper than the one just before it. The road they were on ran up and over each one of the ridges.

"How many ridges can you see coming from that hill?" Jake asked as he pointed.

Chuck pulled his wide brim slouch hat low over his eyes. "Can't rightly tell for sure. Could be three, maybe four. No sign of a town." Chuck lowered his voice. "Too bad, too. You ain't the only one in need of some shoes."

Jake jumped down from the fence, turned around, and looked at his men. They looked more like a ragtag group of outlaws instead of a well-trained, veteran military company. Several no longer had uniform jackets, while a few wore Yankee blue coats. Some wore a faded gray uniform, while a few had the newer butternut, colored with birch dye.

Jake was proud that none of them had holes in their uniforms and most of the patches weren't easily identifiable. In addition, while many of the uniforms were faded and stained, considering they were on the march, most of the uniforms were, overall, pretty clean.

With the havoc that the Yankee blockade of Confederate ports had on supplies, uniforms weren't a major concern, but shoes were. While Jake's shoes might have holes in them, he still had a pair. Several of his men were barefoot or had scrapes of cloth wrapped around their feet.

He hoped the rumors about a supply of shoes in Gettysburg were true. Lieutenant Richard Ewell's Second Corps, leading the Army of Northern Virginia through this part of Pennsylvania, might have "bought" all the shoes in Gettysburg when they came through, but they'd been through Cashtown too. There, they had missed the cellar full of supplies, including enough shoes for all the men of the Seventh Tennessee Regiment.

It was too bad that the friendly local resident had decided to tell the officers of the Seventh Tennessee about the stash of supplies in the cellar of the storeowner's home instead of the men of Turney's First Tennessee. Still, there was hope that somewhere in Gettysburg there would be another hidden supply of shoes.

He lifted his left leg and checked the half dollar size hole in the sole of his shoe. The morning's wet road had played havoc with the newspaper he'd stuffed between the hole and his foot. He knew it wouldn't be long until it gave way and his last pair of good socks would face exposure to the rough road.

He still had one more *Fayetteville Observer* he could use, but he hadn't read it yet. For a spilt second he thought about using it to stuff his shoe, but quickly dismissed the idea. He might be able to get another pair of socks in town or maybe off a dead Yankee, but he wasn't going to get a chance to read the hometown paper again.

"Sir, looky yonder," Chuck said, pointing to the front of the column.

Jake watched as a pair of companies from the Thirteenth Alabama moved forward and over the rise. The morning orders were for a couple of companies from the Thirteenth to join up with the entire Fifth Alabama Regiment to serve as the skirmishers for the whole brigade.

There was another volley from the front of the column. This time, the rising smoke covered a wider area to the right of the road telling Jake that the skirmishers were starting to form a battle line. It wouldn't be long now before they'd move forward.

"Make way, make way!" came shouts from the back of the column. Jake and Chuck both jumped to the center of the road as an officer came riding down its left edge. Behind him, on both sides of the road, came single file ranks of men moving forward at a double quick.

"Davis' skirmishers?" Chuck asked.

"I expect so," Sergeant Major Fitzhugh said as he joined them.

Davis' brigade was following Archer's men up the road. Jake wasn't sure why their skirmishers were moving forward, but he guessed they would be taking up a position on the left of the road.

Jake could make out a scattering of rifle fire. A few seconds later came another blast of an answering volley from the front of the column. The smoke spread out in a line to about a hundred yards to the right of the road. Jake had no doubts about it now, General Archer had deployed his skirmishers to the right of the road and Davis' must be deploying to the left side.

The firing up on the next ridge intensified. Even with the glare of the morning sun in his eyes, Jake could tell that despite the Yankees' steady fire there, very little smoke was hovering over the next ridge. Jake guessed they were using carbines. Rifled muskets coughed out much more smoke than the weapons the Yankees were firing. Thankfully, the fire didn't seem rapid enough for them to be carrying the new repeating rifles or maybe there just weren't that many of them.

Colonel Newton George rode back over the rise, past the remainder of the Thirteenth Alabama, and up to Jake. "The General still think they're militia, sir?" Jake asked as he jumped down from the fence.

Newt slid from the saddle. "He's having second thoughts and wishing he had the artillery in the rear of the column. After Davis' skirmishers get into position on the left of the road, he's going to let the skirmish line move out a few hundred yards before he resumes the march."

"I reckon that's gonna take a while, sir," Chuck stated.

"Sir, why did the General put the dang artillery out front today?" the sergeant major asked.

"I'm guessin' he figured they'd scare the militia away."
Chuck laughed.

Jake climbed back on the fence rail and Newt and the
sergeant major followed him up. Chuck pulled out a wad
of chewing tobacco and stuffed it between his cheek and
gums before climbing up the fence.

The four men stood on the fence and watched as the
skirmish line finally came into view marching through
the waist-high wheat field. The rear rank fired a volley
over the top of the front rank then reloaded as the front
rank moved forward a few yards. The front rank fired
their volley as the second rank moved up to join them.
They kept up a steady fire as they slowly moved forward.

Jake shifted his weight back and forth as he watched
the skirmish line move at a snail's pace.

"Those fellers keep up it like this, it'll take us all day to get
to Gettysburg," Chuck said before spitting on the ground.

"General Heth passed down orders not to bring on
a general engagement. Archer is just being cautious,"
Newt said.

"General engagement? At worst, it's just a bunch of
cavalry! Maybe General Archer should use some initiative!" Jake snapped as he waved his arm toward the
skirmish line.

"You tell them, brother!" Albert yelled out.

Newt just shook his head and patted Jake on the
back. "And you wonder why you can't keep Albert quiet
in the ranks ... you're two of a kind."

Chuck and the sergeant major chuckled at Jake's
expense.

Jake took a deep breath. He wanted to argue with
them, but thought better of it. While he wasn't as bad as
Albert, at times like this, he was finding it increasingly
difficult to keep his own Turney temper under control.

It was the reason he understood why Albert and James were acting the way they were.

His brain was running at high speed with thoughts flashing through his mind. All his senses were on high alert flooding his brain with more information than it could handle. His heart raced, he was breathing faster, but he was in commend of a company and couldn't let any of it show. Unfortunately, he couldn't control how the stress affected his fits of temper and impatience.

He cursed his own failure to keep it under control. He turned back to the hill to the southeast and tried to focus all his attention there blocking out everything else exploding in his brain. He was relieved to see no activity up on the hill, but still it worried him.

"Sir, if the cavalry was screening for their infantry, don't you think that they'd fortified that hill," Jake said as he pointed. "It's the highest one around here. It'd make a formidable defensive position. Dig in some infantry along with a couple of artillery batteries they'd give us hell for sure."

"You need to remember who you're talking about captain. The leaders of the Army of the Potomac just don't seem to know good ground when they see it." Newt laughed.

"Ain't that the truth, sir," the sergeant major spoke up. "I do believe they gave up that dang ridge back at Chancellorsville without much of a fight."

Without saying a word, Chuck jumped down from the fence, spun around, and walked quickly back to the company. Jake knew the sergeant major was right. Most of the Yankee Third Corps had already fallen back when Company K and the rest of Tennessee Brigade skirmish line assaulted the artillery at Hazel Grove.

"If he was here, I think Wright would disagree about it not being much of a fight," Jake muttered.

"Oh God," the sergeant major whispered. He jumped down from the fence and rushed over to Chuck.

Newt shrugged his shoulders. "I forgot, too."

"You got other things on your mind," Jake said.

"No excuse," Newt snapped.

Jake knew there was nothing he could say, so he just stood there in awkward silence.

The chorus of commands from the Thirteenth Alabama broke the silence. It was time to resume the march.

"Get them ready, sergeant major," Newt shouted as he jumped back up on his horse. Jake took his place back in line next to Chuck.

"You all right?" Jake asked.

Chuck nodded.

"Fall in! Fall in!" the sergeant major shouted, following quickly with, "Attention!" Then came, "Right Shoulder Arms," followed by, "Forward March."

As they moved forward, the rise in their front blocked their view of the skirmish line's advance. The regimental band started playing "Dixie" and many of the men sang along with loud, enthusiastic voices, but some, including Jake, stayed silent.

Jake glanced over his shoulder at his two brothers. He knew how Chuck felt. Five sons of Henry Turney joined the First Tennessee and now there were only three. Jake said a silent prayer for himself and his brothers as Albert sang along. "Swear upon your country's altar. Never to submit or falter."

James' head was down, so Jake couldn't see his face. He wasn't surprised; James was the quiet, sensitive one. The closer to a fight they came, the more withdrawn James became as Albert became more boisterous.

"'Til the spoilers are defeated, 'Til the Lord's work is completed."

Jake looked back to the front as they came up over the rise. The Yankee fire seemed to intensify as the skirmish line reached about the halfway point up to the top of the next ridge. If they were using the carbines, which Jake was sure they were, the weapons didn't have the range of the rifled muskets carried by the skirmishers.

A couple of the skirmishers dropped to the ground. The bloodshed had begun.

Jake was just glad it wasn't the First Tennessee taking part in the skirmish line again. He'd had his fill back at Chancellorsville. They'd rushed head long into the artillery covering the withdrawal of the Yankee infantry. While it had been on one of the bloodiest battles for Company K, Jake knew they were lucky in suffering only eight casualties, six wounded, and two dead. He guessed the Yankees had misjudged the slope of the hill causing most of the loads of double canister to go just over their heads.

Jake rubbed his left thigh where a Yankee mini-ball had taken out what had felt like a pound of flesh. He knew he'd been very lucky, just as he was at Cold Harbor where the ball passed clean through without hitting any major organs. James and Albert thought he was nuts to prefer being shot rather than being knocked senseless like he was at Fredericksburg. It was bad enough he couldn't remember the shell exploding nearby, but the whole battle was just a blur.

He noticed one of the skirmishers—one who'd gone down while up on the ridge—was on his feet and limping back down the road. The first of the walking wounded.

Jake wiped the beads of sweat from his forehead. The sky was clear and hazy. He hoped the General would get things in gear before the onslaught of the afternoon's heat.

"Creek, sir," Chuck whispered.

Before Jake could respond, Newt yelled out orders for the canteen detail.

"I want Albert on this detail," Jake whispered to his first sergeant.

"Corporal Zimmerman," Chuck yelled.

"Yes, first sergeant," Zimmerman answered.

"Y'all are on canteen detail."

"Way to go Turney!" a member of Zimmerman's squad snapped.

"Captain, it ain't—"

"Shut up Albert!" someone else snapped, cutting him off.

Jake was surprised at how quickly the other privates shouted Albert down. Why hadn't he thought of this sooner? Suddenly, he felt stupid. Instead of warring with his brother, he'd just turn the problem over to his entire squad.

Jake lifted his canteen strap over his head and handed it to Chuck who passed it along with his own to the right of the column. Jake glanced over and instantly regretted putting Albert on the detail. Albert smiled as he collected Jake's canteen. *Damn it,* Jake swore to himself as he felt his face flash red.

"Albert, you spit in my canteen again and your whole squad will be on canteen detail for a month!" Jake angrily shouted loud enough that he was sure half the regiment heard him. The smile quickly disappeared from Albert's face as the other members of the squad demanded he turn over the captain's canteen.

"You showed him," Chuck whispered.

Hell yes, I showed him, Jake crowed to himself just as the last of the Fayetteville Observer—the newspaper stuffed in the bottom of his shoe—gave way. The change was slight, but very humbling as felt the rough road through the bottom of his sock. Soon, his last pair of socks would be full of holes. He hoped he was right about being able to get another pair of socks and shoes.

"Halt!" Newt shouted.

His command was followed quickly by the sergeant major ordering, "At ease, rest in place."

Newt said something to the sergeant major, and then kicked his horse and guided him along the edge of the road toward the front of the column.

That was the worst part—the standing and waiting. Jake stepped out of line and Chuck took his customary position next to him as Jake looked over his company. They left Tennessee with close to a hundred good men, now they were down to just thirty-eight.

The sweat was now pouring down Jake's forehead. The promise of last night's rain bringing cooler, dryer weather never happened. Instead, the light breeze coming up from the south brought along with it humid, heavy air. The only good thing was the boys on the other side weren't as used to that kind of weather as were his boys from south central Tennessee.

First Lieutenant George Garrett came up from his spot in the rear of the company to join Jake and Chuck.

"Zimmerman ended up with your canteen," Garrett told Jake.

"What about mine?" Chuck asked.

"I think Albert still has it."

Chuck stormed up the road toward the creek. "Turney, if you spit in my canteen ..." he yelled.

Garrett broke out laughing at the first sergeant and several of the men joined him.

"That's enough!" Jake snapped. The laughter decreased only slightly. A couple of men gave him a questioning look.

Jake took three steps past Garrett stepping directly in front of the company as he yelled, "Damn you all! I said that's enough!"

The laughter stopped immediately. Jake looked past the company and noticed James coming back with several canteens and the look of disapproval was unmistakable. James then looked back down at the ground. Jake didn't care.

Jake turned his back on the company and walked over to Garrett.

"Was that really necessary, sir?" Garrett whispered.

"I'm not going to allow anyone to make fun of my first sergeant and that includes you," Jake whispered back.

"Understood, sir. Sorry, sir."

Jake took his hat off and rubbed his face—with the sleeve of his waist-length woolen butternut shell jacket with the infantry blue trim—as he focused on the skirmish line still being very slow and very deliberate.

"What the hell is Archer doing?" Jake whispered.

"Did you say something, sir?" Garrett asked.

"I'm just wondering what's gotten into the Little Gamecock?"

"I guess he's just being careful."

"He didn't earn that nickname for being careful," Jake pointed out.

The Yankee firing from up on top of the ridge, while at times rapid, had no volume. There couldn't be that many of them. Not enough to slow down a regiment and a half making up the skirmish line and certainly not enough to stop two full brigades.

A yell rose up from the skirmish line as they charged up the last twenty yards to the top of the ridge.

"That's more like it," Jake said looking over at Garrett who nodded his agreement. As they reached the top of the ridge, Jake expected the skirmishers to move quickly past and press the attack, but that didn't happen. Instead, they were reorganizing back into a battle line.

"This is going to take all damn day," Jake moaned.

Garrett walked away without saying a word. Jake guessed his first lieutenant had enough of his captain's belly aching.

"Here you go, sir," Corporal Zimmerman said as he handed back Jake's canteen.

"Did Albert spit in the first sergeant's canteen?" Jake asked.

"No, sir. I made sure of it."

"Hugh, you need to do a better job of keeping Albert in line."

"Sir, he's your brother!"

"And he's assigned to your squad. He's your responsibility, not mine and unless you and your squad want to end up on every shit detail there is, you will make sure he behaves himself."

"Dang," Zimmerman whispered. Jake watched Zimmerman's eyes narrow for a few seconds before he suddenly relaxed. "Sir, I do believe I would be of more service to the company by returning to the ranks as a private."

Jake patted Zimmerman on the back. "Nice try, Hugh. Not going to happen. You're stuck with my brother, and I expect you to fix the situation."

"That ain't gon' happen, sir," Zimmerman said then headed back to his place muttering something under his breath.

Jake smiled as he turned back to the fence in time to watch the skirmish line fire off a volley just before starting their advance again. Because of the ridge between them, Jake couldn't hear any answering fire from the Yankees.

He glanced back to the south and there was still no sign of activity up on the top of the large hill. Jake kicked the ground. Just a bunch of cavalry.

Jake took a quick swig from his canteen as the chorus of commands once again echoed down the column. Finally, they were moving again.

To the left of the road, in the front yard of a house that sat at the top of the ridge, a two-gun artillery battery was unlimbering. Jake noticed a civilian come out the front door and say something to the artillery crew. Jake was too far away to hear what the man said, but he was sure it didn't have the effect the man intended, because the entire crew was laughing. Dejected, the civilian went back into the house and shut the door behind him.

Just as the First Tennessee passed the guns, the first one let loose followed by the other one a second later. The acidic, dark gray smoke engulfed the men of Company K. The overpowering smell of sulfur invaded Jake's nose and lungs leaving a foul taste in his mouth.

As he came out of the cloud, Jake saw the first shell explode north of the road, high above a group of four horsemen up on the next ridge. The second shell fell short and exploded harmlessly upon impact throwing up a gray cloud of smoke and dirt. The horsemen rode back over the ridge before the artillery could get off another round.

To his right, Jake noticed a couple of dead Yankees. Jake wasn't surprised to see they'd already been relieved of their shoes. With as much time as it took for the skirmish line to get reformed, Jake was surprised the dead men weren't stripped down to their long johns.

One had the yellow chevrons of a corporal on his jacket sleeve. Jake didn't know what colors the militia might be wearing, but the yellow was a sure sign the man belonged to Union cavalry. Sky blue designated infantry, red artillery, and yellow was cavalry.

The dead corporal's uniform was also worn and dirty as if he'd been in the saddle for days on end.

Not the type of uniform you'd find on a member of a hastily-formed militia.

Also, the resistance the skirmishers faced wasn't what Jake expected out of a militia. There was now no doubt in his mind that they were up against veteran cavalry belonging to the Army of the Potomac.

Just past the crest of the ridge they halted again. The skirmish line appeared as ghostly silhouettes methodically moving through the smoke covering the valley's narrow floor. The Yankees were keeping up a steady fire from the crest of the next ridge, but there was still no volume to it. Jake couldn't figure out why the skirmish line just didn't let out the rebel yell and storm the ridge like the First Tennessee had done at Chancellorsville.

Newt climbed down from his horse and motioned Jake to join him. Since Major Felix Buchanan, the regiment's other field officer, had taken over command of the brigade's sharpshooters, Jake had taken over the role of the colonel's sounding board.

"I think I'm beginning to understand your frustration. I just never thought it would take this long to push them out of the way," Newt said as Jake approached.

"It's just utterly ridiculous. The General seem out of kilter to you?" Jake asked.

"I don't know. He's not doing much talking. I thought about suggesting we deploy another regiment, but I could tell he isn't in a very receptive mood. Did you see Hill this morning?'

"He wasn't wearing a red shirt." Corps commander Lieutenant General Ambrose Hill had a habit of wearing a bright red shirt when combat was expected.

"I think Hill is having stomach problems again and Archer, I just don't understand. He was so sure last evening that Pettigrew was wrong, and now I think he realizes it's Union cavalry in our front and he's worried that the rest of the Army of the Potomac can't be far behind."

"Did you notice the dead Yankees?" Jake asked.

"Yep, well-worn uniforms."

"Hell, sir. Even if it is Union cavalry, we could've deployed the whole damn brigade and just stomped right through them a half hour ago." Jake's voice rose. "You can tell from the sound of their fire, there ain't that many of them. Hell, we did more damage with fewer men at—"

"Captain, keep your voice down," Newt snapped in a hushed but forceful tone.

Jake stared at Newt but held his tongue. Colonel or no colonel, Jake didn't like anyone using that kind of tone with him. Newt starred right back at him. Jake wanted to grab Newt by the shoulders and throw the bastard to the ground and stomp on him, but he somehow kept his emotions in check and after a few seconds he was the first to look away.

The sergeant major joined them breaking an awkward silence. "Sir, any orders for the men?"

Newt looked up to the next ridge. "Hopefully it won't be long now, let's go ahead and load weapons."

After the sergeant major walked off, Jake decided he had better speak first. "Sorry, sir."

"That Turney temper is going to get you into trouble yet," Newt stated firmly.

"I know, Newt, dang it all, we just can't help ourselves."

"Well, at least you didn't shoot my dog." Newt barely got it out before he started laughing, while Jake just stood there embarrassed. His Uncle Samuel, a lawyer over in White County, Tennessee, got so upset after losing a trial that he threatened to shoot the other attorney, thought better of it, then shot the man's dog instead.

Jake's cousin Pete loved to tell the dog story and for some reason, Newt thought it was hilarious and needled

Jake often about the family making a habit of shooting dogs of those they disagreed with. Jake thought the story was an embarrassment to the family and he guessed his reaction to it was one of the reasons Newt thought it was so funny.

"When we advance," Newt said, his tone turning much more serious, "you're going to be my eyes on the right flank. If you need to, you have my permission to turn temporary command of the company over to Lieutenant Garrett. Keep me advised on what is happening on the flank."

"Yes, sir. You can count on me."

"I know I can," Newt responded.

One by one, the other nine-company commanders started drifting forward to talk to the boy colonel. The organization of Turney's First Tennessee was like most of the other volunteer regiments in the Army of Northern Virginia. Ten companies designated by the letters A through I and the letter K, skipping the letter J since on handwritten orders it looked too much like the letter *I*.

Jake stepped over to the fence and took a drink from his canteen as a flash of yellow cut through the smoke below followed closely by a fresh wave of grayish black smoke. A spilt second later, the dull thunder of the skirmish line's volley swept over him.

Glimpses of movement through the smoke told Jake the front rank was reloading. There was another flash of yellow, wave of fresh smoke, and dull thunder as the second rank let loose with their volley.

The front rank moved forward clearing the front of the dark cloud. It looked for a moment like they were going to make a mad dash forward. Jake took off his hat and waved it over his head as he screamed, "Go get them boys."

After just a couple of yards, they stopped and aimed their weapons. Jake dropped his hat to his side and turned away. Newt and the other officers were all staring at him.

"I thought they were goin' to—" The dull thunder of the next volley drowned him out.

Jake put his hat back on and pulled it low over his eyes. *What the hell is the General waiting for?*

Jake turned back to his company. Some of the men were showing sides of frustration, but most just immersed themselves in their own little worlds, shutting out what was going on around them. Many were sitting in the middle of the road. There were a few card games, some were reading, and others looked like they were trying to take a nap. Jake was surprised Albert was one of them.

A few were brewing coffee over small fires built on the side of the road. A couple of men were soaking hardtack in their tin cups.

What sounded like a concentrated volley came from both ranks of the skirmish line, followed by a swelling of the now familiar rebel yell. Jake turned around hoping to see the last of the skirmishers pouring over the crest of the ridge, but he wasn't surprised to see them reorganizing again. "This is going to take all damn day," Jake whispered.

Stephen Brown

The long straw, a piece of nature, food for his father's dairy cows, something to chew between his teeth when he was nervous; it was the long straw that had made all the difference. Funny how something so simple—so small—had done so much to shape his young life.

It was his father's idea to draw straws. Given his age, Stephen thought his father didn't have any business going off to war and he told him so, but when his father pointed out it was going to be a short war, Stephen didn't have a rebuttal.

How could he? The President had called for seventy-five thousand men to preserve the Union, but the call up was for only three months of active duty. Three months was all they would need to take care of the southern problem.

Stephen argued with his Father and pleaded with his Mother that as the oldest son, it was his duty to represent the family. His pleas fell on deaf ears. Finally, his father came up with what seemed to him like an honorable solution to their dilemma. They would draw straws.

His mother took the seat at the head of the kitchen table. Stephen took a seat to her left and his father to her right. Under the soft light of the kerosene lantern, she used a small, sharp knife to cut straw into five equal pieces. The last piece was twice as long as the others. It was the long straw.

She took the straw then stood up turning her back on the two men. It only took her a couple of seconds to arrange the six pieces, but to Stephen it seemed like forever.

When she sat back down, his Father spoke up. "Stephen, you go first. We'll pick until one of us finds the long straw."

His mother held out her right hand and gazed straight ahead focusing on the print of President George Washington on the far wall. Stephen tried to read her face, but her jaw was set and face was totally blank. He waited, hoping she would somehow give away with a glance or a gesture, which was the long straw, but her eyes stared straight ahead. The draw would decide which of her men was going off to war; it was obvious she was determined to play no part in the decision other than to be the vessel holding the straws.

She'd arranged five straws in a circle with the sixth one in the middle. *Which was the long one?* Stephen tried to use some deductive reasoning. Surely, she wouldn't put it in the center; it would be too obvious. Or maybe, she thought that was what both Stephen and his Father would think, so maybe she tried to trick them. Thoughts raced through his brain; his heart started pounding in his chest.

He started to reach then pulled his hand back.

"What are ya waiting for?" his father snapped.

"Do you want to go first?" Stephen asked, making sure not to respond in the same tone his Father had used on him.

"No ... sorry," his Father answered.

Stephen kept his eyes focused on the straws, but no matter how many scenarios he considered, he knew it all came down to his mother and she was remaining steadfast in keeping her eyes straight ahead. No matter how long he waited, it wasn't going to make any difference; she wasn't going to give him a clue.

There was only one thing to do. *Lord, please help me pick the right one.*

The one in the center seemed to call his name. He reached again touching it lightly with his index figure and his thumb. He gave a gentle tug to see if he could get a clue to its length.

"No cheating," his mother whispered.

She might as well have said no stealing, no lying, or any of a number of sins. He knew the only honorable thing to do was to go ahead and pull out the center straw. He tightened his grip and pulled slowly. Even before he had pulled it all the way out, they all knew he had the long straw.

He held it up in the soft light and marveled at how something so small, so delicate, could hold such power, such control.

"Well, it's decided," his mother said as a tear rolled down her right cheek.

"Sir, you want some more coffee? I got a little left in the bottom of the pot," Private Ralph Sturtevant asked First Lieutenant Stephen Brown.

Stephen drained the last of his coffee before answering, "No thanks, Ralph. I've had enough."

Ralph nodded, and then drained the rest of the precious liquid with one long gulp. Stephen stomped out the smoldering ashes of the small fire.

"Give me your canteen," Stephen told his close friend as he reached with his right hand. Ralph pulled out the cork and handed it over. Stephen poured over a cup's worth from his canteen to replenish what Ralph had used to make him the cup of coffee.

"Do you have any food left?" Stephen asked as he handed back the canteen.

"Nope, what about you?"

"Half a biscuit. We'll share it at the next rest break," Stephen said.

Suddenly, drums sounded and assembly quickly followed by Corporal Harlan Bullard, the Thirteenth Vermont's bugler. First Sergeant James Halloway and started yelling out the orders for Company K, Thirteenth Vermont Volunteer Infantry Regiment to get back in formation. It wouldn't take very long for the first sergeant to get the company back into a column of fours. Brigadier General George Stannard had issued orders for the Second Vermont Brigade to stay on the road when they'd stopped for their ten-minute break.

Stephen grabbed his frock coat from the fence post and quickly buttoned up the first five buttons, leaving open the top four.

"Is yours dry?" Ralph asked.

"Still damp," Stephen answered. It had rained most of yesterday and into the evening. While the temperature was rising rapidly, the humidity was also still high and his wool uniform was slow to dry out.

He put his forage cap back on with the gold thirteen surrounded by wreaths of gold. Missing was the big red circle that would have showed they belonged to the First Corps.

Stephen took a step and his right thigh tightened slightly as if it had just been gently slapped by his scabbard. After so many days and miles the nerves in his leg had become so accustomed to the slap and still reacted as if it had occurred. The reaction felt as real to Stephen as the new sensation of the short wooden handle from Ralph's hatchet, stuffed between his belt and pants, rubbing on his left hip.

Robert took his customary position to the right of his commanding officer Captain George Blake. Both tried to look important as they watched the first sergeant and the other noncommissioned officers get the company formed up.

As George had told Stephen on many occasions, the company belonged to the sergeants and when the time came, they would let the officers use it to fight the enemy.

As the men gathered back in formation, Stephen took a deep breath. It was going to be another hot day, but at least they were out front. The Thirteenth Vermont would be the first regiment in the Second Vermont Brigades column and Company K had the honor of being the first company in the column.

Stephen tried to ignore the glances his way and the hint of smiles and gratitude that flashed across the faces of most of the men. The adulation and praise embarrassed him and there was no reason for it. What he had done was something the men should expect from their first lieutenant, nothing more.

Stephen heard shuffling of feet, and without looking, knew that young Second Lieutenant Carmi Marsh had taken his place to Stephen's right. Over the last nine months, they had gone through this routine what seemed like a thousand of times. If nothing else, the men of Company K and the rest of the Thirteenth Vermont were well drilled.

"You have any of your nine days' rations left?" George whispered to Stephen. Stephen instantly noticed the change in George's demeanor. Up until now, the term "nine days' rations" was used by all with humorous contempt, but it was quite noticeable that the humor was gone from George's tone and was replaced with concern.

"Half a biscuit," Stephen whispered.

Stephen was grateful; they only had a few more miles to march, and within a couple of hours they would make it to the camps up on Marsh Creek near the Maryland-Pennsylvania border. Once they joined the rest of the corps, they should be able to finally get resupplied.

More importantly, they would finally meet up with the rest of the First Corps of the Army of the Potomac. After six days of long marches, they would finally catch up to their new Corps Commander Major General John Reynolds and it was none too soon. Last evening, Lieutenant Benedict, Bridger General Stannard's aide had returned to the Second Vermont Brigade with news that General Reynolds was anxious for them to join the rest of the corps. The enemy was close and the prospects for a battle were high.

Until then, Stephen was going to have to deal with an empty stomach. At the start of the march, they were issued "nine days' rations" to be carried in haversacks that were designed to carry no more than four days' worth. Most of the men stuffed their pockets full of food, but even so, they were all running out.

"At least we won't have to worry about water," Blake whispered in a voice steeped in emotion.

Stephen felt awkward and starred down at his feet. He was grateful that Blake stopped there.

When Blake took a step toward the center of the formation, Stephen headed to his customary position at the rear of the company's column; he couldn't help but notice the eyes of the men followed him as he passed by each rank. Many smiled. Some nodded. Stephen locked his jaw and tightened his lips in an effort to keep his expression as neutral as possible.

He took his place next to Ralph in the last rank of the company's column.

"Amazing," Ralph whispered. "Three days ago, they were—"

"Shut up," Stephen snapped in a voice just above a whisper.

Corporal William Church, in line just in front of Ralph, started to turn his head.

"Eyes front," Stephen snapped at him before he had a chance to say anything.

As far as Stephen was concerned, what he did two days ago was no different than what he'd been doing for the last nine months. An example had been set for him to follow. The expectation was clear and there should be no praise or gratitude for doing what was expected. As he had told Ralph on numerous occasions, it didn't matter if the men appreciated his help or for that matter if they made fun of him behind his back. Their reaction didn't change what was expected of him.

Yes, sometimes their jokes had hurt his feelings, but that was his weakness not theirs. He hadn't done anything expecting praise or recognition. He did whatever needed to be done, because it needed to be done and because of the example that was set for him to follow.

The drums beat, the orders were shouted and they stepped off again down the dusty road. He couldn't help but notice the difference in the way the men marched. They stood more upright and their steps were more determined. Stephen knew most of it was because word of General Reynolds' request had spread through the company. He also knew that what he had done for them had lifted their spirits. While as a Christian, he was embarrassed by the praise and recognition he'd received, as an officer, he was pleased with the change in their demeanor.

He took a deep breath and shook his head slightly. What a difference a couple of days made. Two days ago, it was stifling hot and they were running out of water. Then yesterday, it had rained all day and the muddy roads were a bit of a problem, but today the heat and the humidity came rushing back, but he was confident water wasn't going to be a problem again.

With each step, his body started to relax into the now-familiar routine of the march. His eyes became heavy and his eyelids sagged as his eyes fixated on the toes of his shoes. They came in and out of view as his brain slowly drifted into a state between a dream and awake.

"Watch your step!"

Stephen's eyes sprang wide as he looked around the column. The lines looked straight, no heads bopping out of the ordinary. It took a few seconds for him to realize it was just a dream.

Sweat rolled down into Stephen's eyes, the salt causing them to sting. He took off his forge cap and wiped his eyes on his uniform sleeve. Once he had his cap back on his head, he glanced at the men around him making sure they were all still sweating. Unlike a couple of days ago, all of them were.

"Watch your step." It had become such a familiar call that it had filled his nightly and daydreams. If the subject of the call was close, he might hear a clacking sound then a dull thud before someone yelled, "Watch your step."

For nine months, while the Second Vermont Brigade had guarded the rear of the Army of the Potomac, they had drilled for every contingency; well, at least they thought they had until orders came assigning the brigade to the First Corps of the Army of the Potomac.

The First Corps had a two-day head start in the race to catch up with Robert E. Lee's Army of Northern Virginia. It was expected by higher ups that the Second Vermont Brigade would join the First Corps before they caught up with Lee's army. For most of the men, this was their first experience with the summer's heat and humidity south of the Green Mountains of Vermont. Even the boys who spent the summer with the First Vermont down on the Virginia Peninsula never had to march twenty miles in one day, let alone day after day.

When the first man collapsed in the middle of the column and the next three men tripped over him, causing the entire regiment, then the rest of the brigade to stop in their tracks, it became obvious—painfully so for some—that they had never addressed what to do when a man passed out in the middle of a marching column.

There wasn't a command in *Hardees Infantry Tactics* to deal with this situation, so Colonel Randall, the Thirteenth's commanding officer, settled on the command "watch your step" to be shouted out by anyone in the regiment at the first sign someone was going down.

To avoid being stepped on, men were encouraged to sidestep out of the formation before they collapsed. Some had used it as an opportunity to try and slack off, so the colonel had put a detail at the rear of the column to shame them back into formation.

For the first few who had done as the colonel had asked and stepped out of formation before they collapsed, their shame and embarrassment was painfully obvious as they stood or laid on the edge of the road watching their friends and family continue without them.

The debate quickly spread through the regiment and the rest of the brigade, if it was more honorable to do as the officers wanted, step out of the column, or march until you collapse face first in the dirt.

Stephen decided that it wasn't so much of a question of honor than it was pride. There was no way he was going to stand or sit on the side of the road and watch the rest of the brigade march past. He would rather have the detail at the end of the column drag him into the regiment's wagon then deal with the shame of standing on the side of the road.

Even with aching muscles, bleeding and blistered feet, and a lack of food—surprisingly, "watch your step" rarely rang out in the mornings and averaged just a couple an hour through the afternoon, but that all changed two days ago.

"Watch your step," echoed through the regiment every few minutes. Stephen remembered Corporal William Church looking over his right shoulder. "Sir, when are we going to stop for water?"

"We'll get food when we join up with the First Corps," Stephen answered, raising his voice so he could be heard by most of the men in the rear of the column hoping the thought of food would distract them from thinking about the lack of water.

As he had hoped, many of the men clapped and cheered as the talk of joining the First Corps raised their spirits.

"Lieutenant Brown, keep order in the rear of the ranks," came Captain Blake's sharp rebuke.

"Yes, sir!" Stephen yelled out and immediately all the men quieted down.

William glanced back over his shoulder with a pained expression, but all Stephen could do was shrug his shoulders. He didn't know when they would get any water.

When William looked away, Stephen bowed his head slightly and under his breath, slowly and silently recited the Lord's Prayer. With the words *give us this day our daily bread*, a sense of peace fell upon Stephen. He smiled as an inner confidence filled his soul. He knew the Lord would provide. He didn't know how, when, or where, nor did he care about the details. Those he would gladly leave to God. He just needed to be ready when the opportunity came to ensure that his men were given the gifts from on high.

He also knew that God didn't always provide what he wanted, like the night he pulled the long straw, but Stephen knew that God would provide what he needed and right now, he and his men needed water.

The thud was followed closely by clacking metal, then shouts of "watch your step." Stephen looked up along the right side of the column. He couldn't see any gaps in the line or anyone on the ground. He glanced back to his left in time to see Private Oliver Parazo step over a body sprawled out face down on road with his weapon, surprisingly, still tucked in at right shoulder arms.

From the sound of the thud and the few calls of "watch your step," Stephen knew the man had to be from Company K and with no chevrons on his sleeve, he must be a private, but from the backside, Stephen couldn't tell who he was. It was better this way—not knowing who they were leaving behind.

"Watch your step," came another cry from somewhere in front of the column. The calls echoed down the formation growing louder with each step Stephen took. Up ahead, he caught a glimpse of a man doing his best to crawl out of the way, pushing his rifle in front of him toward the edge of the road. Once he was clear of the column, the man rolled over on his back. With stricken, pleading eyes, the man whispered over and over, "Water."

No one stopped. No one offered him water. Orders were clear. Leave them where they fell. A rear guard would be along soon to gather them up.

He gave his canteen a quick shake. From the feel and sound of it, he still had a little left in the bottom. He knew many of the men were already out.

"Halt!" The command was a welcomed relief, but then the orders came for the company to rest in place in the middle of the road under the hot noon day sun.

The moans and groans were met instantly by the first sergeant's expected shouts of "quiet in the ranks." Stephen could tell the first sergeant didn't have his heart in it and was only making a token effort to keep the complaining under control.

Stephen didn't blame the men for complaining. If he wasn't an officer, he'd be complaining to, but it was his duty to be an example to his men, so he kept his opinions to himself.

"Sir, you got any water left?" Private Ralph Sturtevant, standing at Stephen's left elbow, whispered.

"A little," Stephen answered.

"Forget I asked," Ralph quickly said.

Stephen lifted his canteen over his head then handed it to his friend and former classmate.

"I can't drink the last of your water," Ralph protested feebly.

Stephen took a close look at Ralph's face and he was stunned at what he saw. Ralph's eyes were sunken in and his lips cracked. Stephen wondered how Ralph had managed to stay on his feet.

"Drink," Stephen said with this best command voice, knowing full well that the little bit left in his canteen would do little to help Ralph.

After a couple of swallows, Ralph handed back Stephen's empty canteen, then said, "I don't think I can take another step."

"Me either," William Church said as he turned around to face Stephen.

Stephen glanced around and saw the same look in the faces of many of the men who now turned to their lieutenant for help. Only Oliver Parazo, one of the strongest men in the regiment, still looked to be in fairly good shape. The rest of them looked like dead leaves waiting for a strong wind to knock them to the ground.

Stephen noticed a couple of men starring to the right and followed their gaze to a well, its white walls shinning under the afternoon sun. Next to the well, a lone cavalry sergeant sat on his horse holding a saber across his saddle.

Stephen rushed to the front of the company.

"Sir," Stephen said to Captain Blake, "the men need water." Stephen dropped his voice to a whisper and said, "I'm surprised half of them are still on their feet. Maybe the general will modify his order and let us send out a canteen detail."

"Captain Wilder already tried. The General ordered him back to his company," Blake whispered back.

Stephen took off his cap and rubbed his eyes. Captain Wilder from Company B was a good man, so Stephen wasn't surprised that he was the first officer to ask the general to change his orders.

Brigadier General George Stannard was also a good man and Stephen understood the pressure he was under. It had been five days since he had received orders to join Major General John Reynolds' First Corps of the Army of the Potomac. Rumors ran through brigade that the confederates were close, and Reynolds could engage the enemy any day now.

Yes, Stephen understood General Stannard's reasons for pushing the men, but while most of them could handle being without food for a couple of days, they couldn't survive without water for even a couple more hours.

Stephen noticed that Captain Blake's forehead was dry. "You've stopped sweating," he whispered.

"I'm fine," Blake snapped.

"You have any water left?" Stephen asked.

Blake shook his head. Stephen glanced back over at the well. He was amazed how the white wall shone in the afternoon sun. He looked back at Blake.

If I was captain, I'd send over a canteen detail, he thought to himself then instantly regretted it. The general's orders were clear with no wiggle room. As captain of the company, George Blake had to follow orders. With the regiment likely going into battle for the first time any day, the men of Company K needed their captain. If Blake violated General Stannard's order to keep his men in formation, he risked arrest.

The company needed its captain, but ...

"Sir, let me have your canteen," Stephen said.

"Why?" Blake asked obviously confused.

"You don't want to know," Stephen whispered as Lieutenant Marsh and First Sergeant Halloway and joined them.

Blake raised his left eyebrow as he was known to do when he was concerned.

"You can't. We have our orders."

"If I don't we'll lose half the men before we make another stop. Please, let me have your canteen."

Blake stood there for several seconds with his left eyebrow raised high before it slowly lowered back even with his right. He pulled his canteen over his head and handed it handed it to Stephen. Stephen looked over at First Sergeant Halloway.

"I'll give you a hand, sir."

"No, you won't," Captain Blake snapped.

"First Sergeant, give him your canteen," Blake ordered.

"He can't do it alone, sir," Halloway said.

"Don't worry, I won't," Stephen said.

Halloway and turned over his canteen and without saying a word Marsh did the same.

"You goin' take Parazo with you?" Blake asked.

Stephen smiled then turned his back on the three of them. A sense of urgency fell over Stephen. Time was short and he had a lot to do. He walked quickly up to Private Oliver Parazo, the strongest man in the company.

"Oliver, I need your help."

"What can I do for you, sir?"

"I need you to start at the front of company and collect the canteens of those who are out of water. I will start at the rear."

"Sir, isn't that against the General's orders?" Oliver asked confused.

"You're under my command. You only have to obey my orders."

"What about you, sir?"

"Oliver, don't worry about me. Give your rifle to Ralph and get going."

Ralph looked confused when Oliver handed him his rifle and hurried away.

"Give me your canteen," Stephen said to Ralph.

"Stephen, what are you doing?" Ralph whispered.

"None of your concern," Stephen snapped. "Now give me your canteen."

Ralph did as he was told, and Stephen moved quickly through the column collecting the canteens of those who were out of water. He met Oliver about halfway with the big man carrying close to forty-five canteens while Stephen was carrying thirty.

Stephen headed directly toward the well and Oliver fell in behind him. Stephen guessed that Oliver thought it was safer to stay behind his first lieutenant and with the look the cavalry sergeant on horseback was giving them, Stephen didn't blame him. To tell the truth, he would rather be following someone else, anyone else to the well instead of leading Oliver.

The cavalry sergeant stared right at them with no reaction almost as if he was looking right through them. Halfway to the well, the cavalry sergeant pointed his sword at Stephen then shook his head twice.

Stephen held his stare on the sergeant. The man's eyes were cold; clearly this was a man who'd used the sword for more than just pointing at a couple of men wanting water. Stephen's heart pounded in his chest. He knew everyone in the company was looking at him. His stomach seemed to roll over and he swallowed back the vomit that filled his mouth.

For nine months, he thought about a moment like this when he would face the enemy for the first time, but he never dreamed his enemy would be wearing blue.

"Sir, you can't get water here!" The sergeant shouted.

Parts of Stephen's brain shouted for him to let Oliver take the lead or even better yet run back to the safety of the company. Instead, he kept his jaw locked and starred at the sergeant as each step took him closer to the point of the sword.

As he got closer, the sergeant's tone turned harsher as he said, "Sir, I was put here under the general's orders to safeguard the well. You can't get water here." Then the sergeant shifted his sword to his left hand as his right moved to the grip on his pistol.

Stephen smiled. He had no idea why or even how, but he could feel it spread across his face.

The sergeant gave his horse a quick kick and the animal lurched between Stephen and the well.

"Sir, I have orders. You can't get water from this well."

Stephen stopped a few feet from the horse and rider. He took a deep breath and it was almost as if he could smell the water in the well.

"Son," Stephen said to the sergeant who was at least ten years older than he was, "I understand your orders, but my men are in desperate need of water and I'm not going back to them without it. I love you like a brother, but if you try to stop me," Stephen wiped the smile from his face and lowered the tone of his voice, "I'll kill you. I swear. I'll do it. As I see it you have two choices, you can go report that First Lieutenant Stephen Brown of Company K, Thirteenth Vermont violated the general's orders and got water for his men or you can stay here and die. You choose."

Stephen was using all the self-control he could muster to keep from pissing his pants, but he kept his gaze locked on the cavalry sergeant. Stephen relaxed slightly, when the sergeant's right hand moved away from his pistol grip and to his horse's reins. But his heart felt like it stopped when the sergeant raised his sword out to his side then spun his horse twice around. Stephen stood his ground and prayed Oliver was doing the same.

Again, he locked eyes with the sergeant and prayed he was doing the right thing. Sunlight flashed off the blade of the sword temporarily blinding Stephen. *Am I going to die?* Stephen braced himself as he waited for his vision to clear and it did just in time to see the sergeant slide his sword into the scabbard and slowly turn his horse from the well and ride away.

Oliver patted him on the back a couple of times. "You did it, sir. By God you did."

They quickly got to work. Stephen cracked up the bucket and held it pouring the cool water into the canteens that Oliver held but after the second one they both new that was a mistake and they switched.

As Oliver was filling the first canteen that Stephen held, Stephen glanced at his reflection in the water bucket. His beard was longer than it ever been. He looked and suddenly felt old.

They got into a rhythm with Oliver pouring and Stephen switching out the canteens. They worked quickly hoping to finish before the general had a chance to send a squad to stop them and put Stephen under arrest, but no one came.

With the last one filled; Stephen took a sip from his own canteen. Stephen motioned to Oliver. "I'll follow you back."

"You sure you don't want me to carry a couple of more," Oliver asked already weighted down with twice as many canteens as Stephen had draped across his body.

"I'm fine," Stephen lied as he fought to stand straight under the weight of the canteens.

Oliver nodded then turned his back on Stephen. Stephen slowly followed along behind taking baby steps in order to keep his balance. He kept his eyes glued on the ground making sure he didn't step in any animal holes. After several steps, he glanced up to see that he was keeping a pretty good pace staying right behind Oliver. It only took a couple of seconds for him to realize Oliver was the one doing a good job keeping the pace slow enough so Stephen could keep up with him.

Halfway back to the company, three men including Ralph ran up to Stephen and took the canteens from him. None of them said a word, not even Ralph, which was very surprising under the circumstances.

As he turned over his last canteen, Stephen noticed the cavalry sergeant, his horse's reins in his left hand, standing next to Captain Blake.

Stephen straightened up and marched right up to Blake and saluted. Blake returned the salute.

"Lieutenant, the sergeant has orders from General Stannard."

"Sir," the sergeant interceded. "I'm sorry, sir. I have orders to place you under arrest."

Stephen cocked his head slightly. *Why are you sorry? I threatened to kill you.*

"The general ordered me to take your sword, sir, but you are to remain with your company."

Stephen unclipped his scabbard from his belt and handed it and the sword over to the sergeant.

The sergeant took it with his left hand, faced Stephen, came to attention, and then saluted. Stephen was caught off guard, but he returned the salute. The sergeant then jumped back on his horse and rode off.

Blake looked at him then sighed. "I should have done it."

"Sir, the men need their captain. They don't need the first lieutenant ... if the roles were reversed, I would have followed orders just as you did."

A slight grin spread across Blake's face then it faded quickly. Stephen wondered what it might have meant, but he wasn't going to ask. When Captain Clark was elected Major for the entire regiment, Stephen was convinced he would be elected company captain. Most likely he would have been if it wasn't for Third Sergeant Blake declaring his candidacy for promotion.

George Blake had experience severing as a sergeant in Company A, First Vermont Regiment. After the election, Stephen hid his disappointment and was the first one to walk up to Blake and congratulate him on his promotion and told him he was the best man for the job.

Blake took a step closer. "I only hope I would have been brave enough to do what you just did," Blake said as he patted Stephen on the back. Stephen's eyes were drawn to the men in line and the smiles and nods and he was instantly embarrassed.

With the shouts of "Regiment ... Company ... Fall in," Blake hurried back to the front of the company. As Stephen took his place back in line, William turned around and stuck out his hand.

"Thank you, sir." William said as they shook hands. He took a step toward Stephen and whispered, "I was wrong and I'm sorry."

Stephen was about to ask about what, but then it dawned on him.

"William, you weren't wrong, and you have nothing to be sorry about."

William nodded. "Thank you."

Stephen forced a smile. "You're welcome," he said as the memories and emotions flashed through his brain.

According to military etiquette and tradition, First Lieutenant Stephen Brown was the logical choice to setup and take Captain Clark's place once the captain was promoted to major of the regiment, but there were a large number of men who served in Company A of the First Vermont, including William Church, who wanted one of their own to be captain.

For over an hour, the men gathered in groups outside the Johnson Hotel and debated who would be the best man to take Captain Clark's place. Ralph Sturtevant had warned Stephen that Blake was gaining support, but Stephen had discounted Blake's chances.

Friends of Second Lieutenant Marsh were anxious for him to move up to first lieutenant; First Sergeant Morey's friends wanted him to move up to second lieutenant. The only way that was going to happen was if Stephen was promoted to captain. Promoting a third sergeant all the way up to captain would take away Marsh and Morey's chance for advancement.

It all seemed logical to Stephen, but he underestimated the bond of the men from the Company A, First Vermont Volunteer Infantry Regiment, his father's old company. They wanted one of their own to be captain and they found the perfect candidate in soft spoken, seriously minded George Blake.

It wasn't until later that Stephen was surprised to learn that his longtime friend Corporal William Church had been a very persuasive advocate for his former sergeant. William later told Stephen that he felt the company needed to be led by someone with more experience.

Stephen's left foot slipped into a hole; his brain flashed awake from the thoughts of yesterday as he stumbled forward. Suddenly, he felt a pull on his belt holding tight as he quickly regained his balance.

He glanced over to Ralph.

"Got to watch them holes," Ralph said with a smile.

"Yeah, thanks."

"When you going to give me my hatchet back?" Ralph asked.

"When I find something better," Stephen responded.

"You can't be serious about going into battle with just that thing."

Stephen shrugged. He might not have any choice.

Like many of the officers, he decided a long time ago not to carry a pistol. Except at close range, they were very inaccurate. Plus, he found them hard to load and to keep clean.

More importantly, the position of the company's first lieutenant, as dictated in *Hardee's Infantry Manual*, behind the right center of the second platoon, meant he had two ranks of men with rifled muskets between him and the enemy. With the effective range of the company's .58-caliber Springfield rifle muskets at three hundred yards, at long range he had no need for a pistol.

Even if they did become engaged in close combat with the enemy, Stephen didn't think he would be able to steady the pistol enough to hit anything. Even at twenty-paces, he only hit the target a couple of times. He knew under the confusion of combat; he'd have no chance of hitting anything he was aiming at and could even end up killing one of his own men.

Over the last nine months, he had spent many a morning refining his skills with the straight edge of his 1850-foot officer's sword. While not quite the swordsman as Captain Blake, he could on most days hold his own, routinely besting Second Lieutenant Marsh.

He shook his head. Their nine-month enlistment was rapidly ending and the closest he had come to any combat was dueling swords with Blake and Marsh. Not what he expected when he answered President Lincoln's call for service. Still, despite the cat calls they'd received a few days ago when they crossed paths with the Army of the Potomac's Sixth Corps, Stephen didn't consider the men of the Second Vermont Brigade to be green.

He'd seen the look in their eyes when they faced off J.E.B. Stuart at Fairfax Court House, Virginia back in late December. Stuart had led a division across the Rappahannock River and gotten around the Army of the Potomac with the hope of raiding the Union's supply lines. Instead, at Fairfax Courthouse, he found three regiments of the Second Vermont Brigade along with support from four guns from a Connecticut artillery battery.

Up the road, the confident rebel cavalry came only to be greeted by a volley from a couple of companies from the Twelfth Vermont, serving as pickets out front of the main line. After firing, the pickets made a hasty retreat, but they had done their job and had stopped the rebel advance as Stuart sized up his opposition.

For good measure, the Connecticut battery let fly with a couple of shells, then the two sides settled into a starring match. As they waited, Stephen and Blake walked among the men offering words of encouragement, but Stephen could tell they weren't really necessary.

It wasn't that they weren't scared, he could tell that they were all just as scared as he was, but there was also something else in their eyes—determination. This was why they'd left their homes and their families. This was why they'd traveled down from their Green Mountains; it was time for them to fight for their country, but Stuart didn't give them the chance. He thought better than to attack infantry in a line of battle and the rebels moved off to the east and then back across the river without accomplishing much of anything.

While the generals had seen fit to regulate Vermont's Second Brigade to guarding supply lines and holding them out of the great battles at Fredericksburg and Chancellorsville, their own senior officers were determined that if they ever got the opportunity to face the enemy they would be ready. When not on picket duty or taking care of the needs of camp, they drilled, took part in target practice, and attended classes on how to be a soldier.

Stephen guessed Stuart had also determined there was something different about the troops in his front. While their uniforms and flags showed little sign of wear, they didn't act like green troops and besides there were so many of them.

Spared from any combat and with many of the officers having experience in camp life, they'd lost less than two hundred men to illness, disability, or desertion the

Thirteenth Vermont alone numbered close to 750 men. The same was true of the brigade's other four regiments. From what Stephen had seen when the First Corps had marched past them, he guessed the Second Vermont Brigade was double the size of any of the corps' other brigades.

Inexperienced under fire—yes, that was true—and their flags and uniforms didn't show the signs of combat. But Stephen knew and he guessed Stuart knew that the Second Vermont Brigade wasn't going to act like a green brigade when the shooting started.

He still wasn't sure how or why he thought of Ralph's camp hatchet, but with the looming battle he needed something to defend himself just in case it came down to hand to hand combat. Stephen glanced over at Ralph and chuckled.

"Why ya laughin'?" Ralph whispered.

"No reason," Stephen whispered back as he remembered Ralph's reaction when he asked to borrow his hatchet.

"What in the hell do you want with my hatchet?" Ralph blurted out in a high-pitched tone that carried across half the company. Stephen couldn't help but laugh as did the men around him. Their laughter brought a quick response from the first sergeant, who spun around and took a couple of steps backward as he shouted out in his shrill voice, "Sturtevant, Hagan, Church, quiet in the ranks!" Then he directed a dirty look at Stephen before he spun back around and went quickly back into step.

Without saying another word, Ralph pulled out his hatchet and handed to his right. For close combat, the hatchet was a little short, but the wide head might give him some advantage in warding off an attacker's blows. Stephen spun it in his hand, and he liked the feel of it. It was lighter than his sword and he should be a bit quicker with it.

He raised it over his head and made a quick chopping motion out to his right.

"What in the hell are you gonna do with that?" First Sergeant James Halloway shouted. Laugher boomed through the company as the first sergeant back stepped with an embarrassed look on his face, helpless in trying to quiet the men in the ranks.

With many of the men glancing back at him, Stephen knew he had to say something, so as his cheeks flashed red, he held the hatchet high over his head and shouted, "Why first sergeant, I'm gonna use it in defense of my country."

The expected laughter, claps, and yells spread through the company. Stephen was sure most of them probably thought he'd lost his mind. As the laughter died down and the first sergeant regained his composure and resumed yelling at the men to quiet down, Stephen decided that if they did get into close combat, his only hope that whoever he came up against would have the same reaction as the first sergeant. He'd be so caught off guard by the sight of a hatchet yielding officer that Stephen would have a few precious seconds to get the advantage on his foe.

"I can't believe we did it," Ralph whispered.

"We haven't made it yet," Stephen cautioned Ralph, but it was hard not to be excited. After nine months, they were finally going to join the Army of the Potomac and face Robert E. Lee's Army of Northern Virginia and none too soon.

Like the rest of the brigade, the Thirteenth Vermont was a nine-month regiment. Next week, their enlistment ran out and they were going home to Vermont. Up until last week, they had assumed they would go home without firing a shot at the enemy, but the orders came to join John Reynolds for at least for a few days and become a sister brigade to the fabled Black Hats of the Iron Brigade, First Brigade, First Corps, Army of the Potomac.

Through what seemed like endless days of marching, it was very much in doubt if they would catch the First Corps before they had found the enemy. Every night around the campfires, it had become the prime topic of conversation. Over the last few days, the conservation had changed from "we might be able to make it" to "we will catch them."

While they had never been on a forced march before and they had a big learning curve, they'd adapted quickly. In just six days, they had made up the First Corps' two-day head start. Unless the First Corps got into a battle this morning, and based on the messages to General Stannard from General Reynolds last evening, that was very unlikely, they were going to pull off what had seemed impossible just a couple of days ago.

They would fall into the long column of the First Corps and be there when they finally got an opportunity to fight Robert E. Lee and the Army of Northern Virginia. Stephen thought it was fitting that the Thirteenth was going to get the opportunity to stop this invasion of Maryland and Pennsylvania, after all, an invasion was the reason they have all joined in the first place.

President Lincoln had put out a call for additional troops to deal with Lee's invasion late last summer, but before the Second Vermont Brigade had left Vermont, the fighting at Sharpsburg, Maryland on the banks of the Antietam Creek sent Lee and his army back into Virginia. Stephen guessed it was one of the reasons the Second Vermont Brigade had ended up guarding the rear of the Army of the Potomac, they were a nine-month brigade and the reason for them organizing was gone.

What a difference a week had made. While they only had a week left in their enlistment, they had once again found their purpose. They were going to help the First Corps and the rest of the army stop Lee's second invasion on northern soil.

Ralph was right; he couldn't believe they had done it. First Corps was waiting for them about five miles ahead and Stephen could feel the excitement starting to pulse through his veins. Ralph was right, they'd done it.

Jacob Turney

The drums beat, the artillery boomed, the skirmishers to the north of the road let loose with another volley. It was starting to sound a bit like a battle. Captain Jake Turney, Company K, Turney's First Tennessee, had lost track of time, but he guessed it been a couple hours since the first shot and it was becoming increasingly clear the Yankee cavalry was fighting a delaying action, but delaying for what? Speculation ran rampant through the regiment, and Jake guessed the entire brigade, on the purpose of the delay.

Jake's theory, that the Union cavalry was giving the infantry and artillery time to fortify the large hill to the southeast, was proven wrong when the skirmishers took the hill's summit. Jake was very relieved he was wrong. The steep ridge and commanding position of the hill would have made an excellent defense position.

For over an hour, Jake, Colonel Newton George, First Sergeant Chuck Tuley, Sergeant Major John Fitzhugh, and First Lieutenant George Garrett, as well as many of regiment's company commanders had argued and debated various theories. With Jake finally proved wrong, it allowed his mind to focus back on the real question all of them wanted answered, why was Brigadier General James Archer playing into the cavalry's hands?

The brigade was still in a column of fours and slowly moving up the road from Cashtown toward Gettysburg. Why hadn't Archer deployed the entire brigade and pushed rapidly forward? While the Union cavalry was carrying carbines, which fired more rapidly than the musket loaders carried by Archer's brigade, they didn't have any of the new repeating rifles.

While the volume of fire had picked up as they moved farther to the east, it was clear to Jake, and he was sure to all the men in the brigade, there wasn't that many of them. Certainly not enough to give an infantry brigade much trouble let alone two brigades. Davis' brigade was still bringing up the rear, just behind the Seventh Tennessee.

Jake watched the first of the artillery batteries reach the top of the next ridge and he was surprised and pleased to see it make a right turn on to the road that ran along the crest of the ridge. As the third artillery piece started to make its turn, its left wheel came off and continued rolling straight ahead. Three men raced after the wheel and one launched himself face first and got just enough of a hand on it to change its direction into the rail fence. Jake joined the laughter of the rest of the company.

The remainder of the Thirteenth Alabama (a couple of their companies, along with all of the Fifth Alabama were serving as the skirmish line) followed the artillery around the corner. Jake was pleased they were finally getting off this road, even if it was only to take a different one.

On the crest of the ridge was a large brick two-story building with a white front porch running across its entire front. As Jake got closer, he could make out the sign on the side of the building "Herr's Tavern."

There were wounded men wearing blue, gray, and butternut uniforms, crowded on the porch. The pockmarks covered the west side of the porch's pillars with a few streaks of red.

The First Tennessee followed Lieutenant Newton George, riding his large brown horse, around the corner staying right behind the Thirteenth Alabama. As Jake passed the tavern, he saw a Yankee private lying sprawled out near the back porch his brain's oozing from a large hole in the back of his head. More importantly, the private still had on his boots, which looked to be in good condition, with no holes in the soles.

Jake glanced to his front to see Newt, turned in his saddle staring in his direction. They made eye contact and Newt shook his head once. Jake glanced back at the private just as his own left woolen shock gave way allowing the rough surface of the road to grate against the ball of his foot. The private's boots look like they were about his size. Jake looked back to the front. Newt smiled and turned back around in the saddle.

Jake took quick glimpses of the next ridgeline that looked to be about a half mile away. Back near the road from Chambersburg, a thick wood lot covered the face of the next ridge, but it thinned out to the south. To the north, on the other side of the road, there were open fields.

As Jake scanned the ground between the ridges, he saw a beautiful white horse, with a rider slumped over, splash into the creek running through the valley. The horse turned to the left as it came up the opposite bank and there was a bright red streak running down its side. Two men darted out of the woods then led the horse back into the cover of the trees.

It was clear to Jake that the cavalry was going to use the woods to their advantage, but this time it looked like they would have more to handle than just a skirmish line. Finally, James Archer was going to deploy the entire brigade.

As the column passed the artillerymen struggling to reattach their lost wheel, Jake heard Albert yell out. "Y'all loose somethin'!"

What looked like a very frustrated corporal yelled, "Shut the hell up you son of a bitch."

"Who you callin' a son of a bitch, you no' count—"

"That's enough!" Corporal Hugh Zimmerman demanded, cutting Albert off.

As Jake waited for Albert's expected response, he resisted the urge to turn around instead he started counting his steps. Two, four, six and still there was no response from Albert. Jake suddenly felt very stupid as he realized Albert was his fault. He'd treated him as a brother instead of a soldier under his command. No more, he decided. Albert was now Zimmerman's problem. If Zimmerman couldn't deal with Albert, then Jake would deal with Zimmerman.

The rest of the artillery was unlimbering along the crest of the ridge starting near the tavern. Jake hoped they were planning to blast the woods before the brigade started their attack.

Jake jumped as a shell exploded behind the regiment. He stepped out of line and looked behind. Out of the corner of his eye, he saw two puffs of smoke from the fields just north of the woods on the next ridge.

The first shell exploded short of the artillery near the tavern, but the next one was a direct hit, blowing a canon from its gun carriage and knocking down most of its gun crew.

Within seconds, the entire ridgeline exploded as the confederate guns returned the Yankee artillery fire. The dark, angry smoke belched and danced around the guns shutting off Jake's view of the enemy.

Jake turned and ran to catch up with his company. Just as he took his place in line, three men on horseback rode up from behind them and rode past the company at a full gallop, led by Division Commander Major General Henry Heth. Jake noticed brigade commander Brigadier General James Archer and his staff sitting on their horses just ahead on the side of the road. As Heth pulled up next to Archer, Jake wondered what'd taken him so long to get up to the front.

For the first time since the advance started, Jake got a good look at James Archer. He didn't look like himself. There was no fire in his eyes, and he almost looked timid or even nervous. This was so unlike the man who so impressed the Tennessee Brigade that they'd nicknamed him the "Little Game Cock."

As the regiment marched past the two generals, Jake overheard Archer tell Heth, "Sir, I don't know what's up in those woods. We need to shell them first before—"

Jake never expected to see Archer like this. For God's sake, the man had fought alongside a young Lieutenant Thomas Jackson at Chapultepec, Mexico during the Mexican War and had led the brigade boldly during many battles since taking over for Brigadier General Hatton after the Battle of Seven Pines.

To Jake, Seven Pines seemed like a lifetime ago. As the sunset, bayonets fixed and their voices joined the overpowering cry of the rebel yell, the four Turney brothers had madly gone into battle.

Jake remembered glancing to his right and seeing General Hatton leading the Seventh and Fourteenth Tennessee to the east as the First Tennessee continued to the north. Jake was too far away to hear what he was saying, but Hatton, looking every bit the distinguished southern gentlemen, was obviously urging his men forward. The memory had stuck in Jake's brain as if it was yesterday.

Jake remembered checking Company K's front rank and made eye contact with his younger brother Henry. "Eyes front," Jake snapped. Henry just smiled then nodded.

General Hatton and Henry—Jake couldn't think of one without the other as he remembered the last moments, he'd seen both of them alive. The former congressman from Tennessee and his younger brother charging into battle, seemingly without a care in the world.

Jake glanced over his right shoulder. He wasn't surprised to see Albert glaring back at him while James had his eyes fixed on the shoes of the man in front of him. Five Turney brothers had left Tennessee and now there were only three. A month after Seven Pines, Joel was killed at Cold Harbor or as he heard the Yankees were calling it Gaines' Mill.

"Shit," Jake said under his breath.

He glanced back over his left shoulder at Archer. He was shaking his head at Heth. He just didn't look like his normal confident self.

Jake looked back to the front in time to see a large, growling golden retriever come around a house on the right of the road heading directly for the front of the Thirteenth Alabama's column. The dog stopped short, barked, growled, and then lunged at one of the men. The man used his rifled musket to beat back the dog, but the animal appeared even more determined rocking back on its hind legs as if preparing to launch itself.

Almost on cue, two men lowered their rifles and shot the dog. The animal whimper took a few steps toward the house then fell dead just as a heavyset woman in a long white dress with her hair in a bun came running out the house's front door.

She reached the dog just as the last ranks of the Thirteenth were marching past. She lunged at one of the sergeants who pushed her and she fell over an ash hopper. The men laughed as a small cloud of black ash drifted over her, surely ruining her white dress.

Next in line was the boy colonel.

"Those bastards shot my dog!" she screamed at Newt.

Newt did what Jake thought was the honorable thing under the circumstances and ignored her. His placid response just seemed to fuel her anger. "You son of a whore, bushwhacking, son of a bitch—" she screamed at Jake.

"Well, lady, what is he a son of a whore or a son of bitch?" Albert yelled back at the woman.

"You bastard!" she screamed at Albert.

"Keep it up, lady, and we'll shoot you down like they did your dog!"

Jake could feel his face flash red as most of the company laughed at Albert's remark. He stepped out of line, swirled around, and glared at Albert whose face went suddenly blank as Jake's right hand reached down to the handle of his pistol. "One more remark out of you and I'll shoot you myself!" Jake screamed at Albert.

The woman laughed. "You tell 'm!"

Jake turned to her while keeping his hand on his pistol. When she saw Jake's expression, she went suddenly silent. Jake glanced back toward Albert, but Zimmerman's disapproving glare stopped his eyes cold. *Damn, I did it again,* Jake thought as he realized he had just undermined Zimmerman's own authority.

Jake jogged back up to his place in line feeling like a fool. He glanced up to see if his commanding officer had seen his performance and he was relieved to see the colonel had obviously missed it. But all his men had seen it and he felt even more foolish.

Orders came quickly as the brigade shifted formation from a column of fours to a line of battle facing to the east. The entire brigade stretched out down the road in two ranks. Woods along the road now blocked Jake's view of the next ridge, but at least forming into a line of battle and facing in the right direction was a start. The next orders caused Jake's heart to skip a beat.

"Forward March."

Jake noticed the change as soon as the line marched into the woods; there was coolness to the humidity. After hours of the slow dragging march in a line of battle, moving under the comforting shade of the woods perked up Jake's spirits.

Being a managed wood lot with wide spaces between the trees and no underbrush (due to livestock being allowed to graze among the trees), it was no problem for the men to keep good order to the lines even as they had to step around the trees. About halfway into it, Newt called a halt.

Jake and most of the other company commanders kept right on marching forward up to the edge of a zig-zagging worm fence bordering the woodlot. They knew it wouldn't be long before they advanced and they all wanted to get a look at what was in front of them. Newt left his horse with an orderly and joined them just on the edge of the woods.

As Jake leaned on the fence, he scanned the ground in front of him. There were two more worm fences running north and south across the ridge, separating two fields of waist high wheat. While the fence he was leaning on was likely out of range of the Yankees, the other two weren't. Having to climb two fences while under fire was a less than ideal situation, but it wasn't that much of a problem. The second rank would lay down covering fire while the first rank climbed over each fence then the first rank would do the same for the second. He noticed that beyond the third fence there was nothing but tall grass all the way down to the creek.

He shifted his focus to the far right. The Thirteenth Alabama had their right flank on an east west road. Down by the second fence, there was a farm lane with a house and barn. The farm lane served as border for a large apple orchard that covered most of that regiment's front. Jake didn't think the buildings would be too much trouble, but the orchard, with its low branches, ran all the way down to the creek. While it would provide them some cover, their lines would be ragged by the time they made it to the creek.

On the other side of the creek, in front of the Thirteenth Alabama, the woods thinned out and Jake was disappointed to see a couple of Yankee artillery pieces unlimbering. He hoped Pegram's guns would take care of them before the advance began.

To Jake's left, down by the creek, he noticed something odd. There was a large area of taller grass mixed with several patches of cattails.

"Damn. Swamp land," Jake said.

"Are you sure?" Newt asked.

"Yep, see the cattails?" Jake said pointing.

Newt turned to Captain John Bevell of Company D, at thirty-four, he was the oldest of the regiment's ten captains.

"I agree with Jake, it's got to be a swamp," Newt said. "Maybe, with as hot as it's been, it's all dried up, but if not, you're going to have to deal with it."

Jake nodded in agreement. The cattails were thick in front of the companies to the left of the regimental colors. If the ground was wet, the regiment's left division would have to deal with it.

"Is it going to be a problem for you?" Newt asked Bevell pointedly. Being the senior captain on the left, Jake assumed Newt had given John the same speech he'd gotten earlier. Newt was depending on John to keep an eye on the left flank for him.

John hesitated for a moment before he said, "I reckon we can handle it." Jake could tell John wasn't sure of himself.

"Sir, just to make sure, we could go in by divisions. The left division can follow the right and we can spread out once we get across the creek and up on higher ground," Jake suggested.

"We don't know what's up in those woods, we go in by divisions it will open a hole between us and the Fourteenth Tennessee it could open us up to a flank attack," Newt said.

While Jake didn't think it was likely, it was possible and there wasn't anything worse than having a regiment in a line of battle attacked on their flank. Even with the divisions stacked, the best they could do would be to bring maybe twenty guns to bear. A line of only fifty men making a flank attack could do considerable damage.

"Even if they don't attack on the flank, it takes half our guns out of the line and allows them to concentrate fire. We might not have a right division by the time we reach the creek," Newt said.

Jake knew Newt had made up his mind. He thought it was a mistake, but he also knew that once Newt had made a decision he wasn't going to change his mind. It was a personality trait he shared with many of the Turney's.

"John, we will just have to deal with the swamp the best we can."

"Yes, sir. We'll do our best."

Newt smiled. "I know you will. I know you all will."

A more concentrated volley of artillery fire from Pegram's guns slammed into the woods across the way. There was no way to tell if it was doing any good. No way even to know if there was even anything in the woods to shoot at.

John pointed to the left. "The skirmishers are moving forward." Jake saw Major Felix Buchanan in the mix of men. He must have talked the General in to allowing the brigade's sharpshooters to be part of the skirmish line.

"Gentlemen, it's time." Newt said in a hopeful tone. "Good luck to you all."

The captains returned Newt's good wishes and shook hands among themselves, and then hurried back to their companies.

Newt mounted his horse then took a position in the center of the regiment and yelled, "Men of Turney's First Tennessee!" The entire regiment quieted down. "Today, we march into history! Today, we will defeat the enemy on their own soil. Today, we take from them what they have taken from us. Our land, our homes, and our freedom."

Jake cheered at the top of his lungs right along with his men. Nashville had already fallen. The Army of Tennessee was defeated back in December at Murfreesboro and the Union army cavalry had even ventured into parts of Lincoln County. This was their chance to take the fight to the enemy's back yard.

The boy colonel sure knew how to get the men ready before a battle. Jake's cousin Pete was the same way, but he didn't have the knack for the economy of words like Newt, and Jake didn't know any lawyers, including his Father, who did.

"Company, Attention," Jake ordered. The men snapped to attention like the veterans they were, even his brother Albert stood perfectly still. Jake expected nothing else from men tested at the battles of Harper's Ferry, Sharpsburg, Fredericksburg, Cedar Run, Chancellorsville, and many others. They knew what was expected and he knew none of them would let him down.

Jake noticed Newt take his hat off his head and beat it against his right leg. He knew the feeling. Jake was relieved the waiting was almost over, but he was scared half to death. He tightened his lips as he looked over the company of thirty-six men trying to present an air of confidence. Including his sergeants and corporals, they were down to just thirty-two enlisted men with sixteen in his first platoon and fourteen in the second.

As prescribed by *Hardee's Infantry Tactics*, the two ranks of the Second Platoon were on the right side of the formation. Zimmerman's squad made up the second rank of the second platoon with James and Albert on the opposite sides of the line. Jake had purposely placed them there, so it would be difficult, if not impossible, for one artillery blast to take out all three of the remaining Turney brothers.

With their squad being in the second rank, both his brothers had their own bullet catchers in the first rank. Short of detailing them behind the lines, it was the best he could do at being his brother's keepers without being obvious to the rest of his men that was what he was doing.

Jake exchanged glances with First Lieutenant George Garrett in his position four steps behind and centered on the second platoon. It was George's job to look out for the left of the company during the advance and fighting.

To George's right, stationed in the center of the company's formation, was his Junior Second Lieutenant John Farrar. Farrar flashed Jake a nervous smile and Jake nodded. John had no assigned duties other than to help George with the Second Platoon.

With the company down to just thirty-six men, Jake had placed his two platoon sergeants back in line, instead of at the back of the formation with the two commissioned officers. Sergeants Bill Oldham, first platoon, and John Harden, second platoon, had flipped a coin to see who got the bullet catcher's spot in the front rank and Bill lost.

While the sergeant's first responsibility was to maintain order in their platoons by putting them in line, Jake had added some additional firepower to the company's formation. Jake cut short Bill's complaints about being John's bullet catcher when he pointed out that he served as the first sergeant's bullet catcher.

Behind the center of the First Platoon and to John Farrar's right was Second Lieutenant James Holland. While Holland was technically responsible for the First Platoon during an attack, First Sergeant Chuck Tuley was in charge of the first platoon and James helped out where ever Chuck needed him.

Jake knew he was extremely fortunate to have three of the company's four lieutenant slots filled as well as seven of the eight non-commissioned officer positions, also known as non-coms. Some of the other companies were down to just a couple of officers and less than half of their non-coms. Jake expected that after the coming fight, the colonel would transfer some of his men to other companies, but for now they were his men and he was glad to have them.

Jake joined his men by unbuttoning his shell jacket and the first couple of buttons of his shirt. While it was important for the officers to lead by example and be in proper uniform, on a hot day like today, it was more important to make sure no one passed out from heat exhaustion.

Cheers from the left came as an officer on horseback weaved through the trees waving his hat and yelling. Jake knew it was almost time to go. He made another quick scan of his men and everyone looked ready, even Albert was still standing at attention with his eyes front.

Newt took his place behind the colors near the drummer boys as the sergeant major shouted out orders for right shoulder arms. As the regiment stepped off, the regimental band started playing "The Bonnie Blue Flag." It was a fitting song to send them off into battle, but Jake would have rather had them play Dixie again just because he liked the tune better.

As they got over the first fence and cleared the woods, there was a yell to the right as the color bearer of the Thirteenth made a mad dash forward twenty yards in front of the regiment. There he stood waving the nine-foot staff back and forth and yelling urging on the regiment.

For a movement, Jake wondered if Willey Wood, the First Tennessee color bear, was going to make a similar mad dash, then a Yankee volley exploded from the woods, the angry smoke pointing a line toward the Thirteenth Alabama. Suddenly, their color bearer became very stiff then a second later made a beeline back to the relative safety of the ranks.

Jake was surprised the color bearer was still on his feet. While the cavalry's single shot carbines could lay down a more rapid fire than the infantry's rifled muskets, they weren't as accurate at long range.

Jake heard the high-pitched whistle of artillery flying overhead. He glanced to the right and up on the next ridge in time to see two shells burst in front of the Union artillery.

The Union guns returned fire and Jake heard those shells pass overhead on their way toward the Pegram's guns. Jake hoped the Union guns would keep up a duel with Pegram's artillery and leave the infantry alone.

The second rank laid down a covering fire as the first rank climbed the second fence. Jake kept as low as possible as he went over the top rail. He quickly got the first rank back in line and laid down covering fire for the second rank.

At the third fence, things went much the same with no problems as the Yankees continued to focus on the Thirteenth Alabama. Just as the Thirteenth disappeared into the orchard, things started to change. Jake saw a yellow flash through the woods—on the other side of the creek—as the Yankees let loose another volley, but this one was in the direction of the First Tennessee.

A heartbeat later, Jake resisted the temptation to duck as bullets zipped by him. He glanced to his left and was glad to see no holes in the front rank, but he was surprised to see the colors had stopped back a few yards. Then as the sounds of the volley died away he could hear the drummer boys beating out halt.

"Company!" He shouted at the top of his lungs straining to make himself heard above the sounds of the growing battle.

"Halt!" Jake commanded.

He trotted out a few steps to get a better view of what was happening on the left and was disappointed to see the left division mired in the swamp. He chuckled when a man lost his balance and fell face down disappearing into the grass, but this wasn't a laughing matter. Thirteenth Alabama was still moving forward and now there was a hole in the brigade's line.

The woods in their front exploded in a volley directed toward the left division. A couple men fell down into the tall grass, but this time Jake wasn't laughing. Mired in the mud and muck, the left division was a sitting duck.

Newt was doing his best to rally them and get them moving, so Jake drew his sword and yelled at the top of his lungs as he ran toward the center of the right division. They needed to lay down covering fire for the left division.

"Front rank, order arms!" He yelled. The other officers understood what he was doing and relayed the orders.

"Ready. Aim!" he shouted, and then added, "Aim at the edge of the woods boys."

Zip. The bullet was much too close for comfort. Jake sprinted through a gap between companies as more bullets zipped by him. As he cleared the first rank he yelled, "Fire!"

The thunder of the volley slammed against his eardrums. "First rank, reload. Second rank. Order arms. Ready. Aim. Fire!"

The enemy fire slackened. "Second rank, reload," Jake shouted as he sprinted back through the gap and though the coking smoke. The left division had moved forward about ten yards, when there was another volley from the woods.

Jake waved and shouted, and the right division moved forward keeping up with the left. The pop, pop, pop of enemy fire resumed. Several men in the front rank fell to the ground including Private Bob Davis from Jake's own Company K. Onward the line went as it shifted to the right filling the gaps left by the fallen men. Jake glanced back at Davis and was relieved to see that he was still moving.

A shell exploded to the left in the middle of the Fifth Alabama. The Yankee artillery, near the Chambersburg Road, was shifting their fire from the artillery to the infantry. Jake glanced back to the right and was very happy to see the two Yankee guns to the south had had enough and were pulling out.

On the other side of the swamp and to the left of the First Tennessee, Major Felix Buchanan sprinted out in front of the sharpshooters and urged them forward as the next shell sailed long. Jake guessed it was a combination of Felix's daring and the shellfire that inspired the skirmish line and the sharpshooters, for they surged forward with the now familiar rebel yell, rushed down the slope, and splashed through the creek to disappear into the woods on the other side.

"Reload!" Jake yelled.

From the woods in their front drifted a lone faint bugle playing "Saddle and Mount." Jake turned around in time to see the Thirteenth Alabama emerge from the orchard and join the rush through the creek and up the slope; a few yards then disappeared behind the trees into the woods.

"The colors, sir!" First Sergeant Chuck Tuley cried out.

Jake spun around to see the First Tennessee colors moving slowly forward again keeping pace as the left division drugged their way through the swamp. With the building sounds of battle, there was no way he was going to hear the drummer boys and he knew he was going to have to keep a closer eye on the colors. Where the flag went, so went Company K and the rest of the First Tennessee.

Jake heard the zip as his coat wiggled on his left side. He looked and wasn't surprised to see a neat, new hole in his uniform coat. He grasped his side but thankfully there was no blood.

As they got closer to the creek, the fire intensified. Fifteen yards from the water, Newt started shouting and waving his arms and the left division hit the ground. Jake yelled and waved and the right division did the same lying down in the tall grass.

Jake lifted his head and saw Newt spin his horse around. A few gallops and the horse sailed over the third fence and he just as easily cleared the next one as Newt headed back toward General Archer. A few seconds later, one of Archer's aides spurred his horse and took off at a full gallop toward Company K. The aide's horse stumbled after the second fence but cleared the third one with no problems. The officer came around the end of the line as he headed to where the Thirteenth Alabama had disappeared into the woods on the other side of the creek.

The enemy's fire shifted back in the direction of the right division. Bullets zipped through the grass and two bullets slammed into the ground on each side of Jake's head.

"That was close," Chuck said.

"Ah shit," Lieutenant George Garrett cried out in anger.

Jake rolled on his side so he could look to the rear and through the grass made eye contact with George who was obviously in pain. "How bad," Jake mouthed. George just shook his head as he clutched his right hip. *Damn, shot in the ass.* Jake wanted to laugh but this was not the time.

"Lieutenant Holland!" Jake shouted.

"Yes, Sir," came James Holland's expected and immediate reply.

"You take George's spot in the line!" Jake ordered, moving Holland from the first platoon to the second platoon. Holland immediately started crawling over to George.

"Lieutenant Farrar!"

"Yes, sir!"

"You have the first platoon!" Jake ordered him to take Holland's place at the center of the First Platoon.

"Yes, sir!" Farrar replied not bothering to hide his enthusiasm for the opportunity to take on more responsibility.

Jake was pleased the company was keeping up a steady fire. The men would lay on their backs to reload their muskets, roll over on to their stomachs, take aim, fire, then roll back on to their backs to reload again. Shooting through the grass and into the trees, he had no idea if it was doing any good, but it gave everyone more confidence to shoot back at those shooting at them. He wanted to join them, but his pistol was only accurate to up to about twenty yards, so he seldom, if ever, pulled it from its hostler.

A volley thundered from the woods, but this time the billowing smoke rising up and through the trees was farther to the right telling Jake the Thirteenth Alabama had changed direction and were now coming in on the flank of the enemy in front of the First Tennessee.

Immediately, there was a slacking in the enemy's fire. Jake glanced to his left; Wood had the colors up again.

"Company, on your feet!" Jake ordered. Once they were all on their feet, he followed with attention. They were ready to go.

It took less than a minute for the rest of the regiment to get back into formation. Willey Wood waved the colors back and forth twice then rushed forward.

"Order Arms. Forward, March" Jake shouted the orders. He paused. "Double quick step! March!"

Sword raised high and yelling at the top of his lungs, Jake led the right division down to the creek and they splashed through knee-deep water. Out of the corner of his eye, he saw Albert slip, catch himself, stumble, then throw his rifle up on the bank as he gracefully fell face first into the shallow water.

The whole line broke out laughing as they scrambled up the opposite bank. Jake wasn't surprised to see James grab Albert and drag him to his feet. Jake was surprised to see James and even Albert laughing just as hard as everyone else was.

The trees were denser than he expected. Another yell from up ahead to their left then a blast of another volley. The dark angry smoke danced among the trees obscuring Jake's view of what was in that direction.

As they scrambled up the slope, the rush slowed to a more cautious advance. About hundred yards up through the woods, Jake caught sight of a rail fence. Suddenly, the fence exploded with flame and smoke. A split second later, a different set of sounds greeted them as bullets tore through leaves, it slammed into and splintered tree trunks. Jake glanced, no holes in Company K's ranks.

Up ahead and to the right, the Thirteenth Alabama let loose another volley. There was no enemy reply. The humidity held down the smoke from their volley and the acidic, thick cloud swirled and danced through the trees and flooded over the men of Company K as they moved forward.

Jake stepped over a dead Yankee with yellow cavalry stripes down his pant legs and new boots. Two more dead cavalrymen were lying near by both, with boots in much better condition than his shoes. He hoped he'd be able to find them again after the fighting was over.

His men were firing at will and with each shot; the smoke cloud grew angrier. Jake's eyes were watering and the snot was running from his nose, but Jake hardly noticed the common effects of combat, but the visibility was a problem.

"Damn it!" Jake cursed not being able to see. He took a chance and knelt down, and he was pleasantly surprised to find a layer of clear air within three feet of the ground. They were fifty yards from the rail fence that ran across the crest of the ridge and he was relieved to see there weren't any troops behind the fence.

He was about to order his men forward at a double quick when he noticed legs, lots of legs, moving in what looked like a column fours behind the fence line heading to the north toward the advance position of the skirmish line. He knew it had to be infantry, at least entire regiment.

"Lieutenant Holland, report! Lieutenant Holland, report!" Jake shouted as he left his place in line and cut behind the second rank.

"Here, sir!" Holland yelled as he rushed up to Jake.

"There is enemy infantry up ahead."

"How do you know?" Holland butted in.

"Shut up and listen," Jake snapped. He didn't have time to explain.

"I have to report to Colonel George. You have command until I get back."

"Me, sir?"

"Yes, you damn it." Jake snapped as First Sergeant Tuley joined them. "James, just do whatever Chuck tells you to do," Jake whispered. "And you'll do fine."

"Yes, sir," Holland replied as Jake hurried away.

Jake took two quick steps, caught his foot on an edge of a boulder protruding just a few inches above the ground, tripped, and slammed into a large tree, dropping his sword. His right shoulder hurt like hell and he scraped the skin off his left palm, but at least he hadn't fallen on his ass. He glanced around and was thankful no one noticed him.

He knelt down and picked up his sword as he sucked in some of the clear air close to the ground. As he stood back up, he glimpsed at the regiment's color through the smoke. He hurried toward it but this time he took care to watch out for the rocks and boulders.

After a few yards, it was clear there wasn't a horse near the colors. He hoped Newt had decided to dismount and sent his horse to the rear.

"Private Wood," Jake shouted as he ran up to the colors. "Where's the colonel."

"Up ahead, sir," Willey Wood replied, as another volley thundered through the woods releasing another cloud of angry smoke. He couldn't see but ten yards to his front and there was too much noise to try to shout for Newt.

He guessed that General Archer would have moved forward by now and decided it might be easier to find him down by the creek. As he took off at double quick, he started to have second thoughts. Maybe he should have tried harder to find Newt.

As reached the creek, the smoke started to clear and twenty yards to the north was General Archer wading across.

"General Archer," Jake shouted as he quickly closed the distance. "Sir, I saw Yankee infantry up on the ridge coming up from the south," Jake said as he pointed best as he could with all the smoke, to where he'd seen the troops.

"Captain, I doubt it. General Davis is to occupy the timber to our left and I'm sure you saw his men getting into position."

Jake was flabbergasted. Davis' brigade was to their north. "But, sir, they're coming up from the south."

"I'm sure that is what you thought you saw captain, but it had to be Davis' men. Now return to your company."

"Sir!" Jake tried to protest.

"I'm ordering you to return to your company, captain."

Jake was so surprised by the way Archer dismissed his report that all he could bring himself to do was stammer, "Yes, sir."

Jake spun around, hurried along the bank of the creek, and with each step his wits came back to him. He reran in his mind what he'd seen. The fence ran across the crest of the ridge running north and south. The troops were coming from his right to his left. They had to be coming up from the south and there was no way they were Davis's men.

Jake spun around, but Archer was gone.

"Damn-it! Jake shouted as his Turney temper returned with a passion. Jake knew his opportunity to get Archer to listen to him was already gone.

"I'm such an idiot." Jake muttered as he hurried along the creek bank. With each step, he prayed that Archer was right and it was Davis up on the ridge, but he knew it couldn't true.

He left the bank and headed back up the hill into the swirling smoke.

"Damn trees," he muttered, followed by, "damn smoke."

Just then, he saw a flash of blue and red and he knew he was behind the center of the regiment, and then he got a glimpse of a horse.

A yell went up along the line that caused the hairs on the back of Jake's neck to stand up. The flag and the horse pushed forward disappearing into the smoke as the regiment surged forward. Jake ran to catch up as his confidence returned. Yankee infantry be damned. Flash of yellow then the muted thunder of the First Tennessee's concentrated volley.

As the thunder faded, he could hear the shouts of encouragement yelled down the line as they pushed toward the crest of the ridge. They were doing it. Whoever the Yankees were, they were too late to stop them from taking the ridge.

As Jake ran, Junior Second Lieutenant John Farr emerged from the angry smoke. Jake scanned the line; both ranks were reloading. In a few seconds, they'd be ready to dash forward and take the ridge. John smiled at Jake as he passed by. "We got them on the run, sir!" John shouted.

As Jake came around the right flank, he yelled, "Lieutenant Holland, repor—"

From his left, to the north, came an explosion that drowned out his words. While he couldn't see anything through the smoke, it was clear from the direction of the sound that the volley had been fired at them. There were more shouts from the left division, angry, blood curdling sounds of fear and death.

"Damn it!" he shouted, cursing himself. He knew he should have followed Newt up the ridge and warned him about the Yankee infantry. He let Newt and the regiment down and now men were needlessly dying and it was his fault for not warning them.

"Fire at will!" Holland hollered.

Jake glanced at the second rank and was pleased to see his brothers were still on their feet. He then dropped to his knees to get another look up the ridge and suck some clean air into his lungs. To the north, Yankees were pouring over the rail fence as flashes of yellow streaked through the smoke. Out of the corner of his right eye, he saw movement. He quickly shifted his gaze and was shocked to see another Yankee battle line taking position behind the fence about thirty yards directly in front of Company K.

Peeking between two of the rails was a Yankee officer doing exactly what Jake was doing, getting a look under the smoke. Jake couldn't help but laugh when the Yankee waved at him. Jake waved back and for a moment it was like waving to a neighbor on the other side of a field. Time seemed to stop as the two men shared the peace of the clean air below the ranging battle.

It took a couple of seconds before Jake noticed the Yankee was wearing a black hat. Chills went up and down his spine. Only the Army of the Potomac's First Corps, the Iron Brigade, wore the black hats.

Jake was the first to break the peace. He wasn't going to let his men down the way he'd let down the brigade and the rest of the regiment.

He started yelling before he stood. "Cease fire, Cease fire."

Lieutenant Holland and First Sergeant Tuley were surprised at first by the unusual order while in the mist of battle, quickly joined Jake in repeating it. "Cease fire! Cease fire!"

Jake rushed in front of the first rank, shouting, "Both ranks, reload, both ranks, reload."

Jake's yelling got the attention of Captain Henry Hawkins of Company I, the next company in line; Jake emphatically waved his right hand in the direction of the advancing line as he shouted, "Black hats."

For a second, Hawkins face went blank. The reputation of the Black Hats of the Iron Brigade was well known and well earned. Hawkins quickly recovered and started shooting orders to his men as Jake turned back to his own Company.

"Damned black-hated fellows again," Albert shouted out.

"Both ranks, ready, aim," Jake shouted as he waved the direction for them to aim. "Let's give it to those Black Hats," Jake yelled as he dropped to his knees, just before he yelled, "fire!"

As the roar of volley swooped over Jake thundering against his eardrums, he dropped down and looked back up at the fence. Just above where one man's legs disappeared into the smoke, there was a bright yellow flash. A spilt second later, happening so fast Jake wasn't even sure he had really seen it. A leg blew free, and then a billowing curtain of reddish gray smoke formed a veil, as the other pieces of the man's body fell to the ground. Jake had heard about carriage boxes taking a direct hit and exploding, but he'd never witnessed it before.

A second later, the Yankees answered with a volley of their own. Jake looked up and was surprised to see no holes in the line. The smoke swirling though the trees was a curse as well as a blessing. The Yankees, not being able to see any better than his own men, must have under estimated the slope of the ridge and fired high. He glanced back up the ridge and he wasn't surprised to see the Yankees climbing over the fence.

"Reload! Reload, fire at will," Jake shouted as he scurried between the ranks then around the company back to his place in the line.

Jake sent Lieutenant Holland back to his position in the line as he returned to his own spot. The boys were firing at will into the blinding smoke not knowing if they were hitting anything. The Yankee fire wasn't too bad on this side of the line, but from the shouts to the north, Jake could tell the left division was taking a beating.

Suddenly another volley exploded this one from directly in front of them. Jake froze as a he felt a bullet whiz by his right ear. It was much too close. He dropped to his knees and he wasn't surprised to see the Yankee line was over the fence and moving down the ridge toward them. Hard to judge the numbers but it looked like it could be the entire regiment.

Another volley blasted down the hill, but this one was from the south in the direction of the brigade's right. Shouts and screams from the direction of the Thirteenth Alabama, answered the volley. The only thing Jake could make out was the dreadful word "flank," repeated over and over.

The Yankees were pressing the First Tennessee across the entire line and now shouts from the Thirteenth Alabama about Yankees flanking them.

A yell from in front of them told Jake the Yankees were making a dash down the hill. Jake admired the guts of the Yankee officers who ordered their men to charge into the smoke. He wished Archer had shown similar courage earlier in the morning.

"Cease fire, cease fire," Jake yelled as he stepped in front of the line again. "Reload boys, quickly now, they're a comin' and we're gonna give it to them."

"Both ranks. Ready, aim!" Jake added, "Steady boys; let's wait until we see their flag." The seconds seemed like minutes to Jake. Raised high above his head, his sword felt like it weighed fifty pounds as he struggled to stay perfectly still waiting for their flag to emerge. Suddenly there was a flash of red, white, and blue of the national color followed immediately by the dark blue of their battle flag.

"Fire!" Jake screamed as he made a sweeping motion with his arm toward the Yankee flags.

For a couple of seconds the Yankee battle flag disappeared into the smoke. Their national color seemed to rise up higher in the air, then crashed back earthward. A cheer went up along the regiment's right division, but the celebration was short lived as the Yankee flag rose up again from the smoke and started to move toward them.

"Fall back! Fall back!" The shouts came down the line. Someone shouted, "Back to the creek." Jake looked for the First Tennessee's color, but he still couldn't see it through the smoke. Jake got a glimpse of the Thirteenth Alabama's colors moving back down the hill.

"Fall back. Back to the creek!" Jake shouted as he ran across the front rank far enough to make sure all the companies on the right were falling back.

"Keep in line boys. We ain't gonna show them our backsides!" Jake yelled as he headed back to his own company. A man in the back rank of Company B dropped his weapon, turned tail, and ran for it. A couple of others started to turn when an officer brandished his sword giving them just enough encouragement to keep their places in line.

The Yankee flags flashed through the smoke about thirty yards in their front. Jake wanted to make a stand. He thought about ordering the right to fix bayonets and charge, but there were shouts from the north now as well as those from the south repeating the dreaded word, "Flank."

"Back to the creek boys!" Jake shouted instead.

With Archer's Brigade retreating, as the Yankees moved forward, the volume of musket fire had died away. Jake got a glimpse of the Yankee flags; they were closing the distance. Soon, the Yankees would overrun the right division; then it dawned on Jake that the thick smoke over that part of the ridge had turned from a curse into a blessing. The Yankees had no idea what was in front of them.

Jake turned around to Chuck. "Passed the word down the line, when I give the order, we're goin' to give them the rebel yell!"

Chuck looked flabbergasted. "We're gonna charge, sir?"

Jake smiled. "No, but they don't know that," he said as he pointed in the direction of the Yankees. Chuck nodded as Jake spun back around and ran back down the front rank relaying the order to the other captains of the right division. In less than a minute, all was ready.

"Fix bayonets," Jake shouted with all he had. The other captains repeated the order.

"Double quick step! Charge!" Jake shouted. The entire right division erupted in the wonderful sound of the terrible, frightening, rebel yell. Through the smoke, Jake could see the shadow of the Yankee flags stop, then leaned forward slightly as if to brace against the expected charge.

From the south, a few men came running through the trees, then several more. The Yankees had routed the Thirteenth Alabama. From the yells to the north, it appeared the same thing was happening there, too. Jake knew it was time to let go of his pride, take a practical approach to saving his company before the Yankees in his front discovered his ruse.

He turned to Chuck. "Keep it quiet, pass the word, we're going to do about face and sneak out of here. Don't stop until you reach the woods on the next ridge."

"Back where we started?" Chuck asked, obviously disappointed.

Jake nodded. "I'll catch up to you," he said as he headed north to pass the order to the rest of the companies of the right division.

Jake dashed to the left to Henry Hawkins of Company I.

"Henry let's get the hell out of here. Quietly, pass the word to do an about face and let's see if we can—"

Yells from their front cut Jake off. The ruse was up. He turned back just in time to see the Yankee flags dash forward.

The opportunity to sneak away was gone and he had no choice but to swallow his pride.

"Retreat! Retreat! Retreat" Jake shouted as he waved his sword above his head. Henry didn't waste any time and Company I was already on the move rushing to catch up to his own Company K, which was rapidly disappearing into the smoke.

Jake could see the rest of the right division was turning tail and moving back down the hill. It was now time for him to look out for himself, so he trotted after Chuck and the rest of his company.

As he came down the slope, he noticed a Yankee cavalry soldier lying face down with two gaping, bloody holes in his back. Jake's eyes darted to the soles of the dead man's shoes. No holes. Jake's left foot hurt like hell. He slid down on his knees and stopped next to the man's body. He wanted—he needed—those boots.

A bullet slammed into the tree, just above and his right shoulder, showering him with pieces of bark.

"Damn it!" Jake shouted as he realized it was either the shoes or risk injury, death, or even worse, capture. He heard two more bullets zip by his head. As he jumped to his feet, he noticed a clean white handkerchief lying so out of place in the mist of the blood, smoke, and death, next to the dead man's body. Jake reached down and grabbed it, slipped, then fell on his back just as several bullets zipped past.

Jake rolled on his stomach and half crawled, half ran on all fours, for a few yards before getting back on his feet and embarking on a full out run down the slope. The veil of smoke pulled away, revealing the entire brigade was in a rout.

Up ahead, Company K splashed back through the water, Jake was pleased to see some resemblance of the two ranks, but they were one of the few companies that appeared to be in any kind of order.

Shouts came from his left. "Surrender! Surrender or we'll shoot!"

Jake glanced over his left shoulder, to the south; two Yankees had weapons trained in his direction. He would rather die than go through the embarrassment of capture again. He planted his left front, took a quick step to his right, hoping to throw off their aim. Then he put his head down and darted toward the creek.

To the north, he was horrified to see Yankee colors and a mass of blue troops already on the other side of the creek. As he splashed across there were more shouts of surrender. The Yankees had overrun both flanks and were surrounding the brigade.

To the north in the middle of a wheat field, Jake saw a regimental color waving back and forth. General Archer was nearby and it looked like he was having some success at rallying a jumbled mass of men around him. Jake wasn't surprised to see Newt standing in the middle of the mass of men helping Archer with the rally.

Hope surged through Jake. The Division's other two brigades, led by Brigadier Generals Brockenbrough and

Pettigrew should be up by now. If Archer could rally the brigade and Brockenbrough and Pettigrew moved forward, there was still a chance they could drive back the Yankees. Jake changed direction to join them, just as the Yankee's let loose another volley at Archer's group.

The regimental color crashed to the ground. Some of the men darted up the slope, while most of them just dropped to the ground. The rally was over. Jake changed direction again, toward the safety of the woods.

Jake, covered in sweat, pushed through the pain of his cramping leg muscles as he labored back up the slope struggled back over the top of the first fence he came to. As he got over the top, he glanced back again.

He saw a man pulling the regimental color from its staff. Better to destroy it themselves then to let the Yankees capture it. Jake hoped and prayed it wasn't the First Tennessee's color. They'd already lost one color to the Yankees; the embarrassment of losing another one would rank right up there with being captured again.

Jake crawled through an opening between the rails of the second fence, and then he collapsed against it trying to catch his breath. He couldn't help but look back again. General Archer was struggling to get over the first fence when a Yankee grabbed him and pulled him back. When Archer got back to his feet, he broke his sword over his knee and threw it to the ground.

Many men around Archer were throwing down their weapons and surrendering. The good news, if there was any, was that the Yankees weren't pursuing those who made it over the first fence.

"First Tennessee! Men shouted from in the woods. After a couple of minutes, Jake finally caught his breath and then went to join what was left of the regiment.

Stephen Brown

"Where are they?" Private Ralph Sturtevant whispered.

"I don't know," First Lieutenant Stephen Brown whispered back.

Thousands of smoldering campfires made it obvious this was the First Corps camp from the night before, but they were already gone.

"I thought we were going to get some food?" Corporal William Church said looking over his right shoulder.

"I guess someone forgot to tell the First Corps we were hungry," Ralph said.

"Fall out!" came the order from Captain George Blake.

Stephen walked up to Blake. "I thought they were going to wait for us?"

"So did the colonel," Blake answered.

"I wonder if we can see them from up there," Second Lieutenant Carmi Marsh said pointing up the road to where it crested over the top of the ridge they were on.

Stephen thought Marsh might be right. If this ridge was like the others they'd marched over today, they should be able to see for miles to the north.

With all the marching they'd done over the last six days, Stephen shocked himself when he looked at Marsh and said, "Let's go find out."

"I was hoping you'd ask." Marsh looked at Captain George Blake, "You want to come, sir?"

George shook his head. "I better stay with the company. Don't be gone long, not sure how long we are going to be staying here."

Stephen led off and Marsh fell into step next to him. With all the marching they'd done, it had become second nature for both of them. Whenever any of them walked together they naturally just fell into step.

As they came to a crossroad, Stephen noticed the fence lines in both directions as far as he could see were devoid of all their rails. The fence posts looked like lonely soldiers guarding the roads. While on the march, Stephen had seen fences stripped of their rails for fire wood but nothing like this.

Stephen noticed Private Ralph Sturtevant was using a stick to stir up some smoldering embers from an abandoned campfire. Ralph looked up as they passed.

"You want to come?" Stephen asked.

"Where ya going?" Ralph asked before adding a belated sir.

Stephen pointed up the road. "Want to see how far ahead the First Corps is?"

Ralph shook his head. "No thanks, I rather have some coffee ... how long do you think we will be here?"

Stephen shrugged his shoulders.

"You're a lot of help," Ralph called out again adding another much belated, "Sir."

Stephen let out a big laugh.

"He should treat you with more respect," Marsh snapped.

"He said, sir," Stephen said knowing what was coming next as he enjoyed Marsh's irritation much more than he knew he should have.

"But it sets a bad example for the rest of the men," Marsh protested. Stephen ignored him.

"You got nothing to say for yourself?" Marsh snapped.

Stephen stopped in his tracks. "Sir!" he snapped a bit more harshly than he intended.

"What?" Marsh asked obviously confused as he stopped and turned around to face Stephen.

"If you're going to be rude to me, you better say 'sir' when you do it."

"Oh," Marsh said as his face went totally blank.

"Oh what?" Stephen demanded being careful to keep his voice under control. Marsh just stood there with a blank face without a clue what he was talking about.

"I expect to hear a 'sir' whenever you address me," Stephen demanded.

"That's crazy," Marsh protested, before adding, "Sir."

Stephen smiled and resumed walking. "Now you know how Ralph feels," he said as he went past Marsh.

"It's not the same thing," Marsh protested as he came alongside.

"I outrank you," Stephen reminded him.

"Yea, but we're ..." Marsh's words trailed off as it obviously dawned on him that he wasn't going to win the argument.

"We're what?" Stephen asked, not letting Marsh off the hook.

"Ah, ah, fellow officers?" Marsh mumbled more as a question than a statement of fact.

"So, we're not friends anymore?" Stephen asked.

"Well, ah, that too," Marsh stammered. Then getting to what seemed to Stephen as a second wind, he said, "But Ralph is—"

"But Ralph's what?" Stephen cut him off. "A longtime friend? Why yes, he is and next week we are both going to be private citizens again. In the meantime, if he wants to treat me as a friend as he obeys orders, I have no problem with that and neither do you."

"I guess you told me, sir," Marsh said.

"Yes, I did ... and stop calling me sir," Stephen laughed as he slapped Marsh hard on the back.

Stephen and Marsh spilt apart clearing a path for a couple of officers on horseback coming up the road from the north. Stephen recognized one of them as being on the general's staff. He guessed they were doing the same thing as him and Marsh, getting an idea how far ahead the First Corps was.

"Wait up," came a shout from behind them.

Stephen spun around to see Corporal William Church running up to join them. Stephen glanced back at Marsh who had stopped a couple of feet ahead.

"How come you invited Ralph to join you but not me?" William asked joining up with Stephen. He glanced over at Marsh and added a belated "Sir."

"Don't worry about calling me sir," Stephen told William.

"You sure?" William asked as he glanced over at Marsh knowing full well how Marsh felt about being called sir by the enlisted men.

"As long as we aren't around the company, yes I'm sure," Stephen said as he glanced at Marsh.

"It goes for me too," Marsh added.

William fell into Stephen's left with Marsh on his right and quickly the three of them fell into step with each other.

As they came up to the crest, to the northeast, down the slope, and across a creek sat several hundred parked wagons. *Thank God, food,* Stephen thought to himself.

"There are our wagons," Stephen said as he pointed.

"Our wagons?" Marsh questioned him.

"It's got to be the First Corps wagons and we are now part of the First Corps," Stephen reminded them.

"We're going to eat tonight," Marsh said.

"I was thinking the same thing," Stephen added.

"So where is the Corps?" William asked

William was right, there were no troops. Stephen looked for rising dust of a marching column and he was surprised that there was none, except out on the horizon there was a bit of grayish white color.

"Is that smoke?" he asked as he pointed to the north.

"Looks like a cloud to me," Marsh said.

"I can't tell," William added.

"So, where are they?" William asked again.

"They must have got an early start," Marsh said.

Stephen heard a horse coming up from behind. He glanced over his shoulder and wasn't surprised to see the Thirteenth's executive officer Lieutenant Colonel Bill Munson riding up to join them. Munson and Stephen were a lot alike, they were always interested in what was going on around them, but of course, the colonel had a big advantage in having a horse to ride.

"So, where are they?" Munson asked as he pulled up next to them and jumped down from his horse.

"Must have got an early start, sir. Can't even see any dust on the horizon, "Stephen said.

"I meant the wagons?" Munson asked obviously annoyed.

"Over there, sir," Stephen pointed. "If you don't mind me asking, sir, what's wrong?"

"The General has orders to leave two regiments behind to guard those wagons."

The words hit Stephen like a bolt of lightning. *Oh God, no. I can't be left behind again.* The emotion of that night came storming back down upon him.

The lamplight flickered shadows across the walls and ceiling. His mother's stoic expression as she held out her hand, not wanting to give any indication of which one was the long straw. One of her men was going off to war. One was staying behind and the long straw would decide which one would stay behind with her, the love of her life or her first born son.

Stephen knew instantly he had the long straw and he was being left behind. His father was in his forties and war was no place for a man of his age, but his father was firm. He didn't want to be left behind, either. If it wasn't for his mother demanding that one of them stay behind to help work the farm, both of them would have gone.

Of course, both of them knew she was right, but that didn't help Stephen's feelings any when he pulled out the long straw. God had not answered his prayers and had left him behind.

Of course, for a short time he was angry with God and he could relate to Job when it seemed like God had turned his back on him. Those ugly feelings came back because of his experience with Company A, First Vermont, his father's old company, when Sergeant George Blake was elected captain of Company K.

Now it was happening again. The Thirteenth Vermont was a nine-month regiment and for nine months they'd been guarding the rear of the army. Next week, their enlistment was to run out and they were all going home. The coming fight would be their only opportunity to take part in the in defense for his country. *God, why are you doing this to me?* Stephen pleaded.

"They gonna make us guard wagons, sir?" Marsh asked, obviously as worried as Stephen; he forgot to add in 'sir' when addressing the colonel.

"I'm sorry, boys, not us ... the Twelfth and Fifteenth regiments got the duty."

Stephen took a deep breath and felt instantly guilty. *I'm sorry, Lord.* He had done it again, doubted God. Another sin. He was very glad God had sent down to earth his son to take away his sins and not hold them against him.

Then he instantly felt guilty for not thinking of the men in the other two regiments. They were in the same boat as the Thirteenth Vermont. Their enlistments were running out and they weren't going to see any combat if they were stuck guarding the wagons behind the lines. Then it dawned on him. *If we aren't staying behind then ...*

"So why are you upset, sir?" Stephen asked.

"The wagons are staying behind," Munson responded.

"Oh," William said.

"Will there be time—" Marsh started to say.

"No." The colonel cut Marsh off in a very angry matter-of-fact tone; Stephen guessed it was the same response that the colonel had gotten when he had asked the very same question just a few minutes before.

"Any of you have any food left?" Munson asked.

"Half a biscuit, sir," Stephen said.

"I have a whole one," William spoke up.

"I'm out," Marsh added.

William reached into his haversack and pulled out his last hardtack biscuit. "Let me borrow your hatchet, sir."

Stephen handed it over and William walked over to a fence post to chop the biscuit in two as Marsh followed along behind.

"You don't have to do that—" Marsh started to protest.

"I know I don't," William said, firmly cutting off Marsh.

As the two of them walked away, the colonel asked Stephen, "Why are you carrying that hatchet?"

"They took away my sword when they put me under arrest. I thought the hatchet would be better than being defenseless."

Munson raised his right eyebrow a little as if to signal Munson's brain was recalling the events of the afternoon before.

"How many men dropped out of your company's formation after you got them water?" Munson finally asked.

"None, sir," Stephen answered with a sense of pride.

"So, you think it was worth getting arrested?"

Stephen hesitated. He didn't want to seem like he didn't think it was important to follow orders, especially if they would be soon involved in combat, but he couldn't hide from the truth.

"Yes, sir. It was. If I hadn't gotten them water, many of them would have collapsed on the road."

"Like what happened in the other companies," Munson said almost as if he was talking to himself. He pulled his horse up to him and climbed back up on the animal's back.

"You should get back to your company, we will be heading out soon," Munson said.

"Yes, sir," Stephen said then saluted. The colonel returned the salute and rode back the way he came.

"Give me the small piece," Marsh demanded.

Stephen was shocked when William snapped back in a high-pitched voice obviously angry. "It was my fault; I'm taking the smaller piece." He didn't remember William Church ever raising his voice to anyone.

"Corporal!" Stephen snapped.

William turned around. His cheeks, just above his stumble of a beard, were a blazing deep red. "He can't order me to give him some of my food!"

"I never," Marsh protested.

"Sounded like you did to me," Stephen interjected.

"I want—" Marsh started to say.

"You're going to take what I give you and say thank you or I'm going to throw both pieces away," William said as his anger gave way to a sense of desperation. "It was my fault one piece is bigger than the other."

"Fine, I'll take the bigger piece ... and thank you for sharing," Marsh said.

William handed over the larger piece then slipped the other piece back into his haversack. He walked over with the hatchet stretched out in front of him. "I should have waited and used a knife," William said as he handed it back to Stephen.

"What did the colonel say to you?" Marsh asked.

"He wanted to know how many men dropped out of formation after I got the company water."

"You know the men—"

"I know," Stephen cut him off. He didn't want to hear it again. Yes, the men appreciated what he had done, but there was no need to go over it again and again. He had just done what was needed to be done and he was happy that he was in position to do it.

Stephen turned his back and started back down the road to the company camp. Marsh fell in on his left and William on his right.

Stephen stopped in his tracks as the thoughts of the long straw flooded into his brain.

"What's wrong, sir?" William asked.

"Nothing," Stephen answered as he started walking again. The long straw had put him in position to do what he had done yesterday. If he had gone with the First Vermont, his father would have been in his place yesterday, that is if he would have been able to keep up with the march. Obviously, he wouldn't have been the company's first lieutenant; he hadn't been interested in being part of the leadership of the First Vermont.

Since he was the only officer in the regiment and for that matter the entire brigade to disobey the General's order, without him his men wouldn't have gotten water. God had had a plan all along. Then it dawned on him that God might have more opportunities in store for him over the next few days. He hoped and prayed he would be up to them.

Stephen's stomach growled loud enough he was sure the other two had to hear it. He pulled his canteen over his head and took a long drink of water hoping to quiet down his stomach.

Obviously, it wouldn't be too long before they got back on the march. Ralph would have coffee ready by now and Stephen guessed he would have saved some in order to soak up the piece of biscuit Stephen had promised him.

Stephen decided he would let Ralph cut the biscuit and give him whatever piece he wanted. He wasn't going to argue if Ralph wanted to give him the bigger piece. While he knew it was a matter of principle for William, Stephen was too hungry to care about principle.

With the First Corps wagons staying behind only God knew when they would eat again, but he wasn't going to complain. Given a choice between being left behind or going hungry, he would put up with being hungry.

Marsh broke the silence. "It looks like we did it,"

"Did what?" William asked.

"Caught up with the First Corps before they went into battle," Marsh answered with a sense of pride in his voice.

William took a deep breath. "We haven't caught them yet," he whispered.

"They can't be that far of ahead of us and the rate we'll been going today, I'm sure we will catch them soon enough."

"I don't know," William answered.

"You don't know?" Marsh asked as he raised his voice in obvious frustration. "You don't know about—"

"Marsh, that's enough!" Stephen snapped, cutting him off.

Marsh flashed Stephen a dirty look. Stephen was about to say something but thought better of it. No sense in aggravating the situation.

William went to his right between the naked fence posts, weaving between groups of men, heading toward Ralph's little fire. Stephen followed along, while Marsh kept going straight up the road.

"Wait up," Stephen said to William. William stopped but didn't turn around. It only took a couple of steps for Stephen to catch up.

"What's wrong?" Stephen whispered not wanting the men around them to hear.

William looked down at the ground. "I have a bad feeling."

"About what?"

"Everything ... the march, joining the First Corps ... going home."

It was Stephen's turn to take a deep breath. "Everything's goin' to be—"

"You don't know that!" William cut him off with a whisper that was harsh and desperate.

"Fine," Stephen finished his sentence, and then thought better of it. "You're right, I don't know, but God does."

"But what if it is my time?"

Your time? Stephen guessed the expression gave away what he was thinking when William added, "My time to die."

Time to die? What is he talking about? Stephen was about to say something when it hit him, they were going to get into a fight. There was a chance any one of them could die. He felt a shiver flash up and down his spine. He quickly chased the thought out of his mind finding, instead, comfort in his favorite Bible verse.

Stephen put his arm around his friend. "To everything there is a season, and a time to every purpose under the heaven."

"A time to be born, and a time to die ..." William added.

"A time to plant, and a time to pluck up that which is planted." Stephen continued, "A time to ..." and instantly regretted it.

"You going to finish it?" William asked.

"I should have stopped sooner," Stephen stammered.

"A time to kill," William finished it for him. "What if it is my time?"

"Then you'll get to the paradise before me," Stephen said trying to put a positive tone in his voice. Until this moment, while beautiful, he had never really thought about the true meaning of the passage. *What if it is my time?* Again, he chased the thoughts from his brain.

"I guess you're right," William said as his sprit seemed to lift a little. "I love my life but going to heaven doesn't sound that bad either. I guess there is no sense worrying about it."

"I think I read that somewhere," Stephen said with a smile.

"Me too," William whispered as if he was trying hard to believe it.

"You can't tell anyone," William whispered.

"Tell them what?" Stephen said with a smile.

"I'm serious," William said. "Don't tell anyone," he pleaded.

"Nobody else's business," Stephen said with a straight face making sure there was no doubt in William's mind his secret was safe with him.

"Lieutenant," the call came from behind them. Stephen glanced around to see Corporal Harlan Bullard, Captain Blake's clerk and the regiment's bugler hurrying toward them. Stephen stopped, but William continued.

"What's wrong with Bill?" Harlan asked when he joined Stephen.

"Nothing," Stephen lied. He couldn't tell if Harlan believed him or not, but he was happy when Harlan changed the subject.

"I've gotten some requests that we sing tonight."

"We'll have to wait and see," Stephen replied, not sure if it would be appropriate to hold even a makeshift concert on a battlefield.

"That's what I told them ... I just thought it was nice that despite everything many of the men were thinking of us."

"Or they are just looking for a distraction and we are the best they've got," Stephen chuckled.

Shortly after they left Vermont, Stephen, Harlan, and George Blake found they harmonized as Ralph liked to say, "In a delightful melody." Many in the regiment thought they were the best trio in the brigade.

"Maybe so, but it might also steady some nerves," Harlan pointed out.

"I didn't think of that. We'll just have to wait and see what happens," Stephen said.

"You have any food left?" Harlan asked.

"One biscuit." Stephen hesitated. "I promised to share with Ralph," he said sheepishly.

"I guess I better join you," Harlan said with a smile. "Ralph is sharing his coffee with Merritt and I know he is out of food, too."

Stephen forced himself not to show any disappointment. Of course, he would gladly share what he had with Ralph's close friend and their old school mate Captain

Merritt Williams of Company G, but a third of biscuit wasn't going to amount to much.

"Don't trouble yourself, Stephen," Harlan said with a smile obviously reacting to Stephen's failed attempt to hide his disappointment. "I have a couple of biscuits left to put into the mix."

Stephen felt instantly ashamed and embarrassed over his disappointment of having to share his last biscuit three ways. "Thank you, Harlan, we all are very grateful for your generosity."

Jacob Turney

First Tennessee, along with most of Archer's Brigade, rested along the road that ran across the face of the Herr's Traven ridge. Pettigrew and Brockenbrough Brigades had joined Archer's sharpshooters down in the woods and were trading shoots with the Yankees up in the woods on the next ridge.

Jake had heard a rumor that they were waiting for Lieutenant General Richard Ewell's Second Corps to come down from the north before they resumed the attack.

"How far to the south do you want me to go?" Jake finally asked.

A tired and worn Lieutenant Colonel Newton George said, "Far enough to make sure we avoid a repeat of what happened this morning."

"But the Thirteenth is going to be on—"

"I don't care!" Newt snapped, cutting Jake off. The Thirteenth Tennessee was on the flank this morning and the entire brigade including the First Tennessee had been flanked by Yankee infantry.

"No more surprises," Jake said.

"The rest of the regiment is counting on you and Company K," Newt said.

"We won't let you down, sir," Jake said.

Newt looked over at Private Willey Wood, standing alone in the middle of the road holding the First Tennessee's colors. "... If you see anything, send three runners back to find me. Tell them, I'll be with the colors."

"It was my fault, sir," Jake whispered.

Newt sighed. "I should have stayed with the colors."

"And I should have tried harder to find you and Archer should have listened to me. It was more our fault than yours."

"It doesn't change the fact that we're missing 104 men," Newt said as he looked down to the ground. He took off his hat and beat it against his left leg. "Half my regiment ... it's just gone," Newt muttered.

Jake felt for Newt. With the First Tennessee going into the morning's fight with 373 men, it was closer to a third rather than half of its men that hadn't returned. Still, it was still a devastating blow to the regiment and its young commanding officer.

Jake also knew there was something else bothering Newt than just the loss of so many men. Avoiding capture by crawling on his hands and knees through the waist-high wheat field had tarnished his pride. As Jake knew all too well, earlier he'd tried to tell Newt there was nothing worse than being captured, but Jake could see in the young man's eyes that his words had no effect.

Jake reached over and touched Newt on the shoulder. "And I know the worst part was you lost your horse."

Newt spun away from Jake and glared at him with a rare showing of his temper. Jake kept a straight face as long as he could then let out a laugh. "And you say I have a temper."

"This is no time to be joking around!" Newt snapped. "We lost 104 men."

"It doesn't matter when you tell that damn story about my uncle shooting that dog; you always think it's funny."

"That's different," Newt stammered.

"How?"

The anger seemed to drain from Newt's face and a twinkle returned to his eye. After a few seconds, he started to chuckle. "Still can't believe he shot that dog," he finally said. Newt looked up the road and saw the men lying on the ground, many of them sleeping, around the colors. Jake could see the life just drain from his face.

"I lost half my men," Newt finally said.

"Sir, it was closer to a third," Jake said.

"That doesn't make me feel any better," Newt responded.

"Is Tom okay?" Jake asked.

Newt nodded his head then looked over to Company G. Jake followed his gaze over to Newt's younger brother.

"If this attack is successful, we might be able to get back some of those who got themselves captured," Jake added.

An officer on horseback rode up yelling, "Colonel George!"

Several men, some of them obviously angry over being awakened, pointed toward Newt and Jake. Newt waved at the horseman.

"Sir, Colonel Fry sends you his compliments. General Heth received a head wound in this morning's attack, so General Pettigrew is temporary command of the division. The brigade will be moving out shortly and Colonel Fry wanted to remind you that you're going to be the senior officer on the right of the brigade."

"I understand, lieutenant," Newt said as his face flashed red. Newt turned away from the young officer and Jake could tell Newt was doing his best to hold his tongue. With the captured of James Archer, the command of the brigade fell on the senior colonel, which was the Thirteenth Alabama's B. D. Fry.

As Newt stomped away, Jake thought he was overreacting. It was obvious Newt took the reemphasizing of his orders as a lack of trust by the new commanding officer, but Jake thought Fry was feeling guilty about what happened this morning. If Fry had reported to General Archer about the Yankee infantry in his front, maybe Archer might have had time to prepare the brigade for the Yankee counterattack. There was more than enough blame to go around for the morning's rout.

The young lieutenant gave Jake a questioning look.

"Anything else to report?" Jake asked.

"Only that the colonel wished the Colonel George and the regiment Godspeed."

"I'll tell Colonel George. You're dismissed," Jake said as he saluted the young officer.

The young man returned Jake's salute, spun his horse around, and headed back the way he came, and Jake turned back to the regiment.

"First Sergeant Tuley!" Jake shouted as he walked back to where his men were resting.

"Company K, on your feet!" First Sergeant Chuck Tuley yelled. Jake watched while Chuck, the other sergeants, and the corporals got the company organized back into a column of twos and his two young lieutenants took their place in the rear. Company K was typical of the other companies in the regiment with a third of their men failing to rejoin the company, including their first lieutenant and two corporals.

Being down to just two corporals and two sergeants, Jake had decided earlier to reorganize the company. Jake thought it was important to keep the four squads intact, so Chuck recommended they have Sergeants John Harden and Bill Oldham temporarily fill the two empty squad leader roles.

The two young lieutenants would take over the positions of platoon leaders. It made sense to Jake that Holland and Farrar could keep their new positions at the back of the line of battle, while his sergeants would just return to the ranks on the right of their respective squads. Jake let Chuck explain it to the sergeants while he went over their new duties with his lieutenants.

"We're going to have to reorganize the company—"

"Don't have any choice," Holland cut Jake off.

Jake gritted his teeth to hide his irritation.

"John and Bill will fill the squad leader slots and the two of you will take over their positions," Jake continued.

"I'm going to be a platoon sergeant!" Holland snapped.

"Much obliged, sir," Farrar jumped in obviously happy to be informally in command of something even if it was a role normally filled by a sergeant.

Holland sucked in his stomach, rolled back his shoulders, and stuck out his chest. "Sir, I'm a lieutenant. I don't think a platoon sergeant's role is appropriate for an officer of my rank."

Jake took a deep breath. "What role do you think would be more appropriate?" he asked, fighting to keep his tone even.

"First lieutenant and company executive officer," he stated firmly.

"And who do you suggest I use to lead the Second Platoon?"

"With me as executive officer, you could move the first sergeant to platoon leader."

Jake turned to Farrar. "You're dismissed," he said then saluted. Farrar, obviously surprised, and Jake guessed relieved, returned the salute and hurried away.

When Jake turned back to Holland, he noticed the young lieutenant had slumped over a bit and there was a slight tremor in his clenched right fist.

Jake stepped forward coming eye to eye with Holland. "There is only one man in this company who is not expendable, and that ain't you," Jake said in a very sharp biting whisper. "This is Chuck Tuley's company. He is their father and their mother. He makes sure they're fed, clothed, armed, and ready to fight when I need them.

"I need my first sergeant; I don't need an executive officer. "Am I making myself clear?"

"Yes, sir," Holland snapped.

"Son, you use that tone with me again and I'll have you back in the front rank with a musket."

Holland's eyes became wide as he slumped over. "Sorry, sir."

"You're dismissed," Jake said then turned his back on Holland without bothering to wait for a salute.

Jake waited to hear Holland walk away before he took a deep breath and kicked the ground. This type of leadership was against his nature. He was much more suited to yelling, screaming, and then beating them up. He'd seen other officers do just that and quickly lose the respect of their men and their commanders, so Jake tried hard to keep his emotions in check.

In spite his best efforts, he knew most, including Chuck and Newt, still thought he was a hothead. He wondered what they would think if they knew what he really wanted to do.

Jake took off his hat and ran his fingers through his hair. If only his older brother John was here. Like James, John had somehow escaped the Turney temper, but unlike James he had retained the Turney confidence. John would have made a fine soldier—that is, if he would have joined the First Tennessee.

John, like their father Henry, was a strong Union man. It was possible John would have sat out the war or maybe worse, joined up with the Yankee regiment's forming over in East Tennessee.

Jake spit on the ground. Nah, no matter his politics, John would never turn his back on his younger brothers. He might not have gone off to war with the rest of them, but he never would have turned against his brothers.

There was only thing Jake was sure of: if John had joined the First Tennessee, the boys would have elected him captain of Company K. John was such a natural leader, something Jake knew he would never be.

Jake didn't know why he did this to himself. John was dead and the burden of command and his father's proclamation, "You are your brother's keeper," was his and his alone. Thinking about what could have been or should have been was a waste of time, but that didn't stop him.

John should be captain. Henry and Joel should be standing shoulder to shoulder with Albert and James. Cousin Peter should still be in command of the regiment. General Hatton should still be in command of the brigade and Jackson still in command of the corps.

Jake turned back to his company. He wasn't surprised when Chuck told him that both the sergeants thought of it as demotion. Instead of being in command of two corporals and about fifteen men, they were now in the position of corporals and in charge half as many men. Jake was pleased that while they thought of it as a demotion, they understood he didn't have any other options.

There were so few of them now. He hoped that if the coming attack was successful, Company K might get back some of their missing men. Even so, he knew some of them wouldn't be rejoining the ranks anytime soon, if at all. First Lieutenant George Garrett's wound would keep him out of action for quite a while. The same was with Private Bob Davis, while you could never tell for sure—Stonewall Jackson had died from a wound to his arm—Jake thought both George and Bob would recover from their wounds. Chuck told him that Private Marion Sharp wasn't so lucky. While Jake was searching for Newt and General Archer, Marion went down with multiple wounds to the chest.

Corporals Hedgepeth, Massey, and Privates McKinney, Moore, Abbott, and Pleasant Hampton were all missing. Hampton's cousin Manoah reported that Pleasant had tripped on the way down the slope and slammed head first into a tree. Jake could tell that Manoah felt terrible for not stopping to help his cousin. Jake hoped they would get them all back soon.

Jake scanned the column. He wondered if he looked as tired to them as they did to him. He made eye contact with Albert and instantly regretted it.

"Captain, sir. I'd be much obliged if I could have a word with you in private?" Albert asked raising his voice.

Jake guessed everyone within earshot was looking at him. Even James was looking on with anticipation. Jake glanced to his right and was surprised to see Newt had stopped what was he was doing and had focused on the two Turney brothers.

Jake took off his hat and wiped the sweat from his forehead for what seemed like the thousandth time today. He didn't want to do this now, but waiting wasn't going to make it any easier.

"Come with me," Jake finally said. Then he added, "James, you too."

"Why me?" James blurted out.

"Private, because I said so!" Jake snapped, instantly regretting it.

Jake turned his back and walked twenty yards before turning around to face Albert and James.

Albert, with his dander up, spoke first. "Jake, I want out of Zimmerman's squad. He's starting to make my life miserable."

Jake chuckled, "Funny, he said the same thing about you. In fact, he asked me to bust him back down to private, so he wouldn't have to deal with you anymore."

Jake was glad to see James look up and smile, while Albert snapped back, "Why that son-of-a-bitch!"

Jake leaned forward and clenched his fists. "I won't have you or anyone else talking that way about one of my non-commissioned officers! You do it again and it will be five lashes with a cane."

"You wouldn't dare!"

"Both of you shut up!" James snapped. Jake and Albert looked with disbelief at their younger brother. "You're making fools of yourselves."

"Am not," Jake said.

James grunted and rolled his eyes. "What do you call threatening to shoot him? The two of you are just alike and I'm tired of this constant bickering," James said then turned his back on his two brothers and stomped toward the company.

"I can't believe he said that," Albert said.

"Me either," Jake agreed.

"You think little brother is finally growing up?" Albert asked.

"Maybe or maybe he is just sick of the two of us."

Albert sighed then stuck out his right hand. "Sorry for the way I acted."

"Me too," Jake said as they shook hands.

"Company K! Attention!" First Sergeant Chuck Tuley yelled out. Albert nodded to Jake then hurried back to his place in the line.

Jake motioned Lieutenants Farr and Holland as well as Chuck to join him.

"We're going to be covering the brigade's right flank—"

"What's left of it," Chuck blurted out, cutting Jake off in mid-sentence.

Both the young lieutenants took a step backward as if to avoid the coming blow up, but Jake looked down at the ground instead. *I should have demanded that General Archer listen to me.* Jake took a deep breath.

"What's left of it ... let's make sure we don't get surprised again," Jake said as he walked back to the company. This time, instead of taking his customary position on the left of the first rank, next to First Sergeant Tuley, Jake positioned himself in the center of the company, four paces in its front.

"Company!" Jake yelled as drew his sword, and then hesitated as he raised it over his head. He knew he was being much more dramatic than was required in the situation, but he was hoping to raise the men's spirits. With his arm fully extended, he yelled out the command, "Forward!" then as he pointed his sword to the front he yelled out the final command, "March!"

The Fifth Alabama would again be serving as the brigade's skirmish line, but Newt didn't trust them to cover the right flank, so he was sending Jake and Company K out to do it. He left it to Jake to decide how far out to the right to take his company.

As they stepped off, the brigade's drummers started sounding assembly. The First Tennessee drummers joined in, as did one of the buglers from the regiment's band. While it was customarily for the drummers to relay orders to the infantry, Jake liked the bugle calls of the cavalry better and he enjoyed it when the horn players in the band joined in with the drummers.

General Hill was worried about another flank attack, so he was sending Archer's entire brigade out to guard the flank. They were the logical choice. After the beating they'd taken in the morning, it would be too much to ask for them to spearhead another attack. From what Jake heard, Davis' brigade had suffered even more causalities than their brigade, so the men from Tennessee and Alabama were picked to cover the southern flank. As they passed the Thirteenth Alabama getting back in formation, Jake noticed a few strange looks from their officers. For a moment, his eyes locked with Colonel Fry sitting on his horse along the side of the road. Newt hadn't said if the new brigade commander knew he was sending a company to cover the flank. Fry nodded and Jake smiled then turned his head back to the front.

The woods, where they had started their morning advance, curved to the east away from the road. Jake thought about having his men climb over the fence and cut the corner to the east-west road up ahead, but instantly decided against it. He was tired of climbing over fences.

Within a minute the drummer boys of the Thirteenth Alabama, following behind him, took up the beat of the march. As Jake turned the corner on to the road to the east, he naturally fell into step with the drums. Out to his right he noticed a confederate brigade coming into line just in front of the woods.

At first, he thought it was odd. The remainder of Heth's Division, now in commanded of General Pettigrew, was going to lead the attack on the south side of the Chambersburg Road. The Union infantry had established a reinforced position back on the ridge where Jake had waved at the Union officer this morning. Pettigrew and Brockenbrough's brigades had moved forward to the east bank of the creek.

He heard that two brigades, from Pender's Division, were on the eastern slope of Herr Tavern ridge, just in front of the woods where Archer's Brigade had started their advance. They would serve as reserves to continue the attack where opportunity presented itself. Jake glanced to the right again and recognized Brigadier General James Lane. The third of Pender's four brigades was up and getting into line on the far right of the line.

General Hill must be looking for the opportunity to do to the Yankees what they had done to Archer's Brigade that morning and attack on their right flank. Archer's Brigade would move farther to the south to cover Lane's men from a similar attack.

The road was good and the walking was easy. It took just a couple of minutes before the road entered into the same woods where the morning attack had started. While Jack welcomed the shade, the air was heavy and very humid, nothing like the cooler morning air.

He came to a V in the road the left one went straight while the one on the right took a gentle curve turning to the south. He turned back to the company and gave the first sergeant a look. The first sergeant immediately ordered the company to halt and at ease.

"Corporal Zimmerman, report with two volunteers," Jake ordered.

"Yes, sir!" Zimmerman responded.

Jake was surprised that before Zimmerman could even ask for a volunteer, Albert spoke up. "I'll volunteer!"

He was even more surprised when James said, "Me too."

Once Zimmerman, his brothers and Chuck joined him, Jake pointed, "We're going to take the road to the right. You and my brothers stay behind to make sure the Colonel Fry knows which way we went. Once you report to him, then I expect you to catch up."

"You want us to run in this heat?" Albert protested.

"Shut up, private," Zimmerman snapped.

Jake couldn't help but smile as he turned to Chuck and nodded. As Chuck ordered the company back to attention, Jake stepped off. Sweat rolled down his forehead and into his eyes. Both of his jacket sleeves were black from where he'd rubbed the sooty sweat from his eyes and forehead during the morning's fight.

It felt good being out front by himself especially in the shade, so he picked up the pace leaving the company behind. As he came to the edge of the woods, the road had completed its turn and now headed directly to the south and formed the western border to the woods.

Jake stopped at the edge of the shade and decided to wait for the company to catch up. He unbuttoned his jacket, pulled out his shirttail, and used it to wipe his face. Now he almost wished he hadn't used the dead cavalry soldier's handkerchief to wrap his left foot. Maybe, this afternoon, he'd find a new pair of shoes before the handkerchief had worn all the way through and tomorrow he could use it to wipe his face instead of protecting his foot.

He looked to the left and he had a perfect view of the ground between the ridges where they had made their morning's advance. Men in gray were spread throughout the valley down by the creek, with the reserves in battle-line across the ridge covering ground all the way to the north to the Chambersburg Road.

With Lane's brigade, five brigades would try to make up for the disaster of the morning's fight. Ewell's Corps was coming down from the north to cover the ground of Davis' morning attack.

Suddenly, he heard a crack of a branch and several birds made loud squawks above his head. A small branch fell to the ground as the offended birds flew out of the tree. Above the racket of the birds, Jake thought he heard something else.

He looked up the road to the south just in time to see, about ten feet away, a bit of dirt jump up in the air. This time he clearly heard the crack of a rifle fire. He glanced up the road and next to a small log house a cloud of smoke gave away the position of three Yankees.

Jake froze as a yellow flame reached out toward him instantly followed by another crack of a rifle. He did his best to squeeze his bladder to keep from pissing himself as he waited and after a couple seconds he relaxed. They'd missed.

One of the Yankees waved at him. Jake took off his hat and waved back. At least the people trying to kill him were friendly or maybe thought he was brave by standing his ground. If they only knew he was too scared to move. The three of them disappeared behind the house.

He squeezed his hat with his right hand as hard as he could, hoping that it would keep his hand from shaking as his heart pounded in his chest. As the muffled steps of the company grew louder, he put his hat back on and then stuffed his shirt back into his pants.

Before he turned back to the company, he set his jaw in the now-familiar battle face, hoping not to give away the fear that raced through every nerve in his body. He made eye contact with Chuck, who had a questioning look of concern. Jake knew he must have heard the shots.

Jake smiled back at him and shrugged his shoulders as if to say he'd heard it too, but didn't know where they came from, then he pointed down the road to the south. Jake then headed off down the road while he gave thanks for the Yankees not having any sharpshooters down on this part of the line. He knew if there had been one, with his scope and high-powered rifle, he'd be dead.

Still, the range was only about four hundred yards and he was a standing target. He was surprised the shots weren't any closer. Suddenly, three horses came out from behind the house and headed up the road to the south. "Thank God," he whispered to no one. He was very thankful cavalry carbines weren't accurate at this range.

A light breeze picked up from the south, while it was a far cry from being cool, after the dust of the morning's march and the dense smoke of the battle, any breeze of clean air was a welcome relief. As Jake walked past the small log house, he wondered if the farmer had had enough time to hide his animals from Ewell's men.

Maybe later Company K would have the opportunity to do a little forging and find out. While his men had ample supplies, they hadn't had fresh meat in a couple of days. From what he'd seen back in Cashtown, the residents in the area were very resourceful at hiding their animals and foodstuffs. He had heard that some had even hid their cows down in the cellars of their houses.

Jake stopped at the next crossroads and took in the view. The woods ended at the east-west crossroad and the ground opened up to the west. The ground and the road were much like the road they had used in the morning coming in toward town.

To the east, the ground was also wide open but not as hilly as the ground to the west. A few hundred yards to the east, there was a bridge over a creek. Jake glanced back to the north and he was pretty sure it was the same creek they had crossed twice this morning. Past the creek, the on north side of the road, fields stretched as far as he could see.

On the south side of the crossroad, a large orchard partially blocked his view and extended, he guessed, six hundred yards to the east.

Through the fruit trees, he could see that just past the creek there was another road that made a T from the crossroad to the south that cut through the orchard. Through the trees he could also tell the ground to the south was just as open as the ground on the north side of the road.

From what he could see, there was no danger of being surprised from the east or the west, but to the south it was another issue.

The road they were on continued about three hundred yards to the south then took a sharp right turn to the west as it followed the banks of the creek. The southern bank of the creek was covered with trees and it looked like the woods were about four to five hundred yards wide. While not wide, he couldn't tell how far they continued to the south. Those woods could provide cover for Yankee cavalry and enough infantry.

Jake turned back to the company in time to see his small detail of Hugh Zimmerman, Albert, and James coming out of the woods at a double quick. He felt for them having to run in the heat of the mid-day. He guessed right about now that both his brothers were regretting that they'd volunteered.

"Company! Halt!" First Sergeant Chuck Tuley ordered stopping the men five yards from Jake. Chuck made eye contact with Jake and he raised his eyebrows as if to ask what he was going to do next.

Just then, two riders came out of the woods behind Zimmerman and his brothers. Jake walked back past Chuck and the company. The riders went by the detail like they were standing still. It only took a couple of seconds for Jake to recognize the riders were Colonel Fry and the young lieutenant serving as his aide.

Jake stopped about ten feet passed the company and waited for the two officers. As Fry pulled his horse to a stop he smartly slid from the saddle. Jake saluted. Fry returned the salute.

"Captain Turney, anything to report?"

Jake was surprised Fry remembered his name since they had only met on a couple of occasions.

Just then, the artillery—back near the tavern—let loose with an intense volley. It wouldn't be long now.

"Saw a small squad of cavalry, but they're keeping their distance, sir."

"Any sign of infantry?"

"No, sir."

"Good, good. General Pettigrew wants me to use this road to anchor our right flank," Fry said as he looked all around and pointed to the crossroad.

Jake noticed the detail had slowed to a walk and he didn't blame them. He was surprised they had double timed as far as they had. Behind them the front rank of the brigade's column came out of the woods into the open.

"The only thing I am concerned about is those woods." Fry pointed to the south. Jake wasn't surprised. The dam creek and woods had been their downfall that morning and obviously Fry was going to make sure it didn't happen again.

"Do you think your company can explore them for me?" Fry asked, obviously not used to ordering officers around outside of his regimental chain of command.

He hadn't seen the three cavalry troopers again, so there was a possibility that they were using those woods for cover. With Lane's Brigade just to the west, it was doubtful they had gone that way. To the southeast there was open farmland, so they hadn't gone that way either.

He wasn't worried about three cavalry troopers, but they rarely got too far away from their company and regiments.

"I would be happy to sir," Jake said, doing his best to hide his concern.

"Good, good, thank you," Fry replied as he jumped back on his horse. "No surprises this time," he said looking down on Jake.

"No, sir, no surprises."

Fry nodded and rode back to the brigade. Jake guessed he was going to confer with the commanders of the other regiments in the brigade including Newt.

Jake turned back to the company and First Sergeant Chuck Tuley joined him.

"He looked nervous," Chuck said. Jake's two junior lieutenants also joined him. Farrar looked happy to be included in the discussion while Holland looked like he still had a chip on his shoulder. Jake thought about saying something to him but thought better of it. If something happened to him, command would fall on Holland.

Better to give him some authority to stroke his ego than to badger him again. "The colonel wants us to scout those woods," Jake said as he pointed to the woods on the other side of the creek. "I came across a couple Yankee cavalry troopers back a ways. The colonel is worried they and some of their friends could be hiding in those woods."

Jake started walking and the others fell in behind him. He walked past the company to the middle of the intersection and stopped. The large apple orchard filled the triangle from the crossroads down to the creek. The trees were spread apart far enough that he could see there wasn't any horse among them. On the southwest side of the intersection was a knee-high cornfield. While it was easy to see through the orchard, the low branches would make marching through it difficult. Plus, with so few men there was no reason to have the company spilt on both sides of the road separated by a couple of fence rows.

Jake turned back to Chuck. "Let's form the company into a single line in the wheat field"

"Yes, sir," Chuck replied and walked back over the company and started issuing orders and quickly got the men in line. While there was no danger between here and the creek, he was worried that some troops hiding just inside the woods line could let loose a volley and there was no sense making it easy for them by having the company stacked in a column of twos.

Jake turned to his two young lieutenants. "Take your places, gentlemen." Both hurried off to their place behind the line.

Jake crossed the road and climbed over the fence and waited for the rest of the company to join him. This time, he left his sword in its scabbard.

He raised his right hand and pointed and off he went without even issuing an order.

The field was planted with rows running to the southeast. He'd take a couple of steps then sidestep to make sure he didn't step on the next row. It was more out of habit than anything else as his brain took him back to the days of his youth cutting across his father's fields.

After a few yards, it dawned on him what he was doing and he glanced over his shoulder. He was surprised to see the company was doing the same. Silently, without orders, they just followed along like a group of kids cutting through a neighbor's field.

Suddenly, the artillery fire intensified to the north. Before the echo of a gun would fade, another gun—or two or three—would fire. Such bombardments reminded Jake of a summer thunderstorm back home in Tennessee. The kind you'd get after a south wind had blown up the hot, humid air for several days and then clashed with a cool dry wind from the north. After a time, the thunder would come so quickly it just seemed to blend into one continuous, loud boom. Jake hoped this time the artillery would do some good and soften up the Yankee line making it easier on the infantry.

He climbed over a fence and down into a pasture that ran down to the fence line that boarder the road as it made its turn to the west. He only took a couple of steps when he stepped into a large cow patty, slipped, stumbled, and was on the verge of falling on his ass before he got his balance. He ignored the chuckles in the line behind him, figuring he would have thought it was funny, too, if it happened to someone else.

One good thing was that he'd been right, and Ewell's men hadn't found all the supplies around Gettysburg. The cow dung was fresh, meaning that at least one farmer had found some place to hide at least one cow. As he stepped over the next fresh patty and then another, it looked like there might be more than one cow hidden nearby.

There was a muffled thud along with the clacking of equipment followed by a large burst of laughter. Jake glanced over his shoulder to see Albert helping to pull Corporal Zimmerman back to his feet.

With all the laughter, Jake couldn't make out the context of Zimmerman's tirade, but the more he ranted, the louder the laughter became.

Jake glanced past the company and noticed that Fry had the brigade in two lines of battle with the right flank resting on the crossroads. Jake saw a skirmish line of about company strength move out from the regiment and climb over the fences, along the road, heading to the east.

Jake glanced back at the woods in his front and was thankful there was no movement of any kind. Still, he was taking his entire line blindly into the woods. He decided it was time to give Holland some more responsibility. Jake raised his right hand and the first sergeant ordered the company to halt.

"Lieutenant Holland, report with two men from your platoon," Jake ordered.

"Yes, sir!" Holland yelled out. "McKinney, Eppes, y'all are with me."

Holland trotted up to Jake, with the two privates close behind. Holland snapped to attention, waited a couple of seconds for the others to do the same, and then saluted. "Detail reporting as ordered, sir."

Jake bit his tongue to keep from laughing as he tried to figure out if this parade ground-type demonstration was sarcasm or Holland's attempted to bolster his bruised ego. Either way, it was funny and there were a few snickers back in the ranks.

"As you were!" Chuck snapped.

Jake knew no matter the reason, he needed to support his young officer, so he raised his voice making sure everyone in the company could hear him. "Lieutenant, we can't have any surprises this afternoon. There are at least three cavalry troopers shadowing us and maybe more in those woods," Jake said pointing across the creek.

"I want the three of you to find out for sure. If you see any enemy, report back immediately. Only engage to defend yourselves. Do you understand your orders?"

"Yes, sir."

"Lieutenant, I'm counting on you," Jake said then gave his young lieutenant his best salute. Holland returned the salute smartly. The three of them trotted down to the fence that lined the road, and over they went. They dragged across the creek then disappeared into the woods.

Jake looked back over his shoulder and noticed the first rank of the brigade was already over the fence and starting their advance. Jake turned back to the woods. No sign of Holland and no shots, but Jake was still worried. He decided to make sure the rest of the company was taking this as seriously as he was.

"Company!" Jake barked as he pulled out his sword. "Forward! March!" He ordered as he dipped his sword toward the woods.

He leaned his sword on the fence as he climbed over than retrieved it. He walked forward a few yards than waited for the rest of the company to get over and back into line before heading down the slope and across the creek.

This wood lot was more overgrown than the one this morning cutting down how far up ahead he could see.

Jake took a deep breath of the hot, humid air. It reminded him of walking along Swan Creek back home in Boonshill. He wasn't surprised. It was just another in a series of reminders of how this part of Pennsylvania, with its farm land, hills, woods, heat, and humidity was so much like south central Tennessee with the major differences being the hills back home were more rolling and there were coloreds.

The only darkies Jake had seen since they'd crossed into Pennsylvania were a few prisoners passing by on their way south. He was sure the rest had hightailed it when they heard the Confederate Army was coming and with good reason. The ones Ewell's men had taken captive were now on their way back to their rightful place as slaves.

While capturing runaway slaves was not the reason for the army's invasion of the north, Jake knew that many of the men of the First Tennessee looked upon it as an important moral victory.

For them, capturing runaway slaves was the issue that had started the war in the first place. The northern government had ignored its own Constitution and allowed states to pass laws protecting runaway slaves.

His cousin Peter, the organizer and the regiment's first colonel, was a driving force in getting Franklin County to secede from the Union back in February 1861 after the State of Tennessee's first vote for succession had failed and over two months before the second vote passed.

Jake was at Peter's first major speech on the issue less than a month after Lincoln's election as president. Pete had singled out New York as the most glaring example of a state violating Article IV, Section 2 of the United States Constitution which stated, "No person held to service or labor in one state, under the laws thereof, escaping into another, shall, in consequence of any law or regulation therein, be discharged from such service or labor, but shall be delivered up on claim of the party to whom such service or labor may be due."

New York's state courts had even upheld the laws protecting runaway slaves. What had the federal government done about this gross violation of the Constitution? Nothing. They even allowed the citizens of New York, and the eleven other states, which had passed laws in violation of the Constitution, to vote in the presidential election, and as a result, the Black Republican Lincoln had won and slavery, along with their entire way of life, would be abolished.

At the time, Jake didn't agree with Pete that Lincoln would move against slavery in the southern states. His Uncle John, his father's brother, had practiced law with Lincoln up in Illinois and in his letters, John had assured the family Lincoln wouldn't interfere with slavery where it already existed. Even after the firing on Fort Sumter Jake didn't think Lincoln would move against slavery.

One of the first hints that he was wrong came in June of 1861 with the trial of Nathaniel Gordon up in New York City. In 1820, Congress outlawed the slave trading and imposed the death sentence, but the law wasn't aggressively enforced.

Under a treaty with England, the United States and British navies patrolled the coast of Africa to stop the slave trade. Under the treaty, the British navy had no right to search United States ships and the U.S. navy fleet was small and ill-equipped, so most slave ships would sail without a national flag.

If they sighted British man-of-war, they would hoist an American flag. In a rare case where they did see a ship from the U.S. Navy, they would hoist a flag from either Spain or Portugal that matched a complete set of false registration papers.

Even if the U.S. Navy did catch a slave ship, the courts in the south and even many in the north were very sympathetic. Back in 1839, captives aboard a Portuguese slave trader, the *Amistad*, had killed some of the crew and taken over the ship demanding they be sailed back to Africa. Instead, the ship's remaining crew misled their captors and sailed up the United States coast where a U.S. naval ship stopped them. Instead of prosecuting the remaining crew for serving on a slave ship, the federal government freed the crew and then held the captives for murder.

While the northern courts wouldn't return runaway slaves, they were hesitant to punish whites engaged in the illegal slave trade. President Buchanan had even openly declared he would never hang a slave trader.

With high rewards and low risks, Captain Nathaniel Gordon sailed his ship, *Erie*, from the coast of Africa bound for Cuba with 897 captive men, women, and children. Once they reached Cuba, they'd sell the captives into slavery with most of them being smuggled into the southern United States.

When Gordon sighted a large, fast warship, he assumed it was a British ship, so he hoisted the United States colors. Instead, it was the new steam-powered sloop the *U.S.S. Mohican*. The captain of the Mohican put a small crew on board the Erie and returned the captives to Africa. Gordon was taken to New York City to stand trial while the rest of the crew went to New Hampshire. The government tried the crew separately from their captain. Found guilty of serving on a slave ship, each man was fined a dollar, and then released.

Gordon's trial ended in a hung jury and that should have been the end of it, but the Lincoln administration's new federal prosecutor decided to try again and in November Gordon was found guilty and sentenced to death. While Buchanan had proclaimed, he would never hang a slave trader, Lincoln didn't interfere with the sentence. In February of 1862, Captain Nathaniel Gordon was hung by the neck until dead.

There was no way to know what Lincoln would have done if the states hadn't seceded or fired on Fort Sumter, but that didn't matter anymore. With the signing of the Emancipation Proclamation, those who had proclaimed Lincoln would end slavery got the last word.

With his large plantation and hundreds of slaves, for Cousin Pete, slavery was the only issue. For Jake, deciding to join the southern cause was a matter of principle. The federal government had allowed states to violate the Constitution, the supreme law of the land, and had done nothing to stop it.

Jake's father, Henry, had argued vehemently with Jake and his five brothers about taking up arms against their country, especially when Lincoln County had failed to follow Franklin County and seceded from the State of Tennessee and thus the Union. Jake agreed with his father's point that if they left Tennessee to take up arms while still citizens of the United States then they'd all be traitors, but Jake didn't care.

He felt no loyalty toward a government that wouldn't support its own Constitution. It was only after the fighting at Fort Sumter that Henry finally gave up arguing against secession.

When Jake had returned home on his trip in the fall of 1862, the look in his father's eyes was startling. While he seemed happy and relieved to see Jake, his eyes were deep and dark as if a veil was covering the two windows into his soul. At first, Jake desperately wanted to know what his father's eyes were hiding, but he was too afraid to ask. He was afraid his father blamed him for the death of his two brothers. Jake finally decided it was better not to know.

It was at dinner one night when Albert and Rufus announced, with pride, that they were going off to war with Jake that the veil fell from his father's eyes. As his mother held her face in her hands and cried softly, his Father slammed his fist on the table, looked directly at Jake, and shouted in a haunting, anguishing voice of pain, "No!"

While loud, Jake was at first relieved there was no anger in his father's tone, no hint of blame, then he looked into his father's eyes and saw such pain and despair that it reached deep into Jake's very soul gripping it as it was in a vice. Jake took a deep breath and looked away.

His father turned his attention to his youngest son Rufus, "You're not old enough to fight."

As if he'd expected his father was going to bring up his age, Rufus was quick to reply, "But Jake said—"

"I said no!" His Father shouted as he once again pounded the table with his fist.

As if on cue, Jake's younger sisters, Sarah, Delia, and Anne, all started to cry. His mother wiped her eyes on her napkin then hurried the three young girls from the room leaving the three sons to face their father alone.

Henry then pointed to Albert. "You're not going, either."

Albert pushed back his chair and jumped to his feet as the heavy wooden chair fell over backward with a loud thud.

"You can't stop me!" Albert shouted.

Jake followed Albert's gaze to his father and their eyes once again locked. Jake shuddered under the haunting eyes that pleaded with him to tell his brother no, he couldn't go. Jake couldn't, he wouldn't tell Albert to stay home.

"You are your brother's keeper," Henry finally said, just above a whisper.

No! Jake wanted to shout at his father. He was their older brother, their captain, the man who would have to order them into combat, order them to die. He couldn't also be their keeper. Jake pleaded to his father with his eyes, but Henry didn't back down. Jake finally looked away unable to bear the weight of his father's gaze.

When he rejoined the regiment, Jake shared the story with Newt. While she hadn't said it directly, Newt knew his mother expected him to take care of his younger brother. They both agreed it was a heavy burden to be their brother's keepers.

From the creek, there was a bit of an up slope but nothing like the ground they covered this morning. To the north, the sounds of the battle were greatly intensifying, but above the fray he could hear the sharp crack of two close rifle shots. The lower limbs were too thick for him to see anything up ahead. He worried for Holland and his little squad.

"Company Halt!" Jake ordered as he started a slow trot up the gentle slope through the woods. He glanced back and wasn't surprised to see First Sergeant Chuck Tuley right behind him.

Jake was surprised to see a fence row up ahead and it took him a few seconds to realize it bordered an east-west road cutting through the woods. When Jake reached the fence, he climbed on the lower rail. Holland and his two privates were down on the ground, in the middle of the dirt road, weapons pointed to the west. None of them looked injured.

Jake glanced first to the east. It was about 150 yards to the edge of the woods and there was no sign of any activity. To the west, it was about two hundred yards to a small bridge that took the road over the creek that formed the western border of the woods. Jake caught sight of something large moving amongst the trees then there was a bright yellow flash. He tightened his grip on the fence as he waited for the bullet. *Oh God, not again.*

A split second later, there was a loud smack and the fence rail vibrated in his hands as the bullet threw up splitters a few feet to his left. The sharp crack of the musket finally caught up with the bullet.

Suddenly, two men on horseback came out of the woods and continued to the west.

"Fire," Holland shouted in a high-pitched voice more fitting for a schoolgirl than a lieutenant in Robert E. Lee's army. Smoke and flame belched from the two muskets and Holland let loose with a couple of wasted shots from his pistol.

Jake wasn't surprised as the two riders crossed a small bridge over the creek and turned to the south and disappeared behind the woods. At less than two hundred yards, the range wasn't that long for a musket but fast-moving targets, even something as big as a horse, wasn't an easy shot.

Holland got to his knees and looked back up at Jake. "They fire the other shots, too?" Jake asked.

"Don't know, sir. Two shots hit the tree next to me as I climbed over the fence. I didn't see where they came from. Scared me half to death." As the two privates chuckled, Holland's face went totally blank as it sunk in he'd just admitted to being scared.

"I meant they surprised me, sir," Holland stammered as he looked down at the ground. Chuck joined Jake at the fence and shook his head twice.

Jake took a deep breath; it was too bad Holland had slipped in front of the privates. When they got back to the company, everyone would know Holland admitted to being scared. While they were all scared, it wasn't something anyone talked about openly and he knew the men would ridicule Holland behind his back. Jake couldn't let that happen, so he had no choice but to make a bold move.

"Well, getting surprised like that, I think it would have scared the shit out of me," Jake said as he climbed over the fence and down onto the road.

As he climbed up on the fence, Chuck raised his voice and said, "Would've scarred the piss out of me." With that, the privates became suddenly quiet.

Jake had seen it in the faces of all his men; they were all scared at one time or another. Sure, they all hid it, including him, but being scared was just another part of the war.

For Jake, being scared was an old friend, a comfort, a reminder that he was still alive. Maybe it was time they all just let down their guard and admitted they were all scared. Scared of getting shot, scared of dying, and scared of getting captured by them damn Yankees, it was all part of living through the war. For the veterans of the First Tennessee, who had proven time after time that they could face their fears, there should be no shame in admitting it.

Things were different early in the war when at the first sound of musket fire, some men would throw down their weapons and turn tail and run. For them being scared was an enemy, an enemy they couldn't overcome.

When the privates went back to the company, they would talk about how even the captain and the first sergeant were scared. Both Jake and Chuck had proven themselves many times over in combat, so maybe it was as good a time as ever to let the truth out of the bag, everyone was scared.

"How many were there?" Chuck asked.

"Two—they rode that way," Jake said pointing to the west. "I'm not worried about any infantry in that direction. I'm sure Lane has scouts out covering his flank. Fry ordered me to check out the woods, so I think we will do just that. Go ahead and bring the company up."

"Yes, sir," Chuck responded then disappeared back into the woods.

Jake turned back to Holland. "I doubt there are any more cavalry hiding in these woods or infantry for that matter, but we need to make sure."

Jake looked up and down the road again. He guessed the woods were still about six hundred yards wide, but he had no idea how long it was. He did his best to gage the direction the woods ran then made a best guess and pointed into the woods.

"Lieutenant continue in this direction; I'm going to keep in closer contact and not let you get so far ahead of the company. Keep check to make sure you can see me."

"Yes, sir," Holland responded doing his best to hide his nervousness. If nothing else the shot had knocked some of the cockiness out of his demeanor.

They disappeared into the woods as the company climbed over the fence line joining Jake in the road. Jake noticed that they seemed a bit jumpy. He wasn't surprised after what they had gone through this morning.

"Just a walk in the woods, boys," Jake said, raising his voice. "With a couple of scared Yankees taking a few pot shots from behind trees."

He got the chuckles he was hoping for. "Nothing for us to worry about," he added as he climbed over the next fence and headed off into the woods. He was pleased to see Holland give him a wave from about fifteen yards out in front of him. Jake waved back as he prayed that there weren't Yankee infantry men taking a walk through the same woods.

Stephen Brown

"We almost to the top?" Ralph asked. Stephen glanced to his left and noticed Ralph staring at William's heels.

"Why don't you look for yourself," Stephen asked.

"I'm afraid we aren't that close."

"Oh."

"So how close are we?" Ralph asked.

"Do you really want to know?" Stephen asked.

"I guess not," Ralph whispered.

Stephen knew Ralph had made a good choice and he wished he didn't know that they were only half-way up the steep ridge. It wasn't that the ridge was that high or that they weren't used to walking over hills or climbing the green mountains back home, but they never did it in this much heat and humidity.

Stephen pulled off his forge cap and used his coat sleeve to wipe his forehead hoping to keep the salty sweat from reaching his eyes again. He knew it was a losing battle, but he wasn't going to give up.

"Watch your step!" The call came from behind him. He hadn't heard the familiar clang as the man down with all his equipment. The man, who was now most likely lying face-first on the road, must have been a couple of companies back.

Stephen forced himself to lean backwards slightly to avoid bending over into the hill and restricting the air going into his lungs. He knew he was much luckier than the men under his command not having to carry a heavy rifled musket, cartridge box, and knapsack.

He guessed that even having his sword taken away was kind of a good thing; the camp hatchet was much lighter than his sword and scabbard. He almost laughed when he thought back to the first day of the march. Besides stuffing their pockets full of food, most of the men had tried to carry all the items that had accumulated while they were in camp.

One man in Company A even tried to carry a small wood cage with a couple of chickens inside. Stephen remembered the man boasting about how he would have eggs every day on the march. That evening the cage was used as firewood to roast the chickens.

From the troops that had occasionally passed from other corps, Stephen figured they were now the lightest brigade in the army. They were going home soon. They didn't have to worry about needing any extra equipment next week.

He wondered if the roads back in southern Maryland were still littered with the supplies and extra equipment that the brigade had discarded. On the second morning, orders went out making sure that the knapsacks wouldn't be thrown away. Stephen guessed it was a good thing.

While the company wagon would carry the officer's extra equipment, Stephen found it a pain waiting for it to get unloaded. He'd talked Ralph into carrying his half of their fly tent and coffee pot in his knapsack.

Besides his extra pair of socks, Stephen had discarded his extra clothes. He carried the extra socks, tin cup, a bag of coffee, and half a biscuit in his nearly empty haversack. Gone were his books, writing set, playing cards, tin plate, and even his fork.

On the second day of the march, he tore up his letters from home. They didn't weigh much, but he figured he would tear them up before he went into battle, so why carry them through the state of Maryland.

Besides his haversack, his hatchet and rubber blanket (he hated sleeping on the wet dew-covered grass) were stuffed into his belt. His canteen was the only other thing he was carrying.

"Watch your step," voices yelled from behind them. Stephen glanced at Ralph, sweat was pouring down his cheeks. William's neck was fresh with sweat and so were the others around him. It was rough, but it looked like all those in Company K were going to make it to the top.

As Stephen came over the top of the ridge, he noticed a horse and rider coming down the next ridge at an amazingly fast pace. A chill went down his neck. While during the march, it was common for General Reynolds, the First Corp commander, to send riders back to General Stannard, rarely had they come riding so quickly.

Stephen kept his eyes transfixed on the messenger. As he came closer it was obvious, he had pushed his horse so hard the poor animal looked to be on the verge of collapsing.

The drummers beat out the orders and the entire brigade quickly came to a halt. General Stannard followed by his staff and Colonel Randall, the Thirteenth Vermont's commanding officer, rode ahead to meet the rider.

The messenger saluted and Stephen could see an anxious expression on his face even before he started talking, Stephen knew they had failed.

"What's going on?" Ralph asked.

"A messenger for General Stannard."

"Good news?"

"No," Stephen whispered as he cut around behind Ralph. He hurried forward to join Captain George Blake. He reached him just as Colonel Randall rode up to Blake.

Randall waved and the other company commanders came running forward. Stephen stepped back out of the way so the other nine company commanders could all hear the colonel.

"The First Corps met the enemy this morning about ten miles up the road just outside the town of Gettysburg. They held their ground but Reynolds was killed. Abner Doubleday is now in charge of the corps. He has ordered us forward at best possible speed. He is expecting the rebels to resume the attack. It's going to be a hard march. Do your best to keep your companies as closed up as possible.

"We're going to be stopped here long enough to top off our canteens. We don't want anyone running out of water this afternoon." Stephen noticed Randall's eyes dart his way then quickly back to the other officers.

"Send out canteen details as soon as you get back to your companies. We need to make sure we get as many men as possible up to Gettysburg. The rest of the Corps is counting on us. Dismissed."

As the other captains hurried back to their companies, George Blake turned to his first sergeant, but before he could say anything the first sergeant had already started shouting out orders.

After the colonel rode toward the rear of the regiment, Blake turned back to Stephen. "Did you notice the look the colonel gave you?"

All Stephen could do was nod. He didn't want to say anything not trusting what his voice would sound like. He turned away and walked slowly back toward his spot in the rear of the company making sure to keep his head level and his eyes straight ahead. He was determined not to show any emotion despite the way he was feeling.

After nine months of service, they had failed at the first and only real task given to them: reach the First Corps before they had met the enemy in combat. Now Major General John Reynolds was dead and it was their fault.

As he got back to his spot, darkness descended upon him as the sun faded behind a lonely cloud. *My soul is weary of my life*, the opening line of the Tenth Chapter of Job filled his brain. *I will leave my complaint upon myself; I will speak in the bitterness of my soul.*

He looked out to his right across a long, dark pasture and watched the sunlight storm back across the field toward him; then there, in the center of the field, was a blazing patch of orange lilies glowing under the bright mid-day sun. *Consider the lilies of the field, how they grow; they toil not neither do they spin.*

The sunlight swept over Stephen, immediately burning away the fog of despair that had settled upon his heart.

"Thank you," Stephen whispered.

"Did you say something?" Ralph asked.

"Talking to God," Stephen whispered.

"Put in a good word for me," William said.

"Always," Stephen said with a smile that spread across his face.

"Make way," came a call from behind Stephen. He stepped over in front of Ralph, opening up room for Colonel Randall to ride past on his way back to the front of the regiment, followed close behind by his youngest aid, his son Charles. Randall had served as a captain in the Second Vermont Infantry Regiment, and unlike the First Vermont, they'd seen heavy fighting with over sixty casualties at the First Battle of Bull Run.

Back in June, while the Thirteenth was camped near the town of Manassas, Virginia, Randall had acted as a tour guide for a group of officers showing them the Bull Run battlefield. He, of course, took Charles, a second lieutenant in Company G, along with him.

"The colonel showed us where the Second Vermont had been in position." Charles always referred to his father as "the colonel." Despite the fact that Charles was turning out to be a fine officer, everyone in the regiment knew that the only reason he was serving as a second lieutenant, instead of a drummer boy, was because his father was the regiment's commanding officer.

In the light of the fire, sadness came over Charles' face that seemed to make him look much older than seventeen. "Nearby, there were some Union graves."

"How did you know?" Marsh asked.

"We could see the bodies," Charles whispered as if he was afraid of offending the dead. "What was left of them."

"The rebels, they just ... just threw some dirt on them where they lay. The rain has washed most of the dirt away and the bodies, what was left of them, were just lying there."

Charles leaned forward. "None of them were wearing their shoes and some were even striped of their uniforms lying there in their underwear."

General Reynolds was dead and as Stephen stepped back into his spot, the fog returned to his soul. He took a deep breath, there was no avoiding the obvious; it was their fault.

If only they had marched a little faster or marched a little longer each day, they might have made it on time. Well, most of them anyway. Even if only half the brigade would have made it, it might have made all the difference.

Stephen bowed his head and said a prayer for Reynolds and all the men who had died that day. Stephen guessed the troops had carried Reynolds' lifeless body from the field, a privilege of his rank and a blessing to his family, but what about the rest of them?

From the sound of it, there was more fighting to come. He guessed during active combat no one would take the time to bury the dead and he was sure there'd be bodies lying on the field when the Thirteenth finally did get to Gettysburg. He'd of course seen dead bodies before, family and friends who had died of illness or old age. He'd been hunting all his life and had field dressed many of his kills, but this was different.

Of course, the bodies wouldn't be anything like what Charles had described with the rotting flesh giving way to bones. Still, he guessed there would be something different about seeing young men struck down with horrible wounds in the prime of their lives.

Reynolds was dead and for the first time he realized that it could just as easily be him lying up there face down in the dirt with his blood soaking into the dry earth. He had to bite his lower lip to keep from laughing.

Stephen realized it was a very real possibility that he could be killed. He didn't have any idea why, but he found the whole situation funny. They'd be in Gettysburg in just a few hours and just like that, he could be shot down by musket fire or blown up by artillery shell.

One moment full of life and the next a sack of dead meat lying face down in the dirt. He bit down so hard on his lip that tears came to his eyes. He had to fight to keep from smiling. He had no idea why he suddenly found the idea of dying so damn funny.

With them getting the news about Reynolds just now, he knew he didn't dare even utter a hint of a chuckle. He needed to set an example for his men and laughing, no matter the reason, with news of the death of the Corps commander, would be unthinkable.

William glanced over his shoulder at Stephen, his own eyes red from tears; Stephen looked down, trying to avoid direct eye contact fearing he would lose control and burst out laughing. Just an hour before, William had confided that he didn't think he was going to survive the coming battle and while Stephen found that worrisome, right now he couldn't think of William.

He had to focus on himself and the more he did, the funnier the entire situation seemed to him. He turned toward the fence keeping his back to the company making sure to hide the wide smile that was spreading across his face.

"What's wrong?" Ralph asked.

Stephen didn't dare say anything, and then he heard Ralph step toward him. There was no way he could have anyone see him like this. He had no choice.

Stephen threw himself over the rail fence lining the road. He ran through the waist-high wheat as fast as he could. When he reached the middle of the field, he threw himself to the ground and buried his face in his hands and burst out laughing. His whole body shook as the waves of uncontrollable laughter poured out of him.

"What in the hell is the matter with ya?" Ralph's booming voice startled Stephen. He sucked in a deep breath and quickly composed himself.

He rolled over and looked up at Ralph, Oliver, and William looking down on him, each with an expression of confusion and fear.

"You know, we could all be dead tomorrow," Stephen said in a straight face, and then he burst out laughing again.

Ralph's face flashed red. "What the hell is funny about that?"

"God damn it, how the hell should I know?" Stephen snapped back.

For a moment, Ralph seemed stunned. "You took the Lord's name in vain."

"Never thought I'd hear something like that," William said.

"Me either," added Oliver.

Ralph chuckled as he stepped forward and reached his hand down to Stephen. Stephen took it and Ralph pulled him up to his feet. "Capt'n thought you were desertin'," Ralph said.

"Sent the three of you to bring me back?"

Oliver nodded. "Told me to drag you back."

"So how far down do you think they'd bury me?" William asked.

"Depends on whose buryin' ya," Stephen said. "I'd make sure you got put down a couple of feet so the animals wouldn't get to ya."

"Thanks," William smiled.

Stephen started walking back toward the company and the others followed along.

"I don't like thinking about it," Ralph said.

"Me either," Oliver piped in.

"I don't blame you, Oliver, as big as you are you'd be likely to have somebody just threw some dirt over your face," Stephen said with a smile.

"I want to be sent home," William whispered.

"We'll all be home in a couple of weeks," Ralph said.

It was Stephen's turn to pat William on the back. "No matter what happens, we're all going home," Stephen said.

"Good," William answered. "Good."

"So why did you run away?" Ralph asked.

"I didn't want to start laughing in the middle of the column," Stephen answered.

"So why were you laughin'?" Oliver asked.

"I've no idea," Stephen chuckled.

Captain George Blake was at the fence starring at him. *What am I going to tell him? I'm so scared I couldn't stop laughing.* Stephen made direct eye contact and kept a steady pass as he walked straight up to the captain.

"Explain yourself, Lieutenant," the captain demanded in a loud voice, making it obvious he wanted all the company to hear him.

"Sorry sir. I was just so overwhelmed by the death of General Reynolds; I needed a private place to express my grief. It won't happen again." He didn't want to lie, but there was no reason to tell the whole truth.

"Make sure it doesn't," George snapped and stomped back to the front of the column as the drums started beating and orders were quickly issued, and they resumed the march.

Jacob Turney

Captain Jacob Turney noticed the ground flattening out as the woods brightened to his left and to the right. They had made it to the top of the ridge and from the sound of it, his Company K of the First Tennessee was keeping pace with the rest of the attack.

The woods were darker in front of him, but they had reached a spot where the woods were very narrow. Jake stopped and held up his right hand. Chuck Tuley ordered the company to halt.

Jake glanced ahead and saw Lieutenant Holland had halted his little squad about fifteen yards in front of him. The woods they were in looked to be long and narrow heading to the south. He doubted infantry would try to march through it, but there was a chance they could be using it for cover. It was time to give his other junior officer some responsibility. "Lieutenant Farrar, Sergeants Harden, Oldham report," Jake shouted.

"Here, sir," the three answered. Farrar and Oldham were in the center of the line while Harden was on the far right so it took him a little longer to join them.

Jake focused on his young lieutenant. "I want the three of you to check what is west of these woods. Go out far enough so you can see a good distance to the south. We want to make sure infantry isn't using them to cover their advance our flank.

"Post one of the sergeants where come out of the woods, so you won't waste any time getting back to us. We will wait for you here."

"Yes, sir," Farrar responded excitedly and with that he was off with a rush with the two sergeants following right behind. Jake wasn't surprised to hear Oldham and Harden arguing about who was going to be left behind.

Jake looked over at Chuck Tuley. "We will rest here, but no fires just in case there are some Yankees nearby."

Jake turned back to Lieutenant Holland and motioned him to join him.

"James, you're doing a fine job," Jake said just loud enough he hoped the men nearby could hear him without being too obvious he wanted them to. James Holland had earned his promotion from private to junior second lieutenant because of his gallantry at Gaines Mill and Mechanicsville during the Seven Days battles back in '62. When Garrett was promoted to First Lieutenant, Holland was elected to Second Lieutenant and Farrar had stepped up to Junior Second Lieutenant.

Since then, Jake had spent surprisingly little time with his two junior officers. For official duties, Jake had let Garrett take care of dealing with the two junior officers. During what free time Jake had, he spent much of it with both his brothers and Chuck Tuley or with Colonel Newton George.

If something happened to him, Holland would become the new company commander, so without being obvious Jake wanted the company to know he had some confidence in the young officer.

"Jim, I'm having John check the view to the west. Go ahead and take your squad to the edge of those woods,"

Jake said as he pointed to the east. He continued, "And scan the ground to the east, but stay under cover of the woods. If you see any danger, report back immediately. If John doesn't find anything, we will join you shortly."

"And if he finds anything?" James asked.

"We will come get you," Jake said a little embarrassed for leaving out that detail.

Holland nodded and with a wave to his two privates headed for the eastern border of the woods.

Jake flopped down next to a big tree and leaned back against it. Until Farrar got back, there wasn't anything for him to do, so he pulled down his hat over his eyes and within a minute drifted off to sleep.

A sharp kick to the heel of his shoe instantly woke him up. He sat up straight as he pulled his hat off his head.

"Farrar is on his way back," Chuck said as Jake looked up to see him returning to the company.

"How long was I asleep?" Jake asked as he got back to his feet.

"Maybe ten minutes?" Chuck chuckled. "I wish I could fall asleep as quickly as you can."

It was Jake's turn to chuckle as he turned to face John Farrar as the two sergeants went back to join their men.

"Sir, Sam and I went out about 150 yards and we got clear view to the south for what looked to be a mile and we didn't see anything."

"No infantry or cavalry?" Jake asked.

"No sir. We didn't even see any civilians."

"Good, good ... John gave in to Sam?" Jake asked since John Harden was senior to Sam Oldeham.

Farrar leaned forwarded and whispered, "Yes, sir. He said he was tired of listening to Sam whining all the time."

Jake flashed Farrar a quick smile. Everyone in the company knew Sam Oldeham could be a pain in the ass when he wanted to be.

Jake looked over at Chuck and gave him a nod. The first sergeant ordered the men on their feet and back into line.

Jake looked back at Farrar. "Go ahead and take your place back in line."

Farrar nodded and hurried back to his spot in the line.

Jake looked at Chuck and made a motion to the east in the direction that Holland and his two-man squad had traveled. Chuck had the company wheel while Jake headed off toward where Holland had disappeared.

In less than a minute, Jake could see Holland waving at him through the trees. As he got closer to the edge of the woods, the volume and intensity of sound increased dramatically.

As Jake came up to join Holland at the worm fence that served as the border between the woods and a corn field, he held up his right hand and Chuck ordered the company to halt.

Jake threw himself over the fence and walked out ten yards from the woods so he could get a better view. He was surprised how far south they were from the crossroad where he had his conference with Fry.

The road ran northeast into town while his company had moved to the south opening a gap of almost a mile. At this distance and with all the smoke it made it difficult to make out brigade formations, let alone individual regiments.

He could tell the attacked had overrun the ridge line that had been their downfall in the morning and they were slowly moving toward the next ridge, which was dominated by a large building with a small dome on its top.

South of the buildings, woods covered the next ridge all the way down in front of them and as far south as Jake could see. This afternoon's attack was shaping up to be like the mornings, but on a much grander scale. The confederate lines were pushing across a wide depression between the ridges and soon they would be moving up the gentle slope to face the new Yankee line and like this morning, there were woods on the flank that could be hiding Yankee reinforcements.

Jake turned back to his company. He was surprised and pleased to see Holland and his two-man squad patiently standing a couple yards away waiting for him.

Jake walked up to Holland. "James, any concerns?" The question obviously caught Holland off guard, but he quickly recovered and scanned the situation.

"Those woods," he finally said pointing to the woods in front of them.

"They concern me too," Jake said. "Same as before. Keep about twenty yards in front of the company. Looks like that's a spring," he said as he pointed at some cat-tails about thousand yards in their front. "We will stop there and get water."

"Yes, sir," Holland said this time skipping the over dramatic response and salute. As the three of them walked past Jake, he turned his focus to the rest of the company.

First Sergeant Tuley had the men over the fence and in one line again. Jake held up two fingers and quickly Chuck issued orders and the company was back into a standard two rank line of battle.

Jake turned around and with a wave of his right hand, stepped off. "Forward. March!" Chuck ordered the rest of the company.

Jake kept a close eye on the woods in front of Holland's squad. There was no sign of any movement. He was right about the spring and the squad was just about done filling their canteens when he joined them at the water's edge.

He glanced ahead and was surprised to see an opening between the tree line on his right and the one up ahead of them. The woods in front stopped a couple of hundred yards to the south, but the ridge line blocked his view to the east.

Jake made eye contact with Holland. "The three of you keep a sharp look out as you get close to those woods."

"We will, sir," Holland replied with a hint of caution in his voice. Jake noticed that both McKinney and Eppes nodded in full agreement with Holland.

Jake dropped to his knees as he pulled his canteen over his head. He was happy they had found a spring. He bent over and splashed the cool water onto his face.

"Reminds me of a summer day back home," Albert said as he knelt down to Jake's right.

"With thunder announcing the coming of an afternoon storm," James added as he knelt on Jake's left. Jake dunked his canteen down in the water.

"I miss home," Jake whispered. "We win here, maybe we can all go home soon."

"You think so?" James whispered back.

"Hope more than think," Albert stated flatly.

Jake wanted to argue with him, but he was right. It was a hope that if they could beat the Yankees here the war would come to a rapid end as the rebel army threatened the Yankee capital.

"Pray for it," Jake said as he finished filling up his canteen. He hung his canteen once again over his head and pushed his right arm through the strap, so it hung under his right shoulder.

He stood up and watched his men finish up filling their canteens. Once the last of them was done, he walked a few feet to the south and jumped the spring where it narrowed forming a creek.

Holland and his squad followed him and Jake sent them on their way as Chuck got the Company formed up on this side of the spring and once again they were off toward the woods looming in their front.

Jake noticed the closer they got to the words the faster the pace Holland and his little squad took. Jake didn't blame them. While no one said everything, they all knew the purpose of the three men out front was to give the enemy a closer target to shoot at.

Jake glanced to the north as the western extension of the approaching woods blocked his view of the rebel advance. They were once again blind.

When the squad was about twenty yards from the tree line, Jake started to relax. If there were Yankees in the woods, they would have opened fire by now. As the three men disappeared into the woods, Jake said a silent prayer their safety.

Jake spun on this planted right foot, did a 180-degree turn, and took a couple of steps backwards as he scanned the faces of his men. They all looked as worn and tired as he felt. He spun back around as Eppes came back to the edge of the woods smiling, waving, and yelling something Jake couldn't make out.

Jake looked back at Chuck. "First sergeant, halt the company at the edge of the woods." Without waiting for a reply, Jake took off at a trot. He knew there was no reason to run, especially up slope, and his body cried out that he was an idiot, but he just couldn't help himself. He just had to know what Eppes was yelling about.

"They're running. The Yankees are running," as Jake got closer, he could hear Eppes yelling. When Jake was almost up to him, Eppes turned on his heel and trotted back into the woods and Jake followed him.

"Go, you bastards! Run your asses all the way back to Washington!" Holland was standing ten yards out in front of the woods yelling and waving his hat.

Jake walked out to join Holland as his eyes darted back and forth trying to take in all that was happening. To the north there was a farmhouse, barn, and a large orchard. There weren't any signs of anyone around the buildings.

Past the house to the east, the fields and pastures were uneven and went down into a bit of a swell before rising to a north-south road guarded by rail fences on both sides. Jake guessed the road was about a mile away. The road was full of Yankee wagons heading to the south. Jake couldn't help chuckling; the Yankees were fleeing to the south.

He watched the wagons disappear behind a house and barn up by the road then appear again.

For a second, Jake thought about taking the company at a double quick across the fields and try capturing a few wagons, but then he noticed the Yankee cavalry. There were enough of them to make quick work of his little company.

Past the road with the wagons, there was another ridge. Unlike his ridge, the next one, except for a patch straight across from him, wasn't tree covered. The patch of small trees and brush ran to the north along the ridge. Where it abruptly ended, Jake guessed, was the border of some fences, but from this distance, he couldn't tell for sure.

Farther to the north along the ridge, there was a small white house and barn abutting a grove of trees. Jake watched a stream of Yankees swarm past the white house and disappearing into the trees.

Past the grove, the ground sloped up to a large-bald hill with one lone large pine tree. Billowing smoke told Jake that the Yankees had artillery up on that hill. Most likely, they would use the artillery as a rallying point for their defeated army.

While there was still a scattering of rifle fire, it was rapidly dying away. The smoke to the north was dying away too, which told Jake the fighting was in that direction as well. It was a complete rout, just as it had been during the morning, except with much more favorable results.

Jake wanted to smile—he wanted to be happy, but he knew they had some unfinished business. They had left some men behind this morning. He knew Marion Sharp was dead, but he didn't know about the others. There was a good chance that Garrett and Davis were still lying where they fell hot, wounded, hungry, and thirsty. He needed to get the company back into those woods and take care of the men they left behind. Of course, first he had to report back to the colonel.

"Amazing, sir! We beat the bastards again!" Holland exclaimed.

"Yep, it sure is, but it's time to go. Take your squad back to the company."

"But, sir—"

"Lieutenant, we need to report back to the regiment," Jake snapped.

"Sorry, sir," Holland muttered. "I didn't think."

Jake took a few steps out into the pasture that bordered the woods purposely ignoring Holland. He didn't mean it as harsh as it came out, but still, he had issued an order and Holland had protested in front of the enlisted men. That was unacceptable.

He listened as his young lieutenant ordered his squad to rejoin the company. Then Jake again turned his attention to the ground in front of him and started to have second thoughts. Maybe they should move forward and scout the ground around the town. He had fulfilled his orders and he was sure Newt would be wondering where they'd gotten off to. He had men who needed attending to, plus the longer it took them to get back, the less chance that his men, and himself, would be able to get a new pair of Yankee shoes.

Yankee wagons were fleeing on the roads including one that cut over the top of the big bald hill to the east and one that ran right in front of him. As he stood there, he started to have second thoughts about attacking the wagons.

The tree line jutted out to his right blocking his view toward the south. He couldn't help himself. He trotted out, so he could see where the wagons were going.

As he cleared the tree line to his right, he could see the road was sloping up to some high ground to the south. It looked like the wagons were turning there, he guessed they were taking a road to the east, but without binoculars he couldn't tell for sure what he was seeing.

Farther to the southeast, there stood two imposing hills. The shortest and closest one had a bald western face with steep sides. The other was much taller, tree-covered, and rounded in shape. Good thing the Yankees were forming to the north, both of those hills looked imposing.

He turned his focus back to the cavalry along the road. While there were enough of them to stop his small company, a full regiment would make quick work of them. He stood there for a couple of minutes waiting for the attack to resume.

He couldn't understand what was taking them so long. The woods were blocking his view of the large buildings that had marked the last Yankee line.

The rush of blue bellies had slowed to just a trickle. The massed lines of troops in gray and butternut should be coming out from behind the woods pushing forward to crush what was left of the Yankees, but there was nothing but smoke, obviously from friendly artillery, starting a duel with the Yankees up on the big, bald hill to his northeast.

Here was a clear opportunity to push the enemy clean away from the town and there was nothing. It wasn't like the Army of Northern Virginia not to push the attack, but of course he knew the army had changed greatly in the last month.

Jake would never forget that early morning march back in '62. Company K was in their customary position at the head of the column, so when they met up with their guide, even in the dark, he got a good look at the older gentleman with the black beard who seemed out of place on the small pony. Jake wasn't impressed.

He didn't think much of it when the man took the lead of the regiment; after all, he was supposed to be their guide, but he was surprised when just after sunrise, the man suggested to Cousin Pete that they stop for breakfast. Rightly so, Pete ignored the suggestion.

About a half hour later, the gentleman again suggested they stop for breakfast and again Pete ignored him, and Jake became a bit irritated with the old man on the small horse. After another half hour, the man said bluntly, "Colonel, halt your men for breakfast." Knowing the Turney temper, Jake expected to see Pete have a go at the man, but thankfully, he called a halt instead.

When they resumed the march, the older gentleman again interjected himself by telling Pete the regiment was looking a bit raged. Jake expected Pete to tell him to mind his own business, but instead he looked over his shoulder. Jake guessed Pete agreed with the old man because he ordered the regiment to short step.

Before Jake could repeat the order to his company, the old man spun his pony and glared at Pete. "No, that will throw your men all out. It should be slow-step!"

Jake felt his own face flash as he saw Pete's turn several shades of bright red. Before he could say anything, the old man gave his horse a couple of kicks and expertly darted to the left side of the road. As the old man jumped from his saddle, Jake noticed Pete whispering to his adjutant and while he couldn't hear the reply from where he was, he easily and thankfully read the man's lips as he said, "Stonewall Jackson." Jake put aside his temper as General Stonewall Jackson gave the regiment a lesson on how to slow step.

Jake thought it was fitting that on their first meeting Jackson had given the First Tennessee a lesson on how to march, because over the next year, they done a great deal of marching together up and down the Shenandoah Valley and across the state of Virginia.

The march up from Harper's Ferry over to Sharpsburg was the worst with only a third of the First Tennessee still in formation when they went into battle, but that was the point and what Jackson did best. He got his men into the fight.

While the First Tennessee held Hazel Grove back at Chancellorsville, Jackson had marched the rest of the division around Union flank. Jake heard the attack was classic Jackson. He forced the march, perfect positioning of his men, then the surprise attack. Too bad Jackson had gotten out ahead of his troops.

As darkness fell over the wilderness west of Chancellorsville, Jackson and his staff were mistaken for Yankee cavalry and some of his own men shot him down.

They amputated his arm right away and there was hope that he would recover, but he died from pneumonia.

Jake took off his hat and wiped his forehead on his shirt again. He knew that if Jackson was with them, they would be driving the lines forward and pushing the damn Yankees halfway to Washington. Jake glanced back up to the bald hill, and he was sure the Yankees were rallying around the artillery. While the supply wagons were fleeing, it looked like the infantry wasn't.

Jake turned his back and walked toward the woods, leaving behind his dreams of capturing a wagon or two. He needed to join back up with the rest of the regiment and find their wounded and dead from this morning's battle, then if he was lucky, he'd also get a new pair of shoes.

Stephen Brown

Stephen was getting tired of the ridge lines. He took a deep breath as he pushed himself the last few feet to the crest. As the front of the company came over the top, they just suddenly stopped in their tracks. William slammed into the back of the man in front of him. Somehow Ralph sidestepped to the right behind Stephen or he would have done the same to William.

Angry shouts came from Company B walking a couple of yards behind them and Stephen was about to join them when it hit him like a blue northern coming down out of Canada. Even before he realized what it was, the hairs on the back of his neck stood on end and goose bumps covered his arms. A shiver went through his entire body, as his brain registered the low, dull boom of failure.

Stephen stopped dead in his tracks, as shouts of "halt" echoed behind them. He turned around and looked back at the rest of the brigade and he wasn't surprised by the confused faces.

Without orders, without warning, the front of the column had just stopped. He was sure those in the back where confused, angry, but even so, he wished he could trade places with every one of them for the few minutes it would take for the word to spread back through the rest of the brigade. He hated the feeling of failure that the low rumple had brought to his ears as he came to the crest of the hill.

"Artillery?" Ralph asked.

Stephen nodded.

"We failed again," Ralph whispered, then added, "it sounds like more than just one Corps. I heard last night that the Eleventh Corps was also under Reynolds command, could be they joined the First Corps up at Gettysburg."

Stephen was about to tell Ralph that he had no idea what he was talking about but stopped himself. He had no idea what one Corps sounded like and neither did Ralph, but the Eleventh Corps was supposed to be closing on the First Corps and it was possible they had joined up with them.

The campfire telegraph had finally got something right last evening when the reports of the Eleventh being attached to Reynolds had spread through the camp. *It was about time they'd gotten something right*, Stephen thought to himself.

Gossip around the campfires was nothing new, but once they were on the march, it seemed to be more intense and rumors more outlandish. Robert E. Lee's goal was to capture Washington, Harrisburg, Philadelphia, or Baltimore and the British Navy would sail into the city delivering Lee reinforcements. Or he would move north as a British Army would come down out of Canada splitting the north in two.

Over the last year, there'd been plenty of rumors about the British invading Vermont. The textile mills in Burlington, Johnson, and Bennington were competition for the mills back in Great Britain. While the naval blockade of the southern ports had greatly reduced the amount of cotton making its way across the Atlantic Ocean, there was still a cotton highway up the Mississippi River to the mills in New England including Vermont.

With Vermont a long way from any standing army or protection, Stephen wasn't surprised by the rumors about a British invasion, but he didn't take them seriously. Immigrants from Quebec had flooded into Burlington to staff the city's textile mills. He doubted the Canadian government would risk the backlash against them. Besides, attacking Vermont's textile mills wouldn't help the British with their problem of finding a more reliable cotton supply.

Of course, the campfire telegraph would never let facts get in the way of a good rumor, especially one about Robert E. Lee. Stephen guessed it was partly due to the fact that the Thirteenth Vermont hadn't had the opportunity to face Lee's army. The legend of the Army of Northern Virginia had grown to rival stories of the French army conquering the whole of Europe and Robert E. Lee became an American version of Napoleon Bonaparte.

Stephen noticed Colonel Randall and his son Charles dismount and Captain George Blake, and Second Lieutenant Marsh join him at the front of the company. Stephen felt left out, so he walked to the front of the column to join them.

As he came around the front of the company, Blake made eye contact and nodded. Charles followed Blake's gaze and when he saw Stephen his eyes lit up. "You took the Lord's name in vain?" Charles blurted out so Stephen was sure half the company had heard him.

From the chuckles, Stephen guessed it wasn't news to most of them.

The colonel whispered something to his young son while the first sergeant yelled for quiet. Stephen wanted to crawl back to his place in the column, but he strained to keep a straight face and walked up to the other officers.

"Sorry for my outburst, Lieutenant Brown," Charles said, obviously in reaction to his father's whisper.

"An apology wasn't necessary," Stephen responded. "You weren't the only one surprised by what I said."

"Are you really planning on carrying that hatchet into battle?" Colonel Randall asked, seemingly satisfied by his son's apology.

Stephen stared at the colonel and stated firmly, "I've come too far to miss out on facing the rebels, sir."

Stephen instantly regretted the tone of his statement, but there was no taking it back and to apologize might seem like he was backing down from his conviction, so he kept his eyes fixed on the colonel.

"I just meant that it might be better to carry a sword instead," Randall said in what almost sounded like an apology to Stephen. Stephen guessed his confusion was evident to the colonel who quickly followed up with, "Colonel Munson is going to talk to the General about your situation."

"That would be wonderful, sir."

"There are no promises," Randall quickly added.

"Understood, sir," Stephen said as a smile spread across his face, "no promises."

The drums started rolling again. Randall jumped back on his horse and Stephen hurried back to his place in the rear of the company. As he took his place next to Ralph, he raised his voice slightly to make sure William Church could also hear him. "Which one of you told?" he asked.

"Told what?" Ralph said very sheepishly as he looked down at the ground.

Before Stephen could say anything, William whipped around. "Ralph, you told!"

"Ah, ah, I, ah ..." Ralph stammered.

Stephen patted him on the back. "It's all right Ralph."

"You're not angry?"

"No, not really, just embarrassed."

"I'm sorry I embarrassed you," Ralph said, finally looking Stephen in the eye.

"Already forgiven," Stephen said with a smile.

"How do you do that?" Ralph whispered.

"It is much easier than you might think," Stephen said. "You just give it to God and let him worry about it. Makes life so much easier."

"Attention!" The command echoed through the regiment, quickly followed by, "Forward march!" As he stepped off with his right foot, Stephen's brain automatically shifted its focus back to low rumble thunder of artillery coming from the north. Goosebumps rose on his arms and in spite of the sweat rolling down his cheeks. He felt a sudden chill as the survival instinct deep in his brain picked up steam.

The rolling thunder of the artillery was a warning for them to stay away, but on they marched. Left, right, left, right, left his feet moving in cadence with the sound of the regiment's drums.

Beat! beat! drums!—Blow! bugles! Blow! The last stanza of Walt Whitman's poem filled his brain. *Make no parley—stop for no expostulation; Mind not the timid—mind not the weeper or prayer...*

Slowly, a sense of relief fell around him. This was really it. What he had waited for, a chance to do his duty, a chance to defend his country, a chance to make his parents proud.

A warm feeling of calm settled over him. This was his time. With or without his sword, he was going to face the enemy putting his life on the line for what he believed in. Everything that had happened to him since the day he learned of the President's call for volunteers and the formation of the First Vermont Volunteer Infantry had come down to this moment.

The waiting, wondering, hoping; the worries, and the praying were all behind him. Well, maybe not the praying. While he knew the next few days were all in God's hands, he would still pray for guidance. *Please Lord, help make sure I don't do anything stupid to get any of my men killed,* he prayed.

Left, right, left, on he marched.

Jacob Turney

Jake wasn't sure where the rest of the regiment might be, so he decided to head back to the main east-west road they'd crossed earlier and then decide where to go from there. He had the company formed back in a column of twos and marched north across the fields. This time, he took his customary position on the left of the first sergeant in the company's first rank.

To avoid getting the attention of the Union cavalry up on the road coming out of town, he decided to keep to the west side of the woods. With the woods on their right, Jake couldn't see the town or the hills and ridges to the east, but he prayed he was wrong and the Yankees weren't using them as a rallying point.

Ahead on his left, there were troops spread across the fields. Jake expected them to moving forward, but some of the companies had already stacked their muskets by squads and a few large campfires were burning. Details were dismantling the rest of the fences in order to build more fires. It looked to Jake like they were settling in for the evening instead of getting ready to push the Yankees off that big, bald hill.

Jake stepped out of line and looked for Second Lieutenant John Farrar. "Lieutenant Farrar."

"Yes, sir."

"I need to know whose troops those are?" Jake said pointing the men up on the left. "And find out their orders."

John Farrar nodded then trotted silently past Jake with a pained look on his face. They were all hot and tired, so Jake felt for Farrar, but better for one man to go out of his way, instead of marching the entire company over there.

The east-west road ahead was full of troops marching in columns of fours moving toward town, which confused Jake when so many others on his left were settling in. He wondered if the First Tennessee was among those on the road and he didn't see Newt, but that didn't mean anything. Newt could be wounded or even worse. Even with the colors unfurled, he still couldn't read the regiment's name on their flag.

About fifteen yards from the road, Jake halted the company to give Farrar an opportunity to catch up. Jake took a couple of steps toward the fence then yelled out, "What brigade are you?" A common question for troops separated from their commands after a battle.

"Thomas' Georgians!" Several men shouted out. Jake knew they were part of Pender's Division."

Jake was about to ask if they knew where Heth's Division was, when he was distracted by a loud cheer to his right. When Jake turned to see what the cheering was all about and he was surprised to see commanding General Robert E. Lee trotting up on his horse Lucy Long. Jake thought that it was odd that Lee wasn't on his favorite horse Traveler.

Jake turned around and took a position in front of his company. He was planning to join in with the cheering as Lee rode between the company and the road.

As Lee got closer, the men of Company K started cheering. Jake was about to take off his hat and wave it when he noticed the commanding general was riding directly toward him.

"Company K, attention!" Jake ordered and was surprised at how quickly the company quieted down. He guessed the men were just as stunned as he was because the cheering stopped immediately. Jake's heart pounded in his chest as Lee pulled Lucy Long right in front of him.

"Captain, what command are you with?" Lee asked in a fatherly voice of concern.

"Sir, Captain Turney, Company K, First Tennessee."

"What are your orders, son?"

Jake fought to keep his brain from turning to mush. While like everyone else in the army he'd seen Robert E. Lee and he'd cheered him, never did he ever imagine the commanding general would ever talk to him, let alone ask him questions.

"We were covering the right of the advance, sir. Making sure the Yankee infantry didn't get around our flank."

"To avoid what happened this morning," Lee stated.

Does he know it was all my fault? Jake knew the thought was ridiculous, but the guilt remained.

"Yes, sir," Jake mumbled.

"How far forward did you get, son?"

Even though Jake had never spoken to Lee before, he could tell something was wrong with the commanding general. He shifted several times in his saddle and his face gave away fleeting expressions of pain.

"We got on the other side of those woods, sir," Jake said as he turned and pointed to where they'd come out of the woods. "We saw their wagon trains taking roads to the south and to the east. The infantry was falling back to the large bald hill, I think they were trying to rally, but I couldn't tell for sure."

Lee turned to his aides. "I'm afraid they might get away." He then turned back to Jake. "Carry on, captain."

Jake did his best salute as he said, "Yes, sir. Thank you, sir."

Lee returned the salute and rode back to the east, in the direction from which he just came. Jake turned back to the company and couldn't help but smile. Again, the men broke out in cheers and applause and this time Jake joined them. They cheered even louder when Lee took off his hat and waved it a couple of times.

Lieutenant Farrar trotted from up behind Jake.

"Sir," Farrar panted. "What did Bobby Lee want with you?"

Jake couldn't help but laugh about how surprised Farrar seemed that Lee had stopped and talk to such a lowly captain.

"He wanted to know what we'd seen. What troops are those?'

"A couple of regiments from Lane's North Carolinians. His other two regiments are on the other side of the road. They haven't gotten any orders since the Yankee line broke."

Jake wasn't surprised that they also belonged to Pender's division, but he was surprised they didn't have any orders. The commanding general was worried the Yankees were getting away, while a whole brigade was resting nearby and awaiting orders.

He remembered that Major General A. P. Hill, his corps commander, didn't look well this morning. He knew it shouldn't make any difference; Hill didn't look any worse than Robert E. Lee did just now and was a much younger man than the commanding general. It might be the reason Hill had failed to issue additional orders to Major General Pender. Jake knew enough about Pender to know that if Pender had orders to move forward, Lane's men wouldn't be making campfires.

Just then, Thomas Georgina's broke ranks and spread out on both sides of the road pulling out the fence rails as they went. No doubt about it now, Pender's division was settling in for the night.

It was obvious Lee wanted them to press the attack, but to whom would he turn? In the past, it was always Jackson, but now, Jake didn't have a clue. He was glad his only worry was rejoining back up with the regiment and looking after the men they'd lost during the morning's fight.

Jake wanted to take the company over to the large buildings and backtrack over the battlefield. From the smoke he'd seen, it seemed to be the scene of some of the heaviest fighting and there might be an opportunity to get some shoes, but he also knew that the rest of the regiment was more likely back up the road to the west. Going over to the buildings would delay them getting back to the regiment and the way Newt was feeling earlier; the sooner they reported back the better. Newt was probably worried he'd lost an entire company.

"Orders, sir?" Lieutenant Holland asked as he and First Sergeant Chuck Tuley joined him.

"We're going to do a column left. Once we get past Lane's men, we're going to shift to a single line."

"How come, sir?"

"Shoes," the first sergeant said.

"Yep, I'm hoping we will come across some Yankee dead or wounded. Strip everything of military value from the dead, but from the wounded only take shoes and weapons. Also, I don't want to take any prisoners, we'll leave that duty to the provost marshal."

As planned, once past Lane's brigade, Jake spread the company out across a wide front with three squads on the north side of the road and one on the south side. He expected there would be more opportunity on the north side of the road, but more of their own troops had been through the area too, so he put Zimmerman's squad on the south side in hopes of picking up something there, too.

At first, they came across a few of the walking wounded, Yankees struggling to find their own lines, but most had already been relieved of their shoes and weapons. As they went farther to the west, they came across those more gravely injured and the dead from both sides.

Jake was surprised to see several men from Zimmerman's squad, including his brothers, gathered in a circle. As he came up, they parted leaving him a path into the center where a young Yankee sergeant was lying on his back. A huge bloody hole filled with flesh, bone, and pieces of cloth covered the right side of his chest.

The man's eyes were open, but his pupils were fixed and unseeing.

"He's still alive," James whispered.

At first Jake thought he was crazy then he saw a small stream of bubbles break to the surface of the man's chest. Jake didn't think it was possible that someone with such a ghastly wound could somehow still be alive. Then another stream of bubbles confirmed the boy was still breathing.

Jake knelt next to the boy close enough to hear a gurgling sound with the next stream of bubbles. Jake pulled the boy's haversack from around his neck and then his canteen.

"Jake, you said we would leave the wounded food and water?" James said obviously troubled by his brother's action.

"This boy is dead; his body just doesn't know it yet," Jake whispered as he undid the boy's belt and pulled it free. Albert knelt down and pulled off the boy's shoes and socks.

"Let's get a move on," Jake said to the rest of the men and one by one they slowly turned their backs on the dying boy until James was the only one left.

"He might wake up. We need to at least leave him some water," James said.

"He's not waking up," Jake said with a tone of finality.

James took a deep breath then he, too, turned his back on the dying boy and walked away leaving Albert and Jake to finish stripping him of everything useful, but leaving behind his personal items such as his pocket watch and a photograph of a woman about his age holding a small child on her lap. Then they walked away, leaving the boy alone to die.

A hundred yards up the road, they came upon some stretcher bearers helping the confederate wounded, but for right now, the Yankees were on their own. Jake's men left wounded who looked like they would survive or who were conscious with their haversacks and canteens but took everything else starting with their socks and shoes. From the Yankee dead, some of the boys even pulled off their uniform pants.

No one bothered the bodies of their own dead. It was one thing to take from the enemy; it was another thing to take from one of your own men.

Jake left Lieutenant Holland in charge with orders to do whatever First Sergeant Tuley told him to do, then Jake pushed ahead to find Colonel Newton George and the rest of the First Tennessee.

As he walked, his legs started to fight against the long but reasonable incline up the next ridge. As he got to a T road, he had to jump to the side, up against a fence, as a four-gun artillery battery came thundering past.

He wasn't sure he was going the right way until he came over the top of the ridge. At the bottom was a creek and just on the other side was a body of men spread out to the north. There were so many, Jake guessed it was an entire division.

As he looked to the north, he quickly got his bearings. He could see the farmhouse and the orchard that was in the path of the Thirteenth Alabama during the morning's attack. Just beyond, but blocked by the orchard, was the ground Company K had advanced then retreated across, the ground where at least one of his men lay dead.

Jake continued down the road past a farmhouse and another apple orchard. As he got close to the bridge across the creek, he saw Colonel Newton George mount a horse and ride up the road toward Jake at a full gallop.

"Where's your company?" Newt yelled as he came across the bridge almost in a panic.

"Just up the road collecting supplies," Jake said.

Newt's panic flashed immediately to anger. "Captain, where the hell have you been?" Newt demanded as he jumped off his horse right in front of Jake.

"Covering the flank like you ordered," Jake snapped back.

"We were only in the first part of the attack then Pender's Division moved through the lines and pushed forward."

Jake shrugged his shoulders. "I didn't know whose men they were, but you put me on the flank, and I stayed there until they stopped advancing."

A hint of a smile flashed across Newt's face. "There wasn't going to be a repeat of this morning."

"That's for damn sure," Jake said sharply.

Jake told Newt about the wagons fleeing Gettysburg and the Yankee troops moving to high ground southeast of the town. Most importantly, he went over in detail his encounter with the commanding general.

Jake was glad to hear the regiment had only suffered a few causalities during the afternoon's attack and a few men from that morning had made it back to the regiment, including Company K's own Private Pleasant Hampton.

As they were talking, the rest of the company came marching in a column of fours. Most of the men had shoes hanging around their necks. Jake was pleased to see James with two pair and big smile on his face. Jake was finally going to get his new pair of shoes.

Stephen Brown

Trees lined both sides of the road blocking the glare of the late afternoon sun, but the trees trapped and held the worst of the humidity. Stephen lifted his canteen and shook it. The sloshing told him he might have about a pint left. He took a sip then carefully put back his cork.

No question, they weren't going to stop again until they reached Gettysburg and the water was going to have to last. He scanned the men in the last two ranks. Sweat was still streaming down everyone's faces or running down the backs of their necks, staining their uniforms with large dark spots.

He glanced up the road and noticed a dark angry cloud low on the horizon. He thought it looked odd for a storm cloud then the deep growing rumble registered in his brain. Almost like a bad smell, his brain had chosen to ignore the distant artillery and he hadn't even noticed as it had grown in intensity, but now with the dark cloud of smoke, it all came rushing in at once.

Orders were shouted and the drums rolled as the brigade flags at the head of the column were unfurled. Stephen glanced over his left shoulder and watched the unfurling of the Thirteenth Vermont's national color with their name painted in silver across the fourth red stripe. The dark blue battle flag was void of any battle honors. That was soon to change.

He took a deep breath. They had finally made it to Gettysburg. Suddenly, they cleared the tree line on the right and the hills and fields all flooded into his field of view. He turned his head quickly trying to take it all in. On the other side of a field was woods with a gap in the trees and he found himself looking up a slope into a bald face hill with steep sides. Along the edge of the woods, farther to the north, stood a stone house with what looked like its back facing the road they were on.

Suddenly, Lieutenant Benedict, General Standard's aide, took off at a full gallop. Stephen watched him ride up the gentle slope, down into a shallow dip then back up another gentle ridge, past an orchard then disappearing over the top of a small hill.

Ralph let out a low groan. "You all right?" Stephen asked.

"I can't go up another ridge," Ralph moaned.

"Two more."

"What?"

I can see two more ridges, but they aren't that steep, and it looks like there is a large orchard at the top of the second one," Stephen said, trying to reassure Ralph.

"You think the fruit is ripe?" Stephen noticed some enthusiasm in Ralph's whisper. Well, as much enthusiasm as he could have when he was hot, tired, thirsty, and covered in sweat.

"Can't tell from here," Stephen said as he went back to scanning the ground to the east of the road. Back to the south, he noticed a large tree-covered, rounded hill dominating the entire area. While he didn't know much about military tactics, he doubted it would be much of a military objective considering all the trees.

From the road, the ground was sloping away to the east down to a line of trees. A rocky, bare-faced hill loomed menacingly above the tree line. Stephen guessed it would be good artillery position, but the fighting seemed to be much farther to the north, so for now the hill sat empty and alone.

He looked back to the west—his left—and he was surprised the ground was opened up with fields and pastureland sloping away from the road, meaning the road was cutting across the top of a small ridgeline.

As they got closer to the orchard, Stephen could make out lots of green peaches, but none looked big or ripe enough to eat.

"Peaches," he whispered to Ralph.

"Damn," Ralph uttered.

"I told you it was too hard to eat," Stephen said.

"I'm lucky, I coulda broke a tooth," Ralph moaned.

"You should have known better."

"How? Never been hungry enough to try a green peach before," Ralph moaned.

As they got closer to the orchard, whispers grew through the company. They were all so hungry.

"Forget it boys, those damn things are hard as a rock," Ralph yelled out.

Stephen threw his left elbow into Ralph's side as the First Sergeant Halloway shouted for them to be quiet in the ranks.

"What was that for?" Ralph whispered. "I was just trying to help."

"Help get me in trouble," Stephen whispered back.

"I didn't—"

"Lieutenant, you're in the last rank to ensure order in the back of the company," Captain Blake shouted out, cutting off Ralph.

"Understood, sir!" Stephen shouted back, and then whispered to Ralph, "You were saying?"

"Never mind," Ralph whispered.

As the road leveled out, they came to a crossroad that cut through the orchard on the right side of the road. Back a bit from the northeast corner sat a small log house surrounded on two sides by peach trees.

In the doorway stood a man about his father's age with a weathered face and a faded blue shirt. Behind him, peeking over his right shoulder, stood a woman about the same age. Not surprisingly, they both looked worried; the war was suddenly at their doorstep.

Stephen made eye contact, smiled, and nodded. The man nodded back and the woman gave a slight wave and a hint of a smile. Neither really seemed relieved to see Yankees parading past their farmhouse and Stephen couldn't blame them.

From what he'd heard, both armies—except maybe for foragers—left the civilian populations alone. Yes, there had been cases of hoodlums using the uniform to prey on helpless civilians, but for the most part the civilians were left alone, except when the war came to their doorstep.

When that happened, the civilians were left with a difficult choice. Either stay and protect their property the best they could or leave. Obviously, for now anyway, this family had decided to stay. Stephen hoped they had made the right choice and the fighting would avoid their house and orchard.

Across the road ahead, about twenty yards away, stood a large brick house with a large red barn. Stephen didn't see any movement around the farm or anyone looking out the door or the windows. He guessed the family had left at the first sounds of the fighting.

As they came past the house, Stephen noticed the sun low in the western sky slowly diving for the dark rim of a distant mountain range. The bright red was muted by a thin cloud layer.

The sounds of the artillery were louder now and while not as frequent, seemed to be moving closer to them as if the battle was coming in their direction.

As they passed a large whitewashed two-story log house on the right side of the road, General Stannard called the column to a halt. Stephen cut behind the company and walked up to the front. He couldn't help but notice the appearance of First Sergeant Halloway's uniform. He looked like he could almost pass a weekly inspection. There was little dust on it and no wrinkles. Stephen glanced down at his uniform and sighed at the sight of it covered with dust and both his pants and coat were horribly wrinkled. The only good thing was that Captain George Blake, standing next to Halloway, didn't look any better than Stephen.

As Stephen joined them, he jokingly said to Halloway, "Can I borrow your iron?"

A hint of a smile flashed across the first sergeant's face before he pointed to a ragged blue line haphazardly coming in their direction. It took Stephen a few seconds for his brain to process what he was seeing. Then it dawned on him—walking wounded.

Up on the distant hill, a bright yellow flash filtered through the trees, followed closely by an angry dark smoke. As if by instinct, his eyes darted skyward and he quickly picked up the dark speck silhouetted against the bright red sky arching to the west. The distinctive boom reached his ears slightly louder than the background noise of the continuing artillery duel.

"Must be ours," Blake said. "With our colors unfurled, if it'd been rebel fire, it'll be coming in our direction."

Fear flashed through Stephen's entire body; he locked his knees to keep them from shaking. *My God, what have gotten myself into?*

There was a chorus of whispers behind him, so Stephen turned around and as he did, the whispers quickly died away. He was comforted to be greeted by nervous, anxious faces. At least he wasn't the only one scared half out of his mind.

A few hours ago, he was laughing at the thought of dying, but suddenly all he wanted to do was cry. Stephen took a deep breath and forced himself to smile. "Well, boys, this is what we've been waiting for, a chance to get at those rebels."

It was true; this was the moment he had waited for. The memories of the months of frustration tending the farm as his father was down in Virginia protecting the country flashed through his brain, quickly followed by the disappointment of being passed over for command of the company. Then came the frustration as his term of enlistment had ticked down with seemingly no hope of facing the enemy.

Just as quickly, the frustration was swept away by a deep sense of relief. They would finally get a chance to really defend their country. Instantly, relief was chased away by fear.

He turned back around as another angry flash twinkled from the hill. His knees started to shake again, so he quickly locked them again, standing as tall as he could. Yes, as scared as he was, this was the moment he had waited for, to stand in front of a column of his—and, of course, Captain George Blake's—men right before they entered combat. *Thank you, Lord.*

Just as soon as he finished thanking God, he wished he could take it back. As the long line of walking wounded came nearer, they brought with them the reality of war. Of course, he had seen ambulances coming back from the front, but those in the wagons had already been treated for their wounds. This was going to be a much different experience.

"Pass the word through the company to remain in formation," Blake whispered. "We aren't going to be here long, and the wounded are just going to have to fend for themselves. That includes no sharing food and water."

Stephen was at first taken off guard. It was one thing to leave exhausted men collapsed on the side of the road, but it didn't feel right not treating the wounded. He was about to say something, but First Sergeant Halloway beat him to it.

"We should pass the word that there aren't any aide stations behind us."

Stephen was surprised when the first sergeant immediately turned his back on the officers and hurried down the left side of the regiment to quickly relay Blake's orders.

"Shouldn—" Stephen started to say.

Blake cut him off with a firm whisper. "No, they'll find their way to an aide station and get some help. We need to keep focused on our own men."

Stephen took a deep breath. It was so against his nature to see suffering and do nothing to try and help it. He turned back to the column and looked into the anxious faces of the company. He straightened his back, lowered his head slightly, set his jaw as he scanned back and forth across the four columns. Some of the men looked him in the eye with a worried look on their faces while others stared at the ground or just looked away. He just hoped they couldn't tell he was just as scared as the rest of them.

"Pretty flag you got there, boys," a deep, big voice boomed from behind Stephen. "Goes nice with those pretty caps of yours."

Stephen snapped around and looked directly into the sunken eyes of a tall, skinny wisp of a private, which was in stark contrast to his deep, powerful voice. "Don't worry 'bout being green; old Bobby Lee will soon give you some schoolin'," the man called out and Stephen was sure most of the regiment had heard him.

Stephen wanted to say something to the private to defend the regiment's honor, but his eyes fixed on the man's right thigh. The upper part of his pant leg was torn away and the front of his thigh was a bloody mess of torn flesh. Blood was oozing down his leg soaking his pants all the way down to his shoe. The man leaned on his rifle for support.

"It ain't as bad as it looks, sir," the private said with a hint of a smile on his face. "Just a flesh wound. I saw the cannon ball comin' and got turned, but the man behind me, he wasn't quick enough, and it cost him his leg ... Thirteen what, sir?"

"Vermont," Stephen answered him.

"Oh ... green or not, we coulda used you boys this afternoon."

It was only then that Stephen noticed the dull red circle on the top of the private's cap designating his regiment also belonged to the Army of the Potomac's First Corps.

"Where is the rest of the Corps?" Stephen asked.

"Don't rightly know, sir. The line collapsed and it was every man for himself. Any aide stations back up that way?" The private asked pointing back up the road.

"Didn't see any," Stephen said.

"Damn, then where in the hell did those dam wagons go?"

"Not sure," Stephen answered, ignoring the man's disrespectful tone. Stephen guessed if he had nearly had his leg blown off by a cannon ball, he'd be a bit disrespectful, too.

"We didn't see any wagons, but there is a crossroad up by that orchard," Stephen turned and pointed back up the road. "They might have taken it to the east."

"Thankee, sir. I'll head that way."

With that, the man resumed hobbling up the side of the road. "Give them hell for me, boys," he shouted out and was greeted by cheers from the company.

Behind the tall private came many more of the walking wounded, blood oozing from various parts of their bodies. A few had bloody rags wrapped around what had once been a hand or an arm. A few were moaning. A few begged for water, but most walked in silence, keeping their suffering to themselves.

"Watch out!" came a cry from the rear quickly followed by heavy horse hoofs. Stephen stepped back giving room to Colonel Nichols of the Fourteenth Vermont and Colonel Veazey of the Sixteenth riding quickly to the head of the column.

Stephen turned his head to follow their path up the road and was surprised to see them following General Stannard and Colonel Randall in what looked like a race. He was at first confused, but then he saw Benedict coming back their way at a slow trot.

Stephen looked over at Blake.

"It won't be long now, boys," Blake shouted out to the company. "This is what we've been waitin' for."

Stephen went back to his place in the column next to Ralph.

"I'm getting tired of that pretty hat crap," Ralph spouted off.

Stephen took of his cap and beat it against his leg a couple of times knocking off some of the dust. The brass wreath surrounding the large thirteen in the middle with the K just above, was dull and needed some polishing.

Still, it was the type of cap normally reserved for officers and much more eye-catching than the bugle on the
enlisted. The difference with the Thirteenth Vermont
was that every man had the same officer-style cap. Ever
since they'd started encountering the rest of the army,
they had to listen to cracks about their pretty caps.

"You don't think it's pretty?" Stephen needled Ralph.

Hovel beats caught Stephen's attention and before
the officer needed to shout anything, he stepped behind
Ralph clearing room for the horse and rider. The other
colonels were going back to their regiments.

"Company!" The command was quickly followed by
attention, right shoulder arms, and forward march.
The three remaining regiments of the Second Vermont
Brigade resumed journey to join the Army of the Potomac.

Jacob Turney

Even with the full moon, Jake couldn't see the type of his King James Bible. He glanced down into the hole but the dull light of the moon didn't reach down into the bottom and he could no longer see the face of young Private Marion Sharp.

Jake slid his Bible carefully into his haversack then reached his hands out to his brother James standing to his left and to his brother Albert on his right. Quickly, the other seven men followed his lead and they stood in a circle around the grave holding hands. Jake glanced around. It was a pretty spot just a few yards from the slow-moving creek—not that Marion cared, but Jake wanted to have a picture in his mind when he wrote the letter home to Marion's mother. He hoped that knowing her son lay in a peaceful, pretty spot would give her some measure of comfort.

"The Lord is my shepherd; I shall not want," Jake started and the others joined in.

"He maketh me to lie down in green pastures he leadeth me beside the still waters. He restoreth my soul: he leadeth me in the paths of righteousness for his name's sake. Yea, though I walk through the valley of the shadow of death, I will fear no evil: for thou art with me;

thy rod and thy staff they comfort me. Thou preparest a table before me in the presence of mine enemies: thou anointest my head with oil; my cup runneth over. Surely goodness and mercy shall follow me all the days of my life: and I will dwell in the house of the LORD forever."

Jake squeezed both of his brothers' hands before letting go. He reached over and picked up the shovel and scooped into the large mound of fresh dirt, carefully pouring it down over the hole. Jake decided it was better like this to not see the body as it was slowly covered over with dirt.

He then turned the shovel over to Lieutenant Holland. As Jake walked away, back up the slope toward the Herr Ridge Traven, he heard Holland scope up his own shovel full of dirt. Jake knew each man would take his turn throwing in a shovel of dirt until it came to Marion's comrades, the three men who knew him best.

Until that morning, there were four of them—four men who shared everything in this hellish war. They cooked, ate, slept, and fought together forming a bond as strong as brothers. Now the remaining three would finish the job of burying their friend.

It was a ceremony that started and evolved after the Battle of Seven Pines. While the other regiments of the brigade had gone west following General Hatton, Jake's cousin Colonel Peter Turney had taken the First Tennessee to the north to cover the brigade's flank. With the sunlight fading, the regiment halted in a wood lot and lay down. Yankee artillery fire blasted the treetops above their heads raining twigs and branches down upon the regiment.

To their front, across a small wheat field, a line of Yankees with their bayonets fixed. Cousin Peter ordered the regiment to their feet and for fifteen terrible minutes the two lines hammered at each other at close range until it was too dark to see what you were shooting at. When the firing stopped, eight-five of the First Tennessee's men laid wounded or dead. Among the dead was Private Henry Turney.

Before the regiment pulled back, they carried their dead out of the trees, and then buried them in the pasture just past the edge of the woods. Everyone in Company K wanted to lend a hand in digging the grave for the captain's brother. By the time they finished, Jake guessed it was five feet deep.

They carefully laid Henry in the bottom of the hole "then covered" ed his face with his hat. Then the entire company gathered around as Cousin Peter said a few words then he carefully poured the first shovel full of dirt over. He then gave the shovel to Jake. Jake was about to do the same when Joel had stopped him.

"We'll go last," Joel said as he took the shovel from Jake and handed it to Lieutenant George Garrett. Garrett followed Peter's lead and poured in one scoop of dirt, passed on the shovel, then walked away. Every man followed suit until only Joel, James, and Jake were left. The three of them stood silently for a few minutes, and then they took turns finishing the job.

Jake stopped and looked back to watch for a few minutes as Marion's three comrades finished burying him. He knew his company was the only one that followed this sort ceremony and he thought it was a fitting tribute to Joel that it had carried on.

Like Henry, Jake didn't see Joel fall. It was about a month after the Seven Pines at the Battle of Cold Harbor, the second fight during the Seven Days Battle. The first of the Seven Days battles was on June 26, 1862 at Mechanicsville, when the new Commanding General Robert E. Lee attacked the Yankee army.

Lee had taken over from the wounded Joe Johnston after Seven Pines. Mechanicsville was also the first battle for the Tennessee Brigade's new commanding officer James Jay Archer.

At Mechanicsville, the Tennessee Brigade had helped to push the Yankees back, but nightfall cut short the attack. By the next morning the Yankees had pulled back past Gaines' Mill and New Cold Harbor into a strong defensive position.

When Cousin Peter gave Jake and other company commanders their attack orders, they all thought it was a joke. The Yankees had dug in along a tree line just on the other side of a wide creek and an open field. They had excellent field of fire and cover, but it wasn't a joke.

The brigade advanced at a double quick through rifle and artillery fire, but it was just too strong a position for one undersized brigade to take. When they were within twenty steps, the charge collapsed, and they scampered back the way they came.

As the regiment reorganized, Cousin Peter went on a tirade; the regimental color was missing. Jake had other more important concerns. Joel was missing.

Later in the day, eight brigades mounted a successful attack against the same Yankee position. What was left of Archer's brigade followed along in support. After the firing stopped, Jake and James searched for Joel. They first found the color sergeant, gut shot, lying face up with half his intestines lying on ground next to him, but the color was long gone.

A couple of yards to the right of the color sergeant, they found Joel face down with his rifle pointed toward the Yankee lines. Losing their colors was an embarrassment to the entire brigade, but when Jake thought of Cold Harbor, he could only think of Joel lying face down in the dirt. *How can I be my brother's keeper?*

Later that evening, they conducted a similar ceremony as they had for Henry, only this time far fewer men took part and grave was only about three feet deep. Having the captain lose a brother was no longer a novelty.

Jake stopped, turned, and watched Marion's commanders place the board with Marion's name on it at the head of the grave. He knew the company was very lucky in only having one man killed during the morning's attack, but he also knew that at this moment, those three men felt anything but lucky.

Jake glanced up at the full moon. Its smiling face was in stark contrast to the three men who were saying their last goodbyes to their comrade. Jake turned his back and continued up the ridge, feeling guilty for feeling lucky that only one of his men was dead.

Up ahead, the Herr Ridge Traven was now a full-fledged field hospital with men being carried in and out the back door. A few tents were setup around the building, but most of the wounded were lying on the ground waiting their turn to see the doctors or recovering from the hastily performed surgery.

Pleasant Hampton, with a large welt on the side of his head, had made it back to the company, as did Joe McKinney who had a finger shot off. While two had made it back, the company was still missing six men.

Jake hoped that among wounded spread around the tavern he would find First Lieutenant George Garrett, Corporal Cornelius Hedgepeth, and Private Bob Davis. He and a squad had already checked the ground where they fell, and they were gone.

"Captain Jake," George Garrett called out to him from the darkness. "Over here."

Jake saw a man lying on his left side waving.

"In the dark, how did you know it was me?" Jake asked.

"I watched you come up from the ceremony."

Jake glanced over his head; in the soft moon light he could just make out the mound of dirt that marked the grave.

"How did you know it was us?" Jake asked as he sat down next to George.

"It's our ceremony," George said. "I could've recognized y'all from a mile away." He paused for a couple of seconds before asking the dreaded question. "Who was it?"

"Marion Sharp," Jake whispered.

George nodded. "A good man. A good man he was. One of the best men in the company."

Jake noticed George was slurring his words a bit and he was more talkative than usual. He wondered if they'd given him something for the pain.

"How are you doin'?" Jake asked.

"George smiled. "Pretty good for a guy shot in the ass."

"They get the bullet out yet?"

"No need. It took out a hunk of my ass and kept on goin'. The bleedin' stopped on its own and I ain't in too much pain, so I'm down the list a ways to see the doctor."

Jake nodded.

"Have you seen anyone else from the company?"

George pointed behind him to a sleeping man with his neck bandaged. "Davis … it looked pretty bad. Broke his dang collarbone and took out a hunk of flesh. Could've been a hell of a lot worse.

"A little while after the brigade turned tail. He came walkin' out of the woods right past them Yankees. I couldn't believe it when I saw him. His face was a ghostly white with blood just oozing out of that wound.

"The Yankees must have thought he was close to death and didn't pay him no mind. He walked right up and sat down next to me and asked if I had any water. Said his canteen took a bullet right through it so he'd thrown it away. I gave him mine and he took a couple drinks then keeled over. At first I thought he was dead ..."

George yawned and Jake guessed they'd liquored him up pretty good.

"A few minutes later, Hedgepeth dragged himself across the creek using a rifle for a crutch. Never seen anything like it ... the Yankees just let him pass on by, too. Guess they figured with that leg turned every which way, he wouldn't be botherin' them none."

"Where is Hedgepeth now?" Jake asked.

George yawned again and lay down his head. "They took him about ten minutes ago. I think the bullet hit bone."

Jake took off his hat and rubbed his head as he said a silent prayer for his corporal. There wasn't much they could do for a shattered bone except to cut off the leg.

George muttered a couple words Jake couldn't understand then he fell fast asleep. Jake stood up as a wagon pulled up with more wounded.

Jake quietly slipped away and cut across the ridge back toward the Tennessee Brigade's camp. He thought about sending a detail back to help with their wounded, but the company'd had a long day and it wouldn't be fair to those on the detail.

He'd heard that Heth's brigade was most likely going to be held in reserve tomorrow, so he let everyone get a good night's sleep, then he would send a squad over in the morning to tend to their wounded. He glanced back at the mound of fresh dirt. Company K took pride in taking care of their own, in life and in death.

Stephen Brown

Stephen lay on his back on top of his rubber blanket staring up into the smiling face of old man moon. With the recent rains, the ground was soft without being mushy. His head rested on his rolled up uniform coat. His haversack and hatchet lay next to him. He took several deep breaths trying to relax and forget how hungry and thirsty he was.

At least it was comfortable sleeping weather with a light breeze coming up from the south, but the humidity was high, so the morning dew would be heavy. He was debating on if he was going to use his half of the fly tent to cover up tonight. It would make sleeping a bit warm, but it would keep him dry once the dew settled in.

"I wish they'd get back soon," Corporal William Church said.

Stephen glanced to his left. William was sitting up with his rifle across his lap.

"They'll be fine," Stephen whispered.

"I just got a bad ..."

Stephen rolled over on his right side to face his friend. "They'll be fine. We haven't heard any shots fired in a couple of hours."

William let out a loud sigh and Stephen had to grit his teeth to keep from laughing. He watched William laid his Springfield rifle musket to his left side. "I guess you're right," he added as he lay down on his side facing Stephen. "It's just—"

"I know, I know, you got a bad feeling," Stephen chuckled.

"It's not funny, William protested.

"It wasn't funny the first twenty times you said it, but now ... now it's funny."

William flopped over on his back and pulled his cap down over his eyes. "I don't see anything funny about it," he mumbled. "I might be dead tomorrow and you think it's funny."

Stephen sat up and rubbed his forehead in frustration. "I can't believe," his voice raised a couple of octaves before he continued, "you would say something—"

William's chuckle stopped Stephen in mid-sentence. He let up a loud grunt, which was met by William's laughter. "That's not funny," Stephen snapped.

Suddenly, several dark shapes appeared, coming down the road from the direction of the big hill, as if they had emerged from the moonlight. Immediately, Stephen reached with his right hand for his hatchet and slapped William on the leg with his left.

"Hey—" William protested.

"Shut up," Stephen cut him off. William pulled back his hat and sat up. Stephen pointed up the road. William grabbed his musket and flipped open his cartage box.

Coming down from the big hill, Stephen was sure they were Union troops, but this was no time to let his guard down like Edwin Stoughton had back at Fairfax Courtuse back in March. The Second Vermont Brigade's twenty-five-year-old commanding officer, after hosting a party for his visiting mother and sister, had retired to the house he was using as his headquarters only to be awakened by a slap to his rear.

Startled, the Brigadier General sat up in bed and snapped, "Do you who I am?"

To which the voice in the darkness replied, "Do you know Mosby, general?"

A now overly excited Stoughton exclaimed, "Yes! Have you got the rascal?"

"No but he has got you," laughed the "Gray Ghost," Major John Mosby. Mosby and his men took Stoughton prisoner and spurred away several horses. To add insult to injury, the rumor was that when President Lincoln heard of Stoughton's capture, he was more concerned about the cost of the lost horses than the loss of a brigadier general.

It took a few seconds before they heard the faint, hushed call. "Thirteenth Vermont."

"Finally," William said.

Stephen stood up and waved. "Company K," he yelled out. He wasn't surprised by the shouts for quiet and he chuckled under his breath, because those yelling at him were making much more noise than he had, then just as quickly, it dawned on them what Stephen was yelling about and there were a host of people waving and yelling, "Company A, Company H, Company B," making sure their members of the canteen detail could find their way back to their respective companies.

"There's Ralph," William said as he jumped to his feet. "Here, hold this," he said as he thrust his musket at Stephen then stepped between the fence posts on to the road and trotted up to Ralph. Others did the same, giving the canteen detail a reprieve from the burden for the last hundred yards.

Captain George Blake joined Stephen as they waited for their canteens. "You sure we can't start a fire, sir?" Stephen asked his commanding officer. "Sure, could use a cup of coffee."

"Colonel was very clear that he had strict orders for no fires," Blake replied obviously disappointed.

Stephen turned around and looked out to the west past the small white house and barn, across what he guessed was a mile and half of open land of fields and pasture to the long line of woods with the twinkle of yellow and red peeking through the leaves.

Obviously, the confederates were brewing coffee and cooking dinner.

"To victors go the spoils."

"What did you say?" Blake asked.

Stephen pointed across the way. "You think they would share a cup of coffee?"

"Maybe, if you could get into their camp without getting shot and didn't mind being taken prisoner."

"Here you go, sir," Ralph said as he handed Blake his canteen.

"Well water?" Blake asked.

"Sorry, sir, stream. All we could find in the dark. Took a while to find one that was running fairly good and wasn't stale," Ralph said. "I sure could use a cup of coffee," Ralph quickly added. "We got plenty of firewood."

That was true. The first thing the colonel had ordered once it looked like they were finally settling in for the night was to pull the rails from the fence lining the edge of the road. The regiment had an abundance of excellent firewood.

William returned with Stephen's canteen and Stephen gave him back his musket. Stephen took a long drink of the warm water for the first time in many days, not worrying about how much he drank. Unless there was a major catastrophe tomorrow, in which case water would be the least of their worries, they were settled in and would easily be able to find water in the morning.

"Make way, make way," came shouts from the road followed by the hoof beats and wood wheels bouncing up the hard-packed road as the first piece of a four-gun artillery battery rolled past.

"Where does this road go," Stephen called out to a sergeant riding the battery's lead horse.

"Taneytown, Maryland," the sergeant called back.

The Thirteenth Vermont and the rest of the Second Vermont Brigade had come up from the south on the road from Emmitsburg. The one they were camped along went down to Taneytown and he heard the one that ran across the face of the big hill went east to Baltimore.

He'd also heard, when they were up by the cemetery on the big hill just to their north, a couple of senior officers talking about the confederates had come in on the roads from York, Harrisburg, and Chambersburg. To somebody even as inexperienced as Stephen, it was becoming clear the roads had to do with why the two great armies had met at Gettysburg.

"Do we know which command we're assigned to?" Ralph asked.

"Back with the First Corps," Captain Blake hesitantly answered.

"You don't sound so sure," Stephen said.

"It's been a half hour since I talked to the colonel, so it might have changed again.

When the three remaining regiments of the Second Vermont Brigade joined the remnants of the First and Eleventh Corps on Cemetery Hill, there were no cat calls about the arrival of the untested brigade."

Green or not, everyone was happy to see over sixteen hundred additional troops, so much so that as the evening wore on, and the parts of the Third and Twelfth Corps joined the army, the brigade was attached and detached to the various other Corps. They had marched back and forth to so many different positions; Stephen was concerned some of the men might start collapsing due to exhaustion. Finally, they settled in along the road to Taneytown and they were able send out their canteen detail.

"What was the last count?" Blake asked.

"Forty-six," Stephen answered.

"That's better than some of the companies," Blake said obviously trying to find something positive to say about the number of men left in the company. They'd started the march with sixty-eight men including officers and noncommissioned officers.

"There are still some stragglers coming in. We might pick up a few more during the night," Stephen said hopefully. Captain Blake just shrugged his soldiers. Nine months ago, they had left Maine with over ninety men and now when they finally made it to a battlefield and over half were gone.

Stephen let out a big yawn. "I guess we should try to get some sleep. Tomorrow is going to be a long day."

Jacob Turney

Jake had a cramp in his right leg, so he stopped, shifted, stretched out his leg, and then leaned back against the large oak tree. The others spread out on the ground around him waited for him to continue reading. A ray of light from the noonday sun broke through the trees and fell softly on the paper, highlighting the story Jake was reading.

"Old Smith got some miles behind, and while sitting on the roadside, solitary and alone resting and eating his beef and biscuit, he observed a full regiment of cavalry approaching," Jake read aloud.

"He jumped out into the woods and as the Yankees came near he thundered away on his drum, beating the long roll with terrible vim." Jake skipped the part explaining that the long roll was the signal the enemy was near and to form a battle line.

"His trick was successful; for the Yankees supposing, of course, that there was an infantry regiment lying in the thickets, faced about and skedaddled in the regular Bull Run style." Jake stopped reading and let the laughter of his brothers and First Sergeant Chuck Tuley die down. It was one of the funniest stories he ever read from the Fayetteville Observer newspaper.

Before he started reading again, Jake glanced up at his two young lieutenants. Farrar and Holland were still going carefully from tree to tree along the eastern edge of the woods. They obviously hadn't found the initials a Yankee prisoner had claimed he craved yesterday morning shortly after the first fight of the day.

Jake went back to the story. "Old Smith, replacing his drum on his shoulder, came out on the road again with his beef and biscuit in one hand and his drumsticks in the other and resumed his march with his unusual equanimity."

As he flipped the paper over, Jake rubbed his back against the tree taking care of an itch. When he turned his attention back to the paper he noticed the headline, "Tennessee Agent in Virginia."

"We got a new agent in Virginia, a Mr. A. J. Swinebroad. They printed his address in Richmond."

"Better save that part of the paper, sir. We got several boys from families who don't get the paper," First Sergeant Chuck Tuley reminded Jake.

"I'll give it to you when I'm done so you can make sure everyone gets his name and address," Jake said as he turned the page. Families could send packages to the agent, who would then make sure they were forwarded to the men in the field.

"How long are we going to wait for them, sir?" Chuck asked.

Jake glanced up at his lieutenants. "A few more minutes," Jake said as the headline "Deserters!" caught his attention. Company K like the rest of the regiment had had their share of deserters. "Company A of the Forty-first Tennessee is offering a thirty-dollar reward for turning in deserters," Jake commented.

"Dang! How many are they lookin' for?" Albert asked.

Jake quickly counted the names. "Thirteen."

"I always wanted to be a bounty hunter," Albert laughed.

"Didn't the entire Forty-first get captured by Grant at Fort Donaldson?" James asked.

"I think so, but they would have been exchanged by now," Jake said. He expected someone to say something and he was pleasantly surprised that no one did.

Thankfully, the jokes about his capture had run their course. When he was able to rejoin the regiment after his exchange everyone agreed that his capture during his trip home in 1862 was a bad break and not his fault, but that didn't stop the jokes.

Jake thought the jokes were a way for the others to deal with the anger over the number of letters, money, and dispatches that the Ohio cavalry troopers had taken from him. After the losses at Seven Pines and Cold Harbor, Cousin Peter had sent Jake back to Tennessee to recruit more men for the regiment. He'd avoided East Tennessee, the pro-Union movement having taken over that part of the state, by moving down through North Carolina, Georgia, and then into Northern Alabama. He had no idea that a Union Cavalry Brigade had made a daring ride through Tennessee and taken up positions around the Woodville, Alabama area.

Jake and Private John Wilson, who because of his age had mustered out of the service and had joined Jake on the trip home, were riding through Vienna, Alabama when two squads from the Third Ohio Cavalry surprised them. Jake tried to convince them to let John go since he was now a private citizen, but since he was still in uniform, they took him prisoner too. After ten days, the Yankees arranged a prisoner exchange and transportation for Jake and John back to Lincoln

County minus the letters, dispatches, money, and of course their horses.

He'd written his parents about his brothers and as he climbed the front steps he was worried they would both blame him for their deaths, but the look in his Father's eyes was far worse.

His father, Henry Turney Senior, wasn't a stranger to personal loss or war. As a young man of just sixteen he'd joined Brigadier General John Coffee's Tennessee Volunteers and headed down to New Orleans as part of Andrew Jackson's army. He took part in the four days of fighting that became known as the Battle of New Orleans.

In 1820, the Governor of the Alabama Territory had appointed him lieutenant colonel of the Twenty-fourth Regiment of the Militia of the Alabama Territory. Just before leaving, he married Mary Russell and nine months later their first daughter, Nancy, was born

By 1821, his duties took him to New Orleans where General Andrew Jackson picked him to go to Cuba carrying dispatches concerning the peace treaty with Spain and details about turning Florida over to the United States. It was one of the most exciting events of his life.

Later, he served as a member of the first grand jury of Pensacola, Florida, conducted under the laws of the United States. General Jackson took an active role in the business of the court and often conferred with the members of the grand jury.

In 1822, Henry left public service, moved Mary, pregnant with their second child, and young Nancy to the port city of Mobile, and helped form a new merchant business. It was one of the happiest times in young Henry's life, but soon things would change. Mary never recovered from the ordeal of the birth of her second daughter and she died soon after.

Suddenly, his life crashed down all around him and he longed for Tennessee. He sold his part of the business, headed back to the hill country of Lincoln County, and opened a law practice. Family and friends helped with the raising of the girls, but they couldn't help with the void in his heart.

It wasn't until 1827 when he met Delila Pigg that the void slowly began to close. Nine months after they were married, John was born, the first of Henry's seven sons.

It was at John's funeral where Jake saw his father cry for the first time. While he was at first surprised, Jake quickly realized it was a powerful sign of the love Henry had for his children.

It was so much different from Henry's reaction when Jake had returned home. A cloud of despair had settled over his father. *You're your brothers' keeper.* Was it a demand, a challenge, a plea, Jake didn't know and he was afraid to ask.

Jake heard some commotion to his right, so he looked up from his paper. Holland and Farrar were still looking at the trees. To their right came a column of men marching toward town on the road from Chambersburg. The same one the First Tennessee had used yesterday.

"Sir, any ideas who they are?" First Sergeant Tuley asked.

As the head of the column reached the low ground between the ridges, Jake noticed two riders come down from the brick house General Robert E. Lee was using as his headquarters. A cheer spread through the column, so Jake guessed one of the riders was Lee.

"Is that Longstreet with Lee?" Jake asked.

"I think so," James spoke up.

"Then I think it's Law's Alabamians," Jake said. "The colonel told me Longstreet was waiting for them before he moved his Corps to the south."

"This might start shaping up like another Chancellorsville," Albert said.

Jake held his tongue. While Longstreet had a reputation as a fighter, he wasn't creative or resourceful like Stonewall Jackson. The column halted and the men fell out alongside the road while details gathered up their canteens.

Lee and Longstreet continued along the road and disappeared behind the woods. Jake knew the rest of Longstreet's Corps had lined up on the Herr Ridge Road. Jake didn't know the real name of the road, nor did he care, but since the Herr Traven was at the corner of it and the road to Chambersburg, he and everyone else had started calling it the Herr Ridge Road.

"Maybe we should be getting back to the regiment, sir. Even if that damn Yankee craved the initials J.R. on that tree, I doubt those two can find it," Chuck said.

Jake had thought the same thing when Lieutenant Holland had first brought up the idea of seeing the spot where Yankee Major General John Reynolds got himself killed. They'd heard the story while they were visiting Company K's wounded men up at the Herr Traven field hospital.

A wounded Yankee private went on and on about how if Reynolds had lived, the Yankee First Corps would have kicked the whole damn rebel army all the back to Virginia. Everyone did their best to ignore the Yankee, but he had piqued Holland's interest when he started talking about how he'd craved Reynolds initials J.R. on the tree next to where the General fell.

Several men were already claiming they were the ones that shot the Yankee general from his horse. With all the smoke, Jake doubted any of them saw the general's horse let alone him being shot from it. There was a chance that the smoke wasn't as bad on the left of the line and farther up the ridge, so he wasn't about to challenge anyone's claim to the honor.

"Sir, we should be gettin' back," Chuck said. Doing his duty as first sergeant, he prodded Jake.

Jake folded his paper and stuffed it in his coat pocket then stood up. He turned toward Lieutenants Holland and Farrar. Still, it wasn't often that a major general fell in combat and while he didn't want to admit it to anyone else, he too would like to see the spot where Reynolds fell.

"James, go round up our two young lieutenants," Jake ordered instead. Chuck was right. They needed to be getting' back to the rest of the company. While the plan was for Heth's Division to be held in reserve, there was always the chance they could be ordered to take part in the attack. Maybe later, he would come back with the lieutenants and join the search.

Jake pulled his hat low over his eyes before stepping out from under the shade of the trees. The temperate difference hit him immediately. He glanced over at the men of Law's Brigade spread out on both sides of the road out in the open. Too bad they hadn't moved them over into the trees.

He glanced over to the large building that dominated the next ridge. He'd heard last evening that it was a Lutheran Seminary. Jake didn't know much about the Lutherans, there weren't that many in middle Tennessee. He did know that many of their followers had emigrated from Germany and they allowed at least one of their pastors to operate a still.

Jake and his brothers and sisters were raised in the Methodist Episcopal Church, which traced its history back to the Church of England. While the Methodist Church had a rule against buying or selling slaves, there weren't any rules against owning slaves, so it—along with the Baptist Church, which also allowed members to own slaves—became popular in middle Tennessee and across the south.

Like the rest of the United States, the question of slavery had affected the churches. For many years, the issue of slavery caused tension between the northern and southern branches of the American Home Mission Society. Tensions came to a peak in 1844, when the society instituted a policy stating slave owners couldn't be missionaries. As a result, the southern churches broke away and formed the Southern Baptist Convention.

The debate was just as turbulent within the Methodist Episcopal Church. Up in the north, free Negroes had joined and argued for a tougher stance on slavery. Early in the 1800's when it was clear their efforts would fail to change the church; they broke away to from the African Methodist Episcopal Church.

In 1845, the church again faced the question of slavery. Bishop James O. Andrew, one of the five bishops of the church, had inherited some slaves and it became an issue at the annual General Conference. The conference members voted to suspend Andrew from his duties until he freed his slaves. This put Bishop Andrew in a difficult situation since it was against the law in the state of Georgia for him to free his slaves.

A few days later, some southern members drafted a plan for separation. The plan passed by a wide majority forming the Methodist Episcopal Church, South and Methodist Episcopal Church, North.

Jake didn't know what the Lutherans had done about the question, but he guessed any church that allowed their pastors to run a still must be flexible on many issues. Pastor Call up in Lynchburg made some fine drinking whiskey.

Jake looked past the seminary to the large bald hill with the one towering pine tree. He'd heard from a citizen friendly to the rebel cause, that one of the town cemeteries was up on that hill, hence it was known as Cemetery Hill.

He'd heard from Colonel Newton George that Yankee line ran east to the next tree-covered hill and to the south, along the ridge Jake had seen yesterday. In the light of the noon day sun, Jake couldn't see any sign of the disorganized mob of the night before.

The Yankees were dug in and supported by artillery. Jake saw several puffs of smoke up on Cemetery Hill and the confederate batteries around the Lutheran Seminary let loose a volley of their own. The artillery was doing what they always did when they were within range, hammering away at each other. The artillery duel reminded Jake of the line from Macbeth "full of sound and fury, signifying nothing."

The same wouldn't be said when Longstreet's men finally did make their attack. The hill commanded the north end of the Yankee line and it would be hell for the infantry to push them off it now.

As the lieutenants walked up with James, Jake turned back toward the First Tennessee's camp as he remembered commanding General Robert E. Lee complaining the afternoon before about the enemy getting away. Jake glanced back at the bald hill. *Too bad the enemy hadn't gotten clean away*, he thought to himself.

Stephen Brown

"Where are they going?" Ralph demanded.

"Private, I expect you to show your officers the proper respect," Stephen snapped.

"Where are they going, sir?" Ralph snapped back as his cheeks flashed a bright shade of red.

Boom, boom, boom, boom! Four guns, from one of the artillery batteries, fired in quick secession up on the hill. Stephen looked up past the gravestones just below the summit and watched the light breeze from the south push the growing cloud of dark gray smoke to the north.

He resisted the urge to run away when the first shell exploded between the headstones up near the summit throwing up a small cloud of dirt. The Confederates weren't wasting any time returning fire.

Stephen turned back around as the long column was called to attention. He couldn't help but notice that most of them looked dejected, but there were a few who looked obviously relieved.

The drums beat, commands were shouted, and the Fifteenth Vermont started their march to the south, back to guard the wagons of the First Corps of the Army of the Potomac. Stephen felt sorry for Colonel Proctor, Captain Blake told him Generals Stannard and Doubleday had given him an earful about disobeying his orders to guard the Corps' wagons. It helped that General Sickles had encouraged him to come up with his regiment, but Sickles wasn't in Proctor's chain of command.

Stephen felt helpless as the Fifteenth marched to the south. How could the generals order fresh troops away from the fight? Early in the morning, it had quickly become clear how yesterday's fight had decimated the First Corps. The proud black hats of the Iron Brigade were a shell of a fighting unit leaving most of their men dead, wounded, or captured back on the west side of town.

Stephen had his back to the explosion, but the noise was deafening, and a mist of dirt pelted the left side of his head. He instinctively glanced to his left to see commotion around the front rank of Company G where he expected Captain Merritt Williams to be standing. Ralph rushed past him heading toward the commotion.

Stephen followed him. Ralph slid down next to Merritt while Stephen stayed standing and looked down into Merritt's ashen colored face. Lieutenant Albert Clark was giving him what looked like a sip of brandy. Williams opened his eyes and muttered, "I am shot and feel as if my last hour had come."

Stephen glanced around and noticed a couple of the other men were down, one sitting up and the other had his eyes open, but he seemed dazed. Both were being attended to.

The litter-bearers appeared quickly and gently placed Williams on a stretcher carrying him toward the tents with a red flag designating them as a field hospital. Stephen put his right hand on Ralph's shoulder, "we need to get back to the company."

Ralph just stood there not moving, while the three of them had been classmates back at Bakersfield Academy;

Ralph was much closer to Merritt than Stephen was. "Come on, Ralph," Stephen said pushing his friend back toward the company.

"I'm never going to see him again," Ralph whispered.

"You don't know that" Stephen said. "You don't know what God has in store for Merritt."

Five quick explosions up on the top of the hill, then two more down toward the Thirteenth Vermont caused Stephen to jump. He saw a flash of blue and turned surprised to see a flood of blue coats, with the light blue stripes of the infantry, running down the hill toward them.

Colonel Randall saw them too and spun his horse around and quickly rode between his regiment and the onslaught running toward them. He pulled out his sword and started yelling, "See these boys!" The colonel started yelling pointing back at the men of the Thirteenth. "They don't run, and they were never in a battle; you ought to be ashamed to run because of a few shells are being fired over this way!"

A few shells? Those were a few shells? Stephen thought to himself. Stephen wasn't sure if it was the sight of a sword-wielding officer on horseback, the Thirteenth Vermont in a line of battle blocking their path, or what Randall was yelling, but the men in the front drastically slowed giving the units officers and sergeants a chance to catch up and gain back control of their men.

Within a few minutes, they had the men back into a line and heading back up the hill. As they marched, more shells rained down on the summit.

"A few shells," Ralph whispered.

"I was thinking the same thing," Stephen responded.

Just as Stephen got back into line, Colonel Randall rode up.

"How is Merritt?"

Out of the corner of his eye, Stephen saw Ralph turn away. "Hard to tell, sir. I've never seen anyone shot before, but he thinks he is dying."

Randall glanced in Ralph's direction then looked back to Stephen. The friendship between Ralph and Merritt was common knowledge throughout the regiment. "I heard the same thing from some men from the First Vermont, who are walking around today," Randall said forcing a laugh.

Instantly, the colonel's expression changed, and he gave his horse a couple of quick, light kicks. The horse responded immediately, and he leaped forward. Stephen looked ahead of the colonel and saw General Stannard sitting on his horse in the middle of the road talking to their division commander Major General Abner Doubleday.

Randall pulled up his horse next to them then saluted. Doubleday pointed directly over Stephen's head. Stephen turned around following Doubleday's point up past a few gravestones up to the top of hill. Up there three guns fired in quick secession as a couple of confederate shells exploded in the cemetery knocking over one of the gravestones.

"Oh, oh," Ralph whispered.

Stephen turned around and noticed Lieutenant Colonel Munson had ridden up and joined the other officers. The meaning was clear. They were going up the hill.

Stephen walked around the back of the company's rear rank. Second Lieutenant Carmi Marsh gave him an apprehensive look. Stephen patted him on the back as he walked past. He was sure that Marsh wasn't any more scared than he was, but he hoped it wasn't showing on his face.

Corporal William Church glanced his way. Stephen wanted to run over to his friend and give him a big hug and tell him everything was going to be fine, but instead he managed to muster a smile. William nodded then turned back to the front. There wasn't anything else Stephen could do. Shells were falling up on the hill and that was where they were going. If it was William's time, then there wasn't anything he could do about it. He didn't have a reason to order William to stay behind.

As he came to the end of the line, he joined Captain George Blake and First Sergeant Morey. George glanced his way and nodded before returning his stare to the officers in front of them obviously discussing their fate.

Colonel Randall broke from the group first and rode toward the middle of the regiment and the color company with Lieutenant Colonel Munson close behind, waving his hat as he rode. The meaning was obvious; the company commanders were being summoned.

"Come on," George Blake said glancing at Stephen. They trotted over and joined the two senior officers as they jumped down from their horses. It took just a few seconds before the other officers joined them including First Lieutenant Albert Clarke, who was newly in command of Company G.

"Gentleman, we are splitting the regiment," Colonel Randall said obviously disappointed to see his command separated. "I will be in command of the First Battalion."

Stephen exhaled as his brain processed quickly what it all meant. Obviously, Randall would be leading the first battalion up the hill, while he and the rest of the second battalion would be either in reserve or going someplace else. He glanced up the hill feeling sorry for the men in the first battalion.

"The line will make a right face and then a column right to go up the hill," Colonel Munson said. *What?*

Stephen had tuned out Colonel Randall after he thought the second battalion was staying in reserve.

"Good luck to all of you. Dismissed."

Stephen followed George back to the company. George stopped in front of the center of the line. Stephen stood a step behind and to George's right.

"Men," George raised his voice making sure everyone could hear him, "the second battalion is going up the hill to provide protection for our artillery."

"Who is going to protect us?"

The shout came from the back of the company, which was immediately followed by the first sergeant's "Quiet in the ranks!"

"I expect all of you to do your duty. This is why we left home. This is our opportunity to show the rest of the army why we are here."

With that, George headed for his spot on the right side of the front rank of the company. Stephen tried to take a step and he almost fell. His left leg didn't want to move as a rush of fear spread all through his body. Moving meant he would be heading up that hill where the enemy artillery was raining death. Every part of his body was screaming at him not to go.

He took a deep breath and pushed himself to take a step and then another. He was surprised by how quickly fear had rushed over him. He could feel his knees and hands shaking. His breathing was quick and shallow, and he forced himself to slow it down.

More explosions up in the cemetery behind him caused him to jerk his head around. *Who in their right mind would march up that hill?* He looked down to his right hand and he could almost see himself holding that long straw and the disappointment and anger of that moment pushed away the fear.

Yes, he feared being hurt or worse, but that fear didn't compare with the disappointment of being left behind. He gripped his hands into fists and squeezed. Refusing to march up that hill was the smart and safe thing to do, but he wasn't going to be left behind. Whatever fate God had for him up on that hill, he would just have to face and accept, because there was no way he was being left behind again.

Stephen moved to his right and went around the left side of the company, taking his spot behind the left end of the company's second rank.

Just as he got back in position, Lieutenant Colonel Munson rode up. "Lieutenant Brown, the General has decided that you are no longer under arrest, but he does expect you will follow all orders in the future."

"Yes, sir, Stephen responded trying to keep from smiling. With all the commotion, Stephen had forgotten all about being under arrest.

"Unfortunately, they sent your sword to the rear with the baggage, so I guess you are going to have to go into battle with your little hatchet," Munson laughed gave his horse a light kick and rode up to the right side of the line.

Boom, boom, boom, boom!

Another battery let loose a volley. "Right," there was the expected pause as the command was repeated throughout the Second Battalion before the order, "Face!" was shouted out.

"Forward," the command echoed though the column, "March."

They marched to the Taneytown road then a column right was ordered and up the hill they went. When they got in front of one of the batteries, they were ordered off the road and over a stone wall. They marched to the rear of the battery and were ordered to lie down.

Stephen scanned the company; they were all quick learners. Everyone was hugging the ground. He couldn't help but notice Private James Hagan had his legs spread wide apart.

Stephen wanted to join them, press his body into the ground. Captain Blake was still upright, so instead Stephen walked slowly over to Hagan trying to appear as casual as possible when all he wanted to do was run down the hill.

"James, why do you have your feat spread apart?" he asked instead. Before Hagan could answer, two shells fell in front of the battery as a third flew overhead and exploded in the cemetery, between the men of the Thirteenth Vermont and the field hospital tents just down the eastern slope of the hill, knocking over another headstone.

Stephen ducked as fragments from the third shell whistled by. Their battery answered with four guns firing in quick secession. Once the noise died down to the dull roar of batteries firing on the other side of the hill, Stephen asked again, "James, why do you have your feat spread so far apart?"

James looked up at Stephen. It was obvious how scared he was, and Stephen didn't blame him. Stephen was just as scared but doing his best to keep it hidden.

"Well, sir, I figure if I keep them spread apart one shell ain't gonna take off both my legs."

Lose a leg? Stephen had thought about dying, but somehow, he'd never considered the possibility of losing a limb. He of course understood the logic of keeping his legs apart as the other men around James as they too spread their legs apart. "Good thinking James," Stephen finally said.

Out of the corner of his eye, Stephen couldn't help but notice the view. Except for a lone, very tall tree, Cemetery

Hill was cleared and with its large relativity flat summit offering an amazing view across its wide expanse.

Stephen couldn't help but take a view seconds to take it all in. To the northeast was a mostly tree-covered hill where the Union line was obviously extended. The smoke was billowing from the summit where it was being used as an artillery positon. Between the two hills was a small knoll with a battery dug in there too.

To the north, there was a wide-open expanse of farm and pastureland where an attacking line would be vulnerable to crossing artillery fire from both hills and the knoll. Of course, as Stephen had learned this morning from Colonel Randall, at the conference he'd called for all the Thirteenth Vermont's officers, a fast-moving line of infantry could overrun an artillery position. Stephen assumed down the north slope of Cemetery Hill there was infantry in place guarding the artillery.

On the other side of the pasture and farmland he noticed a low dark cloud bank that seemed out of place. It took him a couple of seconds to realize it was another hill covered with artillery. His eyes caught sight of a black speck streaking up out of the cloud. He watched it rise high up into the afternoon sky then it arched over and seemed to be heading right at him.

He unconsciously shifted his weight to his right leg and felt his body start to turn as his brain shouted at him to run. Instead he held his ground and his breath as he watched the rapidly growing speck. He let out a deep breath as the shell fell short, exploding harmlessly in the middle of the road to Baltimore.

The road to Baltimore came up from the west and the town of Gettysburg crossing over the entire length of Cemetery Hill's eastern slope and then tucked behind the small knoll and the tree-covered hill to the north. He had also learned from Colonel Randall that Cemetery Hill was critical because of the roads. The road to Baltimore and the road to Taneytown, Maryland, which was below him crossing the western slope of the hill, were the army's only escape routes. If something were to go terribly wrong, like what had happened just a month before at Chancellorsville, they would need both roads to get all the army out of the Gettysburg area.

Stephen turned away from the smoke covered hill deciding that while he was so exposed, it was better not to watch the shells being in fired in his direction and instead turn his attention to the town. The town of Gettysburg covered the northwest approaches to Cemetery Hill. While the rebels had taken the town, its narrow streets would make it difficult for them to mount an attack from that direction. It looked like a peaceful town with a few church steeples rising above the other buildings.

North and west of town, Stephen couldn't help but notice another large hill with its southern face cleared of trees. The hill looked like a volcano with the belching smoke and flames. He quickly turned away from it too not wanting to know where its rain of death was aimed.

South of the belching hill, there was a ridge with a large brick building capped by a small cupola flying a red hospital flag. There were tents setup in front of the building that were also flying the red flag, but north and south of the building, more guns were belching smoke and flames. *My God, how much artillery do the rebels have*, Stephen wondered.

To the south, the ridge was tree-covered, blocking his view of how far the rebel line extended in that direction. The road they came into town on yesterday separated that ridge from the Union army packed along the ridge running down from Cemetery Hill.

The explosion was right behind him. The area just over the battery's guns and Stephen's back was blasted with dirt. It pushed him over and for a few seconds it hurt like the dickens, but it passed quickly.

When he raised back up, he looked over at the captain. Stephen was relieved when his commander pointed to the ground. Stephen wanted to immediately jump face first to the ground, but instead he went back to the end of the line then slowly lowered himself to the ground.

Once he got down, he of course remembered James' logical advice and spread his legs apart. He could get around with one leg but losing both would surely be a death sentence in more ways than one. If he didn't bleed out before he got help and somehow survived the wounds, he would surely be a burden to his family.

The battery fired another volley followed quickly by three explosions to Stephen's right in the middle of the batteries ammunition line. Stephen was shocked to see one man just disappear as the bag of power he was carrying was set off by the exploding shell. Pieces of his body were thrown high into the air with the dirt and smoke from the explosion.

As the air cleared, Stephen noticed the man's upper body lying on what was left his back, staring up to the heavens. The ammunition line quickly reformed in Stephen's direction a few feet to avoid the man's remains. The gap between each man was now wider with each man having to walk farther up the hill to reach the next man in line before returning down for the next shell or bag of powder.

Before Stephen lay back down, he quickly glanced around, and he was surprised to see Generals Doubleday and Stannard slowly riding between the battery and the Second Battalion. They both looked so calm as if they were on an afternoon ride in the country.

Three more shells close to the battery and Stephen could clearly hear yells of anguish. A couple of litter-bearers trotted past on their way to the battery. They came back quickly, carrying a man on a stretcher with a couple of walking wounded following behind.

The litter-bearers headed to the aide station tent with its red flags waving in the afternoon breeze flying high overhead. Stephen wasn't sure if putting the aide station in the middle of the cemetery was such a good idea, especially so near the summit of the hill, but he guessed the red flags would be enough protection for the doctors and the wounded men waiting to be taken back to the field hospital safety behind the lines.

"Better keep your head down, sir," one of the wounded shouted to Stephen as he walked past. "It's hell up here."

Stephen lowered his head, pressing it down into the long grass as four more shells exploded in around the battery. The gunner was right—it was hell up there and Stephen just prayed the shells didn't start raining down, turning their peaceful patch of grass into another hell on earth.

Jacob Turney

Captain Jake Turney paced slowly back and forth, and as the smoke billowed over the trees to the east, the roar of the battle grew. It started with a massed artillery volley from the north side of town followed closely by infantry volleys from the south.

As the attack wore on, it sounded to Jake like the infantry attack was moving more to the north. While he knew his men needed the rest, he hated being stuck in reserve so far from the fight and not being able to see what was happening.

He stepped back away from the large oak that was giving him shade and glanced up at the sun. From its path across the sky, he guessed it was somewhere between five and six, but he had no way of knowing for sure. All he knew was that the attack had stepped off much later than expected. For some reason, Longstreet had marched south then did a counter march before turning again to the south searching for the Yankee flank.

During the delays, Jake had a chance to talk to a First Lieutenant J.J. Hatcher from Company L, Fifteenth Alabama of Law's Alabama Brigade. Jake was walking past when he overheard Hatcher muttering to himself about the delays. It sounded so much like what he'd done just the day before, Jake couldn't help but chuckle to which Hatcher instantly took offense.

"What the hell you laughin' at?" Hatcher snapped before noticing the three stripes on Jake's collar, and then he quickly added a belated, "Sir."

"I didn't mean any offense, lieutenant. I couldn't help but overhear your complaints ... kind of reminded me of an officer who was stuck in a similar situation yesterday morning."

"Who would that be, sir?" Normally, the bite in Hatcher's tone would have caused Jake's anger to boil over, but it was somewhat refreshing to see someone else lose their cool for once.

"Why that would be me lieutenant?" Jake laughed. After a few seconds, the frustration and anger drained from Hatcher's face. Jake went over the details of yesterday morning, and then Hatcher shared the hectic events of the last few days.

Company L was down to just one officer—a Junior Second Lieutenant named Robert Wicker. While he was well liked by the men of the company, Wicker was twice passed over for promotion. A few days before, the Colonel transferred Hatcher from another company to take over command of Company L.

Jake wasn't surprised to learn that Wicker wasn't happy to be second in command and had shared his frustrations, not much differently than Holland had yesterday afternoon. Both Hatcher and Jake agreed that dealing with young lieutenants could sometimes be just as challenging as charging artillery filled with grapeshot.

Jake was surprised to learn that Law's Brigade had started their march at three o'clock in the morning and had marched twenty miles to make it to Gettysburg before noon. While they only had very few stragglers, Hatcher

knew his men were plenty well spent, then they had to
fall into a column of fours just so they could march ten
feet before calling a halt for fifteen minutes then halting
again for five, so it had gone for the last hour. The old
saying of hurry up and wait had never been truer.

After leaving Hatcher, Jake guessed it was a good
three hours before the first infantry volley. Jake hoped
all the delays were worth it and Longstreet's men had
gained the element of surprise.

Jake glanced around at his men. He could see the
tension on all their faces. He guessed he wasn't the
only one regretting that they were being held in reserve.
Granted, they had a rough time of it yesterday and they
sure could use the rest, one being this far back and not
being able to see was worse than being in combat.

Jake looked to the east again. Above the trees to the
far south the sky was hazy from the rising smoke, but
he couldn't tell much about the direction or the number of men engaged. Up near the large buildings of the
Lutheran Seminary, the artillery kept up a steady fire
toward the bald hill, but there still weren't any signs of
infantry fighting on the north side of the Union line.

"See anything interesting?" Colonel Newton George
asked coming up behind Jake.

"Not a damn thing, sir," Jake replied.

"Put Holland in charge of your company and lets you
and I do some scouting to the east," Newt said with a
twinkle in his eye. Jake instantly knew he meant they
were going to get a closer look at the action.

"Lieutenant Holland report!" Jake yelled.

When Holland didn't immediately reply, Jake glanced
over his shoulder and noticed Lieutenant Farrar shaking Holland awake. Jake waited a few seconds before
issuing the order again.

"Lieutenant Holland report!" Holland stumped to his feet, got his bearings, and then rushed over to where Jake and Newt were standing.

"Sorry, sir," Holland said as he saluted and then came to attention. Jake knew it was more for Newt's benefit than his. Jake returned the salute and looked past Holland to see his Chuck Tuley sitting under a tree nearby watching the three officers intently. Jake made a slight nod of his head and Chuck jumped to his feet and hurried over.

"Lieutenant, the colonel and I are going on a scouting trip. While we're gone, you're in charge of the company. If you need anything—"

"I know, sir," Holland cut Jake off then glanced over his shoulder as Chuck joined the three of them. "I should ask the first sergeant for advice," Holland said in a tone that cut Jake to the bone.

Jake wanted to reach out and slap the boy, but instead said, "Just as I do James."

"And as I do with the sergeant major," Newt piped in. "Always remember, lieutenant, the non-commissioned officers are the backbone of the army."

"Yes, sir," Holland replied as he started to roll his eyes, caught himself, then looked quickly down at the ground.

The lapse was momentary, but noticeable. Newt's checks flashed red, but he held his tongue, turned his back, and walked away leaving Jake to deal with Holland.

Jake glanced in Chuck's direction and he could tell he knew the reaction was about him.

"Sorry, sir," Holland whispered to Jake.

"You roll those green eyes of yours at me again and by God, it will be the last thing you ever do," Jake snapped in a low but unmistakably harsh tone. "Do you understand me?"

"Yes, sir," Holland replied.

"That bit of childishness insulted the colonel, the first sergeant, and embarrassed me. This is your last warning, James. You better keep that damn ego of yours in check, 'cause the next time I see it, I'll bust you back to private and put you in the ranks with a musket. Am I making myself clear?"

Holland looked back down at the ground and muttered, "Yes, sir."

"Lieutenant, I expect you to look me in the eye when you're talking to me."

Holland looked up and his eyes focused on Jake. Jake could tell the young man was shaken and less cocky. *Good.* There was only one thing left to do.

"Now, go apologize to the first sergeant."

"Sir, he didn't see—"

"I don't care. He could tell from mine and the colonel's reaction what you did, now get your ass over there and apologize."

Holland slumped forward and let out a huge sigh. He turned around slowly and walked toward where Chuck was spread out under the tree.

"When did that start? Newt asked as he rejoined Jake.

"Yesterday when George went down, Holland decided he should have the duties of executive officer while the first sergeant should become a platoon leader."

"I'm glad he's your problem and not mine," Newt said as he turned away.

"Thanks," Jake said, following Newt.

It took a couple of seconds for it to dawn on Jake that they were walking to the west away from the fighting.

"Aren't we walkin' up closer to the fighting?"

"Who said anything about walking?" Newt laughed.

Jake looked past Newt and saw two of General Archer's, now Colonel Fry's, aides saddling up their horses.

"God, I haven't been on a horse for over a year," Jake said.

Newt stopped a few yards back from the General's aides. "Not since the Yankees took away your horse down in Alabama."

"Yep," Jake said as he bit his lip.

"Yesterday morning," Newt began to whisper.

Jake leaned over so he could hear better.

"As I was crawlin' on my hands and knees through that swamp grass, all I kept thinkin' about was you getting captured and all the ribbing you took since you came back. I'd rather crawl through quicksand than to go through that," Newt concluded as he patted Jake on the back.

"All ready, sir," said the same young lieutenant that had delivered Fry's message the afternoon before.

Newt walked over, took the reins, and threw himself up on the saddle. "Thanks, lieutenant. I'll take good care of her."

Jake walked in front of Newt's horse and took the reins to the other aide's horse. He too thanked the young officer and promised to bring the horse back in one piece.

With a light kick of his heels and a shake of the reins, Newt expertly guided his horse through the trees up on to Herr Ridge Road. Jake clumsily followed behind having to duck several times to keep from knocking his head on tree limbs.

Once up on the road, Newt spun the horse a couple of times as the rider and horse got a feel for each other, then they were off at a full gallop. Jake's horse reluctantly followed behind. Jake knew it had far more to do with being rusty in the saddle than anything to do with the horse. Jake watched with envy as Newt glided around the first corner taking the road to the east.

Halfway through his turn, Jake had to grab on to the saddle horn and hold on with all he had to keep himself from being flung to the ground.

At a Y in the road, they followed the sound of the infantry and took the road to the south. It was the same road they both had taken the day before to the right of the division. Jake started to get a feel for the saddle and urged his horse forward, finally falling into step just behind Newt.

As they came up to the crossroads where Jake had formed Company K the day before, Jake yelled out, "Right!" He did a better job of following Newt around the corner.

At the next road, Jake yelled, "Left!"

Newt looked over his shoulder.

"We came this way yesterday," Jake said.

It was a very sharp turn, so Jake slowed his horse and remembered to lean into the turn. As the road made a bend to the left bordering the woods, they'd spent a lot of time scouting, Newt yelled out, "You did get pretty far to the right yesterday."

"I was just following orders," Jake said with a smile. "No damn Yankees were going to get around me."

Jake recognized the rider coming from the opposite direction first and pointed him out to Newt. "One of Hill's aides."

Both men pulled on the reins and slowed their horses to a walk as they waited for Hill's aide to join them.

"Captain, what are you orders?" Newt barked out in his best command voice.

"Sir, I'm carrying orders to General Pettigrew to move Heth's Division to the front."

Without hesitation, Newt turned to Jake. "I'll go back with the captain; you go forward and scout out the ground. We'll be along shortly."

"Sir, I should be with my company."

"You don't think your first sergeant can do a little march without you?" Newt laughed.

"Hell yes, he can!" Jake snapped.

Newt pulled his horse around. "Then we're in agreement. Go find out what's going on and report to me when the division comes forward."

Without waiting for a reply, Newt touched the side of the horse with his boats and he was off in the direction they just came, with Hill's aide struggling to keep up with him.

Jake urged his horse forward at a trot, past a farmhouse and barn. Concerned about rabbit or ground hog holes, he kept the horse at a slow walk as they cut across a pasture to the next road. As Jake rode, he tuned out the sound of the fighting. The artillery and musket fire blended into a roar that his mind just chose to ignore.

Just past a house and barn, the road ended, so Jake slowed his horse to a walk to make sure he could avoid any groundhog holes. They cut across a creek and back up on the road at the other side and rode up to the top of the ridge.

Where the road took a turn to the right, Jake found a gap in the fence line and cut into the woods. He found himself on the left flank of what looked like an entire brigade in a line of battle.

Jake rode up next to a middle-aged first lieutenant with a black beard showing a few streaks of grey, standing in his customary position behind the rear rank on the left of the regiment's formation.

"Lieutenant, what regiment is this?" Jake asked.

The lieutenant pulled his slough hat down over his eyes before looking up at Jake, who had the bright afternoon sun peeking through the trees at his back. The lieutenant chewed what Jake guessed was a wad of tobacco a couple of more times, and then spit on the ground before answering. "Twenty-second Georgia, Wright's Brigade," he said in a slow, deep southern drawl.

"You, sir?" the lieutenant asked.

"First Tennessee, Archer's Brigade."

"Y'all gonna be our support, sir?"

"Not sure, lieutenant."

"Well I sure hope so, sir," the lieutenant said then spit again. "General Anderson's got the whole division spread out. From what I hear, McLaws from Longstreet Corps is to our right and they're lined up in a two-brigade front with two brigades in support." The lieutenant stepped closer to Jake's horse and lowered his voice. Jake leaned down to hear him better.

"Not us, sir. The General's got the whole damn division spread out into one long line, but I guess it don't matter as long as y'all come up in support."

Jake looked over the two ranks of men. Veterans all, but he noticed several of them looking around as if they were nervous. Jake knew how they felt, this was sounding all too familiar.

Suddenly, the roar of the fighting intensified to the south. The lieutenant took his place back in line as the orders flew through the Twenty-second Georgia. "Attention, right shoulder arms, forward, March."

As they stepped off, the lieutenant spun around and looked back at Jake. "I'll look for you up on the next ridge." He yelled at Jake. Jake wanted to say something—anything—to the lieutenant, but instead he just nodded his head. Heth's division wasn't going to be up in time to provide them any support. He doubted they would make it up before dark.

After Wright's men cleared the trees, Jack guided his horse to follow along at a slow walk. As he cleared the trees, Jake realized that they had come out within a few feet of where he was yesterday afternoon. To his left, there was the large farmhouse, barn, and orchard. Jake saw some movement in one of the windows and wondered if it was the farmer or maybe the Yankee skirmishers.

As another brigade cleared the woods and headed directly toward the farm, Jake knew they would find out shortly if the Yankees had come this far forward.

Up ahead, smoke was already billowing from the fence line along the Emmitsburg Road. Last evening, Newt borrowed a map from Colonel Fry, the new brigade commander, and Jake had traced out, the best he could, the route Company K had taken during their movement forward. It wasn't hard identifying the north-south road he'd seen yesterday, and was now in front of him, as being the Emmitsburg Road, since it was the first of only two roads coming out of Gettysburg toward the south.

Wright's skirmishers were already returning fire from the Yankees behind the road's fence. Jake was surprised and disappointed the Yankees hadn't stripped the fence of its rails for their campfires last night. Climbing over those fences under heavy fire was going to be a problem.

Past the road, up on the ridge in front of a copse of trees, a few puffs of smoke marked a Yankee artillery position. As Jake studied the ridge, he started make out the shapes of Yankee flags. Each Yankee regiment carried two flags, the National color and their blue battle flag. From the pairs of flags, Jake could follow the Union line running to the north past a white farmhouse and disappearing into the trees beyond. Smoke to the north told him the Yankee artillery, up on the bald hill, was still belching out its death song.

"Bam!"

Jake and the horse flinched at the sound of a close-by musket volley. He was surprised to see smoke rising from around the house and barn to his left. He glanced at the front row of the next brigade and wasn't surprised to see holes in the line and several men on the ground.

The brigade halted and orders were quickly issued, and their ranks exploded with an answering volley of smoke and fire. Smoke from the Yankee volley had settled around the house and barn, so it was impossible to tell if the answering volley had any effect.

As the ringing in Jake's ears from the brigades' fire died out, he could make out a steady *pop, pop, pop* coming from the house and barn, so it looked like the Yankees weren't going to give up their position without fight.

As the smoke started to clear around the buildings, the good news was Jake could only see a few Yankees around the house; even if the house and barn were full of men, they couldn't hold much more than a regiment. He was sure the brigade would quickly over run them then continue up to the Emmitsburg Road.

He heard a zip from a bullet as it whizzed by. The high pitch noise spooked his horse and it spun around twice before Jake got him back under control. When he did, he spun around back to face the farm and was stunned to find the brigade hadn't moved and were returning fire in a manner that suggested they weren't going to anytime soon.

With superior numbers and the enemy having restricted field of fire with so many of their men having to fire through doors and windows, it would be easy for them to just double-quick down there and overwhelm those inside. A brigade should make quick work of the smaller force. Jake took off his hat and rubbed his right hand through his matted hair. That's what he'd thought yesterday too and the generals delayed just long enough for the Yankees to bring up reinforcements.

This time, he had a clear view all the way up to the Yankee line. Those in the house and barn wouldn't be getting any support. Anderson's other brigade fired another volley into the house. The smoke belched and cried in anger and while the Yankee fire from the house slackened slightly, it didn't seem to have any real effect. The Yankees still held the house and barn.

Jake glanced back to the front. Wright's brigade kept going uninterrupted. Thanks to the Yankees in the house and barn, the left flank of the attack had ground to a halt. To Jake, this attack was shaping up to be another fiasco just like yesterday morning.

The center of Wright's brigade was taking a bead on the brick house and red barn on the other side of the Emmitsburg Road. The Yankees' pickets were still giving the skirmish line trouble, but they would do little to slow down an entire brigade.

Almost on cue, a loud boom from behind him signaled opening volleys of their own artillery. A few seconds later shells started exploding up along the road among Union skirmishers. If nothing else, they would provide some cover for Wright's men as they advanced through the open fields and drew fire from the Union artillery up on the ridge.

Just south of the barn and back a bit from the road there was a blast of artillery fire. Jake caught a glimpse of a shell flying to the south, but because of the trees he couldn't see the intended target. Jake strained to hear the concussion form the shells as they exploded, but they were either firing solid cannon balls or his hearing wasn't what it used to be.

Thankfully for Wright's brigade, for now, the artillery had a more tempting target farther to the south. Jake guessed that would change if their own artillery failed to silence the guns once Wright's men got within range of the artillery's canisters. The giant shotgun shells filled with balls slightly smaller than a fist were devastating against massed infantry.

Jake started his horse on a slow walk toward the front. As the tree line to his right started to thin, Jake could see, from the smoke of firing, the enemy's disjointed line. Up on the ridge, he could see the line just suddenly stop, but a bit farther south it continued right up to the Emmitsburg Road leaving a huge gap in the line.

As Jake cleared the trees, he got a good look of two more confederate brigades to the right keeping pace with Wright's men. Farther to the right, another line, slightly in front of them, was already pouring on the fire against the Yankees along the road. Just then another line emerged from the trees. Jake guessed it was Longstreet's supporting brigades.

Further to the south and east, smoke was rising above the trees marking another battle line. Through the smoke, Jake saw glimpses of three hills dominating the ground to the southeast. A smaller one in front, then one larger behind it, with its western face cleared of trees, then a much larger tree-covered one to the south. Even from this distance and through the smoke, it seemed to Jake for the attack to succeed, Longstreet would have to take and hold all three of those hills.

From the smoke, it looked as if he was trying to do just that. The smoke was rising along a wide path back to the southeast pointing like an arrow toward those hills. Jake wondered where in the mass of smoke, shot, and shell was Lieutenant J.J. Hatcher and the Fifteenth Alabama regiment. Since they were last in line, Jake guessed they were in Longstreet's second wave getting ready to advance against the Yankees along the road.

Counting Wright's, five of Anderson's six brigades were advancing, all expecting Heth's Division to come up and support them. Even if they came up at a double quick, it was doubtful Heth's Division was going to make it up in time. They'd issued the orders just too late for the division to move forward in time to support the attack.

The artillery along with Wright's skirmishers started having an effect on the Yankees along Emmitsburg Road as their fire noticeably slackened. The artillery to the south of the barn continued their fire against Longstreet's line, but Wright's main line was rapidly closing the distance and Jake was sure the artillery would soon change targets.

From north of the brick house up on Emmitsburg Road, Jake caught sight of another blast of artillery. He watched the shells with their lit fuses arch through the sky over the road, orchard, house, and barn exploding among the brigade on his left, the one stalled in front of the house and large barn. Shortly afterward, with shouts and yells, the brigade's colors made a mad dash forward. Finally, they were going to use the weight of the entire brigade against the Yankees inside the buildings.

Within seconds, Yankees came streaming out of the house and barn hightailing it back toward Emmitsburg Road. Jake couldn't help but laugh out loud. Within minutes, members of the attacking brigade were pulling the few remaining Yankees out of the buildings.

For the first time since the attack began, Jake felt his sprits lift. Anderson's last brigade must have been waiting for the house and barn to be captured before they started their advance. With that finally being done, it would join the other brigade in supporting Wright's left flank.

Suddenly, the artillery across the road turned their attention to Wright's men. Four blasts in quick succession tore holes in the Twenty-second Georgia. Jake couldn't tell if the first lieutenant was still on his feet. As the brigade answered with a volley, a rider dashed from the formation and came at a full gallop back toward Jake. Jake pulled on his reins and stopped his horse just as a few rounds of artillery, fired from up on the ridge, exploded in the center of Wright's men.

The officer pulled up next to Jake.

"Sir, have you seen General Anderson?" the young lieutenant shouted excitedly.

"I haven't seen him," Jake said.

"Damn!" the lieutenant snapped then gave his horse a quick kick and resumed his mad gallop up the slope and to Jake's left. Surprised and confused by the lieutenant's reaction, Jake spun his horse around. While he hadn't paid any attention to where Anderson was, it shouldn't be that hard to pick out a group of officers on horseback watching the attack.

Besides the artillery, Jake was stunned to see the tree line was void of anyone. Jake watched the lieutenant disappear into the woods just north of where he'd come upon Wright's brigade. At least during yesterday's attack, General Heth had had a bird's eye view of the opening stages of the attack. He'd gotten so close that he suffered a head wound, forcing Pettigrew to take over command of the division.

As Jake spun his horse back around, he noticed to the south the line was storming across the road driving back the Yankee line. Just then a familiar figure on horseback came out of the woods waving his hat. Even from this distance, Jake easily recognized the First Corps commander, Major General James Longstreet.

Jake's sprits brightened. Lee's old warhorse had broken the Union line as Anderson's right two brigades lent support to the attack. Wright's bridge was spilling over the fence along the Emmitsburg Road as the artillery fired another barrage with the Twenty-second Georgia taking the blunt of the fire.

The right of Wright's brigade returned fire and several of the artillery horses along with some of the men fell to the ground. The rest of the gunners struggled with the remaining horses, trying to save their cannons from capture as the remnants of the Twenty-second poured over the second fence and rushed the guns joined by the regiment to their right. The gunners ran for it leaving their cannons behind.

Jake took off his hat and waved it. They were doing it. They were driving back the Yankees again. Jake's smile spread across his face. A great victory on northern soil. Maybe, just maybe, the north would finally just leave them alone.

Stephen Brown

"Here comes another one," Ralph pointed to the west.

Stephen followed the point of Ralph's index finger and quickly picked up the little back speck. Stephen watched it rise higher and higher as it slowed down slightly. Then down it came right toward them.

"You think it is going to be long?" Ralph whispered.

Before Stephen could answer, it was obvious that—thankfully—this one was also going to be long. He heard the whistle as it flew directly overhead and exploded in the cemetery. Thank God the generals had decided the second battalion could do a better job of covering the artillery from a position behind a stone fence along the Taneytown Road than lying in the middle of the cemetery.

"Look, the rebels are crossing the road," Ralph said excitedly pointing this time to the southwest. It was hard to really tell what was going on with all the smoke rising up, but it was obvious, even to someone like him who had never seen a battle before, that the rebels were making headway with their attack. Smoke was rising up from the large hills to the south all the way up the road they came into town on yesterday.

They had overrun the Union line up near the small house surrounded by the Peach Orchard and they were pushing the Union line back farther and farther, but still that action was more than a mile away from them and Stephen was more concerned with what was happening just behind Company K. One of the artillery guns they were protecting had stopped firing.

He spun around, making sure to keep low behind the stone wall, resting his back against it. The other guns were keeping up a pretty steady fire, but the one directly behind them was silent. There were a couple of men standing next to the gun, but they were just standing there.

He knew he should just stay with the company slouched down behind the stone wall. It was the safe thing to do. The rebels were firing long, and the wall was excellent protection from musket or sniper fire. He knew he should stay right where he was and not worry about why that one gun wasn't firing, but he couldn't help himself.

A couple of bullets had blasted away bits of the stone wall, so they were well within range of the enemy sharp-shooters. He scooted to his right toward Captain George Blake.

"Where ya goin'?" Ralph snapped. Corporal William Church looked at him with a questioning look.

"To see the captain," Stephen said. After a couple of feet, he decided a duck walk wasn't going to be as hard on the bottom of his britches. He ignored the curious looks as he waddled down the company's line.

When he caught Blake's attention, Stephen pointed to the silent gun with the lone officer standing next to it. Blake nodded, so Stephen switched directions and headed for the gun keeping with the duck walk until he was on the other side of the road, and then he sprinted up the rest of the hill back up toward the summit and the silent gun.

As he got close to the gun, he immediately noticed a field of dead horses. Of course, he'd seen many a dead horse over the years having succumbed to diseases or old age, but he'd never seen any with holes blown into their sides or half their heads missing.

He walked by one horse with a mangled right leg and a neat round hole in its head just above the eye. It was the only humane thing to do, putting the horse out of its misery.

Of course, the worst thing about a dead horse was getting rid of its carcass before it started to rot. He didn't have time or energy to count the number of dead artillery horses lying across the hill, but in this heat, it was obvious it wasn't going to be long before they started to stink and the flies and other insects invaded their soon to be bloated bodies. He just hoped the Thirteenth Vermont was long gone before then.

The next thing he noticed was the officer, a first lieutenant, with blackened face, weary eyes, and infantry stripes down the sides of his trousers standing like a statue next to the silent gun and not appearing to notice Stephen's approach. Only once Stephen was within a couple of yards did the officer even bother to make eye contact.

"Lieutenant, why'd you stop firing?" Stephen shouted wanting to make sure he was heard over the roar of the battery's other guns firing nearby.

The lieutenant nodded toward a couple of privates sitting down, with their backs against the gun's wheels. "There's just the three of us, the caisson's empty, and our limber is down there," the lieutenant said as he pointed through the cemetery. "Our horses are either dead or scattered."

Stephen walked past the gun about three yards until he could see down the backside of the hill far enough so he could see a row of limbers. To his left, there were a couple of lines of men passing ammunition up the hill, but it was obvious they barely had enough men to supply their own guns let alone this one. He was about to ask the lieutenant where the rest of his men where when he notice a mangled arm lying a few feet away.

In several other places the grass was turned a shade of red. While there wasn't much that could be done about the dead horses, litter barriers had done a fairly good job of removing the wounded and dead men from the hill.

Two men carrying a stretcher caught his eye, and he followed them as they carried a man toward the aide station on the summit of the hill. The red flag was still flying but it now had several holes in it. The tent also had some holes in it. While it provided protection from the afternoon sun, it did little at stopping shrapnel.

Just before the stretcher reached the aide station, another shell exploded just in front of it. The blast knocked down the two men and the stretcher flipped over dropping the injured man face first onto the ground.

The red flag fluttered to the ground, its staff shattered, slowly followed by the front of the tent collapsing. Men, who were nearby, rushed to the aid station to help those inside.

Those in the ammunition lines remained in their posts, passing powder and shells up the hill allowing their guns to keep up a steady fire while this one sat silent. Stephen turned around and hurried back to his company. As he passed the lieutenant, he shouted over his shoulder, "I'll get you an ammunition detail." He didn't give the tired officer an opportunity to respond.

As he got close to the road, a buff of dirt exploded a foot to his left. It took him a couple of seconds to realize he'd just seen the impact of a sniper's bullet at his feet. He changed direction to the right and as he got close to the road bent over hoping the slant of the hill and the stone wall would give him a little cover.

He looked ahead at the wall and every eye in the company was trained on him as if they were all monitoring his every move. He bent way over and sprinted the best he could the last few yards, then slid down next to Blake like he was sliding onto home plate. Baseball was becoming a popular pastime when they were in camp.

"Sir, there're only three men left manning the battery and their ammunition is down the hill. Permission to put together a detail to carry it up for them."

"Shells are still falling up there," Blake said glancing up past the battery. "Ask for volunteers, I don't want to order anyone to go up there ... and make sure they got plenty of water. I don't want any of them passing out."

Stephen glanced back at the silent gun. He didn't know what he would do if he didn't get enough volunteers.

He shouted out, "I need volunteers to carry—"

"Count me in," Henry Meigs shouted out excitedly cutting Stephen off. "I'm tired of hidin' behind this damn wall."

Stephen instantly had the happy problem of having too many volunteers as everyone started shouting out at once that they wanted to join his detail. Meigs was a strong farm boy from Highgate. He was an easy choice. He glanced down the line picking out the strongest of the bunch.

"Meigs, Decker, Manahan, Hagan, Prouty, make sure you've got plenty of water. Get your friends to share if you need to." Stephen sat down on the road and waited while those around the volunteers shared a bit of their water and within a couple of minutes all of them had full canteens.

"Spread out, I don't want to give any sharpshooters an opportunity for a lucky shot," Stephen said once he had all the detail gathered around him. As he ran back up the hill, Stephen noticed the sloshing in his canteen, and he realized he'd failed to take his own advice and get his friends to help him fill up his own canteen.

He looked ahead to the gun and noticed the two privates were standing next to the lieutenant and none of them looked very happy to see the approaching detail. Once Stephen and the detail reached the gun, the mood of its crew didn't improve.

Boom, boom, boom! The next three guns in line fired one after another and within a few seconds came the answering fire from the other side, but none of the shells were anywhere close to their gun. It then suddenly dawned on Stephen why the small gun crew wasn't happy to see them. Once they started firing again, they would surely attract the attention of the enemy artillery and once again become a prime target.

Fear rushed down Stephen's spine. *What have I done?* His men and he were now once again going to be artillery targets, too. He wanted to just tell them all never mind, forget I said anything, and run back down to the relative safety of the stonewall. Instead, he looked the acting artillery officer in the eye. "Anything we need to know, lieutenant?"

Stephen wasn't surprised when the young officer let out a big sigh as he resigned himself to once again becoming a target. "Bring up the shells one at a time and make sure you don't drop any. If one lands on a rock it could explode." Stephen expected the other lieutenant would take charge of the detail, so he waited a couple seconds for that to happen and when it didn't, he headed past the gun to the down slope of the hill.

He pointed down to the limber. "Spread out along the hill and pass the powder bags up first up to the next man then the shell. This is not a race, so don't rush. As the crew starts firing, we will get an idea of the pace we need to keep up with them. Any ques—"

"Sir, look!" Henry Meigs shouted out. Stephen followed Meigs point down the hill to the south to see Colonel

Randall leading the rest of Thirteenth Vermont up the ridge past a small white house with a slightly larger white barn. Over the top of that ridge was the advancing rebel infantry and it looked like the First Battalion was finally getting into the fight.

Stephen turned back to his men and said, "The rebels started their attack from the south and if they keep coming it won't be long before they are attacking this hill and our friends behind that stone wall. Let's make sure if that happens, this gun will be ready to give them support."

With that, his men quickly spread out down the hill. Stephen wasn't going to stand around and watch his men work so he took the last place in line making him the closest to the gun and the closest one to being a target of the rebel artillery.

The powder bag was heavier than Stephen expected, but not a problem to carry up hill. The lieutenant barely looked at Stephen when he took it from him.

When Stephen was back with the shell, he couldn't help but notice the difference in the lieutenant's man's demeanor. His eyes were brighter and there was a determined look in his face, while he might not have been looking forward to getting back into the fight, now that he was, it was obvious to Stephen the officer was going to take his work seriously.

"I hate to do this," the lieutenant said as he cradled the shell in both arms like it was a baby.

"Do what?" Stephen asked surprised.

The officer nodded toward the other side of town to a large building with a small copula on top. On either side were artillery batteries, but just in front there were a couple of tents with a red flag flying overhead. It then dawned on Stephen, the lieutenant was pointing at the red flag and it was obvious he didn't relish the thought of firing on an aide station.

The lieutenant must have noticed the look of concern on Stephen's face. "I don't like it either," the lieutenant said as he turned away, "but enough is enough."

Stephen stepped back from the gun as the lieutenant slid the shell down the barrel, one of the privates, this one with the red stripes of an artillery man down his pant legs, rammed the shell down the barrel as the other private, this one with the blue stripes of the infantry, finished getting the fuse ready. The two privates then rolled the gun to the right a few inches as the lieutenant sighted down the barrel.

The privates took their places several feet on each side of the gun as the lieutenant took the wood handle of the lanyard and gently pulled it out to its full twelve-foot length. As he did, Stephen stepped back a couple more yards to make sure he was clear of the recoil of the gun.

The lieutenant glanced his way then back forward making sure everyone was clear, then he turned away as he pulled the lanyard. Stephen had seen other guns fire and had seen the recoil but seeing it at a distance wasn't anything like being near the gun. The hunk of metal and wood turned into a fire breathing monster with the flame followed closely by the smoke and the roar as the gun leaped backwards several feet.

With his ears still ringing, Stephen was able to pick out the black speck as it reached its arc, just as it started down the light breeze from the south blew the smoke clear and he stood transfixed as he watched the shell fall from the sky. It exploded right in the middle of the tent knocking it and the red flag to the ground.

A direct hit, he wanted to shout and yell and jump for joy, but he couldn't bring himself to do it; no one did. The two privates got on each side of the gun and quickly pushed it back in place as the lieutenant stared at him. "Where's my next shell?" the lieutenant finally yelled at Stephen.

Stephen turned around to find Meigs nearby holding the powder bag.

"Did we hit anything?" Meigs asked as he handed over the shell.

"An aide station," Stephen said without any enthusiasm.

"On purpose?" Meigs asked obviously surprised.

"Pay back," Stephen said as he turned away and hurried up to the waiting lieutenant.

He passed over the powder bag and rushed back to Meigs who was waiting with the next shell.

"Don't run with the damn thing," the lieutenant shouted at Stephen.

"Sorry," Stephen said sheepishly as he handed over the shell.

The lieutenant grunted when he took the shell. One of the privates was ready with the rammer when the lieutenant slid the shell down the barrel. Stephen noticed how the sponge end was still dripping water.

Stephen turned away this time and was ready for Meigs when he passed over the next powder bag. A second later, the gun came alive again with flame, smoke, and roar. Stephen hurried back up with the bag.

After the fourth shell, they started to fall into a rhythm and Stephen delivered the powder bag just as the privates got the gun back in place. When he got back with the shell, they were ready for it and Stephen went back down as the gun roared again. They all fell into a rhythm and Stephen lost count of how many shells they fired.

Stephen took a shell, turned around, and took two steeps when the ground opened a couple of yards in front of him like a volcano throwing out flame, smoke, and dirt. Time seemed to suddenly slow way down. Stephen found himself surprisingly calm and clear thinking. If the shell he was holding hit the ground, it could explode. He twisted his body while making sure he had a firm grip on the shell, making sure to put his own body between the shell and the ground.

When he hit the ground, the pressure of the shell knocked the wind out of him. It took just a few seconds for him to get his wits back. He glanced over his shoulder to see Meigs lying on his back several yards down the hill. He was about to yell at him, when Meigs jumped to his feet, obviously no worse for wear.

Stephen pushed himself on his right elbow into a sitting position and was trying to figure out how to stand up on the slope without the use of his hands when a voice came to his rescue.

"Hand me the shell, sir," Decker said bending over next to him. Stephen carefully passed the shell up and climbed to his feet as Decker carried the shell up to the gun.

"You all right, sir?" Meigs asked coming up next to him holding his hat in his hand.

"I think so," Stephen said. "You?"

Meigs handed Stephen his forage cap. Where the top of the K used to be, there was now a jagged hole.

"Let me see your head?" Stephen snapped. Meigs leaned over and Stephen parted his dirty, matted hair down to his scalp and after a quick search was surprised to find only a small cut that wasn't even oozing any blood.

"You're lucky," Stephen finally said.

"You both are," Decker added as he went past heading back to his place in line. The gun let loose with a roar and smoke as Meigs followed Decker back to his place. Within a few seconds, Stephen had a powder bag and back up the hill he went to the waiting lieutenant. Stephen was expecting the lieutenant to recognize his brush with death and was stunned when he took the bag and turned away like nothing unusual had happened.

Stephen felt his face turn red as anger boiled in his brain. He let out a loud sigh that he hoped the lieutenant had heard, but there was no response. Stephen shook his head and turned away disgusted with the lieutenant's obvious lack of concern.

Before he had gotten all the ways turned around, he noticed it again. The palm up, five fingers spread out as if reaching out for something, the wrist that disappeared into the blue fabric, and a slight bend at the elbow and then torn cloth and bloody flesh. It hit him like a rock between the eyes. Why should the lieutenant be concerned about his brush with death when the arm of one his men lay just a few yards away?

Stephen was instantly disgusted with himself and as he walked down to Meigs for the next shell, he whispered under his breath, "Lord forgive me for judging him." The gun roared as Stephen took the powder bag from Meigs and again back up to the gun he went.

As he came back up to the gun, Ralph was standing next to the lieutenant.

"We're moving out, sir," Ralph said adding the sir, obviously, because another officer was there.

"Get the rest of the detail for me," Stephen said as he handed over the last bag. "Make sure they bring up the last shell."

It was hard to tell, but it almost looked to Stephen like the lieutenant was relieved when he took the shell. Stephen stepped back out of the way, the detail joined him, and they stood there and watched the crew load and fire the last shell. He watched it streak toward an artillery piece near the large building with the copula on top. The shell exploded close to the gun, but it was too far away to say what effect it might have had.

"Return to the company," Stephen instructed the detail then he walked back to the gun.

He stuck out his hand to the lieutenant and said, "It was an honor serving with you lieutenant."

"Abercrombie, John J.," the lieutenant introduced himself. He must have noticed Stephen's odd expression and laughed as he added a "junior," as if Stephen would confuse him for his more famous father.

"Stephen Brown."

"Good luck, to you Stephen Brown." Abercrombie glanced at Stephen's hatchet. "I've been meaning to ask—"

"They took it away when I was arrested for getting my men water during our march up here," Stephen cut him off.

"But a hatchet?" Abercrombie asked as their hands parted.

"Only thing I could think of."

"Lieutenant Brown, we got to go," Ralph yelled up at him.

"It was a pleasure serving with you," Stephen yelled over his shoulder as he started back down the hill to his company. He wished he had more time to talk to young Abercrombie to find out how a general's son from an infantry regiment ended up commanding an artillery gun at Gettysburg.

Jacob Turney

As twilight slowly engulfed them, Jake fought to keep the emotion from his voice as he described to Colonels Fry and Pettigrew along with Newt, what he'd seen of the attack across the Emmitsburg Road. He could feel his cheeks flash red when he described Posey's Brigade—whose name he'd learned as he was riding back—overrunning the farmhouse and barn then stopping their attack on the edge of an orchard halfway to the road.

From there, they'd watched Wright's Brigade cross the Emmitsburg Road alone and storm the ridge behind. Wright's men overran the two artillery batteries capturing some guns, then advanced up the ridge. With all the smoke, Jake couldn't tell how far they'd gotten, but they didn't stay long. Yankee counterattacks forced them back down to the road.

For a short time, it looked like they were going to hold positions along the Emmitsburg Road and still Posey's Brigade held their position. Jake kept looking for Generals Andersons and Hill to order Posey forward, but they never did.

It wasn't until Jake rode back up the ridge and through the woods that he saw Anderson and Hill on the back side of the ridge. It looked to Jake like they'd stayed less than a hundred yards from having a clear view of the attack. While he was sure they'd received reports from underlings, reports can only tell just so much about how things were going or how close they'd come to over running the Yankee line up on the ridge.

Posey's men could have provided Wright with much need support and Jake still didn't know what happened to Anderson's missing brigade. They never did show a presence on the battlefield.

When the Yankees counter charged down the ridge and forced what was left of Wright's men from the road, as well as recapturing the Yankee guns, Jake had seen enough and had turned his back on the fighting. Just like yesterday morning, delays and a lack of support had snatched victory from the Army of Northern Virginia.

"What about Pender's Division and Ewell's Corps?" Pettigrew asked. "What could you see of their attack?"

The question surprised Jake. He knew Pender's men held the town and Ewell's men extended the line to the north and east of town.

"Sir, other than artillery fire, there wasn't any attacks from the north."

"Are you sure, captain?" Pettigrew asked, obviously bewildered by Jake's answer.

"Pender was supposed to attack along with Anderson and Ewell was supposed to step off at the sound of Longstreet's attack," Pettigrew said.

As if a sign from providence, there was a blast of massed musket fire from the north. The four men looked at each other. They all knew it was unlikely the Yankees would launch a counter attack so late in the day.

"It must be Ewell," Pettigrew finally said as he shook his head. Jake forced himself to hold his tongue. All four of them knew that an attack an hour before might have made a difference but at this late hour it was a nothing more than stupidity.

Jake gritted his teeth. He had to get away from the colonels before he embarrassed himself and Newt. Out of the corner of his eye, he noticed the young lieutenant standing nearby looking anxious to get his horse back.

Jake turned to Newt and in a very formal, controlled tone said, "Sir, with your permission, I would like to return to my company." He heard himself say it while in his mind, he was shouting, *Ewell is a horse's ass. Why doesn't somebody just shoot him and put him out of his misery.*

Before waiting for Newt's response, Jake saluted then turned his horse toward its owner and rode off before Newt could respond. Jake was grateful none of the colonels tried to stop him.

He pulled up next to the lieutenant, jumped off the horse and stomped off toward the column of infantry without saying a word. With each footstep, his anger built.

He walked up to the head of the column stopped in the middle of the road and he was disappointed not to find Archer's brigade. Jake didn't recognize the officer leading the first brigade and had to ask the captain of the first company whose brigade it was.

He was surprised to learn it was Brockenbrough's. Jake hadn't heard that Colonel John Brockenbrough was wounded yesterday, so he naturally wondered why he wasn't at the head of the column. He knew the colonel's brother was killed in yesterday afternoon's attack, but surely that wasn't the reason Brockenbrough had someone else leading his brigade.

As he walked, his anger slowly started to ease. As he walked past an apple orchard with branches heavy with green fruit, he almost laughed at a captain yelling at his company to stay after from the damn fruit. He'd had enough of stragglers shitting themselves half to death from eating unripened fruit.

As he cleared the last of Brockenbrough's regiments, Jake's mood darkened again as he recognized Jefferson Davis' nephew Brigadier General Joe Davis leading the next brigade. From what he heard, Davis' Brigade had just as rough of a time yesterday morning as had Archer's Brigade. A couple of regiments were trapped down in an unfinished railroad cut and were beat up pretty bad before they surrendered in mass.

Orders where shouted down the line and drums began to roll and the column started to march forward. Jake thought about just waiting for the regiment, but decided he'd been away from his men for too long. Besides, the brigade should be next in line.

It was getting dark as he cleared Davis' last regiment. He called out to the head of the next column, "Which brigade are you?"

"Marshall!" shouted out someone at the head of the column. The officer on horseback nodded to Jake. *Marshall, who in the hell is Marshall?* Jake wondered before it dawned on him that it was Pettigrew's Brigade. With Heth down with a head wound, Archer—the Senior Brigade Commander—captured, Pettigrew had taken command of the division.

Heth's injury wasn't serious and Jake doubted he'd be away long, so Marshall would step back down and turn the brigade back over to Pettigrew. Until then, Marshall, probably a colonel in charge of one of Pettigrew's regiments, would have the opportunity to show what he could do in charge of an entire brigade.

Jake's mood darkened even more when he discovered the First Tennessee wasn't leading Archer's Brigade.

Archer's Brigade had a nice ring to it, but now command had fallen on Colonel B. D. Fry of the Thirteenth Alabama. It didn't seem right to Jake that an Alabama officer would be leading what was still known as the Tennessee Brigade. While Archer wasn't from Tennessee either, he'd at least been regular army before the war and had attended West Point.

Jake took a deep breath, and then started to notice the pressure in his bladder and yet at the same time felt suddenly thirsty. He shook his canteen and was surprised that it was empty. As he watched the fighting, he'd become so engrossed sitting on the horse under the hot afternoon sun, he hadn't even realized that he'd drank all of his water.

Jake climbed over the fence, walked a few feet into the pasture, and relieved himself. He glanced to the east and marveled as the deep orange moon hung low in the sky.

When he was finished, he climbed back over the fence and waited for the First Tennessee to come to him. As he waited, he glanced back up at the moon bringing back memories of home. He remembered how he and his brothers use to cut across Doctor Woods, land, across Swan Creek and up the hill on the other side.

They'd play on the hill pretending to fight battles from the past. Bunker Hill from the revolution was a favorite with them arguing about who was going to get to say, "Don't shoot until you can see the whites of their eyes!" Since their father had known General Andrew Jackson, they'd also do the Battle of New Orleans even through it didn't really fit in with geography. Since John was the oldest, he always claimed the right to be Jackson.

Jake nodded as the sergeant major walked past, then Jake took his place in line next to First Sergeant Chuck Tuley.

"You okay, sir?" Chuck asked.

"Fine," Jake said dejectedly. Jake guessed Chuck recognized he wasn't in a particularly good mood, because the first sergeant marched on in silence. Other than the sounds made by marching men carrying their weapons and equipment, the entire company was very quiet.

The column halted as Newt came riding back to the regiment and took his place at the front of the column. Newt climbed down from the horse then signaled for Jake to join him.

"You're keeping the horse?" Jake asked as he came up next to his commanding officer.

"One of the privileges of rank," Newt said. "I've never been so surprised in my life," Newt added in a whisper.

"About what?" Jake was confused.

"That you didn't have a heart attack back there," Newt chuckled.

"Sir?"

"Your face was so red; I thought you'd drop dead from a heart attack ... I am grateful you kept your composure in front of Fry and Pettigrew."

"I did my best, sir. I didn't want to embarrass you."

"How bad was it?" Newt asked.

Jake listened as the artillery blasted to the north as the massed muskets of infantry continued uninterrupted.

"It was a damn nightmare!" Jake snapped keeping his voice down making sure the first rank of the company couldn't hear him. "Longstreet held some ground on the right, but what should have been the center of the attack was pushed all the way back to where they started. If they would have had support on their left and if Ewell would have attacked at the same time, and if we had gotten orders in time maybe..." Jake stopped himself.

"That's a lot of what ifs," Newt said.

Jake nodded. It was a complicated plan requiring a great deal of communication and coordination across a wide area. Maybe with Jackson here and the army still organized into two Corps, then maybe, just maybe, it'd been possible to pull together that much coordination, but Jackson wasn't here.

"Ewell and Hill are new to corps command," Jake finally said.

"I think it showed today," Newt added. Drums rolled; orders shouted. Jake took his place back in line. Chuck must have noticed the change in his mood.

"You need anything, sir?" Chuck asked.

"I'm out of water," Jake replied.

Chuck handed over his half-full canteen and Jake took a drink making sure not to take more than half of what was left.

"Albert's got your bedroll, sir," Chuck said. Jake glanced back at Albert who actually smiled for a change. Jake started to take a step to get his bedroll and most of his processions, but Albert waved him back and mouthed, "I got them."

They marched a few yards then halted again. Jake took the opportunity and got his bedroll back from Albert. Just as he got back in line, came the shouts of, "Forward, march."

With each step, his legs started to ache, his muscles confused about whether he needed them to hold him on a horse or march down the road. To the right of the road, the remnants of Wright's Brigade were reorganizing and settling in for the night. Here and there a few hospital tents were already up and doctors, under lamp light, where already performing surgery.

Litter-bearers were coming out of the tree line carrying the wounded, a process Jake guessed would last well into the night. He was sure that stretcher-bearers from Heth's Division would join in and help out.

As they passed the orchard, the sergeant major shouted to the men to stay away from the fruit, a chorus echoed by the other sergeants. Just past the orchard, they made a column left and cut across a pasture with a section of rail fence already missing. Jake guessed they were about thirty yards from the tree line, up on the crest of the ridge from where Wright had started his attack.

Up ahead about ten yards from the tree line, he noticed the brightly lit tents that marked A.P. Hill and Anderson's headquarters. He'd first noticed them when he rode back through the tree line. Jake couldn't understand how Anderson expected to lead a successful attack from the backside of the ridge. Both he and Hill should have known better. Just thirty yards away, they would have had a view of almost the entire battlefield and would have been in position to see for themselves the effectiveness of their orders, but neither man had bothered to take a look and the attack failed.

The column halted and orders issued for the men to go into camp for the night. As always, Jake let Chuck take charge of getting camp organized. First came the stacking of weapons by comrades of four. The comrades of four were the backbone of the entire army. Yesterday afternoon, Chuck took charge of reshuffling the men of Company K to rebalance the comrades of four considering the losses the day before. It was a common occurrence after every battle.

When the war started, three Turney brother privates along with Wright Tuley, the first sergeant's younger brother, made up their own comrades of four and now James was the only one left. It helped that Albert had joined him, but still, Jake knew it was hard on his youngest brother to be the last one standing.

The Turney brothers weren't alone in forming their own family of comrades. The four Massey brothers and cousins were their own family comrades early in the war. It was fitting that when Private John Massey returned to duty after recovering from his wound at Cold Harbor, that Chuck assigned him to the Turney brothers' comrades.

Jake eased over to where John Massey was tending the glowing embers of a fire while James and Albert were gathering firewood. John's cousin, Corporal James Massey, was captured the morning before. His brother William had lost an arm at Cold Harbor and was discharged. His other cousin, John Robertson had transferred to an artillery battery then elected first lieutenant before he became ill with chronic bronchitis forcing his discharge.

Jake squatted down next to John. "My brothers better hurry back with the firewood."

John blew on the embers then looked up at Jake. Even in the pale light Jake could tell John was worried.

Any word about James?"

"I'm afraid not. We just have to hope and pray he is uninjured, and they will exchange him soon."

John nodded then turned his attention back to the fire.

"John, get your axe out!" Albert yelled as he and James approached carrying several rails from a fence.

John reached into his bedroll and pulled out a small axe.

"Jake, ah, sir, Corporal Zimmerman and Sam are bringin' enough wood for the officer's fire," James added.

"Captain Jake!" Private Tom George, the colonel's younger brother, called out from the darkness. Jake waved him over.

"Sir, Newt, ah, I mean the colonel, wants all the company captains to join him for dinner."

Jake stood up and Tom came up close and whispered. "He got a ham from Colonel Fite."

"Tell him I will be there shortly," Jake replied then Tom hurried away. While looking for some fresh hay for bedding back at Cashtown, the Seventh Tennessee stumbled upon a cache of food supplies under the hay. Jake was glad they were sharing some of their bounty.

To the northeast, the artillery and infantry fire continued. Jake couldn't speak for anyone else, but it just didn't feel right. From the sound of it, another division was continuing their attack unsupported while a couple of miles away they were making camp for the night and he was going to be eating ham of all things.

While the center of the line was pushed back, over on the right it appeared that Longstreet had some success. Jake doubted Lee was going to pack up the army and leave Gettysburg. If he stayed, it was likely he would attack again.

"Maybe we'll have better luck tomorrow," he muttered.

"Was it that bad, sir?" Chuck asked walking up behind him.

"Yep," Jake replied.

"I'm going to be having dinner with the Colonel this evening." Jake took a deep breath. "How did our lieutenants behave this afternoon?"

"No problems, sir," Chuck said with a laugh. "I overheard Farrar telling Holland they were damn lucky to have a first sergeant like me to take care of all the shitty duties and he better get off his high horse before you put him back in the ranks. Since then, Lieutenant Holland's been a right perfect gentleman."

Jake couldn't help but laugh as he walked away.

Jake joined Newt and the company commanders, including two newcomers from yesterday, to the group.

First Lieutenant Donaldson took over Company F yesterday morning, when Captain Jim Thompson turned up missing. Captain Davis Clark was wounded, and First Lieutenant Jim Manely had taken over command of Company G temporarily. Major Flex Buchanan also joined them too.

All though dinner, they avoided conversation about what might happen tomorrow and instead rehashed stories that they'd told hundreds of times before but were new to the two lieutenants. Jake enjoyed watching their faces when Buchanan spoke about seeing Cousin Pete Turney down at the hospital in Richmond after both were wounded at Fredericksburg.

Buchanan had gone down first, and everyone was sure he was going to die. Pete went so far as to issue strict orders that Buchanan's grave be well marked. Shortly afterwards, Pete went down with a ghastly wound to the face which broke his jaw.

Jake had seen him being carried from the field and was sure his cousin was going to die and as Pete told Buchanan later, so did he.

Buchanan kept a well-practiced straight face as he repeated what Pete had told him. "As they carried me into the hospital, I thought I was dead. Then I saw you, and I knew you were dead."

Some of the stories were solemn like how General Hatton had led them at a double-quick past old Jeff Davis and they had saluted the President of the Confederacy with a rebel yell. A few minutes later, Hatton was dead. Jake swallowed hard as he remembered his brother Henry falling during the same attack.

The mood lightened back up as they all laughed about James Holman and his camels. Back in '57, Holman took a commission as a second lieutenant in the army.

They assigned him to duty in the frontier out in the middle of Texas. In 1860, he was put in charge of a topographical expedition. Given ten men, they set out from San Antonio with the only herd of camels ever brought over by the U.S. Government from Egypt. Jake could almost picture Holman riding across the Texas plains on a camel.

After the war started, Holman came back to Tennessee and joined the First Tennessee as its first lieutenant colonel. A year later when the regiment reorganized, James Shackelford defeated him in the second election taking over the role of the regiment's second in command.

Holman was just one of many officers who were defeated during that second election including Newton Davis as captain of Company K. Davis had also gone back to Tennessee and last Jake heard he was a lieutenant in the Fourth Tennessee Calvary.

Jake shared memories of his friend Joe Davidson. A second lieutenant, Davidson had tried to break up a fight between Joe Taylor and another private, whose name Jake couldn't remember. Taylor was drunk and had shot Davidson and killed him. Everyone knew Taylor did it, but no one had actually seen him fire the pistol, so the case against him was dropped and he was sent packing.

Taylor went home to Boonshill with a chip on his shoulder. It was a few weeks later that Jake got the letter from his father explaining that Taylor got home on a Monday and by Friday the town had had enough of him threatening fellow citizens. Whether they could prove it or not, they all knew Taylor had killed Davidson and it seemed clear to everyone that if they didn't stop him, he was going to kill again, so they arrested him.

During the town meeting on Saturday, they argued back and forth about what to do with Taylor before concluding that hanging him would be an act of self-defense, so that is what they did.

As the evening wore on, the officers slowly started excusing themselves until it was only Jake, Newt, and Newt's brother Tom still around the campfire. It was then that Tom pulled a flask out of his haversack and passed it to Newt, who took a drink then passed it to Jake.

Jake took a whiff and enjoyed the unmistakable smell of good whisky.

"Where did you get it?" Jake asked.

"Mother sent it to me," Tom said.

"She was up to Lynchburg with Daniel and stopped by Pastor Call's dry goods store," Newt added.

"I've been saving it for a special occasion," Tom said.

Jake took a slow drink of the whiskey. While the Methodist Church he belonged to wasn't a bunch of tee-totalers like some of the Baptist Churches, he doubted any of them were running a still and selling whisky like Pastor Call of the Lutheran Church.

"Man, he makes good whiskey," Jake said.

Tom held out his hand and Jake passed it over to him.

"That he does," Tom said then took a drink.

"Mother wrote that Pastor Call is talking about selling his still," Newt said.

"I'll have to write my father and tell him. It might be a good investment."

Tom laughed. "Daniel already thought that. The Pastor didn't seem interested in talking to him about it."

"Did she say why?"

"Yep, he told her if he does decide to sell it, he's going to give the boy first chance at it," Newt said.

Jake shook his head. "The boy can't be more than thirteen. I met him right after the Pastor hired him. He could read and write ... seemed pretty ambitious for a ten-year-old, but I just don't see him being up to running a still alone."

"Mother said she got a chance to talk to the boy and she thinks Jack Daniels is a very impressive young man."

"How is your Mother doing?" Jake asked.

"Fine." Both Tom and Newt answered together, then smiled at each other. Tom continued, "Daniel and David are watching out for her."

Daniel and David were the two oldest brothers in the George family. After their father died, they'd stepped up to manage the family interests and take care of their mother.

"Plus, all our sisters are nearby," Tom added.

Newt took the flask from Tom, took a drink, and then passed it back to Jake.

"So, what's the special occasion? Jake asked just before he drank from the flask again.

"We're going to drive the Yankees off that ridge tomorrow," Tom said with a smile.

As Jake handed the whisky to Tom, he mumbled, "Or die tryin'."

Newt took a deep breath as Tom took another drink then handed the flask back to him again.

"Or die tryin'," Newt repeated as he finished off the last of Reverend Call's whisky.

Jake decided to take a side trip on the way back to the company and cut back through the woods to the east side of the ridge. The far ridge was full of campfires and Jake could easily see the extent of the Yankee line.

The full moon lit the area between the lines, and he could make out the black shapes moving about. He guessed they were either stretcher barriers still gathering up the wounded or some of the regiments sending out details to bury their own dead. He was sure that on the other side of the Emmitsburg Road the Yankees were doing the same.

As Jake studied the Yankee lines, it reminded him of the position of the Army of Northern Virginia back in Maryland on the west side of the Antietam Creek. The more he thought about it, the more today's fighting reminded him of the Battle of Sharpsburg.

That battle had started on one flank and had swept across the entire line of the Army of Northern Virginia. Jake had heard the stories and seen the results of the morning's attacks at Sharpsburg with bodies piled in a cornfield and in the middle of the Sunken Road. The First Tennessee along with the rest of Jackson's Corps had started the day overseeing the surrender of twelve thousand Union troops at Harper's Ferry before starting on one of the hardest marches of the war.

The Union Army had unexpectedly caught up with Robert E. Lee and the main branch of the Army of Northern Virginia on the high ground just north of Sharpsburg. Fortunately, the Army of the Potomac delayed their attack giving Lee a chance to concentrate his army.

It'd been close. Late in the afternoon, A.P. Hill led the division through Sharpsburg just in time to stop a Union break through on the army's right flank. The next day, there was a truce, so both armies could bury their dead and care for their wounded. Jake and Newt had walked across much of the battle tracing the Union attacks by the dead and wounded they'd left behind.

One unsupported Yankee Corps after another had attacked the heights on the west side of the Antietam Creek and while the Army of Northern Virginia had bent in several places, the Yankees couldn't break them.

Outnumbered and outgunned, at the end of the day the Army of Northern Virginia still held the high ground. Jake took a deep breath. Yes, today was much like the fighting at Antietam. The Yankees might have bent in a few places, but at night, they still held the high ground. While they had not broken, the Army of Northern Virginia suffered mightily at Sharpsburg and was in no position to take on the Yankees again, so during the night, Lee headed back toward the Potomac and safety of Virginia. It was the only time Jake could remember when the Army of Northern Virginia had left control of the field in the hands of the Yankees.

Of course, it was the only other time, until Gettysburg, when they'd fought outside of the state of Virginia. Then like now, they were the invaders. In this war, at least in the east, fate had not so far smiled on the invading armies.

For a second, Jake had a fleeting hope that during the night the Yankee army would pull out and leave the battlefield like Lee had done at Sharpsburg. Jake chased the thought away. They were on their home soil and had the high ground. As he turned his back on the enemy, he knew that they would still be there in the morning.

When he got back to camp, he found his brother's and the rest of Zimmerman's squad embroiled in a game of poker. Jake stood twenty yards away in the darkness and watched his brothers enjoying themselves seemingly without a care in the world. Albert was more like himself—not so loud—and James was much more outgoing and laughing along with the others. Jake knew that tomorrow things would be different.

Tomorrow, he knew they would either drive the Yankees from that ridge or die tryin'.

Stephen Brown

I'd be scared too, but I saw his foot, he wasn't hurt," William whispered. "What did Jerry say?"

"That he found a safe place for Mollo to—"

"To hide?" Private William Church cut Stephen off.

Stephen gave him a dirty look, which even in the light of the campfire, Ralph couldn't help but notice.

"Sorry," William said.

"—to recuperate from his ordeal," Stephen finished.

"Stephen, I saw the ball coming, it hit the rock Mollo was standing on and bounced off without exploding. Sure, it knocked him down, but he didn't even have a scratch on him."

"Captain said the same thing," Stephen whispered as Captain George Blake walked up with the big hole in his left trousers. With a little breeze, it looked like his leg was waving like a flag.

"What did Jerry say?" Blake asked as he sat down on the other side of the small campfire.

"That he is recuperating," William snapped.

"Corporal, he was talking to me!" Stephen snapped back at William.

George just laughed. "The two of you sound like a couple of schoolgirls."

"I don't see anything funny about it," William snapped. "He is hiding some place because he got scared by a cannon ball. Hell, you almost had your whole leg knocked off by a ball and who knows where poor Bill is. Is he captured, wounded, dying, or dead? We have no idea. It just ain't right, I tell you, it just ain't right."

Stephen and George just looked at each other. Stephen wanted to say something, but he didn't know what to say. William was right. It wasn't fair that Corporal Bill Skinner was wounded, dead, or captured by the enemy. Detailed to serve with the regiment's color guard, he had gone forward with the first battalion, but didn't come back. It wasn't fair that Bill was missing while Mollo was hiding because he was scared.

"Do you want me to have Jerry take me to Mollo, so I can bring him back to the company?" Stephen asked George.

"Hell—"

"Shut up, William," George snapped before Stephen had a chance to.

Even in the dull light, Stephen could see William's cheeks flash red, but he was smart enough to hold his tongue and sit there in silence and fume.

"Do you think he is going to be any use to us if we bring him back? George finally asked.

And that was the question. Private John Mollo was obviously scared almost half to death by the bouncing cannon ball that slammed into the small boulder just as he stepped up on it. While Stephen had gotten himself back up and continued in spite of his near-death experience with the artillery shell, he wasn't Mollo.

"No," Stephen finally answered.

William grunted obviously not pleased with the answer.

"Corporal, so you think in his present condition he would be an asset to your squad?" George snapped.

"No, but—"

"There is no 'but,' if he isn't going to be an asset to your squad, then we don't need him in the company. Leave him where he is," George said firmly. Stephen could see the fight drain from William's face. Stephen knew his outburst had more to do with the missing Bill Skinner and the premonition of his own pending doom than Mollo hiding somewhere behind the lines.

George's gaze went over Stephens' head and a big smile flashed across his face than he became suddenly very reserved.

"Hey Doc, can you look at my leg?" George shouted out sounding like he was in pain.

Stephen looked over his shoulder and saw Surgeon Nichols coming their way.

"What happened to your leg?" Nichols asked as he came up to the fire.

George stuck out his left leg and held his pant leg showing the gaping hole just below the knee. "A cannon ball blew a hole in it. Can you save it?" George said with such concern that Stephen almost believed him.

Nichols just stood there obviously dumbfounded looking for something to say when both George and Stephen burst out laughing.

"Yeah, very funny," Nichols finally chuckled then turned away.

"That wasn't funny, that ball almost took your leg off," William snapped.

"And if I had seen or even felt it when it happened, I might be just like Mollo hiding in a corner somewhere instead of sitting here laughing about it."

"You should have let me go with them," William whispered.

"And this is why I didn't let you. If he is out there, Ralph and Jim will find him, but..." Stephen hoped William would get his meaning without him having to say it.

"But what?" William snapped.

Stephen took a deep breath. "Without taking unnecessary risks to get themselves killed."

"I would never," William said in a huff.

"You still think you're going to get killed here?" Stephen whispered.

William sat there for a few seconds and Stephen watched the anger totally drain from William's face. He was right; William still thought he was going to die during this battle. If William was killed as part of his normal duties, Stephen could live with that, but he wasn't going to order or even allow William to take any unnecessary risks like searching for Bill Skinner out in front of the Union lines.

Sergeant Jim Halloway and Stephen's good friend and the owner of his little hatchet Private Ralph Sturtevant had both volunteered to search for Bill and Stephen knew both would be thorough and still careful. He could only imagine the risks someone who already thought they were going to die would take not only endangering themselves but anyone who was with them.

"I hate waiting," William finally said after all the anger had drained from his face.

Stephen patted him on the back. "So, do I ... so do I."

Corporal Harlan Bullard walked up and looked down on the three of them. "It's too quiet," Harlan said.

"What do you suggest?" George asked as he got to his feet.

"All quiet along the Potomac, seems to fit," Harlan answered.

Harlan was right, compared to just a few hours ago, it was incredibly quiet. Just the low dull hushed voices of thousands of men were the only sounds that cut through the growing darkness. The sounds of war had been put to bed for the night.

Stephen got up and took his place to the right of Harlan. While George might be captain of the company, when it was time to sing, Harlan was the obvious choice to lead their trio.

"You sure this is a good idea?" Stephen asked.

"I think so," George replied. "Give the men something else to think about."

Harlan started, "All quiet along the Potomac, they say..."

George and Stephen joined in with, "Except now and then a stray picket." It had been a week since they'd sung together. Last night, they were all too tired after the long march to bother. Stephen knew they should be rusty, but he thought they sounded fairly good. He guessed he wasn't alone because they quickly had an audience as men from all around drew up around them in a wide circle.

"Not an officer lost—only one of the men, moaning out, all alone, the death rattle." Stephen glanced down to William who had buried his face into his hands. On second thought, maybe this wasn't the best choice of a song, but it was too late now.

"While stars up above..."

Stephen glanced up and the sky was bright with stars and the full moon rising above the eastern horizon. As he sang, he scanned the faces of those gathered around the fire. Harlan was right, they all needed this reprieve.

He glanced back down to William, but this time his gaze was past Stephen and to the right. Stephen glanced over his shoulder and in the dim light he could see Ralph and Jim standing in the back of the crowd. Skinner wasn't with them but that didn't mean anything.

William got up and made his way through the crowd. Stephen didn't want to cause any undue attention to Ralph and Jim, so he looked away for a few seconds. When he glanced back, Jim and Ralph were talking to William and no one was smiling. Whatever the news, it wasn't good.

Stephen did his best to keep his focus on finishing the song without messing up any of the words, but as soon as they finished, he started back through the small crowd even before the applause had finished.

"Sergeant, report," Stephen said to Jim trying to use a military manner to hide his nervousness.

"Sorry, sir, we didn't find any sign of him. We went out between the lines as far as we dared without coming under fire ourselves and there was just no sign of him."

George walked up obviously hearing the bad news. "Did you find any dead bodies?"

"Yes, sir. Lots of them," Jim replied obviously a bit haunted by what he'd seen. "Some were in pieces, sir." Ralph whispered as if he was afraid of offending the dead.

"Did you raid their haversacks?" George asked pointedly.

"Why would we do that?" Jim asked obviously confused.

"The dead don't eat," George snapped.

Stephen was suddenly very hungry. "My fault, sir. I sent them out and I didn't give them orders to bring back food."

"No, damn it ... it was my fault." George snapped again. The colonel told me this morning to look for the opportunity to get food out of the haversacks of the dead and I forgot to tell anyone."

"Sir, I wouldn't trouble yourself. I heard the Twelfth got a food ration a little while ago," William spoke up.

George's mood suddenly lightened up. If their sister regiment in the Second Vermont Brigade had gotten a food ration, they should be getting theirs soon enough. "I'll go check with the colonel," George said as he rushed off into the darkness.

"How far forward did you go?" William asked turning his attention back to Jim and Ralph.

"William... we went as far as we dared," Jim answered him.

"Our sharpshooters up at the house warned us not to go any farther or risk getting shot," Ralph added as he pointed out to where the house sat on the road to Emmitsburg.

"You coulda—" William started to say.

"They did what they could," Stephen snapped, cutting off William. In the dim light of the fire, it was hard to see William's expression, so Stephen just waited, wondering if William was going to say he would have gone farther forward despite the sharpshooter's warning. Instead, William turned away and went back to the fire.

"What's the matter with him?" Ralph said obviously aggravated.

"He's just worried about Bill," Stephen said.

"I'm worried about Merritt and you don't see me acting like a jerk," Ralph snapped.

Stephen chuckled.

"What?" Ralph snapped again.

Jim patted Ralph on the back. "If you listened to yourself, you would have a different opinion."

"What ... no," Ralph stammered.

Stephen turned back to the fire and Jim followed him as Ralph stammered, "Really?"

"Really," Stephen laughed.

Stephen sat back down next to William. He had his head down seemingly staring at the fire.

"You were right," William whispered.

Stephen patted William on the back. "He might have been captured. If he was, good chance they will parole him."

"I hope so," William said as Stephen looked around taking in the view of thousands of campfires spread across the ridge. The red and yellow glows reminded him of a more pleasant time sitting around the fire with his family. It was such a warm, inviting, and peaceful sight in the midst of so much suffering and death.

He turned back to Ralph, who was looking toward the Emmitsburg Road.

"You see something?" Stephen asked.

"No, just thinking," Ralph said. Before Stephen could ask about what, Ralph glanced at William. "I'll tell you later."

George walked back up into the light of the fire and he motioned Stephen to join him just out of ear shot of anyone else. Not surprisingly First Sergeant Sidney Morey suddenly appeared out of darkness to join them.

"William was right, the Twelfth and a few of our companies got a food ration. Not much, not enough to share. The colonel didn't know if they ran out of food before they got to us or we were just missed the rest of us."

"Most of the men are also running low on water again," Morey said.

"Go ahead and send out a canteen detail and have them keep an eye out for food," George ordered. Morey nodded then disappeared back into the night.

"You want me to send a detail back down to the road to see what they can get off the dead?" Stephen asked.

"Didn't they say there were sharpshooters down around the house?" George asked.

"Yes," Stephen answered then he realized they most likely had missed their opportunity. The sharpshooters would have picked the bodies clean of anything of value including food.

"You want to sing a couple of more songs?" Stephen asked. "Might take the men's minds off of how hungry they are?"

"The men?" George asked with a hint of a smile in the dim light.

"Us too," Stephen chuckled.

"But first go tell William that Bill is over at the aid station."

"Is he all right?"

"He took a round in his belt buckle, I couldn't see well, but he looked pretty bruised up and he says it hurts like hell, but yes it looks like he is going to be fine."

"Good, good," Stephen said as he headed over to tell William his friend was going to be fine.

Jacob Turney

Jake sat straight up. His mind still foggy with sleep, he reached for his belt and holster as the muted artillery fire echoed around him. It wasn't until he drew his pistol that he realized they weren't in any immediate danger. The sky was brightening to the east, but it was still a ways to go before the sun would be up. He guessed there was just enough light for the artillery to see outlines of enemy positions silhouetted against the brightening eastern sky. Just as suddenly there was the expected enemy response as louder explosions peppered within the muted fire.

Several others around him sat up or stirred including his brother James, but Albert didn't move. Jake wasn't surprised, Albert had developed the ability to sleep through almost anything.

James looked over at him, but his eyes were glazed over and he flopped back down without noticing Jake looking at him. The other men around him did the same as they all realized it was just an artillery that had invaded their sleep.

Jake lay back down and closed his eyes. Artillery duels were more sound and fury than anything else. The muted *boom, boom, boom, boom* told him a friendly four-gun battery had let go with a volley. Being on the other side of the ridge, woods between him and the artillery, and most important, the guns facing in the opposite direction, the friendly fire was loud but muted.

He couldn't hear the muzzle blast sound of the enemy's answering fire, but he could tell what kind of shell the enemy was using based on the sound of its explosion. With sound waves traveling in all directions, the exploding enemy shells were much louder than the friendlies firing toward the east.

The louder shells were timed fuses exploding in the air. They didn't do much damage to equipment, but they played hell with men and horses spreading shrapnel over a wide area. The louder ones were exploding higher in the air. The trick was to have them explode high enough to spread shrapnel over a wide area but not so high that the mini projectiles had lost all their power by the time they hit the ground.

The more muted explosions were likely percussion shells designed to explode upon impact with the ground, a cannon, limbers, or caisson. While a hit on a cannon would knock it out of commission, hitting a limber or caisson and exploding the ammunition inside could cause a spectacular explosion spreading death and destruction over a much wider area.

Of course, some of the duller explosions were timed shells where the fuse was too long, and the shell had hit the ground before exploding. Sometimes when that happened, the force of the impact with the ground would put out the fuse and only those close by would hear the dull thud as the shell dug a hole into the ground.

Jake tensed up as a far-off familiar *pop, pop, pop* of musket fire joined the chorus of death. Jake waited for the drums and bugles that would call the

First Tennessee into formation, but they were silent. Whatever infantry that had joined the artillery wasn't part of a general engagement.

Jake rolled over on his side and closed his eyes. Whatever was going on, for the moment, it didn't involve or concern the men of the First Tennessee. He guessed that would change soon enough, but for now he would get some sleep.

Stephen Brown

We used my shelter half and tried carrying him that way but he cried out in such pain that we had to set him down. We then tried to carry him upright, but that wasn't any better." Ralph wiped a tear from his eye. "He told us that the battle wasn't over and they were going to be coming again today and he was worried if we left him behind he'd be crushed by horses or cannons, but what could we do?"

Stephen patted Ralph on his shoulder. They'd seen wounded men up around the cemetery but there were aid stations nearby and the litter bearers were quick to carry them off to the rear.

"He's probably still lying out ..." A shell exploded about fifty feet above horse team about twenty yards to their right cutting Ralph off mid-sentence. One of the horses screamed in agony and flopped down on the ground. A member of the gun crew pulled out a pistol and shot the suffering animal in the head as the other members of the battery rushed to settle the rest of the team and unharnessed the dead animal.

Another shell exploded high above them and—a second later—small pieces of it fell all among the men of the Thirteenth Vermont. The shell exploded so high the shrapnel pattern was so spread out by the time it hit the ground amazingly no one in the regiment was injured. Stephen tried to push his butt deeper into the wet soft ground as he slid his shoulders lower down along the low stone wall the regiment was hiding behind. To their left the Fourteenth and Sixteenth Vermont were down in brush and rocks hidden from the sights of the enemy artillery, but the Thirteenth was out in the open with only a low stone wall keeping them safe from the enemy fire. Stephen took a deep breath; he didn't like being a target today any better than he did yesterday up in the cemetery.

A boom then a loud screech closely followed by the sharp smell sulfur as a friendly shell flew overhead on the way toward the ridge to the west and hopefully bringing death and destruction to the enemy. Stephen stuck his fingers in his ears as five more followed in quick secession and the rest of the battery let loose with a volley.

As he pulled his fingers from his ears, he was greeted with dull whistles as the air around him danced and swirled from the six cannonballs disturbing the calm morning.

"I love that sound," Stephen said to no one in particular.

"I heard it yesterday. Didn't know what it was at first," William said.

"I think I was too scared to notice it yesterday," Stephen chuckled as he glanced at Ralph to see if he had any interest in continuing his story. Last evening when he and Jim had gone forward to find Bill Skinner they had come upon a wounded rebel private from Georgia who'd been shot through both legs. It didn't take long for the man to identify himself to Ralph as being a fellow Mason.

Stephen knew how badly Ralph felt about leaving the man alone, wounded, between the lines, but he had done what he could to help the man. All through the night in the dull light of campfires, Stephen had seen litter bearers coming back into lines carrying the wounded and he was sure the other side had done the same. There was a good chance that during the night the man had been given some much-needed attention, but that didn't matter to Ralph. He still felt guilty about leaving a fellow Mason behind even if he was one of the enemy.

Down the line a man crawled over the stone wall dragging four canteens behind him. Stephen said a silent prayer wishing him well. Several men poked their heads over the wall and they were quickly rebuked by their sergeants reminding them that sharpshooters were looking for an opportunity to blow their brains out.

"Do you have any water left?" William whispered.

"About a quarter of a canteen?" Stephen answered. "You?"

When William didn't answer immediately, Stephen pulled the strap over his head and handed his canteen to William.

"I just want to wet my lips," William whispered.

Stephen's stomach growled. He never remembered going without food for two days, but the excitement of being on the battlefield was helping him overcome his hunger pangs, but water was different. It wouldn't be long before the sun would be peeking over the trees to the east. While being on a battlefield was exciting and everything he had dreamed about since the night he drew straws with his father, none of them was going to last long out in the open in the baking sun without water.

Stephen took off his forage cap.

"What are you doing?" Ralph asked.

"Stephen don't!" William snapped.

Stephen ignored both of them. He turned his head sideways so he could poke just the right side of his face above the wall just far enough to see. He had to know how the private with the canteens was doing. His nose brushed against the rough rocks of the wall as he slowly eased his head up. He was so close to the wall his eyes couldn't focus on the rock. As his right eye cleared the wall, he closed his left bringing the scene in front of him into sharp focus.

"Hey you! Get your head down," Bill Skinner yelled at him obviously not recognizing his first lieutenant. Stephen ignored him. It took him just a couple of seconds for his eyes to dart to the low ground in front of them with the cattails outlying the small spring.

The private seemed to be having a rough time crawling as he dragged the canteens behind him. Suddenly the man flattened himself to the ground. Above the other sounds of the fighting, Stephen couldn't hear the sniper's bullet but obviously the private had. It was a few seconds before he started crawling again. Stephen noticed he was keeping his butt a bit lower than before.

While keeping low made it harder for the sharpshooters to see him, crawling also meant he spent a lot of time exposed to their fire. Plus, all that work just to fill up four canteens.

Stephen lowered his head and then spun back around settling his butt back into the soft damp ground. "He's over halfway there," Stephen said loudly so that it would be passed down the line to the private's friends.

"You could have gotten your head shot off," Ralph snapped.

Stephen ignored him. The sky was brightening, and the sun would be up soon and it would give him an opportunity. It would be risky, but there was no way he could sit by and do nothing while his men ran out of water. He knew it was a foolhardy idea, but there was a chance with the sun just coming up above the tree line that if he moved deliberately it just might work.

There was a sharp crack of something striking the stone above his head as small pieces of rock showered down on him.

"See? That could have been your head!" Ralph snapped.

It dawned on Stephen that the artillery had stopped firing. There were still some distant explosions and musket fire to the northeast and there was smoke rising around the tree-covered hill that was the anchor of the Union line.

He glanced around and there was little movement around them by the experienced troops, which told Stephen that whatever was happening over there wasn't anything for them to be too concerned about. He took a deep breath and closed his eyes as he tried to decide the best way of telling Ralph and the captain about his plan to get water.

Jacob Turney

To the east, the pale gray sky was brightening as the sun crept toward the horizon. To the west, the full moon hung low just above the South Mountains. The air was heavy to breathe with hardly any hint of a breeze. He'd hoped that yesterday's southeast wind meant there was a chance of cool air and maybe some rain coming in from the west, but instead the day was dawning even more humid than the day before.

Jake yawned, and then lay back down resting his head on his rolled-up jacket. The drums sounding reveille would come soon enough. He stretched his arms over his head and arched his back.

When he closed his eyes, he could almost see the smoke on the ridge and Wright's Brigade streaming back defeated.

Jake knew that Lee would again press the attack just as he knew the First Tennessee would play a part. While no orders were issued the night before, from where they were placed so late in the day in the center of the army, Jake and Newt had concluded Heth's Division was going to attack. The only question in their mind was who was going to join them.

For some reason, Jake didn't know why Pender's Division had also sat out yesterday's fight. Jake guessed the fact General Pender was severely wounded early in the battle might have played a part in their attack falling apart.

Pickett's Division from Longstreet's Corps, which had guarded the rear of the army at Chambersburg, had made it to Gettysburg late yesterday afternoon and had also missed the attack. There were at least three divisions available with two of them being fresh.

While Heth's Division had rested yesterday, the division had suffered mightily in the first day's attacks. From what Newt had learned from Pettigrew, the First Tennessee had faired pretty well in only losing a third of their men.

If they did attack, Jake had no doubts about their objective. He took a deep breath. Alone and unsupported, Wright's Brigade had pushed past Emmitsburg Road and assaulted the ridge beyond. Maybe three divisions might have a chance to break the center of the Yankee line.

Jake chased the speculation from his mind. Maybe old Bobby Lee would have a few tricks up his sleeve, something much more clever than a full frontal assault on the Yankees' center. Surly, he had learned a few things from the Yankees' folly last December at Fredericksburg.

First one drum, then another, all through the camp one after another joined in with reveille. A few bugles joined in along with the shouts of sergeants and corporals making sure all their men were awake.

As Jake got to his feet, he felt a pressure on his bladder, so he joined in with the growing line of men headed for one of the open ditch latrines the shit detail had dug late last evening. Early in the war, most regiments hadn't bothered with such nonsense like digging ditches to relieve themselves, but with so many men gathered together, the unsanitary conditions played a major role in disease running rapidly through the camps.

Company K was lucky to lose only seven men, while some of the other companies had lost more; it wasn't a major problem for the First Tennessee. Some regiments had lost over half their men to disease, death, or disability before they had ever fired a shot.

Jake knew that it helped that the First Tennessee had reported for duty in Richmond in May after the weather had warmed. It also helped that they learned drill under the cadets of the Virginia Military Institute. Thanks to their guidance, the regiment established good sanitary practices right from the start, which helped to cut down the instances of disease.

Company K had left Tennessee with ninety-seven men and now they didn't have enough men to fill out a full platoon, but it was combat not disease that had greatly depleted their numbers. Thirteen were dead and another fifteen disabled because of their wounds.

Some of the men had transferred to other regiments or duties such as teamsters. Some had second thoughts even before they'd left Tennessee and four had deserted from Company K. Some were either too young or too old to deal with the physical strain of army life and had been discharged early in the war.

There were many reasons why Company K could only muster thirty-one men this morning, but the dead and seriously wounded were by far the leading causes. Many of the men still with the company had also suffered some sort of wound during one or more of the battles. Bill Oldham at Cold Harbor, Chuck Tuley, Felix Royales, and Mike Denham at Seven Pines, and the list went on and on with almost half the men being wounded at one time or another.

With wounds from Cold Harbor, Fredericksburg, and Chancellorsville, Jake had fought through his share of pain, but he thought of himself as being one of the luckiest men in the regiment. None of his wounds were serious enough to keep him away from his Company for awfully long.

When he finished, Jake turned back to the company. Chuck, James, and Albert were sitting around a small fire, laughing as they waited for the coffee to finish brewing. Five Turney brothers had left Tennessee and now there were three. Two Tuley brothers had left Tennessee and now there was only one. Jake wondered what tomorrow would bring. How many Turney brothers would answer muster tomorrow morning?

"Coffee ready yet?" Jake yelled.

"Almost," James said as Jake walked over to join them. Halfway there, he noticed Albert was tending a skillet with fresh eggs frying.

"Where did you get those?" Jake asked.

"I found them in the woods yesterday afternoon. Looked like the farmer had turned the chickens loose in hopes of catching them later," Albert said.

"Where are the—" Jake started to ask but Chuck and James laughter cut him short.

"Shut up!" Albert snapped.

"What happened?" Jake asked.

"I'll drop the eggs in the fire," Albert threatened.

"No, you won't ... go on tell him," James laughed.

"No," Albert protested, but not very forcefully.

"Either you tell him or I will," Chuck said in his first sergeant's voice of authority.

Albert pulled the eggs from the fire and used a fork to slide a couple of eggs on to a tin plate James was holding, who then passed the plate to Chuck.

"You shouldn't even get any eggs," Albert said to James as he slid a couple of more eggs on a plate, then James handed Jake that plate.

"Ah, I ... ah," Albert said as he slid a couple of eggs on to the next plate. "I heard a noise up in the woods. Thought it was chickens, but I wasn't sure, so I snuck in all careful like, then I seen them. Must of been at least thirty hens. About the same time I seen them, they seen me and all hell broke loose with them running around sqawkin' up a storm. So, I took a bead on one and rushed after—"

James' and Chuck's laughter drowned out the rest of Albert's sentence.

"So, what in the hell happened!" Jake demanded.

"Go ahead and show him!" James commanded.

Sheepishly, Albert pulled back the hair from his forehead revealing a knot the size of a small fist. "Low branch," Albert added. "Knocked myself silly. By the time I got my wits about me, all those damn chickens were gone ... but I did find some eggs."

"Only 'cause you didn't have to chase them down." James laughed.

As their laughter died away, Jake noticed the musket fire to the east had also died down. As he took the first bite of his eggs, he hoped that whatever old Bobby Lee had planned they get to it pretty soon, before the sun got high in the sky.

Suddenly the sky brightened as the sun climbed above the horizon. Few clouds, high humidity, and a bright July sun were going to make for a long, hot day.

Jake turned to Chuck. "After breakfast, send out a canteen detail. I'm expecting we will be moving out soon and I want to make sure we aren't low on water."

Chuck nodded as James and Albert looked at each other. All knew what "moving out" meant and Jake was sure that after what had happened two days ago, none of them were looking forward to another attack on the Yankee line, but he also knew that each of them, as well as the rest of his men, would do their duty.

"Hey Albert, isn't that your buddy over there?" James said as he pointed to a corporal sitting on the lead horse of a six-horse artillery team.

Jake hadn't paid any attention to the commotion going on around him. The army had so many men, horses, wagons, and artillery pieces that there was always commotion going on, but until the regiment's drums started pounding none of it had anything to do with them.

Early in the war, Jake had been vigilant making sure of taking note of everything going on around him wondering what the purpose of moving of a regiment or a battery from one place to another and how it was going to affect the First Tennessee or more importantly Company K.

He quickly learned that more often than not, the movements had nothing to do with anything of consequence and he found himself worrying over nothing at all, so he learned to tune out the noise around him, so he was a bit surprised to look up and see a line of artillery pieces coming from the east. It looked like General Lee was bringing up more artillery and there was only one reason for doing so.

"I don't know him," Albert said obviously a bit confused.

"Oh, sure you do," James said with a laugh. "You exchanged a few words a couple of days ago, he said something about you being a son of a—"

"Was that him?" Albert cut off James.

"I do believe so," James replied. "Why don't you go ask him about his wheels?" James laughed.

The artillery team moved forward up through the trees and Jake turned back to his eggs. If there was any doubt about it, the General was massing artillery to soften up the Yankee line before sending the infantry.

"Eat up, boys, I got a feeling, things are going to be getting busy pretty soon," Jake spoke up. "Mighty busy."

Stephen Brown

As he expected, the sun was bright and hurt his eyes as he looked to the east. He was sure it would be in the eyes of the rebel snipers, so sure, he was willing to bet his life on it. Once again, his men needed water and once again it was his duty to make sure they got it, but this was different. While he was willing to bet his own life, he wasn't willing to bet the life of another. This time, he was going to have to do it alone cutting down the number of canteens he could carry.

Each filled canteen weighed about two pounds, and while he could carry thirty on level ground a short distance a few days ago, this was much farther, and he hadn't eaten for two days. It would do no one any good if he got out there but couldn't get back with all the canteens, so he decided the safe bet was to carry twenty and at least they would all have some water to share.

"I need twenty empty canteens!" Stephen shouted at the top of his lungs. He didn't really need to shout, but he figured the more aggressive he was about this the fewer protests he would have to endure from William, Ralph, and most importantly from the captain.

"You can't—" Stephen was ready for Ralph's protest and his "As you were, private," had the just right amount of harshness to cut Ralph off at the knees. He glanced at William and the harshness in his voice had also caught William off guard and for a moment at least he sat there with a blank expression on his face.

Stephen leaned forward and glanced to his left and right and was not surprised to see everyone staring back at him like he was crazy. "Hurry up before the sun gets up too high," he shouted out. This time several men started passing their canteens his way and not surprisingly Captain George Blake was duck walking quickly down the line.

"Hurry it up." Stephen shouted again trying to put a bit more bite into his voice. "Give me yours too," Stephen snapped at Ralph and William.

Stephen was a bit surprised when both readily handed over their canteens without protest. He was even more surprised when he glanced up and saw George dragging several canteens behind him.

"How many you gonna try to carry?" George asked as he flopped down next to Stephen.

"Twenty," Stephen said. "I did thirty the other day, but this is a little different."

"I think you should go alone; you should draw less attention that way," George added.

"I was thinking the same thing."

As Ralph and George helped Stephen gather the canteens, Stephen tried to erase his mind of what was out there waiting for him. Even so, his heart was racing, and his knees were starting to shake. This was foolhardy and he knew it, but he also knew that it needed to be done. While the artillery duel was over, there was no sign the enemy was leaving. In fact, there was more rebel artillery being put into position across the way.

It wouldn't be long before it started again and as George had said last night, it wasn't like old Bobby Lee to leave a battlefield in the hands the enemy. Being a long way from home with spread out supply lines, he couldn't wait this time for the Yankee army to come to him. Unlike at Antietam and Fredericksburg, if he wanted to engage the enemy at Gettysburg, like yesterday, he was going to have to be the aggressor.

There was no doubt Lee would attack and Company K sat right in the middle of the Yankee line. While there was little hope the company was going to get any food before that happened there was no way they could also go into battle baking in the hot sun with no water.

Ten canteens went on each shoulder and as light as they were, he could have carried all twenty on one shoulder, but on the uneven ground, it was better to be careful and balanced. He sat there for a few seconds taking a couple of deep breaths to calm his nerves.

"You don't have to do this," Ralph said.

Stephen looked over at him and smiled. How could he explain to Ralph or any of the others that it was the moments like this that had drove him since the evening he drew the long straw? Moments to literally stand up and make a difference, to be a servant to the men under his command, to live the example set by his Lord and Savior.

Greater love hath no man than this, that a man lay down his life for his friends, came right after the last commandment, *that ye love one another, as I have loved you.* Yes, he told himself, he was doing this mostly out of love, but it would be a lie to say it was the only reason.

He took one last deep breath and stood up slowly then faced the low stone wall. Two steps, right hand on the wall, and he quickly bounded over. A hint of a smile flashed across his face. He quickly set his jaw wiping it from his face and he immediately felt guilty that he was doing this as much for himself as he was the men whose canteens he carried.

He had enough of being stuck behind the stone wall. This was his first and only chance to be in combat with the Thirteenth Vermont, he didn't want to waste it sitting behind a wall. He was happy and excited to be doing something helpful.

Suddenly, the excitement vanished. Stephen couldn't believe he hadn't noticed it until now, but at the far end of the field just before the spring was a wood rail fence with all the rails still in place. He was shocked that during the night the rails hadn't succumbed to the numerous campfires.

The canteens wouldn't be a problem; he'd just slide them between the rails. The problem was how he was going to on the other side without getting shot.

The pasture grass was above his knees making it almost impossible to see any groundhog or other animal holes, so he walked much slower than he would have liked, but it wouldn't do him any good to step in a hole and break an ankle or a leg. He knew from the rock outcroppings near their line that in many places that there wasn't much dirt covering a rock layer, much like home, but still, even in rocky areas, groundhogs were very resourceful in finding places to dig a den leaving a hole large enough to swallow a man's foot.

He glanced to his left and he could see the fresh dirt marking an active groundhog hole. Out of the corner of his eye on the other side of the groundhog hole there was a patch of blue laying on the ground with a small pile of canteens next to it.

He turned back to the front and focused on the problem at hand, the freshly dug holes were easy to see and were nothing to worry about, but where there was an active hole, there were going to be many more abandoned holes nearby. He stepped on his right foot and he felt solid footing, but then his toe started to slide. It was a familiar feeling and he took a short step with his left foot and quickly lifted his right avoiding the hole, just like he had done thousands of times in his father's pasture.

At first, he thought it might have been a humming-bird zipping by his left ear, but he quickly realized the pitch was too high. He hoped it might have been a large bumble bee, but he knew that it wasn't.

He planted his left foot and took a quick step to the right, hoping his foot wasn't coming down into a ground-hog hole, but it was better to break a leg than to have his brains or another part of him blown all over the ground. Two steps forward then another quick step, this time to the left. He was glad there was a gradual slope down to the low ground with the high grass and cattails, and once he got down there they would provide him some cover to fill the canteens, but they were also a large sign telling everyone for a mile around where he was going.

Another step to the left, the zip wasn't as loud as the first one and he didn't even want to believe he had heard what he had heard. He glanced back to the left and there was a man crawling on his hands and knees heading back to the bushes covering the rest of the brigade pull-ing a couple of canteens behind him.

The man glanced in Stephen's direction. Stephen almost laughed as the man's expression exploded in sur-prise and his lips said, "Oh my God." *Yes, that is right, I'm an idiot for doing this*, Stephen thought to himself.

Four steps forward then the next step was back to the right. He was going to have to vary his steps as much as he could so the snipers wouldn't be able to lead him. He glanced up. There was high ground near the road and he was now lower than it. It was doubtful there were any snipers up by the road. His eyes followed the road up slope to the south past the houses they had marched by a couple of days ago to the small house in distance to where he had seen the family standing in the doorway.

The rebels held that ground including the peach orchards that surrounded the house. He took a quick step back to the right. He guessed those trees were about a half mile away, and if he could see them, anyone hiding in the trees would be able to see him.

Three steps forward and a quick step back to the left. About a half mile away was his guess, about 2,600 feet. If memory served him right, a bullet traveled at about 950 feet a second, so the sniper would have to guess where he was going to be three seconds after the shot was fired.

Sweat was pouring down into his eyes. He had a sudden urge to drop to his knees, forget the whole thing, and crawl back to the stone wall. Three seconds was all that stood between life and death. No one would blame him for giving it up. They would all understand, but instead he took another step and then another.

The next step was to the right as he started counting seconds in his head instead of worrying about his steps. *One thousand one, one thousand two.* He took a larger step to the right as it dawned on him that it didn't do any good to vary his steps if he always took the same size step to the right or the left.

He picked up the pace slightly as he stopped worrying about counting steps and counted, *one thousand one, one thousand two*, then took a short step to the left. If every two seconds he took the same size step to the right or the left the sniper or snipers had a fifty percent chance of hitting him.

Large step back to the right and the zip was much louder this time. His heart was pounding so hard he thought it might pop out of his chest, but the counting helped him ignore how scared he was. Thank God, two more steps and he was at the rail fence and he dropped to the ground.

The high grass on the other side lined the creek banks that flowed from the spring—about twenty feet to his right—gave him additional cover. He started to relax a little with the rails and grass giving him protection from the sharpshooters.

The rails were too close together for him to slide through them, so he grabbed the lower rail and pulled as hard as he could. It slipped a little. He shifted around to get some leverage with his legs. The rail started to move. He pushed harder with his legs and he didn't notice that his head rose up above the grass. The bang was at his left ear with wood chips blown into his face. He collapsed to the ground.

He lay there with his body shaking uncontrollably. He wanted to cry out but all he could do was let out a low growl like a mad dog. The left side of his face started to hurt. He reached up expecting a massive wound and half his face gone, but instead there was a little blood from a few wood splinters. As his hands stopped shaking, he pulled the splinters out then he looked up to the fence rail to find an inch-wide, round hole that wasn't there before.

How close had the bullet been to his head? He was glad he didn't know. Another sharp bang made him flinch. The upper rail vibrated as small pieces of wood rained down on his face. No doubt the sharpshooter wanted him to know they hadn't forgotten about him.

As crazy as it might seem, he decided that his best option was to go over the top of the fence. He got himself together and pushed the canteens through the rails. He then crawled about ten feet to the south away from the spring.

He reached under the lowest rail to make sure it was soft ground with no rock outcroppings. He then got into a squatting position making sure to keep his head below the high grass. He took a deep breath, then launched himself catching the top rail with both hands and did a flip over the fence landing on his left side on the soft ground.

He struggled crawling away from the spot where he went over the fence just in case, they tried a wild shot into the grass. He flipped over on his back and tried to get his breath back and to calm down.

When his breathing returned to normal, he rolled over on his stomach and crawled back to the canteens. As he gathered them up, it dawned on him how stupid an idea this was. The odds were good he wasn't going to make it back and his men would have no hope of getting any water since he had their canteens.

He put the canteen straps over his head with half of the canteens under his right shoulder and the other half under his left. He started crawling dragging them behind him through the high grass. He pulled himself forward with his left hand and when he reached out with his right he pushed into cloth with no give. He pulled himself forward slowly and came face to face with a bearded man in gray.

His eyes were open but locked in a death stare. He must have been part of yesterday's attack and got missed by the burial parties that were sent out last night.

Stephen slide past him and crawled a few more feet before angling over toward the spring. His right hand splashed into the cool water. He peeked through the grass and glanced to his left. He couldn't see the trees. He took a deep breath as a sense of relief flooded over him. He looked carefully at the water. No red. About five yards to his left there was a man lying on the opposite bank with his shoulders and head under water as if he was taking a refreshing dunk in the cool water, but his arms floating to his side told a different story.

Stephen double checked the water to make sure the spring was flowing to the left, then it suddenly dawned on him how ridiculous he was being. He risked his life to get his men water and even if the man was upstream what was he going to do? Walk all the way back without any water just because there was a little blood in it?

He took off his forage cap then slowly scooted his head farther out through the grass making sure that he still couldn't see the peach trees up on the high ground. He told himself that was the only way a sniper was going to see him was if he could see the trees.

He took a deep breath, closed his eyes, and slowly lowered his face down into the water stopping when the tip of his nose touched something solid. He could feel the water was just past his eyes but not quite to his ears. It wasn't very deep, but the water was cool and clean. Too bad it wasn't deeper. He would have gladly stripped down to wash away the dirt and sweat of the last week. What would it be like to feel clean again?

He opened his mouth and let it fill with water. Then he quickly forced shut his jaw trapping the cool life-giving liquid just before he raised up his head. He breathed through his nose a couple times before he swallowed the water.

He started with his own canteen pushing it flat to the bottom. The neck was just an inch below the surface, but that was all he needed. The bubbles streamed from the neck. When they slowed to a trickle, he pulled it out. It was about three quarters full. The water wasn't deep enough to tilt the canteen, so it would fill completely, but three quarters was much better than nothing.

He took a long drink of the cool water. The privilege of risking his life was he got to drink first and as much as he wanted. He took a breath. His stomach cried for food, but water would have to do. He took another long drink, then pushed the canteen back into the water and filled it again.

Once the cork was secure in his canteen, he turned his attention to the other nineteen. As he was finishing the last canteen, he realized he was going to have another problem. He had to pee. Pretty obvious that standing up and taking a piss was not an option. He quickly decided that pissing his trousers was something he also had no interest in doing. He was wet enough as it was covered in sweat and he didn't want to do anything to add to it.

He pushed himself back a foot from the spring and lay on his side, so he was facing down the slope. He undid his buttons and fumble with his pants pulling them just enough to be able to relieve himself. "Please God, don't let me die like this." He could hear the laughter of the burial party with his Johnson flapping about as they threw him in the hole.

When he finished, he carefully lay out the canteens ten to a side with their straps overlapping. Dragging full canteens back to the fence was going to be difficult and he didn't want anything to make it any harder than it needed to be.

He crawled straight for the fence so he would be several yards north of where he had jumped it the first time. Once there, he pushed the canteens through the rails. He crawled a few feet and took a couple of breaths before launching himself back over the fence.

This time he landed flat on his back knocking the breath right out of him. As he lay there stunned, he was thankful there were no bullets flying into the fence over his head. He was hoping the sharpshooters had found someone else to give their attention too.

He rolled over and crawled back to the canteens. Once again, he carefully lay them out ten to a side. Then he rolled on to his stomach between them, wrapping the straps over both shoulders. He pulled up both legs to his side as close as he could, almost like a frog. He was careful to keep his butt and torso low down as he pushed himself back so he was resting on his knees and bracing with both arms out in front of him.

He took a deep breath and pushed on all fours, first up on his toes then battling through the weight up on his feet. He steadied himself then took a step to the right. Three zips came a second later to his left. No time to think about that. Two steps forward, another one to the right.

The slope and the weight slowed him more than he expected, so he took a sidestep after every step forward. When he got within one hundred feet of the stonewall, Ralph and William ran out and grabbed the canteens from him and they all ran back jumping over the wall.

Stephen was surprised and embarrassed by the cheers and the claps on the back from his men. He was grateful when George yelled at them to quiet down and get back in line.

George scooted over to him. "Should I send someone else?"

Stephen shook his head. "Too dangerous."

George pulled Stephen's face to the right. "That looks like it hurts," he said.

"Did I get all the splinters?" Stephen asked.

George looked carefully. "I don't see any." George pulled on Stephen's coat pulling it away from his body on the left side. Stephen looked down and saw two clean holes in the side of the coat.

"Beats me how they missed you," George said.

"I guess God was looking out for me," Stephen whispered.

George patted him on the back then scooted away.

"You were lucky," Ralph said.

Stephen flipped around and settled with his back against the wall ignoring Ralph. He could feel his knees start to shake as his heart pounded in his chest as it dawned on him how close he had come to dying. He pulled down his forge cap to shade his eyes from the sun, more importantly covering his face just in case the fear he was feeling was noticeable.

Jacob Turney

Jake walked behind Company K. They were lying in two rows facing toward the Union line. Fifty yards down the western slope from the summit of the ridge, through the trees, he couldn't see anything of the Yankee position just over a mile away. No matter, he'd gotten a good look at it yesterday.

He took off his hat and beat it a few times against his leg. He hated waiting. He was thankful that at least they were waiting in the woods instead of lying under the open ground under the noonday sun.

"Shouldn't be long now," Colonel George said as he walked up to Jacob.

"Where's your horse?" Jake asked.

"Back with a private from Company A. "

"Good idea. No reason to give the Yankees an easy target. Do you know who is going with us?" Jake asked

Pender's Division with Trimble in command will be on our left with Pickett's Division on our right."

"Puts us right in the center of the line," Jake said as he put his hat back on his head. "An attractive target for their artillery."

"We just have to pray the coming barrage will take care of them for us. We've moved every gun into position.

Unlike us tucked away in woods, the center of the Yankee line is all out in the open including their artillery," Newt said with a hint of confidence.

"Your men have full canteens?'

"Yes, sir."

"Good, good, I doubt we will have any time to get water once the artillery starts firing."

"Good afternoon, gentlemen." Jacob recognized Colonel Birkett Fry's voice. Jacob turned around and joined Colonel George in returning Fry's salute.

"I've sent word for the rest of the regiment's commanders to join us. If I remember right, Captain Turney, you have command of Company K?"

"Yes, sir, but to be honest, with only thirty-two men left I'm more in command of a platoon than a company."

"No different than the rest of the companies in the regiment," Newt added.

"I'm afraid you both are no different than the rest of the brigade. We all took a beating a couple of days ago."

Jake was surprised how frank and somber Fry was with them, but the facts were facts and with what they were facing today, this was no time to hide the truth. The brigade was at about half strength and they were going to be the center of the attack.

The other colonels joined them quickly. Jake turned to go back to his company and was surprised when Fry told him to stay.

"Gentlemen, let's take a walk."

The brigade's colonels and Captain Jacob Turney followed Colonel Fry up the sloop and over the top of the ridge into the open. Halfway to the road up ahead, the house and barn that had held the Yankee troops that had caused so much trouble for Anderson's men yesterday were just smoldering ruins.

Up past the road to their left was a small white house and barn. To the right, on the road, stood a larger brick house and a small red barn. Both would be obstructions for someone to go around but Jake hoped not Company K.

"Gentlemen." Fry sounded so formal, so polite. Jake guessed he was trying to gain the respect of the other colonels through kindness. Jake was grateful, some newly promoted officers could be such jerks.

"After discussing with Generals Lee, Longstreet, and Pickett, our objective is that group of trees." Jake shaded his eyes to get a better view. There was what looked like a row of small trees, with a few large ones to the right side.

"We are on the right of the division. Pettigrew's brigade with Marshall in commend will be to our left. Davis and Brochenbrough's brigades will be next line and Scales' and Lane's brigades will be providing support.

"Captain Turney, you are the guide for your regiment and the entire brigade. General Pettigrew and the rest of the Division will guide on our brigade. Pender's Division, now under the command of General Trimble, will guide on us from our left and Pickett's Division will work around to join us on our right.

"In other words, Captain Turney, your small company is the center of the entire attack and the guide for three divisions."

"Oh shit," Jake whispered thankful no one seemed to hear what he said.

"Captain, make sure all your officers and sergeants know our objective, just in case."

Fry didn't have to finish the "just in case," as Jake looked across the mile of open ground between them and the Union line. He just prayed the coming artillery barrage worked, otherwise they'd be lucky if any of the men from Company K made it to the Yankee line.

It took a couple of seconds before Jake realized that Fry was just trying to make him feel more important than he really was. While the regiment dressed to the right, Jake followed the flag. He was going to go where the flag went and they would be following orders from Colonel Newton George.

If something happened to him, no matter who took his place, they too would just follow the flag. Everyone was replaceable. If the color sergeant, Willy Wood, was shot down, another of the color guard would take his place. If Colonel Newton George went down, it would be Captain Jake Turney who would take over command of the regiment and Lieutenant Holland would be the new company captain.

Jake stood and stared across the open ground, but he was more concerned by the leadership changes in the army brought about by the attack two days ago. The division was now being led by Pettigrew taking over for the wounded Heth. Fry was taking over for a captured General Archer. General Trimble was an experienced officer, but not at all familiar with the chain of command in Pender's Division.

His job was easy: follow the flag straight toward those trees. The only question was how much of the rest of the army was going to join him. Were all these officers new to command going to be up for the task at hand? Maybe such a full-frontal attack wasn't the best idea, but what did he know? He was just a captain.

As he looked at the ground in his front, he noticed they were going to be descending a slope for a while, giving whatever Yankee artillery fire was left a clear field of fire. The ground leveled out and it looked like it was much lower than the ground along the road. That was a very good thing. It would give him and the rest of the regiment a chance to dress lines.

"Orders will be to fix bayonets and to hold fire until we cross the road. There are fences on both sides of the road. Hard to tell how many of the rails are still in place."

Jake hoped there weren't any. With so many men getting to the fence at the same time, there would be lots of targets making it hard for the Yankees to single out anyone, but still, no one wanted to climb two fences under heavy fire.

"If the fences have rails, go fast, keep low, no stopping to shoot, once over, don't worry about the formation just go," Fry stated firmly.

Jake nodded; trying to dress the lines would just give the Yankees a minute of target practice.

"Right before the road, there is some low ground. We should be able to dress the lines and get ready for a dash for the fences," Fry added.

"Let's just hope our artillery takes out theirs or it is going to be a ..." Fry just let his voice trail off. There was no need to finish the obvious. "We better get back and you brief your regiments," Fry added as he turned around and headed back toward the woods.

Jake starred at the road for a couple of seconds more, hoping that he was wrong about the rails. He prayed that last night some adventurous Yankees had gathered up the rails for campfires. It would make things much easier. He then turned and followed the others back into the woods.

Stephen Brown

"It's almost done," William said as he shook Stephen awake.

Stephen yawned and stretched his arms about his head. "How long was I sleepin'?

"Not long, about a half hour," William answered.

"Any trouble with sharpshooters?" Jake asked.

"Not much. A few shots, but the boys kept low. Seems like the sharpshooters have other things on their minds than firing at a few privates."

Still, Stephen decided to be cautious; he spun around and slowly got on his knees, peeking over the wall. The work party—a hundred yards to his front—while crouched down, was much more in the open and a more inviting target than he was.

The work detail was pulling out rails from the upper parts of the fence he'd vaulted over when he'd gotten water. They were using them to fill in the gaps in the lower sections forming a makeshift breastwork.

Stephen guessed William was right. The work detail was much more in the open than he was and there was no evidence of anyone shooting at them. Could be the rebel sharpshooters knew what was coming and decided to get out of the way.

"You think this is a good idea?" William asked with an obvious frown of concern.

"What do you care?" Stephen chuckled. "You're the one who is so sure he is going to die."

William's face flashed red then he punched Stephen hard in the arm.

"You son of a bitch, that hurt!" Stephen snapped.

William's face went blank, immediately followed by a big smile. He just doubled over with laughter.

"What's so funny?" Ralph asked.

"None of your business," Stephen snapped, instantly realizing he had just made things much worse.

"The fine Christian Lieutenant called me a son of a bitch," William said, laughing so hard it took Ralph a couple of seconds to realize what he was saying.

"What's gotten in to you? Yesterday you took the Lord's name in vain and now you cursed at one of your men?" Ralph said in a voice of utter surprise.

"Not only cursed, he called my dear sweet Mother a bitch," William said suddenly and seriously with a straight face, but he could only hold it for a couple of seconds before laughing with Ralph at Stephen's expense.

When Captain George Blake asked what was so funny, that was enough for Stephen. "I'm going to check the breastworks!" he snapped.

Stephen jumped over the stone wall and stayed low as he rushed forward. Unlike earlier, he didn't hear any zips from bullets going by him. William might be right that the sharpshooters were clearing out from the no man's land between the lines.

Still, not wanting to tempt fate, he hurried and stayed low, but the laughter chased after him. He couldn't believe he had let his anger get the better of him. He was so embarrassed that he had disparaged Mrs. Church.

"Forgive me, Lord", he whispered. Of course, he knew why they were laughing. In the nine months they've been together, it was one of the very few times he had cursed at anyone. Still, he should have been better than that. He shouldn't have overreacted and he knew he was going to have to apologize to William no matter how much he laughed at him. He was wrong and he needed to own up to it.

Stephen knelt about ten feet from the breastworks. There were a few stones and a couple of logs, but for the most part it was just made up of fence rails. While the hay behind the fence was mostly trampled down by the boys building the works, the grass in front was about the same height as the breastworks. Obviously, the plan was for the regiment to lay down behind the works. For infantry coming their way, it would be almost impossible to see the regiment.

"What do you think, Lieutenant Brown?" Colonel Randall asked as he came up on his right side.

"Someone is in for a surprise when we stand up, sir."

"That is what we are hoping for."

"Sir, it isn't going to be much protection from artillery."

"That is true, but if things get hot back by the wall, we can just sneak up here. If they don't see us, they won't be shooting at us. You haven't found your sword?"

"No sir, it is with the baggage in the regiment's wagon," Stephen said, trying not to sound dejected.

"You might not get it back ... so if I was you, if you get the opportunity, I would relieve one of the rebel officers of his sword."

"I will do that, sir." Stephen smiled.

"And don't let any of the higher ranks give you any bull crap about only surrendering their swords to an officer of equal or greater rank," Randall said firmly.

"Any suggests on how to do that, sir?" Stephen asked.

"I think that hatch will be all the encouragement they will need," Randall laughed.

"I think they have stopped laughing at you, so you should get back to your company."

"Yes, sir," Stephen mumbled embarrassingly.

"I'm sure George is going to talk to you about the importance of maintaining discipline in the ranks."

"Yes, sir."

"And you better pray Mr. Church never hears what you called his wife," Randall chuckled.

"I didn't—"

Randall's laughter cut him off. "I bet about now you wished you'd stayed with your company. "

"Yes, sir," Stephen mumbled again.

Randall patted him on the back. "You better get back to them."

Stephen hurried back to the wall again staying low, but this time instead of jumping over it he thought better of it and slid around the backside.

George was waiting for him just behind the wall. "The colonel have anything interesting to say?"

"No," Stephen snapped as he felt his face flash red. He flipped back around and sloughed down against the wall as a few scattered chuckles signaled that they hadn't gotten all the mileage out of his discomfort. He pulled his cap back down over his eyes.

After a couple of minutes, the talk and laughter died away. Stephen wasn't surprised. With the artillery moving back and forth, thoughts quickly returned to the coming battle.

Stephen pushed back his cap and glanced down the wall at the rest of the company. He noticed George was peeking over the wall. Everyone else was staying low.

Most lay on their backs with their caps helping to block the sun. If they could fall asleep, they would for a time forget how hungry they were. Some were reading while a few souls were playing cards.

Stephen heard some commotion to his left. He glanced over and saw another battery coming into line about twenty yards away. He was glad there weren't any batteries close to them. He saw firsthand yesterday how artillery was a magnet for enemy fire.

Riding behind the battery and heading in his direction were a few riders. With the sun in his eyes, it took him a second to recognize Captain Randall and General Stannard. They were talking to another officer with several other officers trailing behind the three of them. From the looks of the uniform, he guessed it he was a major general, which meant it, must be the Second Corps commander Winfield Scott Hancock, whom Stephen had heard was commanding this section of the line.

The three of them looked in his direction and Hancock laughed. That wasn't a good sign. It was even worse when Hancock put a couple of quick kicks into the side of his horse and sprinted in his direction leaving the others behind.

Stephen felt like he was going to throw up. *What in the hell do I do now?* Stephen pushed to stand, but Hancock motioned him to stay down. *Do I salute while sitting down?* Stephen debated for a couple of seconds before deciding it might be better not to.

Hancock pulled up next to him. "Lieutenant Brown."

Oh God, he knows my name.

"I hear you had some trouble with your sword."

"Yes, sir. I was arrested for violating the General Stannard's order about leaving formation."

"I heard the story last evening?"

"Sir," Stephen stammered.

"I overheard a cavalry sergeant talking about a young Vermont lieutenant telling him that he loved him like a brother, but if he didn't let him get water for his men, he was going to kill him."

"Yes, sir, I guess I did say something like that." A few chuckles behind him told him that most of the company was eavesdropping in on the conversation.

"Now I hear from your colonel that you are going into battle without your sword."

Stephen pulled out the hatch. "But not unarmed, sir."

Hancock roared a deep belly laugh. "Good for you, son, good for you." Hancock swirled his horse around. "You give them hell son. All of you give them hell."

All the company and about half the regiment let out a yell as Hancock rode back up where the other officers were waiting for him as the regiment's sergeants started yelling for quiet in the ranks. Stephen slid the hatchet back into his belt and turned back around proud but thoroughly embarrassed by all the attention. He'd done countless things for his men since leaving Vermont and he was having trouble coming to grips to why this was so much different.

"Good job, Stephen," William whispered to him as Ralph patted him on the back.

"For what?" Stephen stammered.

"Not embarrassing yourself and the rest of us in front of General Hancock."

"Not a very high standard?" Stephen laughed.

William shrugged his shoulders. "If it had been me, I think I would have pissed my pants," William whispered.

It was Stephen's turn to pat his friend on the back.

Jacob Turney

Jake stood up and stretched his back. Down the slope to the west the large number of horses looked peaceful in the knee-high grass. If it wasn't for the harnesses, they looked like they were enjoying the peaceful pastures of back home instead of being instruments of war.

He guessed it was a good idea to clear out the horses with what was coming. It seemed like every piece of artillery belonging to the Army of Northern Virginia was along the ridge just in front of them. Arranged in four- or six-gun batteries, with their limbers and caissons stretched out behind them, what he could see through the trees, the artillery was ready.

While he'd watched many an artillery barrage over the last three years, he could tell this was going to be different. When he was out in the open with the brigade's officers, there were guns as far as he could see. Even so, he knew there were many more that he couldn't see.

He pushed the small strips of cotton cloth deep into his ears. No question about how loud things were going to become.

"Captain, I got some extra beeswax? You want some?" Chuck asked. Jake looked down on his first sergeant and shook his head. While it worked best in this heat, it would just melt and goo up his ear channel and it would be days before he got it all cleaned out. He glanced over to the center of the regiment. Newt was also standing with his hands on his hips.

For what seemed like the fiftieth time, Jake looked over his men. A few glanced up at him, but most were taking advantage of the quiet and the shade to get some shut eye. Everyone knew what was coming and he guessed most of them were long past worrying about such things as when the attack would come, if at all. While they had never seen so many batteries massed like this before, it had little to do with them.

They were what seemed like a safe distance back behind the guns and the trees would provide some measure of protection from any Yankee shells firing long. Until the barrage ended, there wasn't much for them to do but wait.

He stepped to the back of the company and went back to pacing. He hated waiting. He glanced at Newt; he was also back to pacing behind the center of the regiment. They weren't alone. All along the line, officers were pacing behind their commands.

Jake's eyes met James. It was pretty obvious that James was nervous. Jake forced him a smile. James smiled back. Albert was face down using his hat as a pillow fast asleep.

Jake was surprised. It was not like Albert to fall asleep before a battle. Maybe the extra attention Zimmerman was giving him was starting to have an effect or maybe the knock on the head was affecting him more than they had thought. No matter why, at least things were much quieter with him asleep.

It dawned on Jack how quiet it was. He glanced up into the trees and even the leaves were still. It reminded him of being at church waiting for the minister to start his sermon.

With the cloth in his ears, the gun was a bit muffled, but obviously close. A few seconds later came the second gun. Now the only question was how ready the rest of the artillery was to fire?

He stopped and stared through the trees and waited for the flash and smoke. He would see them just a spit second before the sound. It seemed like it took forever but within a minute the bright yellow flashed through the trees quickly followed by dark gray smoked rising up blanketing the gaps between the trees.

The concussion came roaring through the woods like an angry lion taking Jake's breath away as it hammered against his ears in spite of the cloth. Close behind was a strange feeling running up though his feet as the very ground he stood on vibrated from the blast.

He glanced up and the leaves and branches were swaying as if there was a light breeze sweeping through the trees. The sound alone was vibrating the very air and everything in it.

Jake glanced over at Newt. He had his hands over his ears. Jake turned back to his company. James had buried his face with both hands over his ears. Albert was awake and running his mouth again saying something to Corporal Zimmerman, but Jake doubted that Albert could even hear himself let alone Zimmerman. As quickly as the blast swept over them it was gone and eerily quiet. Then the Yankee reply roared down the slope.

Jake felt an impact on his right shoulder from a small branch. There was an explosion behind him throwing pieces of dirt in his direction.

That was close. Up ahead a shell exploded above the trees. The Yankees were firing a few shells long, so Jake decided to stand up wasn't such a good idea after all. He glanced back at Newt. He was already lying down behind the center of the regiment. It took Jake all his willpower from running back to his place in the formation.

He took slow and measured steps. No need to broadcast to the entire company how scared he was. He laid down next to the first sergeant who said something to him, but Jake just shrugged his shoulders. He couldn't hear anything over the roar.

Chuck smiled at him, so obviously, whatever it was could wait or wasn't that important. The sound continued to pound on his ears and he started to get a headache. Jake rolled over on his back and put his hands over his ears. Looking up into the trees he was amazed as the leaves danced in the shock waves of sound.

From what he heard; the bombardment was supposed to last about an hour. He only hoped the artillery was doing their job and hammering the entire Yankee line. If not, he knew it was going to be a very bad day for him and his company. He closed his eyes and he had a vision of trying to cross the rail fences up on the road under Yankee infantry fire. Yes, it would be a very bad day indeed.

Stephen Brown

It was distant, but a noticeably clear sharp sound of a lone artillery gun. Stephen spun around and peeked over the stone wall. There was another gun, then just as quickly, all returned to an eerie quiet. Heads were popping up all around him. Suddenly, there were a series of flashes across the way so many there was no way he could count them. A billowing angry cloud of gray and white obscured the enemy's guns almost instantly. Within a second, the sound hit him in the face like a hammer driving into his brain.

As the sound swept over him, his eyes saw dark specks jump out of the cloud arching high across the sky. One looked to be heading right for him. He was so transfixed on the shell; the answering blast from friendly artillery caught him completely by surprise, taking his breath away. He lost control of his bladder and pissed himself. The warm liquid flowed down inside of his right thigh.

It took him a second to get his wits about him. The angry dots were much larger in the sky and on the downward part of their journey. Stephen waved and yelled for everyone to get down. George was doing the same on the other end of the company's line.

Stephen dropped down with his back against the wall as the first shell exploded to the regiment's right. There was a shout down the line. Stephen glanced to the right to see the backside of a soldier from the middle of the regiment's center as he ran to the east.

Stephen's brain yelled at him to follow the man, so he crossed his ankles and pushed his back against the wall as two shells exploded not more than twenty yards to the east, directly in front of him, as another exploded high above the regiment.

He ducked down and prayed that his men would all be safe. He glanced up and everyone seemed fine. A few faces looked in his direction. He forced a smile and they forced a smile back at him.

The roar was now constant, and Stephen noticed a strange vibration through his butt as the ground beneath vibrated from the artillery fire. Even with the cotton George had ordered the entire company to put in their ears, the sound was overwhelming. Stephen put his hands over his ears. He glanced down the line to see just everyone else doing the same.

Another shell exploded about ten yards east of the center of the regiment. While most of the rebel shells were going long and far down the backside of the ridge, many were close and that one was too close.

A couple of runners came out from the center of the regiment's line in both directions, as Colonel Randall obviously decided there was no way anyone was going to hear the regiment's drums. The center of the line moved first, men staying low flung themselves over the stonewall.

George and the first sergeant were coming in his direction tapping men on the shoulders and motioning them over the wall. Stephen did the same, tapping William and Ralph on the shoulder. Over the wall they went and so followed the next in line and it spread from both ends and quickly the entire company was over the wall, leaving George and Stephen starring at each other.

Two more shells exploded close by and that was enough for Stephen. He sprang over the wall. He joined the rest of the regiment crawling toward the forward breastworks. More shells exploded behind him, but none exploded in front of him. The rebels were, as the colonel predicted, firing long.

Suddenly, in front of him there was a bright flash on the opposite ridge as smoke billowed high into the sky. One of enemy caissons had exploded. A second later, Stephen was surprised he could clearly hear the explosion above the roar of the barrage.

He stopped to rest lying flat on the ground. It was the oddest feeling how the ground was vibrating under him as if it was one long earthquake. He glanced up. He was about halfway there and the rest of the regiment was leaving him behind. He went back to crawling.

Jacob Turney

Jake rolled over on to his right side trying to get comfortable. He watched the leaves and branches dance as if a strong wind was coming from the east. Suddenly, a large branch spilt.

Under the weight of the end, it swung down and when it reached the end of the crack it broke off. Jake yelled "Heads up!" as loud as he could but he couldn't even hear himself over the roar as he watched the branch fall into the middle of the regiment's formation.

He could see open mouths and angry faces, but he could only guess at what was being said. A couple of men stood up to pick up the branch and carry it out of the formation.

Jake looked back into the same tree just in time to see a shell hit the center of the trunk. The entire tree swayed, and more branches broke off as the shell bounced back then exploded. The two men carrying the branch were knocked down as a couple of others rolled on the ground in pain.

Litter-bearers rushed into the formation and carried away the injured. A couple of the men weren't moving at all but Jake couldn't tell if they were dead or not. Jake felt guilty that he was glad the shell had hit the center of the regiment and not his company.

Farther down the line, another shell exploded just a few feet above the ground. Jake couldn't tell how many were hit and to keep from staring, he rolled the other way and he prayed the shells continued to avoid his little company. He took several deep breaths to calm his nerves. He noticed a small twig on the ground next to him seemingly dancing across the waving blades of grass as they swayed with the vibrations of the ground beneath him.

The two quick slaps on his back startled him. He rolled over to see Chuck pointing to Newt standing in the center of the regiment. For a second, Jake thought the colonel had lost his mind, but then it dawned on him that the Yankee shells had stopped exploding above them. He wondered how long he had been staring at that damn little twig.

Jake pushed himself up. Several in the company looked up at him as if he were crazy. He smiled down to them like he didn't have a care in world as he prayed to himself that Newt was right, and the Yankee guns had gone silent.

Newt and a couple of the other captains started walking forward through the trees and Jake hurried to catch up with them. As they came out of the trees, they were surprised to see the dark cloud on the opposite ridge rising. The Yankee artillery looked to have stopped firing. Near a couple of large trees, Jake could see horses pulling a gun away from the line. They were pulling out.

Jake tapped Newt on the shoulder and pointed to the gun as it went over the top of the next ridge. Newt said something but it was still impossible to hear. Jake just smiled back as another gun disappeared over the ridge. All along the Yankee line the smoke rose higher in the sky.

The lack of Yankee guns would be a big plus during the charge. With about a mile and half distance, being able to cross without having to worry about long range artillery fire would be wonderful and much easier to keep the men in formation. More importantly, for the last 400 to 500 yards their only worry would be Yankee infantry fire. With a mad dash, they might be able to get off a couple of volleys before they crashed against the Yankee line.

It would be much better to face the infantry volley from an entire regiment than a six-gun battery firing off a volley of canister. With each shell containing ninety-six metal balls, one volley could take out half the regiment. Then at closer range, each gun would be loaded with double canister, which would have horrible effects. Jake looked to his left and saw more Yankee guns pulling out. It was a very welcome sight indeed.

Stephen Brown

The last of the guns to his left disappeared over the top of the ridge. Stephen released his hands from his ears. While the noise was still overwhelming, the cotton was enough protection now to keep his ear drums from hurting.

"Do you think they'll be back?" William shouted.

Stephen was surprised he could hear him. "I hope so!" Stephen yelled back.

A few of the Confederate shells had fallen among the artillery knocking a few guns off their carriages and causing a couple of caissons to explode, but for the most part the artillery near them had suffered little damage. Stephen guessed—hoped—the artillery was pulling out to get rearmed before the Confederates started the charge. He guessed since the rebel artillery was causing so little damage, continuing to fire back at them really didn't make much sense, when everyone knew what was coming once their artillery stopped firing.

Stephen looked across the fields in front of him. He guessed it was just over a mile to the next tree-covered ridge and somewhere beyond was the rebel infantry. They had started yesterday's attack on the Union left flank and he guessed they wouldn't do the same. He'd heard the rebels had been beaten back in the morning from a hill on the right flank, so he didn't think they would try there either. If he was right, the attacking force was in those trees across the fields in front of him.

The still smoldering house and barn to his right would cause the confederates little trouble during their advance. The brick house and on the road to his left would also be of little concern. The fences lining the road would be a different issue.

To the left of the brick house, the rails were stripped from the fences. To the right of the house, both fences still had their rails. He pitied the poor fools who were going to have to climb over two fences under fire. Stephen prayed the artillery would be back by then. He was sure some canister fire would make the climb even more difficult.

Well within musket range, Stephen doubted the rebels would try to remove the rails before the advance. Anyone taking the time to try and remove the rails would be an easy target.

"Here comes one!" Ralph yelled out. Stephen glanced up and saw the dot heading right for him. Stephen grabbed hold of the grass in front of him as a reminder to stay where he was. The dot was quickly getting larger, but the angle was widening, and it was going long. Stephen turned his head and followed it down. His jaw dropped when it exploded just on the other side of the stone wall, they had left a short while ago.

"Thank God we moved forward," he whispered, knowing full well that only God was going to hear him. Suddenly, the gray angry cloud that covered the opposite ridge started to lift quickly followed by an eerie quiet occasionally punctured by a lone artillery gun. Now the only question was how long they were going to have to wait for the confederates to join them. Drums and bugle calls from the opposite ridge told him it wouldn't be long.

Jacob Turney

As soon as the guns fell silent, Jake started yelling, "On your feet! On your feet!" He didn't want his men lying on the crowd thinking about what was coming next. Better to get them up and give them something to do.

Jake noticed the dirty look First Sergeant Chuck gave him right before he added, "Company, fall in!"

Getting the men into formation was his duty not Jake's. Once the men were in formation, Chuck took his position on the left of the second rank and waited for Jake.

"Go ahead, fix bayonets and load weapons," Jake said this time letting Chuck issue the orders.

When Chuck barked out fix bayonets, Jake turned his back and looked through the woods and watched the artillery being driven away. The clanks of the bayonets were right together telling him his men were focused and ready.

He turned around with the orders for load and scanned his men while they loaded their weapons. No one rushed—there was no reason to—but everyone was deliberate and focused. No doubt in Jake's mind, his company was ready to give the Yankees hell. Just too bad there were so few of them left.

Once they were all finished, and Chuck had called stand at ease. Jake stepped to the center the formation.

"Boys, we are going to join Pickett's and Pender's entire divisions in visiting the Yankees this afternoon." There were a couple of chuckles, but everyone had time in the early morning to get a glance at the Yankee line on the opposite ridge. They all knew what was facing them.

"We can only hope the artillery has softened them up some for us," Jake continued. "Up near the road there is some low ground that should give us some cover. We will stop and dress the formation. The road has fences on both sides and it looks like the rails are still in place"

That got everyone's attention. "What the—" Albert started to say, but Zimmerman's quick "Quiet in the ranks," cut him off before he could finish what Jake was sure was going to be a whole series of colorful adjectives.

"Get over them as quickly as you can. Once over don't worry about reforming the line, just rush forward as quickly as you can. If you get a clean shot, take it and make sure it counts." He paused for a couple of seconds. Was there anything else he could say? "If we beat them this afternoon, it will be on to Washington tomorrow."

"Hell yes," Albert shouted out and couple of others joined him. Just then the drums started sounding for the regiment to fall in. Like Jack, the regiment's other company commanders had already got their men up and ready.

The call came for the regiment to come to attention. Jake took his place in line on the first rank just in front of Chuck. Forward march came quickly and they were off. The formation would be a bit jagged until they got through the trees, but nothing new for any of them.

As they marched, Jake's heart started pounding. He took a couple of deep breaths. Nothing new here either. His body just reacting to the fear like it had done hundreds of times before. As they got to the tree line, Jake quickened his pace a few steps.

Two entire divisions would be stepping out of the woods together and he was on their flank. Pickett's Division was still in the woods to his right, so for right now, Jake was on flank of two entire divisions.

He turned around and watched as they came stepping out of the woods, flags waving in the light breeze and a mass of thousands. What a sight it was. The company caught up with him and he resumed his place in the line. It would be a few hundred yards before Pickett's men to his right would clear the woods and start their trek to the left to join up with his company putting them roughly in the center of the line.

His heart skipped a beat when he saw the flashes on the hill to his left and the angry dark gray cloud that followed. It was a couple of seconds before the booms reached them. He quickly picked up the specks as they arched across the sky. They were all going north of them toward the line advancing toward the hill. He didn't look as the shells started exploding. He decided he didn't want to know how effective the Yankee artillery fire was being.

"Eyes front," Jake yelled. He didn't want his men looking that way either. Damn, more flashes down the ridge just a little way to his left. What the hell? Two hours of artillery fire and the Yankees still had a line of artillery in front of them?

The explosions were closer, but still to their left. He glanced down the line; there were holes being filled by men shifting to the right and stepping up into the front rank.

Jake stepped a little quicker. Not enough to be considered double time, the ground was too uneven for that, but the sooner they got across these fields the better. He glanced back hoping to see friendly artillery coming back into line, but there was nothing but woods.

He turned back around to see a cannonball bouncing across the ground. "Oh, God," he whispered. The balls would bounce right through both ranks.

The blast was above the center of the regiment. The yells were muffled, but as they stepped out of the smoke, Newt and Willy Wood, who was carrying the battle flag, were both on their feet and the men had shifted to the right filling in more holes in the line.

As they got to the end of the woods to their right, he was glad to see—almost on cue—Picketts' men step out of the woods to join the advance. If nothing else, they hopefully gave the Yankees more targets and cut down on the damage being done to their part of the line.

Stephen Brown

Stephen was looking straight across the fields when they stepped out of the woods like they were on a parade ground with their flags flying high. The unit to their left was already taking a beating from the artillery. Stephen wondered how long it would be before the new line drew the attention of the artillery. The six guns behind him and to his left answered the question just a couple of seconds later.

As he watched the balls fly across the sky, George spoke up. "I'm thinking that is a brigade."

Two of the balls exploded above the rebel brigade showering down a rain of death. A heartbeat later two more exploded within the ranks. The other two either went long, were duds, or were solid cannon balls instead of explosive shells.

"It must be a huge brigade," Stephen said with an obvious questioning tone in his voice.

"They only have three corps. Their brigades are almost as big as our divisions," Captain George Blake answered him.

"My God," William said out loud. "I almost feel sorry for them."

Stephen did too. They had never seen anything like this. Still, the lines kept coming. There didn't look to be as many of them, but they weren't slowing down. They weren't wavering. Thousands and thousands of them were heading their way with a goal to kill them.

"Where's their artillery?" Ralph asked.

Stephen just shook his head. George shrugged his shoulders. They were nowhere to be seen.

"I wonder if they ran out of ammunition," George said.

"I hope so," William stated firmly. "That stuff scarred the crap out of me."

"Me too," Stephen chuckled. Two hours of lying under threat of artillery fire was enough for him.

George patted him on the back and slid to the right of the line giving words of encouragement to each of the men as he went.

The blasts from the artillery seemed to fall into a rhythm as guns all along the line joined in on the fight. He tried counting how many of them there were but he couldn't keep track. The most intense fire seemed to be to their north along the higher ground and up on the hill they'd been on yesterday. To the south, on the bald hill that seemed to dominate that part of the field, there looked to be six guns joining into the action. To Stephen, it looked like an angry volcano.

The direction of fire from the hill was odd. They seemed to be firing much farther to the south, far from the infantry brigades. Hopefully, they were hitting whatever they were firing at. All in all, he guessed over a hundred guns were blasting away at the rebel formation.

It didn't take long to get a sense where the rebels were headed. The line that had come out of the woods first, on Stephen's right, was headed straight ahead across the fields. When they first appeared, there was a great amount of debate as to what it was. They had enough flags to be a full division but based on the number of men they looked to be a large brigade with two additional regiments in support.

As the artillery cut holes in their lines, they stayed the course, heading straight. The right of the brigade was heading toward the taller trees to Stephen's right.

The much larger second brigade was angling to their left (to Stephen's right) as if they were going to join up with the first brigade. Something seemed odd to Stephen.

"I think there are more of them coming," Stephen said out loud.

"Did you say something? Ralph asked, having had trouble hearing Stephen over the roar of the artillery fire.

"I think there are more of them coming," Stephen spoke up as he pointed to the south.

"You think so?" Ralph asked.

Stephen pointed to the brigade in their front making a more obvious move to their left angling over to join the now much smaller first brigade. It was then that he noticed, though the smoke on the opposite ridge, to the right of the first brigade, there was looked like more brigades.

Stephen pointed and as William followed his point, his face went blank. "Do you think it's a full division?" William asked excitedly.

"I don't know but there are sure a lot of them heading this way," Stephen said.

Just then, right behind the brigade directly in front of them, another huge brigade stepped out of the woods with their flags flying. Stephen tried to control his emotions, but he heard his voice crack as he pointed and said, "There is another one!"

Two rebel brigades and what looked like a division were coming and all with the mission to kill as many Yankees as possible. From what Stephen had learned over the last twenty-four hours, they were roughly in the center of the Union line. Yesterday, the rebel attack had started on the left flank of the Union army and proceeded in stages across the entire Union line. In some places, they were more successful than others and the last attacks had happened so late that they had little effect.

The firing on the right flank just before dawn seemed to be an extension of the previous night's attack. The fact it ended so quickly meant it had been a Union victory. Robert E. Lee had tested the flanks and lost and now he was driving a knife toward the Union center and the Thirteenth Vermont.

"They're gone!" William shouted. "Where did they go?" he questioned excitedly. Stephen followed the point of his finger. The brigade on the right was gone.

"There is low ground just on the other side of the road. We won't see them again until they climb over the fence line." Ralph said. "I noticed the low ground along the road last evening when we went looking for Bill."

Just then, Stephen watched as the two brigades in front of them disappeared. They wouldn't see them again either until they crossed the road. The brigades to his left would have an easier go of it since Union campfires had devoured all the rails giving the rebels a clear passage across the road. Not so far to the north, the rebel brigades would have to cross over both the fences lining the road under artillery and musket fire.

"Have mercy on their souls," Stephen whispered to himself.

Jacob Turney

The first thing he noticed was how quiet it was. The high ground up on the road was providing them cover but also served as a natural sound barrier. The flag stopped. The entire regiment, what was left of it, came to a halt. Jake looked to his right and watched Garnett's Virginians come up to join them. As they came to a halt, Jake stepped a few yards to his right and shook hands with a major.

"Glad you could join us," he said, forcing a smile.

It was then that he noticed General Garnett sitting on the horse in the front of his brigade. Jake was surprised to see him still on horseback. He was such an easy target for sharpshooters.

Jake turned back to his own company. Things weren't going well. The artillery fire had been hell on earth. To the north, Yankee infantry had moved across the road and had blasted Brockenbrough's brigade and between them and the artillery the entire brigade had broken and ran back to the safety of the ridge. Jake had half a mind to do the same.

The men finished straightening the lines. While much smaller than when they started, they still looked like a military organization, but instead of a company they were really nothing more than a small platoon.

He looked at his brothers and tears formed up in his eyes. He turned his back on them and looked up to the fence about fifty yards in their front. Once they came back into view, he knew the Yankee infantry would join in with the artillery. He wiped his eyes. The odds were good at least one of them would die in the charge to the enemy line.

He took a deep breath and forced himself to think about the task at hand. He stepped back to the company. "Boys, you got to throw yourselves over that fence. Don't worry about keeping in line or firing your weapon. Just get across the road and over that second fence as quick as you can. Once over, double time up to the enemy line then we will give them hell."

He tried to be as rousing as he could, but they all knew what was waiting for them, so he got little response from the company. The flag moved forward again. "Forward!" he shouted. Two heartbeats later, he yelled out, "March!" Together, they stepped forward. For a couple of minutes, it would be like being back on a parade ground.

As he went up slope, he looked through the gaps in the lower fence rails. First to come into view were the taller trees on the ridge up ahead. Next, there was a stone wall to his left with artillery barrels behind it. If he could see them, they could see him. He was at first surprised they were holding their fire than it dawned on him the fences along the road were a two-edge sword.

No doubt the artillery, as close as they were, was loaded with canister. The rails of the fence were providing them some protection, so the artillery was waiting on them to come over the second fence. *Oh, God.*

The trees grew taller. Another stone wall came into view and this one was directly in front of Jake and the First Tennessee. Another battery of artillery and lots of infantry were waiting behind this wall.

Suddenly, the wall exploded in smoke and fire. Less than a second the splinters exploded from the fence in front of him. Jake clearly heard a few zips as bullets flew past his ears. There were a few screams in the line, but the fence had made an excellent bullet catcher for his company with no holes in their line. He glanced to the left; the flag was still moving forward with Newt at his place next to it.

Two more steps and he would be at the fence. A chill went down his spine. "Keep your asses down going over the fence," he cried out as loud as he could. There was a splattering of laughter.

Left foot on the lowest rail, both hands on the top rail and he threw himself over the fence. Once his feet hit the ground, he quickly spun around surprised he didn't fall on his face. There was another volley from the stone fence and more screams from the line. He hurried across the road and flew over the second fence. He glanced to his left, Wiley Woods was over with the flag, but Newt wasn't with him.

No time to worry about what happened to his commander and his friend. Jake was now suddenly in command of the regiment. Jake stepped aside and let the company pass, then yelled at young Lieutenant Holland, "You're in command of the company. Take my place in the line."

Holland nodded and Jake hurried over to Willey Wood. They didn't have enough men left in the regiment to provide Willey a color guard to protect the flag. They were on their own. Colonel Fry was in the front and a little way to the left in the center of the brigade line. Jake's job was to watch Fry and give instructions to Wood. Where Wood went with the flag, the rest of the regiment would follow.

A few paces farther and they were greeted with another Yankee volley. Fry went down. The brigade kept moving and the front rank made a gap as they marched past their commander. Jake rushed over to check on Fry. He had a wound in his right thigh. It didn't look like they would take the leg, but he was done for the day.

"Captain take command of the brigade. Hold your fire until you get close to their line," Fry shouted to make sure Jake could hear him.

Jake nodded and ran to get in front of the brigade. Once there, he pulled out his sword. The boom of cannons and the awful noise of grape shot and canister exploded on his brain. He raised sword and the best he could and ran for the stone wall. They needed to get down behind that wall before the Yankee artillery and infantry tore them apart. He glanced back and he was relieved that what was left of the brigade was following him.

Stephen Brown

Stephen was surprised when the battle flags of five regiments popped up right in front of them. The advancing brigade looked lightly scratched compared to the bombardment falling on the other brigades to their north. Stephen guessed the slope on their path to the road was steeper and had provided this brigade some measure of protection all the way up to the road.

When the brigade appeared, it suddenly became clear why the guns on the bald hill were firing much farther to the south than the rest of the artillery. They were the only ones who could see what was coming.

The command came down the line to load weapons. Stephen's heart rate quickened. Since he drew straws with his father, this was the moment he had waited for. With no rails left in the fence, the rebel brigade crossed the road in good order. The artillery to Stephen's right started opening fire on them, but the gaps in the line were quickly filled in and the men kept going.

Stephen glanced to his right. The other rebel brigades had made it to the stone wall beyond the higher trees along the ridge. This last brigade was on their way to join them and they had no idea what was looming on their flank.

The other regiments in the Second Vermont Brigade, back up on the ridge, opened fire on the newest rebel brigade, but the Thirteenth Vermont stayed hidden and waited. The seconds ticked by like they were minutes. As their flank became rebel brigade flank came perpendicular to the Thirteenth's line the orders were yelled out to stand, aim, and fire.

While expected, Stephen still jumped at the sound of the volley. The white smoke was over whelming, with the thick smell of sulfur. Stephen squatted down to see and was amazed at the carnage of their first volley. The enemy flank was ripped to shreds with bodies littering the ground. A few of the enemy soldiers fired in their direction, but with the Thirteenth on the rebel brigade flank only a few men could aim in their direction.

The order was fire at will and the smoke was slightly less intense. Stephen waited for the expected turn. The rebel brigade had no choice but to wheel toward this threat on their flank. He rubbed his hatchet knowing that soon he was going to need it in hand to hand combat.

"Take your time boys, make every shot count," Stephen yelled out. It made him feel like he was doing something helpful even though it wasn't really needed. The men were well drilled, and all the training was paying off and of course it helped that the enemy could only train few guns in their direction. Once they wheeled, things were going to be different.

Jacob Turney

Jake slid down behind the wall. He planted his sword into the ground next to him. He felt faint as he tried to catch his breath. He took a quick drink from his canteen then glanced around and he wasn't surprised that he was surrounded by a mass of men without any sign of military organization. He was surprised to see Garnett still on his horse to the south encouraging his men along the wall.

Albert slid down next to him.

"James?" Jake asked his brother.

"I saw him limping to the rear," Albert said as he quickly peered over the wall and fired in the direction of the artillery to their right. Jake took off his hat and spun around and looked for a couple of seconds. To the right and left the Yankees were huddled along the other side of the wall, but he had come into a gap. He was about ten yards to the south of the corner of the wall where it made a turn to the east. The eastern run of the wall was also stacked with Yankees and they were firing into the flank of the men advancing on the stone wall farther up the ridge. If he could get some men over the wall, they could fire into the backs of the Yankees facing to the north.

Jake pulled his sword from the ground and waved it above his head as he yelled, "Hold your fire, hold your fire!"

About twenty men responded.

"Load!" he yelled. Once they were all loaded, he yelled, "We are going over the wall. Form a line facing..." he used his right arm to point to the north, "and fire into their backs."

He pulled his pistol out of its holster with his right hand as he raised his sword with his left and over the wall he went. He quickly was engulfed in white smoke making it hard to see anything. "Fire!" he yelled as he pulled the trigger on his pistol as quickly as he could. There was a scattering of shots from the men around him, which was quickly greeted by enemy fire from higher up on the ridge. Two close yells near Jake answered the enemy fire. The smoke totally engulfed Jake. He yelled, "Retreat!"

"Did you see anyone go down?" Jake asked Albert as they slid back down behind the other side of the stone wall.

"I heard a couple of yells but couldn't see anything after we fired.

Jake turned around and took off his hat again and glanced over the wall. There were two men down where there wasn't any before they went over the wall. He couldn't tell their condition; both were lying flat and not moving.

To the left the Yankee regiment between him and the corner of the wall was pulling back. Jake wondered if suddenly being fired upon from their left flank and anything to do with them pulling back? Either way, it was wonderful seeing the Yankees giving up a part of their line.

He glanced back up the ridge and through the smoke saw a Yankee aiming his musket at him. Jake quickly fired the last of his ammunition at the Yankee as smoke from his musket obscured Jake's view.

A blast of stone fragments exploded a few inches in front of Jake. He jumped back and lost his balance and fell over, landing hard on his back as he dropped his pistol. Somehow, he kept ahold of his sword. Albert reached out his hand. "You hurt?"

"Nope, I'm fine," he said as Albert pulled him back to a sitting position.

"That was too close," Jake said as he reached back and grabbed his pistol and slid it into his hostler. He flipped back around resting on the stone wall. He was heartened to see General Armistead leading his men up the slope to join them.

With so many men up among the Union position, Armistead's men weren't taking as much of a beating as the First Tennessee had suffered. There would be plenty of them left to make another push over the wall.

"I'm reloaded. We goin' try again?" Albert asked.

"Yes, but we will wait on him," Jake said pointing at Armistead.

"Sounds like a plan," Albert said with a faint hint of a smile. "To be honest, I'd rather be back with James," Albert confessed.

"Me too," Jake said as he slapped his brother on the back. "Me too."

"Fire at will over the wall boys!" Jake shouted out. "Let's give 'em hell." Firing from behind the wall was much safer and they would provide Armistead's men some support as they came up the ridge to join them.

Stephen Brown

Stephen was shocked that the wheel never happened. Instead, the rebel brigade just kept marching right past the Thirtieth Vermont. There were still a few guns on the right of the Thirtieth that could still bring fire on the rebels, but the men of Company K had run out of anything to shoot at.

Word had been passed down the line to be ready to wheel the Thirteenth, so they could go after the rebels, but there was a delay. General Stannard was ordering the Sixteenth Vermont forward to join up on the Thirteenth's left flank down close to the road. They stood there just waiting for that to happen.

"Quiet in the ranks," Stephen shouted out hoping to stop the grumbling about the delay. He understood how they felt. The war had just walked right past him and like the first nine months of his enlistment, Stephen was being forced to watch others fight in his place.

Next week, he would muster out of the army and head home. His Mom, Dad, and younger brother would all want to know what he did in the war and he didn't want to tell them at Gettysburg he watched the enemy march right past his company.

Still, Stephen was nervous. He could sense danger to the south. He kept glancing in that direction but there wasn't any infantry following the last brigade. He guessed he was just being silly.

He glanced to the rear; the Sixteenth was finally moving behind the Thirteenth on the way to their left flank. It wouldn't be long now. Stannard was still on his horse about thirty yards in their rear issuing orders to his aides. Stephen took a deep breath and turned back to the regiment. William glanced over his shoulder and smiled at Stephen. "It is almost over."

Stephen smiled back making sure to hide his nervousness. It looked like William wasn't worried anymore about his premonition. Hopefully, it was nothing more than a bad dream.

William pointed past Stephen. "Hancock."

Stephen spun around to see Major General Winfield Scott Hancock sitting tall in the saddle next to General Stannard and he didn't look happy. Stephen guessed he was just as impatient with the delay of getting the Sixteenth in line.

Suddenly Hancock grabbed the inside of his right thigh, wavered, and slid from his horse. One of Stannard's aides was quick and caught Hancock and lowered him to the ground. One of the other aides used his pistol and belt to make a tourniquet.

A blood curdling scream went up to their right as the rebel brigade let out the famous rebel yell and rushed forward. They were crashing into the Union line up by the taller trees, while the Thirteenth stood and watched.

"Fix bayonets!" The order was passed down the line. "Make sure your weapons are loaded," Stephen added as he pulled out his hatchet. It looked they were done waiting for the Sixteenth. Movement on the right of the regiment's line as company by company each was changing front and moving forward.

"Get ready boys," Stephen shouted.

A second later George echoed the drum roll to charge front. Company A paused to let the rest of the regiment come into line with Company K being the last. Once in position, the yell went out as the regiment's flag rushed forward and the line kept pace. Stephen tripped, stumbled, but somehow kept up from falling on his face. They were back in the war.

Jacob Turney

Armistead and his brigade were getting close. Over the last hundred yards, the artillery canister had greatly thinned their ranks but Armistead was still in the front, his hat on his sword raised high so all his men could guide on him.

The last few yards, Armistead's men ran up to the wall crowding in among Jake's men. By the time Armistead joined them it was a mass of men along the wall.

Armistead stood back from the wall for what seemed like forever before Jake heard him tell an officer next to him, "Colonel, we can't stay here."

"Then we'll go forward!" the colonel yelled out.

Armistead looked down the line and his gaze fell in Jake's direction. "Come forward, Virginians! Come, boys, we must give them cold steel; who will follow me?"

Jake and several men within earshot rose up en masse and followed Armistead as he stepped over the wall. Jake was right behind the general as they headed for a couple of nearby artillery guns. Firing to the right was having an effect as the closest Yankee regiment was being forced back from the stone wall. If they drive away that regiment, it will give encouragement to the rest of them men still huddled behind the wall.

Suddenly there was a larger volley from the right. Through the smoke Jake could see that the Yankee regiment had reestablished a firing line. Jake noticed Garnett's horse galloping back toward the road with a large wound on his shoulder with no sign of the general.

"The day is ours, men, come turn this artillery upon them!" General Armistead shouted out. Jake and a few others rushed toward the guns just as the Yankees up on the ridge let loose another volley. Armistead shook and started to fall. Jake reached out and caught him and lowered the general to the ground as several of his own men gathered around.

Jake stood back up; they needed more men. He rushed back to wall and on the other side he found Willie Wood and several other men from the First Tennessee.

"Come on boys, over the wall. Let's give it to them." There was hesitation at first to leave the safety of the wall, but Wood stood up with the colors and bounded over the wall and several others followed him. "Maybe we have a chance," Jake whispered.

Stephen Brown

It was a mass of confusion along the front of the Thirteenth Vermont. On their part of the line, Company K was keeping up a steady fire while there was some hand to hand fighting toward the middle of the regiment.

The Sixteenth Vermont was down by the barn and brick house down the slope along the road moving on the enemy from the rear.

"Forward!" The yells caught Stephen a bit by surprise. "Forward!" he yelled out adding his own voice to the call. He spun the hatchet in his right hand. It was much smaller than a bayonet on the end of a rifle or a sword for that matter. Worst case scenario, he might have to try throwing it like the Indians used to do.

"Keep close to me!" William yelled at him. Obviously, he wasn't the only one worried about the size of his weapon.

"We got you," Ralph added. Stephen was instantly grateful and embarrassed at the same time. The flag rushed faster forward, and the men followed.

A few of the confederates raised their weapons and used them as clubs or stabbed forward with their bayonets, but there were too many of the Vermont men for them to deal with and they were quickly knocked to the ground. The rest of the confederates pulled back. The regiment's flag stopped, and the men quickly reloaded their weapons.

Jake Turney

Jake got the fifty men who joined him to get off a volley against the rear of the Yankees to their north, but there weren't enough of them to have much effect. "Reload!" he yelled out.

"You in charge?" an excited voice yelled from behind Jake. He spun around to find a much younger captain. "Yes," Jake answered him.

"Orders from General Lee, hold this ground at all hazards; General Ewell's men are on the move." *What the hell?* Jake thought to himself. The captain rushed back over the stone wall before Jake could even answer him.

Unarmed Willie Wood was standing next to him with the First Tennessee's battle flag. "Get back behind the wall," Jake ordered him. Wood had a confused look on his face. "Protect the colors and get back behind the wall," Jake told him.

Another volley from up on the ridge knocked a couple of Jake's men to the ground. Men were being killed and wounded under his command, who he didn't even know and for what? Jake looked out to the road and the only men he could see were streaming back to the ridge from where they started. Union artillery was making sure the return trip was about as dangerous as the trip over. The only saving grace was they were running and walking back in small groups making it harder to hit.

The order was direct from General Lee, so retreat was out of the question, but there was no reason to lead these men to their deaths or for him to commit what amounted to suicide. He'd been captured before and been exchanged. It could happen again.

Jake reached into his pocket and pulled out his white handkerchief. He raised it high above his head and started yelling "Surrender! Lay down your weapons! Surrender!"

He glanced to his right and the few men still with General Armistead were doing the same but the rest of them were gone. Some of the men on the other side of the wall took off toward the road taking their chances with the Yankee artillery. Jake didn't blame them.

Jake put his sword back into his scabbard. He would only give it up to someone of equal rank. He looked down into the blank eyes of a young face with a bullet wound to the head. Suddenly, the boy's eyes blinked. *My God*, shot in the right temple and he was still alive. Jake knelt down to the boy. "How are you feeling, son?" Jake asked as he slowly reached around the boy's neck so he could raise his head.

Jake was surprised when he felt something hard just under the skin on the back of the boy's neck. He carefully lifted the boy's head when he was surprised by familiar voice behind him. "You need some help?"

"Glad you're still alive," Jake said.

"Me too," Albert said as he sat down next to him with his right leg curled under his butt and his left leg out straight. Jake noticed Albert's left pant leg was torn below the knee and his blood-soaked handkerchief wrapped around his calf.

"How you are feeling, Maze?" Albert asked the boy.

Maze's eyes brightened as he recognized Albert.

"My leg hurts," Maze said.

Albert reached over for Jake's handkerchief. "Maze, this is my brother Jake."

Albert took Jake's handkerchief and as he carefully tied it around the boy, James', head. "Jake, this is James Maze, he is in Company F."

Jake checked Maze's legs and found a large wound in his right thigh that had already stopped bleeding.

Yankees were quietly hovering over them while they checked over Maze. Jake looked up at them.

"He needs medical care. A bullet is lodged in the back of his neck."

"We will get him a stretcher," a tall sergeant answered Jake. "We got to get you two to the rear." Jake nodded and helped Albert to his feet. "If you hadn't gotten hit, would you have left me up here alone?" Jake asked his younger brother.

"You bet your ass." Albert laughed.

The sergeant looked confused as to why Jake put up with the obvious lack of courtesy from a private.

"Brothers, what can you do with them?" Jake smiled.

The sergeant smiled and nodded his head. "I know what you mean, sir."

Albert put his arm around Jake's shoulder to steady himself and keep the weight off of his right calf and the two of them slowly moved up the slope to the right of the taller trees along the top of the ridge. Jake's adrenaline quickly wore off and he suddenly felt so very tired.

He stopped, took out his canteen and took a long drink of water. "Do you want some?" Albert shook his head, so Jake finished off the last of it.

It dawned on Jake how quickly the air was clearing as the smoke drifted away. Up ahead, he noticed a couple of Yankee flags were bright and clean with no damage. Surrounding them was a mass of bright and smiling faces. It'd been a long time since he had seen anyone so soon after a fight looking so excited about what had just happened.

After years of fighting, win or lose, Jake no longer felt any thrill or excitement by the bloody aftermath of a fight. Jake and Albert joined up with a disorganized column walking past the obvious green troops. A light breeze blew the regiment's national color and Jake caught a glimpse of Vermont between the stripes. The insignia on their forage caps showed the number thirteen. Jake had never heard of the Thirteenth Vermont.

The voice caught him off guard. "Sir, I will relieve you of your sword." Jake looked up to see a young Yankee first lieutenant smiling at him. Jake wanted to punch the smiling bastard right in the mouth or tell him to go screw himself, but instead, just ignored him as he and Albert took another step.

The officer's smile vanished in a spilt second. His right arm shot up and Jake focused on the menacing camp hatchet posed to strike at his head. *What the hell?*

"Sir, I asked you nicely once, I won't ask you again."

Jake peered into the young man's steely gaze. He didn't blink. No hint of a facial twitch or anything to convey a hint of doubt or indecision. He wanted Jake's sword and it was obvious he wasn't going to back down. More importantly, the faces of the men around him had changed too. They were looking at him with pride and respect he had rarely seen men show to such a junior officer.

The young officer had done something to earn their respect and the idea that such a man would then back down in front of them, Jake knew was out of the question. At least he wasn't surrendering his sword to some meanly mouthed Jake Ass.

Jake used his left hand to undo his belt and handed over his sword, scabbard and pistol.

"Thank you, sir."

"Get a move on," someone shouted from behind Jake. He and Albert went back to walking up the slope.

The young officer turned to one of his men and held out the hatchet. "You want this back?"

"Nope, not going to need it anymore," the man replied.

Jake heard a cheer behind him, so he glanced over his shoulder. The young officer had dropped the hatchet on the ground and was holding his sword high above his head and all the men around him were cheering.

"What an ass," Albert mumbled as they started up the slope.

Jake ignored him. "I wonder what in the hell happened to his sword," he replied.

Stephen Brown

When Stephen lowered the sword almost on cue First Sergeant Halloway yelled out, "Enough of that, the lieutenant's got a sword, now let's get to work helping gather up those prisoners."

Stephen felt a little embarrassed as he slid the sword back into the scabbard then buckled the belt around his waist. He checked the pistol, it was empty. No matter, it didn't look like he was going to have much need for it the rest of this day.

"How is the sword?" Captain George Blake asked walking up. Stephen pulled it out and handed over to his commanding officer and friend.

"It looks well used." Stephen shrugged. He once again had an officer's sword; he didn't care what it looked like. When Stephen took the sword back from George, he noticed a funny expression on his face, then George pointed to the south. Stephen followed his point and noticed a large group in the fields on this side of the road.

'What the ..." Stephen let the words fade away. More confederates were coming this way.

"I'll go tell the colonel, you and the first sergeant get the company organized." George hurried away while Stephen spun around the direction, he had last seen the first sergeant. It took him only a couple of seconds to get First Sergeant Halloway's attention and quick point was all that was needed. He started yelling for Company K to form up.

Stephen moved to the south to a vacant patch then pulled out his new sword and once again waved it above his head. The other sergeants joined in with Halloway yelling for the men to form up on the First Lieutenant.

Stephen looked back to the south and they were still coming, but a cheer up along the road got his attention. He was surprised and pleased that the Sixteenth Vermont had changed front and with a shout and cheers were making a charge toward the enemy infantry.

As the sergeants and corporals took their place in the line, the men fell into their places. George hurried back up to Stephen. "I wish it was us instead of them."

Stephen didn't say anything. He had seen enough killing close up for today. Compared to the troops in gray, the Thirteenth was much fresher when they charged with bayonets into the flank of the rebel line. Some of the confederates had tried to turn and meet the charge and for a few minutes blood flowed, but the stand was foolish waste of life.

Stephen started yelling, quickly joined by many others, for the confederates to surrender. After less than a minute, they started laying down their weapons and the Thirteenth Vermont pushed on toward the tall trees rolling up prisoners as they went.

Stephen turned back to the company and noticed Ralph out of line over with First Sergeant Halloway. Ralph looked at him funny. Stephen rushed over to the first sergeant and was surprised to see blood streaming from a large tear in his right pant leg.

"He is refusing to go to the rear," Ralph stated firmly. Stephen looked into the first sergeant's eyes and it was clear he was in a lot of pain. He noticed second sergeant walk up behind the first sergeant. It was clear to him and Ralph they weren't the only ones who thought Halloway needed to get treatment on his leg.

"It looks worse than it is," Halloway protested.

Stephen looked past Halloway and noticed a couple of the regiment's company's escorting prisoners over the ridge to the rear.

"Sergeant, you need to join them and find an aide station and get that wound treated," Stephen said firmly. "Until you find one you can help with the prisoners," he said giving the first sergeant a bit of cover for going to the rear before all the fighting was concluded.

"Sergeant Manzer report," Halloway hollered.

Stephen forced himself to keep a straight face, but a hint of a grin must have given him away.

"What!" Halloway snapped.

Second Sergeant Manzer whispered, "I'm right here Jim."

Startled, Halloway jerked his head around.

"You're both a couple of asses."

To Stephen's left, he heard a voice. "And first sergeant, you are relieved," Captain George Blake stated in a low firm tone that made it clear it wasn't open for discussion. Halloway started to open his mouth, then thought twice about it. "Yes, sir," he said instead as he gave George a rare salute as if he was surrendering.

"Sergeant Manzer, until the first sergeant returns to duty, you will perform the duties of first sergeant." With that, George spun around and marched back to his spot in the middle of the company. Halloway mumbled as he stepped out of line and Stephen walked with him past the back line than took his place on the left of the formation as Halloway limbed up the ridge.

"You need some help?" Stephen called after him, but Halloway waved him off.

Stephen turned back to the company as the rest of the regiment completed falling into line. The Thirteenth Vermont was once again ready for action, but it looked like the Sixteenth Vermont had things well in hand.

After a brief stand, the confederates turned tail, but still, their advance was a concern. How many more were out there waiting to advance?

One of the colonel's aides came trotting up to George. After a brief exchange, George turned back to the company. "Men, Colonel Randall and General Stannard send high praise of a job well done. The regiment is going back into line behind the stonewall where we started this morning.

Orders were given for a left face. More orders were issued, and Company K and the rest of the regiment headed back toward their wall.

The three muffled bangs in rapid succession startled Stephen. He knew immediately what it was. He stepped to his right out of formation so he could get a better look. He looked down the Union line to the south, in the direction he thought the sound came from but there was no telltale smoke. *Oh, God.*

The first explosion hit to his right. He turned to see men in the center of the regiment down. The second shell was much closer hitting the company behind Company K. The force of the blast shook Stephen.

He looked toward his company to see William look over his shoulder, then suddenly he disappeared in a cloud of smoke and dirt.

Stephen took off running quickly losing his cap. He slid down next to the unmoving William. Stephen gently shook him, nothing. He wrapped his arm around William's stomach. It was like putting his hand into the insides of butchered cow. He rolled William over him slowly in his direction. Stephen didn't notice the next artillery volley.

William's head flopped over on to Stephen's lap and Stephen was looking into the fixed, unblinking, lifeless eyes of his friend.

Tears welled up in his eyes. "My God, why?"

The explosion was deafening. The shockwave knocked Stephen down on top of William. He struggled to keep his wits about him, but within a couple of seconds he could feel his eyes roll up into his head and he saw nothing but darkness, then darkness closed in on his brain.

Jake Turney

"I don't want to leave my brother," Albert protested.

The doctor didn't seem to notice or care. "You're not going to be able to walk on that leg, so you'll get put in a wagon. Your brother is going to have walk," he said firmly.

"Besides, we separate enlisted from officers," one of the privates guarding them added bluntly. Another one pointed to Jake. "Time to go, sir."

"Jake!" Albert pleaded.

"They got the guns," Jake smiled as he leaned over and gave his younger brother a hug as he whispered, "Keep your mouth shut and I will see you at home."

Jake turned his back and tried resist wiping his eyes. Once out of the aide station tent, he glanced back to make sure Albert wasn't watching him only then did he wiped his eyes before he looked across the road and back up the ridge. The small farm to his right was covered with dead artillery horses, but the small farmhouse didn't seem to be in too bad of shape, but the horses told a pathetic story of waste and incompetence.

For two hours, the confederate artillery had fired long over the heads of the Union infantry and all to show for it was hundreds of dead horses. While still in the tent he had heard three rounds explode up on the ridge, but it was obviously too little and way too late.

Coming toward him were four men carrying what looked like a lifeless man. As they got closer, he could make out the "13" on their caps. Then he recognized his holster and his belt. The steely-eyed officer was down, and his men weren't waiting for litter bearers; they were rushing him to the aide station carrying him by his shoulders and his feet.

"This way, sir." The private used his rifle to push Jake down the road to the south. After a few steps, he glanced back over his shoulder and watched them carry the officer with his sword into the aide station. Jake didn't notice any blood.

"Get a move on," another private said this one without any military courtesy. Jake hoped Albert kept his mouth shut when they carried that officer with his sword and pistol into the aid station tent. He could tell from the faces of his guards; they weren't going to be in a very forgiving mood to a loudmouth prisoner.

Stephen Brown

It was the singing that brought him slowly back to consciousness. "I need to be with them," he tried to say but while he could feel his lips move, he didn't hear his own voice. He forced his eyes to open, but they were very heavy, and it was dark. He didn't understand.

"I think his lips moved and I am sure he blinked," Ralph said.

"You sure?" George replied with what seemed like a hopeful tone.

Stephen couldn't figure out who they were talking about. It must be someone close. He forced his eyes open, but something was terribly wrong, it was as dark as night. It was only about four o'clock, how could it be dark? He shuddered as it dawned on him that he must be blind.

"His eyes are open," he could hear Ralph say. Stephen glanced in the direction of the sound and there was Ralph's face bathed in red glow.

"Welcome back," Ralph said.

"Where did I go?" Stephen tried to say.

"His lips moved again," Ralph told George.

"Do you want some water?" George asked him. Suddenly Stephen realized his throat was horribly dry. He nodded his head.

Ralph carefully reached under his head and slowly raised him up as George brought a canteen to his lips. He took a couple of sips and started coughing uncontrollably.

Ralph quickly pulled him up and beat him on his back a few times. "You can't swallow and breathe at the same time," Ralph snapped at him, obviously worried. After a few slaps Stephen was able to get his breath again.

"Do you want to try again?" George asked.

"Yes," Stephen replied.

Ralph laughed. "I heard that."

George brought up the canteen again and this time Stephen made sure not to breathe while he drank the warm water. When he'd had enough, he tapped George on the leg with his right hand.

"Stephen, can you move your hands and feet?" George asked as he pulled the canteen away.

The question instantly scared Stephen. "What happened to me?" he asked, and this time he could hear his own voice.

"How bad am I hurt?" Stephen asked with obvious trembling in his voice.

"Try to move your hands and feet and I will let you know," George stated firmly.

Stephen took a deep breath. There was no pain, so that had to be good sign, or was it?

"Am I paralyzed?" Stephen asked.

"Did you try to move?" Ralph asked, obviously worried.

"No."

"How the hell would we know if you haven't tried to move?" George snapped.

It took a second for Stephen to focus on moving his arms and legs and thankfully they responded.

"A shell exploded right above you. The blast knocked you out, but otherwise it looks like you are fine," Ralph said as he lowered Stephen back down.

"Where's William?" Stephen asked.

"You don't remember?" George asked.

"Remember what?" Stephen asked.

Stephen looked up into Ralph's face and saw a tear roll down from his right eye.

Ralph put his hand on Stephen's shoulder. "What is the last thing you remember?"

Stephen closed his eyes and tried to focus his thoughts.. "The look on that Captain's face when I held his sword over my head," he said.

Ralph patted him twice. "After you put the sword away we were hit with artillery fire ..."

Epilogue

The Confederates

Jacob Turney spent the remainder of the war at the officer prisoner of war camp on Johnson Island, Ohio along with his commander Colonel Newton George. He was exchanged in March of 1865 and returned home to Tennessee. Jacob took up farming after the war. In 1870, he married Fanny Klepper. Their daughter Ida was born in 1871. Jacob served as the School Land Commissioner for Giles County, Tennessee.

Fanny died in 1880 after just ten years of marriage.

Jacob married again in 1895 to Mary Taylor. He died March 19, 1909. He is buried in Rose Hill Cemetery, Fayetteville, Tennessee.

Albert recovered from his wounds and was exchanged back to the company in September. Albert and James were both captured in December 1863 near Ackland, West Virginia. At the Military Prison in Wheeling, West Virginia, both took the oath of allegiance to the Union and were sent north for the rest of the war.

After the war, James and Albert also returned to Tennessee. James taught school, but in 1874 he was admitted to a mental health institution. He died there in 1905.

Albert married Mary Tate in 1868. They had two sons, Samuel and John. Albert was a farmer like this older brother Jacob. Mary died in 1908. Albert lived until 1914. He was the last living Turney sibling. He is buried in the Boonshill Cemetery in Lincoln County, Tennessee.

Newton George's young brother David was killed during fighting at Petersburg in 1864. After the war, Newt settled in Fayetteville, Tennessee where he practiced law. He never married and died in 1919.

The Yankees

Shortly after being mustered out of the Thirteenth Vermont, Captain George Blake returned to Gettysburg and found the marked grave of William Church. He dug up William's body and took him home to Swanton Vermont to be reburied.

He then returned to his family ending his military career. He worked in a hardware store for a time and was appointed Postmaster of Swanton in 1891.

With the planning of the Thirteenth Vermont Monument, George Blake led the effort to put a statue of his First Lieutenant Stephen Brown on top the monument. While Captain John Lonergan was the only member of the Thirteenth Vermont to be awarded the Medal of Honor, Blake was successful in his efforts. The veterans of the Thirteenth remembered fondly the young lieutenant who risked arrest and death to get his men water.

The original design was for Stephen holding the hatch, but the Gettysburg Battlefield Memorial Association rejected the design as not being a fitting memorial. The design was changed to Stephen holding the captured sword with the hatch lying near his right foot, overhanging the statue's base slightly.

Ralph Sturevant mustered out of the Thirteenth Vermont and returned to the Bakersfield Academy to complete his education. In 1865, he started his study of the law and opened a law practice in Swanton in 1869. At an annual meeting of the Thirteenth Vermont Regimental Association he was elected to write the history of the regiment. His work, *The Thirteenth Regiment of Vermont Volunteers* is an excellent regimental history.

Stephen Brown mustered out of the Thirteenth Vermont; he quickly enlisted in the Seventeenth Vermont. He was elected captain of the regiment's Company A. The regiment saw combat for the first time at the Wilderness and Brown was severely wounded in the left shoulder leading the amputation of his left arm.

He returned to Vermont to study law, graduating in 1868. He moved west to Chicago. He practiced law and did real estate investing. His law office was destroyed in the Great Chicago Fire.

In 1886, he was introduced to the new Chicago Federal Assistant Pension Agent. Brown remembered the young artillery officer from Cemetery Hill, John J. Abercrombie Jr.

In 1891, Brown returned home to Swanton to take care of his parents. He died in 1903 and is buried next to his friend William Church.

During a visit to the Swanton Vermont Historical Society, I was given access to Stephen Brown's personal scrap book. In it, I found a detailed description of his meeting with Abercrombie in Chicago and their remembrances on Cemetery Hill.

In it, I learned that Abercrombie was an infantry officer (127th Regiment New York Infantry) detailed to an artillery battery. Brown detailed the story of firing on the rebel field hospital and how both men felt bad about it, but under the circumstances, they felt they had to do it. It is a puzzle on which battery Abercrombie served with at Gettysburg. Brown wrote that Abercrombie was assigned to the Third New York Battery. While there is a monument to the battery at Gettysburg, it is reported they weren't engaged. Despite my research, I couldn't find any reports of Abercrombie being assigned to any of the batteries on Cemetery Hill.

Making it more interesting, Abercrombie told Brown that later that evening, the brigade that had replaced the Thirteenth Vermont was overrun and the rebels had reached the battery. Abercrombie was clubbed by a musket knocked senseless. As his eyes came back into focus, he saw a rebel ready to run him through with a bayonet. He closed his eyes expecting to die opening them again to see a gunner, private Stephen Pidgeon knock the top of the rebel's head off with an iron ramrod.

There are no reports of the rebels reaching a battery on that side of Cemetery Hill, which might make us question Brown's story, but I think that would be a mistake. Also, in Brown's scrapbook, I found five sworn dispositions from the Thirteenth Vermont detailing Brown's actions with the artillery battery. I could find no reason for the dispositions other than Brown using his legal training to carefully document what had happened.

What I learned from the Abercrombie and Brown story is that no matter how much we might think we know about the war, there are still millions of stories left untold.

About the Author

Thomas M. Eishen holds a bachelor's degree in secondary education, social studies, with an emphasis on United States history from Indiana University at Fort Wayne. Tom is a member of the Gettysburg Foundation, The American Battlefield Trust, and Sons of Union Veterans of the Civil War.

You can follow Thomas on Facebook and Instagram. His website, tommyeishen.com has an extensive collection of modern photographs of Gettysburg National Battlefield.